THINK
TWICE

ALSO BY HARLAN COBEN

NOVELS

THINK TWICE

HARLAN COBEN

GRAND
CENTRAL

NEW YORK   BOSTON

Copyright © 2024 by Harlan Coben

Cover design by Jonathan Bush
Cover photo by Getty Images and Shutterstock
Cover copyright © 2024 by Hachette Book Group, Inc.

Grand Central Publishing
Hachette Book Group
1290 Avenue of the Americas, New York, NY 10104
grandcentralpublishing.com
@grandcentralpub

First Edition: May 2024

Grand Central Publishing is a division of Hachette Book Group, Inc. The Grand Central Publishing name and logo is a registered trademark of Hachette Book Group, Inc.

The publisher is not responsible for websites (or their content) that are not owned by the publisher.

The Hachette Speakers Bureau provides a wide range of authors for speaking events. To find out more, go to hachettespeakersbureau.com or email HachetteSpeakers@hbgusa.com.

Grand Central Publishing books may be purchased in bulk for business, educational, or promotional use. For information, please contact your local bookseller or the Hachette Book Group Special Markets Department at special.markets@hbgusa.com.

Library of Congress Control Number: 2024930619

ISBN: 9781538756317 (hardcover), 9781538756348 (ebook), 9781538769928 (signed edition), 9781538769942 (special signed edition), 9781538768747 (large print trade), 9781538768426 (international trade)

Printed in the United States of America

LSC

Printing 1, 2024

In memory of Juan "Johnny" Irizarry
I miss the smile and the fist bumps

THINK
TWICE

PROLOGUE

Here is how you destroy a life.

You stand over his bed and watch him sleep. He's a heavy sleeper. You know this because you've been watching him for six weeks now. You don't take chances. You prepare. That's the secret sauce. There is no reason to rush. Anticipation is a big part of life. "It's the journey, not the destination." You remember the speaker at your college graduation said that. It's an old saw of a line, a cliché, but it stuck with you. And it's not completely true, not by a long shot, but it is a good reminder on those long, lonely nights that joy can and must be found in both the waiting and the tedious.

Because you are well prepared, you know that he likes to have a cognac before he goes to bed. Not every night, but pretty close to it. If he hadn't taken one tonight, then you'd have postponed. Don't be in a rush. Don't take chances. If you're patient, you'll get your target with little to no risk.

It's about preparation and patience.

Because you've been watching him, you know he keeps a spare key in one of those gray hide-a-key fake rocks. That's how you gained access to the house this morning to spike his cognac. That's how you gained access again tonight.

He will not be waking up for a while.

He keeps a gun, a Glock 19, in a hard case in the top drawer of his night table. The hard case doesn't have a combination lock. It's biometric and opens via a thumbprint sensor. He's totally passed out, so you lift up his hand, take hold of the thumb, and push it against the sensor. The lock mechanism whirs and pops open.

You take out the gun.

You are wearing gloves. He, of course, is not. You wrap his hand around the Glock, so that his fingerprints will be in the right spots. Then you carefully put the weapon in your backpack. You have tissues and plastic bags with you. You always carry them. Just in case. You dab the tissue against his mouth, making sure to get his spit on it. Then you put the tissue in a plastic bag and put the plastic bag in the backpack next to the gun. You may not need this. It may be overkill. But overkill seems to sell.

He remains on his back snoring.

You can't help but smile.

You enjoy this part. You enjoy this part much more than the actual kill. A kill can be relatively simple and is usually quick.

But this, the setup, this is a work of art.

His mobile phone is on the night table. You set it on silent and then that, too, you put in your backpack. You leave his bedroom. His Audi car keys are on a hook near the back door. He's meticulous about that. He comes home, he puts his keys on the hook. Every time. You grab the keys. For good measure, you take one of the baseball caps he keeps on the coatrack. You put it on your head. The fit is close enough. You don sunglasses. You know to keep your head low.

You drive off in the Audi toward her.

She is staying at an Airbnb on a quiet lake in Marshfield. He doesn't know that she's there. You do because again you've been preparing. Once you saw that she'd gone there—that she planned to hide from him and not tell anyone—you knew it was time. You take out his mobile phone and type in the address of the Airbnb, so there'll be a record of it in his map searches.

The Airbnb she rented is a small Cape Cod. She's been there for a week now. You understand why she's taken this step, but it could only ever be a temporary solution for her. You park on the street. It's late. Two in the morning. You know, however, that she's still awake. So you park down the street, in front of an empty vacation home.

You take the gun out of your backpack.

The kitchen light in the Airbnb is on. That's where she will be.

You circle toward the light and look through the window of the kitchen door.

There she is.

She sits alone at the table with a cup of tea and a book. She's a pretty woman. Her dirty blonde hair is tied back seemingly in haste. Her feet are tucked under her. She looks too thin, but that's probably the stress. She is totally focused on her book. She wears an oversized men's dress shirt. You wonder whether it is his. That would be bizarre and creepy, but so much of life is.

Still watching her through the window, you carefully, slowly, try the knob.

You don't want to make noise. You don't want to startle her.

The door is locked.

You look down at the knob. It's old. The lock looks weak. If you had tools, you could open it quickly. But this is probably better. You look at her through the window again. And when you do, she looks up and spots your face.

Her eyes widen in surprise.

She is about to scream. You don't want that.

Careless. Again. Despite all your planning, you made a mistake the last time. You can't afford to make another.

So you don't hesitate.

You aim your kick for the spot right below the doorknob. The old door gives way easily. You enter the house.

"Please." She stands and puts her hands out, one holding the book. "Please don't hurt me."

You shoot her twice in the chest.

She drops to the floor. You hurry over and check.

Dead.

You remove the tissue from the plastic bag in your backpack. You leave it on the floor. Juries love DNA. They've all grown up with TV shows that exaggerate the miracles of the technology. They expect it in a murder trial. If there's no DNA evidence, a jury wonders about guilt.

You are in and out of the house in less than fifteen seconds.

The gun made noise. No question about it. But most people assume fireworks or backfire or some innocent explanation. Still, there is no reason to hang around. You hurry back to the car. You aren't particularly worried that someone will notice you running. If they do—if worse comes to worst—they'll see a man in a baseball cap running back to an Audi registered to him, not you.

It will, if anything, help.

You start to drive. You feel odd about the killing. It is a thrill, the killing part, more for your beloved than you, but you often feel oddly empty right after. It's a bit like sex, isn't it? Not to be too clinical about it, but the letdown after climax, the moment the French call *la petite mort*—the Little Death. That's how you feel right now. That's how you feel during the first mile or two of the drive, the shooting replaying in your mind, the way her body dropped to the floor. It's exciting and yet a little...

Empty?

You check the clock. He should be passed out for another three hours. That's plenty of time. You drive back to his house. You park the Audi where you found it.

You smile. Here, this part, this is the true rush for you.

This Audi has some kind of tracking system, so the police will be able to see where it went tonight. You enter his house. You hang up the keys. You keep the baseball cap—it may have some of your hairs in it now. No need to take that chance. If the police notice it's missing, they'll figure he dumped it after the shooting.

You head upstairs to his bedroom. You put his phone back on the night table. You even plug it into his charger. Like with the Audi, the police will get a warrant for his phone locations that will "prove" he took the journey to that Airbnb at the time of the murder.

You use his thumb to open the hard case. You put the gun back. You debate just leaving the gun next to his bed, but that feels heavy-handed. There is a storage shed in the yard. You take the hard case with the gun and hide it under bags of peat moss. They'll know that he has a Glock 19 registered in his name. They'll scour the entire property and find it in the storage shed.

Ballistics will confirm that the murder weapon was his Glock 19.

The Audi. The mobile phone. The DNA. The gun. Any two of the four would convict him.

For her, the horror is over.

For him, it's just begun.

CHAPTER ONE

M yron Bolitar was on the phone with his eighty-year-old father when the two FBI agents arrived to question him about the murder.

"Your mother and I," his dad said from his retirement condo in Boca Raton, "have discovered edibles."

Myron blinked. "Wait, what now?"

He was in his new penthouse office atop Win's skyscraper on the corner of 47th Street and Park Avenue. He swiveled his chair to look out the floor-to-ceiling windows. It was a pretty bitching view of the Big Apple.

"Cannabis gummies, Myron. Your Aunt Miriam and Uncle Irv swore by them—Irv said it helps with his gout—so your mother and I figured, look, why not, let's give them a shot. What's the harm, right? You ever try edibles?"

"No."

"That's his problem." That was Myron's mother, squawk-shouting in the background. This was how they always operated—one parent on the phone, the other shouting color commentary. "Give me the phone, Al." Then: "Myron?"

"Hi, Mom."

"You should get high."

"If you say so."

"Try the stevia strain."

Dad: "Sativa."

"What?"

"It's called sativa. Stevia is an artificial sweetener."

"Ooo, look at your father Mr. Hippie showing off his pot expertise all of a sudden." Then back to Myron: "I meant sativa. Try that."

"Okay," Myron said.

"The indica strain makes you sleepy."

"I'll keep that in mind."

"You know how I remember which is which?" Mom asked.

"I bet you'll tell me."

"Indica, in-da-couch. That's the sleepy one. Get it?"

"Gotten."

"Don't be such a square. Your father and I like them. They make us feel more, I don't know, smiley maybe. Alert. Zen even. And Myron?"

"Yes, Mom."

"Don't ask what they've done for our sex life."

"I won't," Myron said. "Ever."

"Me, I get giddy. But your father becomes a giant hornball."

"Not asking, remember?" Myron could now see the two FBI agents scowling at him from behind the glass wall. "Gotta go, Mom."

"I mean, the man can't keep his hands off me."

"Still not asking. Bye now."

Myron hung up as Big Cyndi, his longtime receptionist, silently ushered the two federal officers into the conference room. The two agents stared up, way up, at Big Cyndi. She was used to it. Myron was used to it. Big Cyndi got your attention fast. The agents flashed badges and made quick intros. Special Agent Monica Hawes, the lead, was a Black woman in her midfifties. Her sullen junior partner was a pasty-faced youngster with a forehead so prominent he resembled a beluga whale. He gave his name, but Myron was too distracted by the forehead to absorb it.

"Please," Myron said, gesturing for them to sit in the chairs that faced the floor-to-ceiling windows and said pretty bitching view.

The agents sat, but they did not look happy about it.

Big Cyndi put on a fake British accent and said, "Will that be all, Mr. Bolitar? Perhaps a spot of tea?"

Myron resisted the urge to roll his eyes. "No, I think we're good, thanks."

Big Cyndi bowed and left.

Myron also sat and waited for the agents to speak. The only thing he knew about this visit was that the FBI wanted to talk to both him and Win about the high-profile Callister murders. He had no idea why—neither he nor Win knew anything about the Callisters or the case other than what they'd seen on the news—but they'd been assured that they were not suspects or persons of interest.

"Where's Mr. Lockwood?" Agent Hawes asked.

"Present," Win said in that haughty prep-school tone as he—to quote the opening lines of the Carly Simon song Win's entire being emanated—walked into the party like he was walking onto a yacht. Win—aka the aforementioned Mr. Lockwood—was the dictionary definition of natty as he glided around Myron's new conference table and took the seat next to him.

Myron spread his hands and offered up his most cooperative smile. "I understand you have questions for us?"

"We do," Hawes said. And then without preamble, she dropped the bomb: "Where is Greg Downing?"

The question was a stunner. No other way around it. A stunner. Myron's jaw dropped. He turned to Win. Win's face, as usual, gave away nothing. Win was good at that, showing nothing.

The reason for Myron's surprise was simple.

Greg Downing had been dead for three years.

"I thought you were here about the Callister murders," Myron said.

"We are," Special Agent Hawes countered. Then repeated the question. "Where is Greg Downing?"

"Are you joking?" Myron asked.

"Do I look like I'm joking?"

She did not. She looked, in fact, like she never *ever* joked.

Myron glanced at Win to gauge his reaction. Win looked a little bored.

"Greg Downing," Myron said, "is dead."

"Is that your story?"

Myron frowned. "My story?"

The young agent who looked like a beluga whale leaned forward a little and glared at Win. He spoke for the first time, his voice deeper than Myron expected. Or maybe Myron had expected a high-pitched whale call. "Is that your story too?"

Win almost yawned. "No comment."

"You're Greg Downing's financial advisor," Young Beluga continued, still trying to stare down Win; he would have had a better chance of staring down a duvet cover. "Is that correct?"

"No comment."

"We can subpoena your records."

"Gasp, now I'm terrified. Let me think on that one." Win steepled his fingers and lowered his head as though in deep thought. Then: "Say it with me this time: No comment."

Hawes and Young Beluga scowled some more. "And you." Hawes swiveled back on Myron with a snarl. Myron guessed that Hawes had him, Young Beluga had Win. "You're Downing's, what, agent? Manager?"

"Correction," Myron said. "I *was* his agent and manager."

"When did you stop?"

"Three years ago. When Greg, you know, *died*."

"You both attended his memorial service."

Win stayed mum, so Myron said, "We did."

"You even spoke, Mr. Bolitar. After all the bad blood between you two, I hear you gave a beautiful eulogy."

Myron glanced at Win again. "Uh, thanks."

"And you're sticking with your story?"

Again with the story. Myron threw up his hands. "What are you talking about, story?"

Young Beluga shook his massive white head as though Myron's answer was a total disappointment to him, which, he guessed, it was.

"Where do you think he is right now?" Hawes asked.

"Greg?"

"Stop jerking us around, jerkoff," Young Beluga snapped. "Where is he?"

Myron was getting a little fed up with this. "In a mausoleum at Cedar Lawn Cemetery in Paterson."

"That's a lie," Hawes countered. "Did you help him?"

Myron sat back. Their tone was growing increasingly hostile, but there was also the unmistakable whiff of desperation and thus truth in the air. Myron didn't know what was going on here, and when that happened he had a habit of talking too much. Better to take a deep breath before continuing.

"I don't understand," Myron began. "What does Greg Downing have to do with the Callister murders? Didn't the cops already arrest the husband?"

Now it was the two agents who exchanged a glance. "They released Mr. Himble this morning."

"Why?"

No reply.

Here was what Myron knew about the murders: Cecelia Callister, age fifty-two, a semi-supermodel from the 1990s, and her thirty-year-old son, Clay, were found murdered in the mansion where they resided with Cecelia's fourth husband, Lou Himble. Himble had recently been indicted on fraud charges related to his cryptocurrency startup.

"I thought the case was open and shut," Myron continued. "The husband was having an affair, she found out, was going to turn state's evidence on him, he had to silence her, the son walked in on them. Something like that."

Special Agent Monica Hawes and Special Agent Young Beluga Whale exchanged another glance. Then Hawes repeated in a careful voice, "Something like that."

"So?"

Myron waited. Win waited.

"We have reason to believe," Hawes said, still using the careful voice, "that Greg Downing is still alive. We have reason to believe your former client is involved in the murders."

The two feds leaned forward to gauge the reaction. Myron did not disappoint. Even though this accusation should have seemed inevitable by now, Myron went slack-jawed when he heard it out loud.

Greg. Alive.

How did he process that? After all the years—their on-court rivalry, Greg stealing Myron's first love, Myron's awful payback for that, Greg's even worse payback, the years of reconciliation—and Jeremy, dear sweet, wonderful Jeremy . . .

It made no sense. Every part of his face registered complete and utter bafflement.

And Win's reaction? He was checking the time on his vintage Blancpain watch.

"Please excuse me," Win said. "I have a pressing engagement. My, what a delight to have met you both."

Win rose.

"Sit down," Hawes demanded.

"I don't think I will."

"We aren't finished."

"You aren't, are you?" Win gave them both his most winning smile. It was a good smile, even better than Myron's cooperative one. "I, however, am. Have a most pleasant afternoon."

Without so much as a backward glance, Win sauntered out of the office. Everyone, including Myron, stared at the door as Win vanished from sight.

Win's full name is Windsor *Horne Lock*wood III. The skyscraper they currently sat atop was called the *Lock-Horne* Building. The italics are here to emphasize that the building was named for Win's family and thus big bucks are involved. For many years, Myron's sports agency MB Reps (the M for Myron, the B for Bolitar, the Reps because they *rep*resented people—Myron came up with that name on his own but remained humble) had been housed on the building's fourth floor. A few years back, Myron stupidly sold his agency and moved out and now a law firm resided in that space. When Myron decided to come back two months ago, the top floor was the only available space.

Not that Myron was complaining. The pretty bitching view impressed clients, if not FBI agents.

Over the past two months, Myron had been working hard to woo back some of his old clients. He had overlooked Greg Downing for the simple reason that, well, the whole dead thing. Dead men make poor earning clients. Bad business.

The two agents were still staring at the door. When they finally realized that Win was not returning, Hawes turned her focus back on Myron. "Did you hear what I said, Mr. Bolitar?"

Myron nodded, got his bearings. "You claim a man who died of a heart attack—a man who had an obituary and a funeral and who, as you pointed out, I eulogized—is, in fact, still alive."

"Yes."

Myron looked back at the door where Win had just up and left. Yes, Win loved to play the aloof, elite, above-it-all snob because that was what he was, but Myron still found it hard to believe that Win would just walk out without reason. That made Myron pull up and try to take a more cautious route.

"Do you want to tell me about it?" Myron asked.

Young Beluga did not like that one. "What are you, a shrink?"

"Good one."

"What?"

"The shrink line," Myron said. "It's very funny."

Young Beluga's narrow eyes narrowed even more. "You being a wiseass with me?"

Myron did not reply right away. Thoughts about Greg's family swirled in Myron's head. He fought hard to keep them at bay. Greg's wife, Emily. Greg's…man, it was hard to even think about it…his son, Jeremy. So much past. So much history. So much misery and joy. There are people we stumble across who change things forever. Some are obvious—family and partners—but in the end, when Myron looked at his own life's journey and trajectory, nobody altered Myron's more than Greg Downing.

For the better or the worse?

"You hear me, wiseass?"

"Loud and clear," Myron said, fighting to keep focus. "Can you prove what you're saying is true?"

"About?"

"About Greg being alive. Can you prove it?"

The two agents hesitated, exchanged yet another glance. Then Hawes said, "Greg Downing's DNA was found at the Callister murder scene."

"What sort of DNA?"

Young Beluga took that one with a side of relish: "Skin cells," he said. "Your, uh, 'dead' client? His DNA was found under the victim's fingernails." He sat up a little straighter and lowered his voice à la a conspiratorial whisper. "You know, like when a helpless victim is desperately scratching and clawing to save their own life? Like that."

Myron's head reeled. This made no sense. Young Beluga smiled with teeth too small for his mouth, thus adding to his overall beluga appearance.

"Under which victim's nails?" Myron asked.

"None of your business." It was Hawes this time. "You and Greg Downing go way back, don't you? Basketball rivals. High school. College. Both of you were drafted in the NBA's first round. Downing had a great pro career. Became a beloved coach after he retired." Hawes put on a sarcastic pity pout. "You, on the other hand..."

"...have a cool-ass office with a pretty bitching view?"

Quick backstory: Not long after the draft, during Myron's first preseason game as a twenty-one-year-old Boston Celtics rookie, an opposing player named Big Burt Wesson slammed into Myron, twisting his knee in a way no joint should ever be twisted.

Bye-bye, basketball.

Hawes and Beluga thought this still bothered Myron, that it would be a good way to needle him and get under his skin.

They were two decades late for that.

Hawes's gaze met Myron's. "Let's stop with the games, Mr. Bolitar. Where is Greg Downing?"

"I'm going to have to ask you to leave now."

"You don't want to cooperate?"

"If you're telling me the truth—"

"We are."

"If you're telling me the truth," Myron started again, "if Greg is alive—I can't talk."

"Why not?"

"Attorney-client privilege."

"I thought you were his agent."

"That too."

"I'm not following."

When young Myron realized that his knee would never heal properly, when he realized his playing days were over, he doubled down on "moving on." He had been a good student at Duke. He channeled his basketball focus into studying for the LSAT, aced it, got accepted to Harvard Law School, graduated with honors. After he passed the bar, he opened MB Reps (then called MB *Sports*Reps because—try to follow with help from the italics—at first, he only *rep*resented athletes or people in *sports*). By being a true bar-associated attorney, Myron was able to offer his clients the fullest protection under the law.

It helped, especially when a client had a legal issue.

Like now, he guessed.

"We were told you'd cooperate, Mr. Bolitar."

"That was before I knew what this was about," Myron said. "Please leave. Now."

They both took their time standing up.

"One more thing," Myron said. "If you find Mr. Downing, I don't want him questioned without my presence."

Young Beluga's reply was a scoffing sound. Hawes stayed silent.

Myron sat there as they started to circle around the table. *Greg. Alive. Forget the murders for a moment. How the hell can Greg be alive?*

Young Beluga stopped and bent down over Myron. "This isn't over, asshole."

He had no idea how right he was.

CHAPTER TWO

in's office was one floor below Myron's.

When Myron got off the elevator, he still auto-braced for the hustle and bustle and pure volume of screaming traders shouting out buy-sell orders for stocks and bonds and investments, and, uh, financial stuff like that. Myron wasn't good with monetary instruments and the like, and he was okay with that. Win handled all money matters for the clients. Myron handled the agenting work—negotiating with owners and executives, soliciting endorsement deals, increasing a client's social-media compensation, branding, upping appearance fees, taking care of life's mundanities, whatever.

In short: maximizing earning potential.

Myron's job involved bringing in the money; Win's job was to invest and grow it.

The lack of workplace cacophony had something to do with how trades were made online or via computers nowadays. There was still the occasional shout across the room, but for the most part, every head was down, every eye was on a screen. It was creepy.

Win's private corner office was, not surprisingly, the largest. It faced both Park Avenue and uptown. There was the pretty bitching view, but there was also dark wood paneling and period art and the feel of a nineteenth-century men's club in central London.

"You know something," Myron said.

"I know lots of somethings."

"You're being coy. You're never coy."

"Sometimes I'm coy with the ladies," Win said. Then: "No, wait, I mean coquettish."

"Did you know Greg was alive?"

Win considered that. He spun toward the windows and looked out at his view. This too was something he almost never did. Then Win said, "A columbarium."

"What now?"

"You told the agents that Greg Downing was in a mausoleum."

"Right."

"A mausoleum is designed to hold a corpse," Win said. "A columbarium houses cremated remains."

"I stand corrected. Thanks for the vocabulary seminar."

Win spread his hands. "I give and I give."

"You do. Your point is, Greg was cremated."

"Correct."

"And, what, that makes it easier to fake a death?"

"Let's run the timeline, shall we?"

Myron nodded for Win to continue.

"Five years ago, Greg Downing was fired as head coach of the Milwaukee Bucks. At the time, Greg was immensely popular with a winning record for three different NBA franchises. It would be fair to say he was still very much in demand, correct?"

Myron nodded. "The Knicks and Heat both wanted to talk to him."

"But instead of fielding those offers, Greg, who was still a young man—"

"Our age," Myron added.

"Very young then." Win gave a small smile. "He instead pled burnout and claimed that he wanted out of the rat race. Did you buy that?"

Myron shrugged. "I've seen it before."

"Now who's being coy?"

"It was out of character," Myron conceded. "Greg had always been hypercompetitive."

"Game knows game," Win said.

"Meaning?"

"You were rivals for so long because you are both hypercompetitive. It led to great battles on the court. It led to great catastrophes off it."

Myron had no reply to that one.

"Did you and Greg discuss his decision?" Win asked.

"No. You know this."

"Just reviewing the facts. Greg simply took off. Ran away. Disappeared. He sent you an email."

"Yes."

"Do you remember what the email said?"

"I can find it if you want, but it just said something about needing a change in his life, looking to start his next chapter. He said he wanted to travel alone and find himself."

"Find himself," Win repeated with a disgusted shake of the head. "God, I hope he didn't use that wording."

"He did," Myron said. "Anyway, he started off in a monastery in Laos."

"And we know that how?"

"He told me." Myron considered that. "Why would he lie?"

Win didn't answer. "When did you next hear from Greg?"

"I don't know. I figured he needed to recharge the battery. That he'd be back pretty soon. But a week became a month then two months. He texted every once in a while. He said he was in Laos, then Thailand or Nepal, I don't remember exactly. Then..."

"Two years pass, and we get word he's dead."

"Yes," Myron said. Then: "What aren't you telling me, Win?"

Win again ignored the question. "How hard would it have been to fake his own death? Let's say you are Greg. You write your own obituary and put it in a newspaper. You say you died of a heart attack. You ship ashes—they can be burnt anything, really—in an urn. There's a memorial service. We go to it." Win held his palms to the sky. "Voilà, you're dead."

Myron frowned. "And then what, you sneak back into the country and murder Cecelia Callister and her son?"

Win stared out the window some more. That was when Myron saw it.

"Greg would have needed money," Myron said.

Win still stared.

"All those years away. No matter how frugal he was being. He would need to access his bank accounts. Did you meet with him?"

More staring.

"Win?"

"We have a dilemma."

"That being?"

"Client confidentiality."

"You're not an attorney."

"My word should mean nothing then?" Win turned away from the window. "If a client requests confidentiality, I should still speak freely?"

"No," Myron said, searching for a way around the impasse, "but in the specific case of Greg Downing, I am his agent, his manager, and his lawyer. Whatever he told you can be shared with me."

"Unless," Win said, holding up a finger, "the client told me not to tell anyone, including and specifically you."

Myron took a step back. "Wow."

"Indeed."

"Are you saying you knew Greg was alive?"

"I'm not saying anything of the sort."

"I sense a 'but.'"

"But if I were to review his financial decisions with this fresh perspective, I could perhaps conclude that this isn't the total shock for me that it is for you."

Win didn't have to give the details—Myron got the gist.

"So hypothetically," Myron said, "before Greg ran overseas to, uh, find himself, he may have made some money moves. Opened offshore accounts, transferred assets into less traceable instruments, that kind of thing."

"If he did," Win said, "that's the kind of thing that would remain confidential."

"So Greg planned this."

"Perhaps."

Silence.

Then Myron said, "Greg never fired us."

Win closed his eyes.

"If he is alive, he's still our client."

Win rubbed the closed eyes.

"You know where I'm going with this?" Myron asked.

"It would be hard not to guess without some form of fresh brain trauma," Win said. "You want to help him."

"Want doesn't matter," Myron said. "If Greg's alive, we are obligated to help him."

"Is this the part where I say, 'Even if he's a murderer?'"

"And then I nod sagely and reply, 'Even if.' Or maybe 'Let's cross that bridge when we get to it.'"

"'Even if' is the less hackneyed line," Win said with a sigh. "Do I need to remind you that this will open a lot of old emotional wounds for you?"

"Not really."

"Or that you're not good with handling old emotional wounds."

"I'm aware."

"Your destructive ex. Your career-ending injury. Your biological son."

"I get it, Win."

"No, my dear friend, you don't. You never do." Win sighed, shrugged, slapped his hands on the table. "Okay, fine, let's do it. The Lone Ranger and Tonto ride again."

"More like Batman and Robin."

"Sherlock and Watson."

"Green Hornet and Kato."

"Starsky and Hutch."

"Cagney and Lacey."

"McMillan and Wife."

"Scarecrow and Mrs. King."

"Simon and Simon."

"Turner and Hooch."

Win gasped. "Don't we wish?" Then he snapped his fingers. "Tango and Cash."

"Ooo, good one." Then: "Michael Knight and KITT."

"KITT, the talking car?"

"Yes," Myron said. "Plus, it has to be the Hoff playing Michael. None of these crappy reboots."

"Michael and KITT," Win repeated. "Which one of us is which?"

"Does it matter?"

"It does not," Win said. "So first steps?"

"Follow the money trail from the offshore accounts."

"Negative," Win said.

"Why not?"

"We won't be able to trace the money," Win said. "I'm *that* good."

"Then look at the Callister murders maybe."

"On it already. And you? Where do you go?"

Myron thought about it. "To my destructive ex."

CHAPTER THREE

————————

Emily Downing, the destructive ex, answered the door of her apartment on Fifth Avenue with a wide smile. "Well, well, well. If it isn't the good one I let get away."

"You use that line every time you see me."

"It's what always comes to mind. How long has it been, Myron?"

"Three years. Greg's funeral."

Emily knew that, of course. For a moment they just stood there and let the history wash over them. They didn't try to stop it or pretend that it wasn't happening. They'd met in the Perkins Library at Duke University the first month of their freshman year. Emily met Myron's eye and gave him a crooked smile from across the study table. Boom, Myron was a goner. They were both eighteen, both away from home for the first time, both inexperienced in the ways that teenagers pretend they aren't.

They fell in love.

Or at least, he did.

Standing in front of him now, all these years later, Emily said, "You don't really think Greg's alive, do you?"

"Do you?"

She gnawed on her lower lip, and boom again, Myron fell back to those cooling autumn nights in her dorm room, the lights low, the moon in the window over the quad. After almost four years of college dating, Myron broached the subject of marriage toward the end of their senior year.

Emily's response?

She took Myron's hands in hers, looked him straight in the eye, and said, "I'm not sure I love you."

Yet another boom. A very different kind of boom.

"Greg alive," Emily said in amazement. A strand of hair fell across her eye. Myron almost reached out and pushed it away. "It's too weird."

"You think?"

She gave him the crooked smile again. No boom this time. Barely a nostalgic pang. "Still a sarcastic wiseass."

"I gotta be me."

"Don't I know it. But all of it was weird. Starting with you taking on Greg as a client."

"Greg was a solid source of income."

"More sarcasm?"

"No."

"I never understood it," Emily said. "Why did you work with him? And don't tell me it was just about money."

Myron decided to go with the truth. "Greg had hurt me. I had hurt him."

"So you two were even?"

"Let's just say we both wanted to move past it."

"Greg liked you, Myron."

He said nothing.

"It's why I asked you to give the eulogy. I think it's what Greg would have wanted."

Myron and Greg's basketball rivalry started in sixth grade, moved to AAU when they were thirteen, then high school, then the ACC

to come over. He went. They had sex. The result—though Myron wouldn't know this until some fourteen years later—was a son, Jeremy, who Greg unwittingly raised as his own.

Yep, a mess.

Myron had always blamed Emily. Just as he had started to move on from the pain of losing her, she had been the one to call him that night. She had provided and encouraged the alcohol and made the first move. She had a plan of sorts, destructive as all get-out, and he was just a pawn in it. That was what he'd spent years telling himself. But now, with more distance and objective hindsight, Myron realized that his thinking was old-fashioned. He'd wanted to paint himself the good guy and ultimately the victim. Classic self-rationalization.

Man can justify anything if he puts his mind to it.

"Myron?"

It was Emily. Present-Day Emily. Boy, Win had warned him about letting old trauma back into his life, hadn't he?

"So you two divorced," Myron said, pushing away the past. "But then years later, you got back together, right? You even got remarried."

Emily didn't reply.

"And then, what, Greg just up and ran overseas without explanation?"

"There's more to it."

"I'm all ears, Emily."

She did the lip gnaw again. "I didn't tell the police this. Just so we are clear. I wasn't trying to hide anything. It's not their business. None of this is."

"Okay."

"It's not your business either."

"Okay."

"Greg and I had an arrangement."

Myron waited for her to say more. When she didn't, he asked, "What kind of arrangement?"

"A transactional one."

Most arrangements are, Myron knew, but instead of raising that, he went again with: "Okay."

"Greg was rich."

"Right."

"You know this better than anyone."

"Okay."

"Stop saying okay," she snapped. "Anyway, he promised to take care of me."

"Financially?" Myron asked.

"Yes. It's how I can afford to live here. Greg set up a generous trust for me. For Jeremy too, of course. Win helped him set all that up."

"Seems normal," Myron said.

"It wasn't. I mean, our relationship…" Emily stopped.

"Are you saying you weren't really married?"

"Yes. Well, no. We were legally married. But I mean, what is marriage anyway? Greg spent his life on the road with basketball. That's always been the case. During the off-season, he mostly hung out in South Beach. He only stayed with me when he visited New York, which was, I don't know, maybe a month, six weeks every year."

"And when he did stay, did you two—"

Myron motioned coming together with his hands, accordion style, wondering why he would ask a question like this in the first place. Did it matter?

"We had separate bedrooms," Emily said, "though we sometimes hooked up. You know how it is. We'd go to a fancy dinner party or charity ball. We're all dressed up, we'd have a bit to drink, we'd come home, we'd remember what it used to be like and it's late and it's too hard to find someone else..."

She met Myron's eye. Myron said, "Got it. Go on."

"What else is there?"

"For one thing, why did you want this arrangement?"

"I wanted financial stability."

"And what about Greg?"

Emily turned away from him and headed toward a glass bar cart. "Drink?"

"No, thank you." They were getting to the heart of it now. "Whose idea was this arrangement?"

"Greg's," she said, reaching for a glass with one hand and a bottle of Asbury Park gin. "This part is a little harder to explain."

"Take your time."

"I'm also not sure it's relevant."

"Your 'dead' husband is being accused of double murder," Myron said. "It's relevant. Why the arrangement, Emily?"

She stared at the bottle, but she didn't pour. "At first, I wasn't sure myself. Greg and I still had Jeremy in common. Even after he grew up and joined the military. Jeremy is so strong and brave and heroic and all that, but he's also...there's something fragile about our son." She turned and stared up at Myron. Our son. That's what she said. Our son. And there were two ways to hear that. Emily started pouring. "Really, Greg and I had no real interest in one another. We were long, long over. But once his anger dissipated, you know from what we did to him..."

Myron felt the squeeze in his chest.

"…there was something else there. I don't know what you'd call it. Friendship isn't really accurate. He and I didn't talk much or have a lot in common. But we had trust. And a bond."

She took a sip. Myron finished the thought for her. "Jeremy."

"Yeah, I guess. Whatever, I'm not telling this right. But one day Greg came to me and said that he wanted us to get remarried. He offered up a generous financial package. I took it."

"And he never explained why?"

"He said something about appearances. He wanted to look committed to one woman and that it would be good for Jeremy."

Myron mulled that over. "Did that make sense to you?"

"No. I figured that Greg had gotten himself in trouble."

"What kind of trouble?"

"The kind of trouble where it would look good to be married and have a family. I don't know exactly what, but Greg didn't have great impulse control. I thought maybe he'd met an underage girl in some club. Or maybe he screwed someone's wife again. Yeah, ironic, right? Greg was into that. Sleeping with married women. Lot of them. I told my shrink about it. He's sure that Greg's trauma was a byproduct of what we did to him."

Myron stayed quiet.

"No reply?" she asked.

"No," Myron said. "None."

"Anyway, Greg just said he needed to be married. We would go to events together, play the part of the happy couple for the media, the great redemption story, and in exchange he would set up the trusts. I liked that for a lot of reasons. The money obviously. But socially too. Friends don't invite you places when you're single. Especially me. You once told me I gave off a sex vibe."

"Emily, I was young and—"

"Oh, I'm not offended. Jesus. Everyone gets so weird about everything nowadays. I do give off that vibe. I always have. I know it. Anyway, married couples—well, the wives anyway—they don't want that vibe around their husbands. Not when you're a single woman, even though, ugh, zero interest on my part. Anyway, it worked. Greg and I Part Two. He did his thing, I did mine."

Emily's eyes were everywhere but on his. That wasn't like her. Myron said, "You're not telling me something."

"I'm working up to it. It was Greg's private business. I'm not in the mood to drag it out in the open."

"It's not 'in the open.' You're only telling me."

"That doesn't make it better. You know that, right? But if Greg's dead, what does it matter now? And if he's not dead, if he's somehow alive..." Emily chewed that over for a bit. Myron gave her space. "Let me show you something."

Emily took out her mobile phone, her fingers dancing across the screen.

"As Greg got older, he got weirder. I don't know how else to put it. More reclusive. More online."

"Greg?"

"Yeah, I know. Doesn't sound like him, does it? Anyway, so one day he leaves his phone out on the kitchen counter. He'd been on it nonstop the whole morning and I knew his passcode—he always used the same one for everything. So you can guess what I did."

"Invaded his privacy."

"Exactly. Anyway, I find he's got Instagram. This is so foreign to me. Greg. Can you imagine? Greg has an Instagram account."

"We set it up for him," Myron said. "It helps with endorsement and branding."

"No, not that one. I know about the public one. He never goes on that. Esperanza handles that for you, doesn't she?"

Myron said nothing.

"This is another account. Greg had it under a pseudonym. Here. Take a look."

Emily didn't hand him the phone, so Myron went behind her and looked over her shoulder. Strange how the senses remember better than we do, especially smell. He wondered whether she still used the same shampoo, because for a moment he was back in her freshman dorm, her toweling off after a shower, wearing the raggedy old robe he'd brought from home. It didn't mean anything. It wasn't as though he wanted to act on it. But it was there and inescapable.

The Instagram profile picture had a University of North Carolina tar heel logo. Greg's alma mater. The account's name was UNCHoopsterFan7. UNCHoopsterFan7 followed 390 people—and was followed by twelve.

"It's probably a sock puppet account," Myron said.

"What's that mean?"

"A sort of pseudonym. People pretending they're someone else. Sometimes they do it for marketing. Like they'll be the owner of a restaurant and pretend they're a customer and rave about it. Or political numbnuts who will post 'Oh I'm super independent' and then they'll defend whatever malfeasance their particular candidate is into."

"That's not what this account is. Greg never posted or commented."

"Okay. So maybe it's just a way to look at other accounts and not have anyone know."

"He was direct messaging with someone, Myron."

Emily tapped with her thumb and brought up an account for a

very toned, very muscled, very oiled-up male "Public Figure" and "Fitness Model" named Bo Storm.

Myron's eyes narrowed.

Bo Storm had six thousand followers and followed nine hundred people. Emily glanced at Myron over her shoulder. She wanted to see his reaction. Bo was shirtless in nearly every post in what they used to call beefcake poses. He had a rippling six-pack and the kind of smooth skin that can only come from a serious waxing regimen. His face stubble had been carefully cultivated. His hair was long and frosted. In the top pinned photo, Bo Storm was dancing on what looked to be a nightclub stage in only a thong.

His profile quote read: "Living the rainbow dream in Vegas. Guys, sign up for my OnlyFans account to see more."

Myron had no idea what to make of this.

"How old do you think he is?" Emily asked.

"Twenty-five-ish?"

"Yeah. A lot younger than Greg."

Myron nodded, trying to sort through where Emily was going with this. "So this Bo and Greg were messaging?"

"Yes."

"Did you read the messages?"

"Greg came back into the room, but I saw enough. Heart emojis. Future plans. Intimate stuff."

Myron said nothing.

Emily asked, "Are you surprised?"

"Who cares if I am?"

"I guess it shouldn't matter, should it? I mean, I get it. Or I try to get it. It's a new world, and our generation is still trying to figure it all out. And maybe Greg's constant womanizing was some kind of compensation or outlet or maybe he's bi or pan or omni or I don't know. I really don't."

"It doesn't matter," Myron said.

"Yeah, we can both keep saying that, but it's still a shock, right?"

Myron said nothing.

"And you're right. It doesn't matter. Not in that way. But here's where it gets weirder. Look at the last date this boy—I know this Bo Storm's not a boy, but my God, he's so young—look at the last day he posted."

Myron took the phone from her now and scrolled. The most recent photo was Bo standing on a beach wearing tight bathing trunks and a black tuxedo jacket with no shirt under it. The caption read "Beach Formal for Larry and Craig's Wedding," followed by various emojis of hearts and flames and rainbows.

Myron looked at the date. "He hasn't posted in five years."

"He stopped two weeks before Greg ran off for Asia. And look before that. This Bo guy never went more than two or three days without posting. So, I mean, put it together. Greg is flirting with this young hot guy on Instagram. Suddenly Greg decides to run off. The hot young guy stops posting. So you tell me."

The implication seemed obvious.

"After you read the messages," Myron began, "did you confront Greg?"

"No. At the time . . . How to put this? I was surprised, sure. And part of me was devastated. But part of me . . . I loved Greg. I really did. But imagine how hard his life must have been, Myron—hiding who he really was so he could keep his life in sports."

"It's 2024," Myron said.

"Seriously? Tell me—how many male coaches in pro sports have come out?"

Myron nodded. "Fair point. So you figured Greg ran off with this Bo guy?"

"What else would you conclude under the circumstances? Did you really buy the whole monastery-in-Laos stuff?"

"I guess not."

"And in a way, I was happy for him. Greg was never at peace. Not his entire life. There was something always roiling inside of him. I lived with him and knew him better than anyone and yet I always felt that distance. So I let it go. I had the money. I had the perks of marriage, and I was already used to not having him around. It was all okay. Until he died. Jeremy was crushed."

Myron remembered. That had been the last time Myron had seen his biological son—at Greg's funeral crying over the death of his "real" father.

"We're still missing big pieces," Myron said.

"I know."

"Let's say Greg was attracted to Bo. Let's say the two of them ran off together. How do we go from that to Greg, what, faking his own death?"

"I don't know."

"And then, what, he waited a few years and murdered Cecelia Callister and her son?"

"Well," Emily said, "Cecelia was what I *thought* was his type— beautiful and married. But I don't know what to think anymore. Was Greg gay? Was he into married women? Both? Neither? And now the FBI think he's alive and murdered two people. I can't see it, but people are full of secrets, Myron. You know that."

CHAPTER FOUR

———————

When Myron first returned to the Lock-Horne Building after his too-long hiatus, he would constantly get into the elevator and, out of habit, press the fourth-floor button, his old one. Today he did it on purpose. His old office now housed FFD— Fisher, Friedman and Diaz, a hyperaggressive female-led victims' rights law firm. Created by the charismatic and media-savvy Sadie Fisher, FFD advocated for the abused, the bullied, the battered, taking on this new digital era, trying to get the laws updated and the victims protected.

The front page of their website reads:

> We help you knee the abusers, the stalkers, the
> douchebags, the trolls, the pervs and the psychos right
> in the balls.

The new kick-ass law firm was, alas, busy because insecure and violent men (being factual here and not PC/sexist: The vast majority of stalkers and abusers are men, the vast majority of their targets are women) were very much in vogue. As Win put it when he invested in FFD, "Insecure, enraged men are a growth industry."

The receptionist wasn't at her desk, so Myron knocked on the office door.

A familiar voice said, "Come in."

Myron opened the door. Esperanza Diaz had her back to him. She was on the phone. She stood looking out the same window in the same office she used when this space had been MB Reps. Esperanza had started off as Myron's receptionist and assistant, but by the time they sold the agency, Esperanza had finished law school, passed the bar, and become his full partner. Eight months ago, not long before Myron decided that it was time to launch his sports-and-entertainment agency comeback, Win introduced Esperanza to Sadie Fisher. The two hit it off, and Fisher and Friedman added Diaz to their name. Now Esperanza, perhaps the best ass-kicker Myron knew, had a whole new arena to kick ass in.

She hung up and turned to him. "Hey, Myron."

"Hey."

Esperanza came toward him. She wore pearls and bold colors. Her blouse and skirt were both super-tight. All the senior partners at FFD were dressed likewise. It had been Sadie Fisher's idea. When Sadie first started representing women who had been sexually harassed or assaulted, she had been told to "tone down" the outfits, to wear clothing that was both drab and shapeless. Sadie hated that. It was more victim blaming and she wouldn't stand for that.

Now the lawyers on this floor did the opposite.

"Working a case?" Myron asked.

"Our client is a second-year law student at Stanford."

"Good school."

"Right. Her stalker, a horrendous guy who threatened to kill her on more than one occasion, was accepted to the same law school and insists on going. I'm getting the judge to issue an order of protection."

"Think you'll get it?"

She shrugged. "Just normal news at FFD. In not-so-normal news, is Greg Downing really alive?"

"Maybe, yeah."

"I never liked him," Esperanza said.

"I know."

"You forgave him. I never did."

"Look, I hurt him—"

"And he hurt you. I know. I've heard you say that before. It's bullshit. You took him on as a client because you wanted to show everyone how magnanimous you could be."

"Don't sugarcoat it, Esperanza. Tell me how you feel."

"Greg destroyed your dream—"

"He didn't know how bad the injury was going to be."

"—and now he's faked his own death and murdered someone."

"Uh, you may be jumping the gun."

"Whatever. I don't want to be part of this."

"Oh," Myron said. "Okay."

"Don't make that face. I hate when you make that face."

"What face?"

"The Helpless Bambi one."

Myron blinked and pouted, playing it up.

"Ugh," she said. "Look, I got your message, and I did a deep dive on this Bo Storm for you." Esperanza sat behind her desk and started typing on her laptop. "By the way, how was seeing Emily?"

"How do you think?"

"Not as bad as usual, I imagine. You're happily married now. It's all in the rearview mirror now."

"True. Except."

"Yeah. Jeremy. I get it." Esperanza kept typing. "First off, Bo Storm isn't his real name."

Myron put his hand to his heart. "Gasp. Oh. Gasp. I'm. So. Surprised."

"Yeah, I'm starting with the obvious because after that, it all gets pretty strange."

"In what way?"

"Bo Storm has been off the radar for five years. I mean totally."

"Since Greg supposedly ran overseas."

"Right. He closed it all down. Not just his Instagram account. Bo had a pretty decént OnlyFans following. Good subscriber base, maybe because his rates were cheap."

"When you say OnlyFans and subscriber base—"

She looked up at him. "You don't know what I mean?"

"I don't."

"You pay for access to see him naked."

"Oh."

"And in sex scenes with other men."

"Oh."

"Do you really not know this?"

Myron shook his head. "And when you say 'his rates were cheap...'"

"His monthly subscription fee was only $1.99—but really I think he just used the OnlyFans to advertise his wares."

"Wares?"

"Prostitution. It's not just for us ladies. From what I've been able to find out, Bo worked at a gay sports bar called"—she raised her gaze and met Myron's eye—"Man United."

Myron looked at her. She continued to look at him.

"That's actually a pretty funny name," Myron said.

"Agreed," Esperanza said.

"Do you have a real name for Bo?"

"Not yet but get this: I'm using this advanced facial recognition image search. You know what that is?"

"Pretend I don't."

"I put in a photo of someone's face. It scours the entire internet and finds other photos that person is in."

"Yikes. Talk about Big Brother."

"It's not new technology, Myron. It's been around for years."

"Okay, so what did you find?"

"Bo is in a bunch of posted photos from the clubs. Parties, tourists, that kind of thing. So far, I've found two things that are relevant for you. One, there are no recent photographs of him. Nothing at all in the last five years."

"So," Myron said, "since he stopped posting—"

"No one has posted a photo of him anywhere. That's right. And that's rare. You really have to try to stay that off the radar."

Myron took that in. "What's the other thing?"

"There is one crowd shot of Bo that you'll find very intriguing."

"Crowd shot?"

"As in, he's in a crowd. As in, a sporting event. As in, your friend Bo attended an NBA basketball game."

Myron froze. "As in, a game coached by Greg Downing?"

Esperanza nodded. "Greg's Milwaukee Bucks in Phoenix playing the Suns. Six years ago. I zoomed it in for you and printed it out."

She handed him a photograph. Yep, crowd shot. Bo sat behind the Bucks' bench next to an uber-tan, uber-blonde woman packed into a tight tank top.

"Can't be a coincidence," Myron said.

"Man, you're good."

He smiled. He was happy that Esperanza had found such satisfaction in this new job, but he missed working with her on a day-to-day basis. MB Reps wasn't MB Reps without Esperanza.

"So how do we find Bo Storm after all this time?" Myron asked. "Maybe Man United had his real name for payroll?"

"Already tried that. They're under new ownership and got rid of all the old records."

An idea came to Myron. "Explain that facial recognition search thing you did."

"It's fairly self-explanatory."

"So if you had a photo of me—"

"I could put it through the search engine and theoretically it would find every photograph with you in it on the web."

"Open up Bo's dormant Instagram page for a second."

Esperanza did. Myron started scrolling through it. He stopped and pointed. "This guy," Myron said. "He's in at least a dozen of Bo's photos."

She read the captions out loud: "'*Me and Jord doing our thang.*' '*Jord and me at the club.*' Hmm, both of these guys are hot. Gay guys keep in such great shape. A lot of shots of them at the club shirtless."

"Yeah, but not that." Myron scrolled some more. "Here's one of Bo and Jord at a barbecue in a yard."

"Still shirtless."

"And look—'*Having the boys over for the Super Bowl.*'"

"Still shirtless," Esperanza repeated, making a face. "Who watches the Super Bowl shirtless?"

"Can we put this Jord guy through your search engine?"

Esperanza nodded. "That's not a bad idea."

"Every once in a while."

"Give me an hour, okay?"

"Okay."

Myron just sat there and stared at her.

Esperanza said, "I got something stuck in my teeth?"

"No."

"What then?"

"I miss this. Don't you miss this?"

She said nothing.

He leaned forward. "Come back to MB Reps."

She still said nothing.

"I'll even add your initials into the title."

Esperanza arched an eyebrow. "MBED Reps?"

"Sure."

"That's a terrible name," she said. "Then again, so is MB Reps."

"Fair."

"I'm doing good work here."

"I know."

"Sadie is amazing."

"I know that too. So do both. Half time here with Sadie, half time back with me."

"Do good," she said, "and bad."

"Whatever floats your boat."

She shook her head.

"What?"

"I love you," she said. "You know that."

"I love you too."

"You're my best friend. You'll always be my best friend."

"Same."

"With Win. I get it."

"What's your point?"

"You don't like change, Myron."

Now it was Myron's turn to stay quiet.

"Where's Terese?" Esperanza asked.

That was Myron's wife.

"She's in Atlanta."

"Where she's working."

"Yes."

"While you're in New York."

"She's coming to visit."

Silence.

"It'll be fine," Myron said.

"Will it?"

"I love Terese," Myron said.

"I know you do," Esperanza said, but there was a tinge of sadness there. "Let's find Greg, okay? Then we can talk more about the rest of this."

———————

An hour later, Myron got a call from Esperanza. "I got something on Bo's online buddy Jord," she said.

"What?"

"I'm coming up to show you."

Two minutes later, Myron heard Big Cyndi squeal, a sound that makes children cringe and your cat hide under the couch. But it was, Myron knew, a squeal of delight. Esperanza, he deduced, had arrived. Myron stepped into the foyer as Big Cyndi wrapped her tremendous arms around Esperanza. It would be grossly inadequate to call what Big Cyndi gave those she loved merely a "hug." Big Cyndi's embraces were all-encompassing, all-consuming, like your entire body was being wrapped up in damp attic insulation.

Myron watched and smiled. Years ago, Big Cyndi and Esperanza had been a hugely popular pro wrestling tag-team champion for the famed league known as FLOW, which stood for the Fabulous Ladies

of Wrestling (they had originally been called the Beautiful Ladies of
Wrestling, but a TV network had an issue with the acronym). Their
monikers were Big Chief Mama (Big Cyndi) and Little Pocahontas, the Indian Princess (Esperanza). Both women were Latina, not
Native American, but no one seemed to care. Yeah, it was a different
era. The size difference between the partners—Big Cyndi was six
foot six and flirting with three hundred pounds while Esperanza was
maybe five two and sported a minuscule suede bikini with fringes—
made for a comical and dramatic appearance. Pro wrestling is never
about the wrestling. It's about the plot and the characters. It's a
morality play, almost biblical in its storytelling. Little Pocahontas
would always be skillfully and honestly winning a match when their
bad-guy opponents did something illegal and sleezy—the dreaded
foreign object, throwing sand in her eyes, whatever—and the crowd
would scream and cry and boo and worry because Little Pocahontas
would suddenly be in extreme distress, getting mercilessly beaten,
until Big Chief Mama jumped back in the ring, erupted, threw the
bad guys off her, and then, again using creativity and skill, the two
would come back in the match for the miracle win.

Somehow this was massively entertaining.

Eventually Esperanza wanted out of the wrestling game. She
came to work for MB SportsReps as Myron's assistant and, as mentioned earlier, worked her way up to partner. When they needed a
third in the office to take over the reception desk, they hired Big
Cyndi.

Still holding Esperanza, Big Cyndi started sobbing. She wore
a tremendous amount of garish makeup, and when she cried like
this, her makeup ran everywhere, so that her face resembled a box
of crayons left in the blazing sun on a concrete surface. That was
Big Cyndi. She lived life loud and embraced it all. She drew stares,

no way around it, but Myron remembered years ago, when he still didn't quite get her, Big Cyndi explained: "I'd rather see shock on their faces than pity, Mr. Bolitar. And I'd rather they see brazen or outrageous than shrinking or scared."

"It's okay," Esperanza said soothingly, stroking Big Cyndi's back. "You just saw me this morning, remember?"

"But that was down *there*," Big Cyndi replied. She said the word "there" as though it were something cursed. "But now you're *here*, with us, back where you belong...."

It was true, Myron realized. This was the first time Esperanza had been up to see their new digs. She had probably stayed away on purpose.

"It's nice to see you *here*," Myron added.

Esperanza made a face. Then she said, "Bo's friend Jord? His real name is Jordan Kravat."

"So you found him."

"So to speak. He's dead."

"Whoa."

"Murdered."

"Double whoa." Myron tried to take that in. "When?"

"Guess."

"Five years ago."

"You're good."

"Before or after Bo vanished?"

"Right around the same time."

"So Bo's friend Jordan is murdered—"

"I think Bo and Jordan were more than friends."

"Oh. Okay. Either way, Jordan gets murdered, and Bo vanishes."

"And Greg decides to go off the grid," Esperanza added.

"Obvious question: Was Bo a suspect?"

"They convicted someone else. A local organized crime boss went down for it."

Myron considered that. "Still. The timing. It can't be a coincidence."

"One more wrinkle."

"I'm listening."

"You remember that Bo worked out of a gay sports bar?"

"Man United," Myron said.

"Right. The bar was owned by Donna Kravat. That's Jordan Kravat's mother."

Myron felt that thrum when pieces are starting to land on the table. He had no idea how they fit. None whatsoever yet. But pieces were landing and they mattered and that was a start. Shake the box. Get the pieces out and onto the table. Then you can begin to put them together.

"We got an address on the mom?"

"We do. She's still in Vegas."

"I should probably fly out then."

"I saw Win on my way up."

"Did you mention Vegas?"

"I did. He's already got the jet gassed up and ready to go."

CHAPTER FIVE

Two hours later, Myron and Win sat on Win's private jet as it taxied down the runway at Teterboro Airport in northern New Jersey. The flight attendant, a woman named Mee, gave Win a cognac and Myron a can of a chocolate concoction called Yoo-hoo. Myron had spent most of his life drinking Yoo-hoo, but over the past few years, his desire for a soda that tasted like chocolate milk had deserted him. Still, Mee always brought him one and he drank it because he didn't have the heart to tell her or himself that maybe he'd outgrown his once-favorite beverage.

"I just read an article," Win said, "that a popular new drink mixes Yoo-hoo with absinthe."

"Gross," Myron said.

"I don't know. You know what they say. Absinthe makes the heart grow fonder."

Myron looked at Win. Win looked at Myron.

Win finally said, "I have the file, but fill me in."

Myron did. Win listened in silence. When he finished, Win said, "Do you remember Huey Lewis and the News?"

The non sequitur shouldn't have caught Myron unawares, but somehow it did. "Of course. You hate them."

"Hate is so passé, Myron. People hate bands to sound cool. Like Creed or Nickelback. Let people enjoy what they enjoy."

"I once saw you pull a gun on a wedding band when they played 'The Heart of Rock and Roll.'"

"Come on. When they rhyme 'beating' with 'Cleveland'..."

"Okay, yeah, I get it."

"And let's be fair," Win said. "Who hires a Huey Lewis Yiddish tribute band?"

"With a female vocalist," Myron said.

"What were they called again?"

"Judy Lewis and the Jews." Then: "Is there a point to this conversation?"

"Just that I recently learned the original name for the band was Huey Lewis and the American Express. They changed their name to the News because they worried the credit card company would sue them."

Myron nodded. "In short, there is no point."

"None at all. So let's get to the matter at hand, shall we?"

Win had bought the luxury jet from a rapper who was a Duke alum too. There were sleeping quarters and a shower on board. The carpet was golf-course green with a putting surface in the back right-hand corner.

"Go ahead," Myron said.

Win slipped on his reading glasses. He looked older with them. His beloved blond locks of privilege had streaks of gray now, especially around the temples. The clenched-mouth jowls sagged just a tad more than they did a few years ago. They were aging, Myron realized. Better than most. But no one gets out unscathed. "Greg Downing meets this handsome, too-young-for-him dancer-slash-sex-worker named Bo Storm. Do we think it was online or in person?"

"We don't know for sure," Myron said. "We do know that Bo attended an NBA game in Phoenix where Greg coached."

"And sat behind the bench."

"Correct."

"So we have that. And we know that Greg and Bo were direct messaging via Instagram."

"Right."

"At some point, a man named Jordan Kravat, Bo's boyfriend—we are assuming a romantic entanglement, no?"

"Might as well."

"Either way, Jordan Kravat is murdered. Subsequently, Bo vanishes, Greg claims hermit status and moves overseas—and for a while, there is no sign of either of them. Two years later, Greg purportedly dies, and we inter his ashes. And now, very recently, Greg's DNA is found at a murder scene. That pretty much sum it up?"

"Pretty much."

Win frowned. "I'm still not seeing much here."

"Meaning?"

"What do you figure happened? Greg and Bo fell in love and, what, murdered Jordan Kravat before running off—only to fake Greg's death, sneak back into the country, and murder a somewhat notorious supermodel."

"Step at a time," Myron said. "Someone was arrested for Jordan Kravat's death."

"A career mob boss named Joseph Turant." Win pulled out a sheet of paper. "Everyone calls him Joey the Toe."

Myron frowned. "Joey the Toe?"

"It's a poorly conceived moniker," Win agreed.

"I mean Joey the Toe? If you call a guy 'The Toe,' why not go for the rhyme?"

"Exactly. Joe the Toe."

"Has a much better ring, I think," Myron said. "Joe the Toe versus

Joey the Toe. And what kind of nickname is 'The Toe' anyway? How does someone come up with that?"

Win said, "Joey likes to cut off toes."

"Oh. Then the name kind of makes sense."

"It does," Win said.

"Maybe a tad too literal."

"Agree. And it's only the baby toe. Joey keeps them as souvenirs. They found sixteen in his freezer when they served the warrant."

"Sixteen baby toes?"

"Yes."

"That must be a real icebreaker at a party," Myron said.

"Three of the toes were female, thirteen male."

"Was one of them Jordan Kravat's?"

"Yes."

"This case." Myron just shook his head. "What else do we have on our podophilic friend Joey the Toe?"

"Podophilic," Win repeated. "Good word."

"You're not the only one who can give vocabulary seminars."

Win sighed. "Let's press on, shall we? Joey the Toe ran the Turant crime family. According to this, he has a fairly extensive record— the usual potpourri of extortion, corruption, murder, assault, loan sharking, racketeering."

"'Racketeering' is a nice all-encompassing term," Myron said.

"Isn't it? Anyway, Joey the Toe was arrested and convicted for the murder of Jordan Kravat. He's serving a life sentence in Ely State Prison in Nevada."

"Interesting," Myron said.

"I don't really see what we hope to learn from the victim's mother."

"You know how this works, Win. We knock on doors and stir the pot and muck things up and hope something rises to the surface."

"Our usual carefully crafted plan, then."

"Correct."

"Feels like a waste of time."

"I could have come alone."

"To Vegas?" Win arched an eyebrow. "You know I never miss a trip to Vegas."

"Big plans, Win?"

"Golf and debauchery, yes."

"I thought you didn't do that anymore."

"What, golf?"

"Haha. I thought you gave up prostitutes."

"I did. Sort of. And you need to stop shaming sex workers. 'Support sex workers' isn't just an empty progressive catchphrase to me."

"Yes, you're very enlightened."

"That said, I am much more cautious than I used to be."

"In what way?"

"I make sure that there is no abuse or coercion or trafficking going on."

"How do you do that?"

"We don't need to go into details. But I know." He steepled his fingers. "It's always been a dichotomous issue for me: I want no emotional connection when it comes to the act of sex because I feel that gets in the way of the physical pleasure—and yet I don't want it to be cold or impersonal either. A purely financial transaction doesn't work for me. I need to feel as though the participant—the lucky participant, I may add—is attracted to me. I need to believe I am desired."

Win looked up and waited.

Myron said, "Wow."

"I'm a lot," Win said.

"You realize what you said has several massive contradictions, right?"

"We are all contradictions, Myron. We are all hypocrites. We want black and white. But it's all gray."

Mee, the flight attendant, came over. "We have some goodies if anyone is hungry."

"Thanks, Mee. I'll have the caviar."

She looked to Myron. "The same, please."

When she left, Win felt Myron's eyes on him. Win said, "Never with employees anymore. Never. I think it's why Yu quit."

"Because you slept with her?"

"What? No. The opposite."

Back in the day, Win would have relations with his flight attendants Yu and Mee, in part to make terrible puns, like when Myron would ask Win where he was, Win would answer "Between Yu and Mee."

"Are you saying Yu quit because you wouldn't have sex with her?"

"Perhaps."

"I thought it was because she opened a successful real estate agency in Santa Fe."

"Allow me my delusions, Myron." Win shifted in his seat. "So how did it go with your ex?"

Myron filled him in on the conversation with Emily. At the end, Myron added, "Oh, and one thing I found interesting: Emily used to be friendly with Cecelia Callister."

"So was I," Win said.

"Wait, what? When?"

"A long time ago. We had a weekend."

Myron just shook his head.

"It was glorious, if you must know."

"No, I mustn't."

"She was maybe a tad performative. I find beautiful women can often be performative. Do you find that, Myron?"

"No."

"They need to be in love to really let go."

"That's true of most women. Men too."

Win cocked his head. "You don't really believe that."

"You never told me about you and Cecelia Callister."

"A gentleman never kisses and tells."

"You always tell."

"Well, I'm not a gentleman."

CHAPTER SIX

A few hours later, the familiar sight of the Las Vegas Strip came into view as Win's jet landed at what was now called Harry Reid International Airport. The landing was smooth enough to have been choreographed by the Four Tops. They taxied to a stop. Myron and Win walked off the plane. Two black Mercedes-Maybach GLS SUVs waited on the tarmac. One would take Win and his golf clubs to the Shadow Creek golf course. Win was a scratch golfer, a member of Merion, Pine Valley, Seminole, Winged Foot, and Adiona Island. If you know, you know. Win came from a long line of golfers. His ancestors stepped off the *Mayflower* with top-of-the-line golf clubs and desirable tee times.

The other SUV would take Myron to Donna Kravat's residence.

"Where are we staying?" Myron asked.

"The Wynn. Know why?"

"Because it's a good hotel in the heart of the Strip?"

"Yes, but also the alliteration. Win at the Wynn."

"Oh boy."

Myron's ride to the housing development at Kyle Canyon took half an hour. He hadn't called first, but Win had sent a local private investigator to make sure that Jord Kravat's mother, Donna, would be home. According to the investigator, Donna was now at the condo pool in a chaise lounge by the deep end, wearing a bright pink bikini. Myron's preconceived stupidity told him that anyone with a full-grown adult child had to look a certain age. Yep, sexist of him. Donna Kravat was probably Myron's age, maybe a few years older, and looked fantastic. No doubt that there had been what Myron's mother euphemistically called "work done," but so what? That was common in this era and especially around this pool. Half of Myron's high school class in Livingston had nose jobs. Some people dye their hair. Some people do whatever. Let it go, people. Do what you want. Myron himself had gotten cosmetic veneers on his teeth a few years ago. Who was he to judge?

That said, the "work" here was well done. Donna Kravat was a wee bit faux curvy, but again, so what?

"Donna Kravat?"

She lowered her sunglasses. "I know you."

"I don't think we've met. My name is—"

"Myron Bolitar," she said. "You played ball at Duke."

It was rare people remembered him from his playing days anymore. "Did someone tell you I was coming?"

"No," Donna said. "But I was a senior at Wake Forest when you were a freshman at Duke. Rode the bench for the women's team back in the day." She gave him a big smile. Yep, she had veneers too. "You were a great player."

"Thanks."

Her smile dropped. "When you hurt your knee, I mean, so early in your career..."

"It was a long time ago," Myron said.

"Still," she said. Donna Kravat took off her sunglasses and sat up. "So okay I'm super-curious. Why does Myron Bolitar want to see me?"

They were there now. Myron had rehearsed various ways to

begin the conversation, but how do you come out of nowhere to ask a mother about her murdered son?

Donna Kravat saw it and nodded. "It's about Jordan."

"Yes. If you'd rather go someplace more private—"

"Oh, I'd love to go someplace private," she said, forcing up a hint of a double entendre to mask something that couldn't be masked. "But we can talk here. My son never leaves me, you know. Not for a second. His murder is my constant companion. If you try to push it away, it just waits and jumps out when you're not ready. So Jordan is always right here, right next to me."

"I'm sorry," Myron said.

She picked up her phone. Maybe to answer a text. Maybe to give herself a moment. She typed deliberately. Myron stayed silent. Still looking at her phone, Donna Kravat paused, then asked, "Did you know my son?"

"No. This is about a friend of his."

She nodded. "Bo."

"Yes. How did you know?"

"It's not exactly a brilliant deduction on my part. He's the only friend who vanished after Jordan's murder. Do you know where he is?"

"I was hoping you could tell me."

"I haven't seen him since he testified against Jord's killer. Why are you looking for him?"

Myron wondered how to answer that and settled for, "It's a long story."

"Is this where I say I've got all the time in the world?"

"After I was injured, I became a lawyer and a sports agent."

"I think I read something about that. You were on the cover of

Sports Illustrated after you got hurt. With your knee in a cast or something. They thought you might make a comeback."

"Didn't work out. Anyway, this involves one of my clients, so I have to keep it confidential."

"Attorney-client privilege," she said.

"Yes. If that's okay." Myron tried to keep the conversation going. "Were Bo and your son close?"

"They were a couple, if that's what you're asking. They met through me, actually. I owned a bar."

"This would be Man United?"

"Good name, right?"

"Very."

"I spent a semester in England my junior year at Wake Forest. Became a big fan of Manchester United. That's how I thought up the name. Did you do that at Duke?"

"A semester abroad?"

"Yes."

"Couldn't. Basketball."

"Right, of course. Like I said, I was more a bench warmer. Anyway, my son told me he was gay when he was fifteen, though it was hardly a surprise. I wanted to be supportive of his choices, and I thought I could make a profit with the club. But I was wrong on both counts."

"How so?"

"We started great. I mean, Man United was a big hit. And it was fun. Really. And I tried to keep it clean. Sure, some of the dancers engaged in private deals. Made side money. That's going to happen."

"You mean prostitution?"

"Right, whatever. But then the mob came in. They came in hard.

They wanted a cut of everything. They started pressing the guys to do more. We tried to stand up to them but . . ."

"And Joey Turant was one of those mobsters?"

"He and his family, yes." She shook her head and looked off. "Jordan didn't get how dangerous the Turants were. I told him to back off. But that wasn't his personality."

"I'm sorry."

She nodded, took that in, gave herself a second. "Do you want to know where I think Bo is?"

"Yes, of course."

"I think he's buried somewhere out in the desert. I think they killed him too."

Myron considered that. Donna studied his face.

"You don't agree," she said.

"I don't know."

"But?"

"But I think Bo's alive."

"Why?"

Myron said nothing.

"The attorney-client privilege again?"

"Do you know Bo's real name?" Myron asked.

Now it was Donna Kravat who stayed quiet.

"Donna?"

"You seem like a good guy," she said. "But I don't really know you. I don't know why you're here."

"I told you."

"You found something out about Bo, and now you're looking for him. Like I said before, I think he's buried in the desert somewhere. But if he's not, if he's on the run, maybe a guy like you is part of the reason why."

"It's not. I want to help."

Her face closed down. She put the sunglasses back on and lay back. Myron had to find a way to get her to speak to him again.

"You're a basketball fan," he said.

She didn't reply.

"So you remember Greg Downing, right?"

That got her attention. She lowered the sunglasses and looked over the rims at him. "Of course. I even saw you two go head-to-head in college. I was sorry to hear he died so young. I was a fan."

"Did you ever meet him?"

"Greg Downing? No."

"Did your son ever mention him?"

"No, never." She sat all the way back up now. "How would Jordan have been connected to Greg Downing?"

"Bo may have been friends with Greg."

"What? When?"

She met Myron's eye. Myron just nodded.

"I don't understand. You think Bo and Greg Downing..."

"I don't know. It's why I'm here. I need to find Bo. Please, Donna. What was Bo's real name?"

"No, sorry, that's not how that works," she said. "You come here unannounced. You ask about my murdered son. What aren't you telling me?"

"There's nothing to tell right now," Myron said. "If I learn anything, I promise to tell you. Please."

She stood now and slipped into a cover-up. She put her hands on her hips and let loose a big sigh. "He claimed his real name was Brian Connors."

"Claimed?"

"He wouldn't give me a Social Security number or anything. It was all off the books. So I don't know if it's real or not."

"Did he say where he was from?"

"Somewhere in Oklahoma."

"Do you know if he has any family?"

"He was close to his mother. Her name is Grace."

"Father? Siblings?"

"The parents were divorced a long time. The father's dead. There may be a brother, I'm not sure. Bo was very secretive about his past. I don't know why." She moved closer to him. "How long are you in town?"

"Probably just overnight."

"Do you want to have dinner with me?"

Myron hesitated. She held his eye and boy, it seemed like a come-on, but he really wasn't sure. He raised his left hand feebly, pointed to his ring, and cringingly said, "I'm married."

"Me too."

And then, because Myron was smooth, he said, "Oh."

"But you know what they say: What happens in Vegas stays in Vegas."

"Yeah," Myron said. Then: "That's not really my style."

"Then how about as two former ACC athletes? I think there's more we should discuss. But I can't right now. Where are you staying?"

"The Wynn."

"I'll meet you at Mizumi. Tonight. Eight o'clock."

CHAPTER SEVEN

M yron called Esperanza as he walked back to the Mercedes
SUV.

"There's going to be a lot of Brian Connors."

"Mother is named Grace." Myron slid into the backseat of the car with the phone on his ear. The driver shifted the SUV into drive and started down the road. "He's maybe from Oklahoma."

"I'll get on it."

"Thanks." Myron hung up and sat back.

They'd traveled about two more blocks when Myron realized something was wrong.

"Excuse me," he said to the driver. "Where's Harold?"

"He had to take off. I'm his replacement."

"What's your name?"

"Sal."

"Sal, I'm Myron."

"Nice to meet you, Myron."

"Likewise. Harold said something about his wife being sick."

"Yeah, that's why he had to leave. Sorry for the inconvenience."

"No worries," Myron said.

Myron surreptitiously tried the car door. Locked. Not unexpected. He checked his phone to make sure the phone locator was on. It was. It always was. He and Win shared locations all the time.

Just in case.

Just in case something like this arose. Myron dropped a pin and pressed the silent alarm button on his phone. It would reach Win and let him know that trouble was a-brewing.

Then, with the car stopped at a traffic light, Myron leaned forward, snaked his arm around Sal's neck, and pulled back hard against the man's throat.

Sal made a gurgling noise.

Myron dug in deeper, cutting off the air supply. Sal's hands flew up to the crook of Myron's elbow, feebly clawing at it, trying to find some way to dislodge or loosen the grip.

Myron held tight.

With his mouth close to Sal's ear, Myron whispered, "My driver's name was Fred. And he's single."

Myron flexed the bicep to get an even tighter squeeze.

Sal's body bucked.

Myron spotted the car's key fob on the console between the seats. It was awkward—right arm around Sal's throat, left arm reaching across it—but Myron was able to stretch over himself like in some childhood game of Twister. Once he got hold of the key, he debated how to play it. Did he stay in the car now and get Sal to talk? Or did he just get the hell out of the car and to safety?

All of the calculations went through his head in nanoseconds. Chances were, Sal the Driver wasn't the only one in on this. Someone had gotten rid of Fred, either through trickery or coercion, and if it was coercion, it was important to figure that out and find Fred as soon as possible.

There was also Rule One in the Myron Bolitar Rules of Engagement: Get to safety. Confronting your adversary came later.

Win would want to take on this fight. He would relish finishing Sal off.

Myron not so much.

The light turned green.

Myron unlocked the doors with the fob. He worried that when he released his grip to leave the vehicle, Sal might hit the gas on him. Myron couldn't risk that. Could the fob turn the engine off? He didn't know how. So Myron tried a simpler move.

He reeled back and punched Sal hard in the side of the head—hard enough, Myron knew from experience, to stun him until Myron could get out of the car safely.

But that was not how it worked out.

After the punch landed, before Myron could make another move, both back doors of the SUV flew open.

Two men climbed in, one on the left, one on the right. Both had guns.

This wasn't good.

Myron didn't hesitate. Before the door had a chance to close, with the man on his left still sliding into the seat, Myron elbowed him hard in the nose. He could feel the bones in the man's nose spread and give way.

Myron pushed the man hard and started to roll out.

"Don't move!"

That was the guy entering the vehicle from Myron's right. Myron stopped, debated his play here. Would the guy shoot him? Probably not. If they wanted to kill him, they would have done so. Maybe. They had tried to abduct him. Who were they? And for what purpose? Myron didn't know.

He only knew that his best bet was to get the hell out of the car.

Then again, he'd dropped a location pin and alarm already.

Win would be on the way.

So maybe the answer was to stall?

No.

Myron raised his hands as though in surrender. Here is a truth. Myron was a good fighter. He was well trained. But more than that, he had the reflexes and speed of a professional athlete. No, that's not faster than a bullet. But yes, using the element of surprise as well as his size and strength and genetic gifts, Myron slowed down the hand raise, all the while planning the move. When the time came, when he could feel just the slightest overconfidence and lapse in the gunman's concentration, Myron saw an opening.

Now, he told himself.

The fingers on Myron's right hand formed a spear. He struck cobra-like at the throat. The gunman's eyes widened in pain. Myron's left fist came right behind it. The blow landed flush on the jaw, sending the guy reeling. With the door still slightly open, Myron shoved the man right out of the car.

"Okay, that's enough!"

The voice had come from the front seat. His buddy Sal the Driver. Now Sal had a gun too, and with the roomy backseat of the Mercedes-Maybach, Myron would have no chance to reach him in time. Sal pointed the gun, his eyes wide and full of rage.

He wanted to shoot.

Myron hesitated. And that was all it took.

The man on the left, the one he'd elbowed in the nose, hit Myron on the side of the head with the butt of the gun. Myron saw stars. There was another blow—Myron wasn't sure from where—and then another.

And then there was blackness.

CHAPTER EIGHT

M yron was tied to a chair in the center of the room. His left shoe and sock were off.

Next to his bare foot was a set of pruning shears.

There was also a protective plastic sheet under the foot.

Oh, this wasn't good.

There were four men. One was Sal. Two were the men who'd jumped in from the sides. And there was a new one, clearly the leader, who stood in front of him.

"Saw the pin drop to your friend," the leader said. "Sal stuck your phone in the back of a truck heading west. Your friend is probably tracking you to the California border by now."

The leader's appearance screamed old-school bad guy. He had the greasy two-day growth on his face. His hair was slicked back and his shirt was unbuttoned. He had gold chains ensnared in his chest hairs and a toothpick clenched in his teeth.

"I guess you were some hotshot basketball player back in the day," the leader said. "But I never heard of you."

"Wow," Myron said. "Now you've hurt my feelings."

The leader smiled, gave the toothpick a good chew. "We got ourselves a comedian, boys."

"I'm also a gifted vocalist," Myron said. "Want to hear my rendition of 'Volare'?"

"Oh, I'm going to hear you sing all right."

Again the smile. Myron didn't look away. Rule Two of Engagement: You never show fear. Not ever. That was what Myron had learned. These guys feed off fear. It arouses them. It gives them strength.

Assess. That was what Myron knew to do. Take it in. Figure out what he could. Myron checked out the space quickly. The walls were concrete. There was a tire pump against one wall. A shovel too. There were tools on the wall.

Could be a garage.

He could hear traffic outside, the occasional loud radio as a car speeded by. The leader stepped forward. He kept chewing the toothpick.

"Where is Bo?"

"The toothpick," Myron said. "Don't you think it's a bit much?"

"What?"

"The Badass gnawing on a toothpick," Myron continued. "It's been done. A lot."

That made the leader smile. "Good point." He spit out the toothpick and moved closer. "Let me tell you how this is going to play out, okay? See your foot? The one with no shoe or sock?"

"I do, yeah."

"So here's the thing, hotshot. We're going to cut off your pinky toe. That's not open for discussion. You can't get out of it. It has to happen. It's our boss's thing. Like it's his slogan or something."

"His MO," Sal corrected.

The leader nodded. "Yeah, that's better, thanks. His MO." Then: "What's MO stand for anyway?"

"Operating method, I think."

"Then it would be OM."

"Right," Sal said. "Wait. I think it's Method of Operation?"

"Then it would be MOO."

"Moo," Sal said. "Like a cow."

"Right. And that would be easier to say, right? We would say 'cutting off a toe is his moo.' Moo is one syllable. It's easier to say. MO is two syllables. Who'd abbreviate it and make it harder to say? So it can't be that."

"We can google MO, Jazz," Sal said.

"Right, of course."

Then Myron said, "Modus operandi."

"Huh?"

"That's what MO stands for. Modus operandi. It's Latin."

Jazz liked that. "Look at Einstein the comic vocalist over here," he said.

Sal added, "Einstein without a pinky toe."

"Well, he'll still have *one* pinky toe if he cooperates."

"Einstein with one pinky toe instead of two."

"Kind of a mouthful, Sal." The leader—Jazz—turned back to Myron. "So that's the deal, my friend. You lose the pinky toe. No matter what. Even if you sing like a canary. But if you don't want to lose more appendages—"

"Good word, Jazz."

"What, 'appendages'?"

"Yeah."

"Thanks, Sal. I do that word-a-day thing online." Back to Myron. "Anyway, if you don't want to lose more *appendages*"—he looked back and winked at Sal as he said it—"you'll tell us what we want to know. Where is Bo?"

"How do you know I'm looking for him?" Myron asked.

"Yeah, that's not really important."

"Well, yeah, Jazz—can I call you Jazz?—yeah, Jazz, it is."

"How so?"

"Because if you know I'm looking for Bo, you also know I don't know where he is. If I did know, I wouldn't be looking for him, would I?"

Jazz took that in. He looked at Sal.

Sal said, "Kinda makes sense, Jazz."

The other two goons nodded agreement.

"But you are looking for him, right?" Jazz said.

"Yes."

"Why?"

Myron debated how to play it and decided to play it as straight as possible. "He may be connected to another missing person."

"Who?"

"Who what?"

"Who's the other missing person?"

"Oh," Myron said to stall. "You know what's interesting?"

"Can't wait to hear."

"We both seem to be on the same side here."

Jazz rubbed his chin. "How do you figure?"

"We are both looking for Bo Storm. If we pool our knowledge, we could probably help each other out."

"Oh man, that would·be great, Myron. I so want to help you out. It's what I live for really."

Sal shook his head. "The dude is stalling."

"No shit, Sherlock. Let's clip off the toe and speed this up. Jerry?"

One of the goons said, "What?"

"You got the ice cooler?"

Jerry the Goon brought over a small Coleman cooler, the kind of thing you'd store a six-pack in, and placed it next to Myron's foot. He looked back at Jazz.

"Go ahead, Jerry. Do the honors."

The idea clearly didn't thrill Jerry. "I did it last time."

"So? You're good at it."

Sal said, "I'll do it. I'm still pissed off at him about that choke hold."

This was not good.

Myron tested the ropes. No give at all. Sal moseyed over. Outside, Myron could still hear the cars whizzing by, the snatches of songs on the radio. Sal bent down and picked up the pruning shears. He brandished them right in front of Myron's eyes, slowly squeezing and relaxing the handles, just to show Myron that the shears did, in fact, work.

Myron tried to buck, kick out, move in any way. But there was no give to the ropes.

Sal dropped to his knee by Myron's exposed foot.

"Hold up a second," Myron said, trying to keep the panic out of his voice. "Let's talk this out."

"We will, Myron," Jazz said. "Don't worry about that. But first, the toe has to go."

Sal opened the shears. He showed Myron the curved blade. Myron desperately started to wiggle the foot, tried to squirm or bend or whatever.

Anything so it wouldn't stay still.

"Look, Jazz, Sal, Jerry, whoever—just hold up, okay? I want to cooperate. Tell me why Joey Turant wants to find Bo."

That made Sal stop. "Who said we worked for Joey the Toe?"

"Uh..."

Was he serious?

"Here's the thing," Myron said. "I was going to go to see Joey next."

"In prison?"

"Exactly. Pay my respects. Tell him I want to help."

"This is a cute stall tactic." Jazz smiled. "You don't have a clue, do you?"

It was then that Myron heard a familiar song coming from a nearby car.

"The Heart of Rock and Roll" by Huey Lewis and the American Express/News.

"You talk too much," Jazz said. "Cut the fucking toe off, Sal. He'll be much more cooperative without that toe."

Sal held the foot down. Myron kept bucking.

Sal said, "Jerry, help me here."

Jerry came over. He held the foot down with both hands. Sal opened the clippers. There wasn't much time. The song was still playing. Huey was singing that from what he's seen, he believes them, when the music stopped cold.

Myron stopped squirming. "Sal?"

Sal looked up at him.

"Stop right now or you're going to die."

"Yeah, I don't think so."

Myron closed his eyes and waited.

The first bullet took off the back of Sal's head.

Warm blood and brain matter splattered onto Myron's naked foot.

Myron shouted, "You don't have to—"

But there was no use. Win stepped into the room. While quietly singing that the old boy may be barely breathing, he took out Jerry next with yet another bullet to the head. Then the other goon went down as Win crooned the chorus about the heart of rock and roll, the heart of rock and roll, still beating.

All three shot in the head. All three deader than dead.

Jazz raised his hands. Win pointed the gun at him too while singing, "In Cleveland. Detroit."

Jazz said, "Please don't."

CHAPTER NINE

Three hours later, at eight p.m. on the dot, Donna Kravat sauntered into Mizumi, the sushi place at the Wynn hotel, decked out in a slinky black dress and high high heels. Myron rose and she gave the freshly showered, freshly scrubbed-footed Myron a small buss on the cheek. Donna smelled great. When she sat down, Myron said, "Why did you tip them off?"

"I don't know what you're talking about."

Without warning, Myron snatched her purse from her.

"What the hell—?"

He started rummaging through it, found her phone, pulled it out.

"What are you doing?"

He held the phone up to her face. It unlocked.

"Myron?"

Myron scrolled down on iMessage. "You tipped them off. Right after I arrived. That's who you were texting."

"Myron—"

"Did you know what they would do?"

"Would it matter if I said I didn't?"

"Not really, no."

"I'm surprised," she said. "You still have your toe."

"I'm resourceful."

"I bet you are."

Myron put down the phone. "So why are you helping your son's killer?"

"Because," Donna said, "I don't believe Joey did it."

"Why not? All that evidence—"

"Too much evidence, don't you think?" Donna sat down. So did he. She reached out and beckoned him to return her phone. He did. "Think about it. The fingerprints. The DNA. The weapon. The *toe*."

"Uh, Joey the Toe collects toes. It's in the name."

"Not when he kills someone. He uses it to send a message— a way to intimidate his rivals. Seriously, what kind of idiot keeps a dead man's toe for the police to find? What kind of idiot leaves so many clues behind?"

"Prison is littered with such idiots."

"Joey Turant was senior level of a major crime family. He had no motive to kill my boy."

"You can't know that. Maybe Joey was in the closet and Jordan was going to out him. Maybe Jordan crossed him or looked at him wrong or did nothing—"

"They were on the same side."

Myron didn't get that. "Same side of what?"

"I'm not going into it," she said.

"Yeah, Donna, I think you are. I almost got my toe snipped off because of you."

"So you think, what, I owe you?"

"I don't get it. Why would you sic those goons on me?"

"My son and Bo," she said.

"What about them?"

"Toward the end, their relationship was strained. You know how it is. Two young hot guys trying to commit in a city that's the opposite of commitment."

"One cheated?"

"I don't know. Probably. Probably both. That doesn't matter. Let me ask you something. Put aside your preconceived notions about this case, okay? When a murder occurs, who is always *always* the top suspect?"

Myron saw where she was going with this. "The partner."

"Exactly."

"So you think Bo was involved in Jordan's murder?"

She didn't bother replying.

"Did the police look into Bo?"

That made her chuckle. "Are you kidding? With all that evidence pointing to Joey? They always wanted to nail The Toe—and now a murder case was being served up on a silver platter. I don't even think they cared if Joey did it or not. But one thing was for sure—they weren't going to muddy the waters by looking into other suspects."

That made sense.

"Ever since Bo testified, the Turants have been scouring the planet for him. And they've gotten nowhere. Bo vanished without a trace, without anyone following up, without a single clue. I'd given up. And then, after all these years, you come along—"

"That doesn't mean he had anything to do with your son's murder. Maybe Bo is dead too. Like you said. Maybe Joey got revenge—"

"No. If Joey murdered Bo, why would he be so obsessed with finding him? He'd already know where he was."

Good point.

"Maybe it's like you said before," Myron tried. "Bo was scared. His boyfriend gets murdered. He testifies against the killer. Maybe Bo thinks he's next."

"Maybe. Okay, sure, I doubt it, but who knows? It's possible.

And when we find him, Bo can explain all that. But either way, you, Myron, gave us the first big clue in a long time."

"That being?"

"Greg Downing."

"I'm not following."

"Bo's a good-looking kid. My top dancer for a while. Sexy as all hell. But—how to put this—Bo's belt doesn't go through all the loops, if you know what I mean. He's not that smart or resourceful, certainly not enough to pull off murdering my son and framing someone like Joey the Toe for it." She leaned forward now. "But if someone like Greg Downing was in the picture, if Greg fell in love with those six-pack abs and that tight little ass..."

———————

Win sat in the empty prison visiting room across from Joey the Toe.

"Jazz is your cousin," Win said to him. "That's why I let him live."

Joey sat with his arms crossed. He wasn't cuffed or manacled. There were no barriers between them. It was long past closing hours, but that didn't matter with Joey the Toe. He ran the place.

"So you let him live," Joey said with a shrug. "Is that supposed to mean I owe you a favor?"

"It does not. You sent men after my friend."

"Clearly not my best men."

"I would hope not."

"I should have sent more."

"I don't think it would have changed the outcome," Win said.

"No, I guess not. You had a locator on Bolitar's phone."

"Yes."

"But we moved his phone."

"There's one on his watch too."

Joey the Toe shook his head. "How did my morons miss that?"

"There was also the car."

"What about it?"

"Your guys drove my friend in the limo driver's SUV. The limo company tracks all its cars."

"To make sure none of the drivers takes a little side action," Joey noted with an approving nod. "Smart. So what do you want?"

Win leaned back and steepled his fingers. "You're searching for Bo Storm."

"Duh."

"I can hurt you. You can hurt me. Neither of us needs the headache. So let me explain the situation: We will find Bo Storm. And when we do, we will notify you."

Joey the Toe gave him the stink eye. "Notify me."

Win said nothing.

"Why do you want to find him?" Joey asked.

"He may be connected to another murder."

"Really?" Joey the Toe found that amusing. "Interesting, eh? Then this Jordan Kravat kid, he isn't the only one Bo murdered? Is that what you're saying?"

"I don't know yet."

Joey the Toe leaned back and stroked his beard. "This other murder," he said. "Do the cops like someone other than Bo for it?"

The question caught Win off guard. He considered how to answer the question and decided to go with the truth. "Yes. How did you know?"

"And let me guess. Someone you know—a friend maybe—is about to go down for it?"

"More of a client than a friend," Win said. "But yes."

Joey smiled.

"How did you know?"

"I didn't murder Jordan Kravat. Yeah, yeah, I know you hear that all the time, but I got no reason to lie to you, do I?"

"You don't."

"I got framed. This other murder you're talking about, your client, friend, whatever, he's also being framed. Like me. What kind of evidence do they got on him? DNA? Fingerprints?"

"DNA."

Joey shook his head with a grin. "Hot damn. He's done it again."

CHAPTER TEN

W in's penthouse suite at the Wynn wasn't as palatial as one might think. Oh, it was pretty fantastic and it had the mirror on the ceiling and all of that, but the biggest ones were more homes near the golf courses and Win didn't like that. He wanted to be inside, where the action is.

"I have a lead," Win said to Myron.

"Oh?"

"Correction: Esperanza found the lead. I came up with an inspired idea with what to do with the lead."

"Teamwork makes the dream work."

Win blanched. "Never say that again."

"Right, my bad. The lead?"

"Esperanza didn't find anything on your Brian Connors."

"That's the lead?"

"Does that sound like a lead? As you know, she ran that image search for our friend Bo-Storm-né-Brian-Connors over the last five years."

"And nothing came up."

"So she ran it the other direction."

"Going further backward in time?"

"Yes."

"So photos more than five years old."

"This one is more than ten. Here."

Win handed Myron an 8 × 10 glossy photograph. Myron looked at it. He felt his pulse pick up a step.

"Whoa."

"Always a way with words."

There were two people in the photograph. One was a very young Bo Storm. Myron would guess that he was sixteen, maybe seventeen. He wore a tank top. His muscles were big but not as defined as they would later be. Bo was tall from what Myron could see. Myron was six four and he'd guess that Bo was about the same.

The other man in the photograph made Bo look small.

The other man was enormous—six nine, maybe six ten, and two hundred seventy pounds minimum. He wore an Oklahoma State basketball uniform. Myron remembered him. Good rebounder, good defender, good three-point jumper for a guy his size.

"Spark Konners," Myron said. "With a K."

"Correct."

Myron looked over at Win. "Spark worked as an assistant coach under Greg in Milwaukee."

"Again correct. What else do you know about him?"

"He never made it to the NBA—I think maybe Spark played a year or two in Italy or Spain—but I remember Greg saying the kid was smart. Had a big future in coaching. So Bo is...?"

"Brian Konners," Win said. "Spark's younger brother. Esperanza did a background check. There is no record of Bo or Brian anywhere over the past five years—no credit cards, no bank accounts, nothing."

"What the hell, Win?"

"It is perplexing."

"So maybe Bo and Greg didn't meet online by chance."

"Seems unlikely."

"They met through Greg's assistant coach Spark Konners." Myron looked up. "I wonder whether Spark invited his brother to that game in Phoenix. That's probably where Bo-Brian and Greg met."

"Could be."

"We need to talk to Spark."

"We do indeed."

Myron thought about it. "After Greg quit coaching, Milwaukee cleaned house, so I know Spark isn't working there anymore."

"Esperanza already tracked him down. Spark Konners is plying his trade as an assistant coach at Amherst College."

"Big step down." Myron made a face. "Isn't Amherst a Division 3 school?"

"It's hard to stay on top."

"We have to talk to him."

Win smiled. "Remember I said that Esperanza came up with a lead?"

"And you came up with an inspired idea off it. I remember."

"Spark Konners just arrived in the lobby. He's on his way up."

"He's here? Wait, how?"

"I sent a plane for him."

"And he got on just like that?"

"He may be under the impression that the NBA is creating a franchise in Las Vegas and that he may be in line to coach for them."

Myron stared at Win. "Wow."

"Right? So the impetuous owner of this new franchise sent a plane for him."

"You're the owner?"

"The *impetuous* owner," Win corrected. Then: "I always wanted to own a basketball franchise."

"You don't like pro basketball."

"Too much fouling," Win said. "Too many time-outs. It's so boring after a while. You know what would make the game more exciting?"

"You being one of the teams' impetuous owners?"

"Yes, that, but also—" The doorbell sounded. "He's here. I'll tell you my ideas later."

"Can't wait."

Win called out, "Ladies."

Three modelesque women appeared from the other room. They all worked the same look—shiny, sleek, jet-black hair perfectly transitioning to shiny, sleek, jet-black dresses. They pouted and strutted in perfect, confident unison, as though they'd rehearsed this.

"Why are they here?" Myron asked.

"For appearances."

"I'm not following."

"They're all hot social media influencers with huge followings. And you know who would hang out with hot social media influencers with huge followings?"

Myron saw where this was going. "An impetuous owner?"

Win smiled. "Now you're getting it."

When Win opened the door, Spark filled the doorway like a solar eclipse. The huge man had to bend his way into the room. He gave Win a firm handshake.

"Okay, ladies, time to go," Win said. "Let the boys have some space to talk."

The influencers tee-heed and filed out, giving Spark Konners little waves as they did. Spark waved back with an unsure smile on his face. He wore an ill-fitted dark blue suit with a dark blue tie that was too short on him.

Win introduced himself to the big man. Spark nodded, smiled, and nervously wrung his hands. Perspiration dotted his brow.

"Thanks for coming so quickly," Win said to him.

"Thank you for sending the plane. Boy, that was a treat."

"Was everything on board to your liking?"

"It was great, yeah. I never flew private before. Thank you again."

"It was my pleasure," Win said. He spread his arm to where Myron now stood. "Do you know Myron Bolitar?"

Spark started toward him. "We've never met, but my old boss really admired you, Mr. Bolitar."

"Call me Myron."

Myron shook Spark's gigantic hand. It was like shaking hands with a throw pillow. "And Greg spoke highly of you too," Myron said.

"Which is why you're here," Win said. "Let me just give you some quick background before I leave you two alone. The NBA is hoping to open a Las Vegas franchise. I'll be the majority owner. Myron will be the team's president and general manager. We are now in the process of interviewing coaching candidates." Win looked toward Myron. "Did I forget anything?"

"Not that I can think of," Myron said.

"Then I'll leave you two to it. I promised the influencers I'd take them clubbing."

When Win first left the room, both Myron and Spark just stood there. The room felt suddenly quiet and empty without Win. Win belonged in a room like this. Myron and Spark didn't.

"Have a seat," Myron said.

He did. Myron sat where Win had left the file with the photograph. Myron opened it and saw other sheets of paper. "Your résumé is impressive," Myron said.

Spark's normally ruddy complexion turned a dark shade of aw-shucks red. He tried to make himself comfortable on the sofa, but he was the kind of big where everything around him looked too small for him. "Can I just say something before we start?"

"Of course."

"I don't want to come across as a kiss-ass, but I remember the way you dominated the Final Four your senior year. I was a kid then, just starting to play. You were one of the coolest players I'd ever seen."

Myron didn't know what to say to that, so he went with "Thank you." Then to get to the matter at hand: "It says here you worked three seasons under Greg Downing."

"That's right. All in Milwaukee."

"What was that like?"

"Working with Coach Downing? I learned a lot. No one was better at scouting, at planning, at coming up with a game plan than Coach Downing. He was meticulous in his preparation. A real details guy."

Myron nodded, remembering that that was how Greg had been on the court—the smartest and most prepared player he had ever seen. He could anticipate every play, every pass, every defense, every offensive set. He knew his opponents' strengths and weaknesses and how to counter and exploit them.

"But," Spark continued, "he also knew what buttons to push to get the maximum out of each player. Some guys needed to be coddled, some needed to be left alone, some needed tough love. Coach Downing understood that."

Okay, Myron thought, *enough with this uncomfortable setup.*

"Do you mind if we start with a few basics?" Myron asked.

"Shoot."

"What's your family situation?"

"I'm married to Kendra. We met at Oklahoma State. She works

as a dental hygienist. We have two boys, Liam and Joshua. Liam is eight, Joshua is six. Right now we live outside of Boston. But I already talked to Kendra and we'd be more than willing to move out here. This is an exciting opportunity for me. She gets that."

Myron could see the hope in the man's eyes, and it was crushing. This had been Win's idea. Myron tried to take comfort in that, but it felt like a cop-out. He was participating, wasn't he? He was the one asking the questions. He was the one who was now perpetuating the lie.

It was time to move it along.

"Any other family?"

The blinks gave him away. The smile stayed on Spark's face, but it no longer reached his eyes. "Family?"

"Mother, father, siblings?"

He cleared his throat. "My father died a few years back."

"I'm sorry."

"We weren't particularly close. My mom's alive."

"Where does she live?"

The question slowed him down. "She travels a lot. Right now, I think she's in Rome, maybe Paris."

They were getting close to it now. "Any siblings?"

"No."

Just like that. Fast. No hesitation. He had been expecting the question by now, and he was ready with his answer.

Myron feigned going through the file. "It says here you have a younger brother. Brian."

"He's . . ."

Myron waited.

"It's not relevant. He hasn't been a part of my life in a long time."

"I'm sorry. Where does he live?"

"Is it okay if we don't talk about it?"

"Well, it's not really my decision. This is a new franchise. And it's in, let's face it, Sin City. There will be a ton of scrutiny, and the league is obviously nervous about that. We need to fully vet any possible employees. If there is any hint of scandal—"

"There isn't."

"So where is your brother, Spark?"

The smile fled.

"He lived in this city under the name of Bo Storm," Myron said, dropping the pretense. "You know this. His boyfriend was murdered. No one has seen him since."

"Damn." Spark stared at Myron and slowly deflated. "I should have known."

Myron said nothing.

"There's no team coming to Vegas, is there?"

"No," Myron said. "There's not."

Spark shook his head. "Dick move."

Hard to argue.

Spark put his hands on his knees and pushed himself into a standing position. The man took up a lot of space. "Is your friend going to give me a ride back? I missed Liam's game for this. I'm his AAU coach too."

"I don't mean your brother any harm."

Tears welled up in the big man's eyes. "I'd like to leave now."

"I really need to talk to him."

"You could have just called and asked. You didn't have to drag my ass across the country and give me all this hope."

"I'm sorry about that. I really am."

"I could have told you on the phone. I haven't seen him in years. I don't know where he is."

"No idea at all?"

"I have to go now. Can you get me back home or do I need to book a flight?"

"Win will fly you back. No problem. When was the last time you heard from your brother?"

"Like I said, we hadn't been close in a long time. You want to know the truth? I think he's dead."

"How about your mother?"

"What about my mother?"

"Where is she? Can I talk to her?"

Spark came over at the mention of his mother. He loomed over Myron, his eyes on fire. "My mother doesn't know anything. You stay away from her. You understand?"

Myron made his voice firm. "Take a step back, Spark."

"I'm telling you to leave her alone."

"How about Greg Downing?"

That confused him. "What about him?"

"Do you know where he is?"

"He's dead. But you know that. I'm leaving now."

Myron kept the eye contact. He let Spark break it. Spark headed for the door. When he reached it, Myron called out, "Spark?"

He turned back.

"I'm sorry. Really. But I also think you're lying to me."

CHAPTER ELEVEN

———————

W in met Myron in the lobby. They hopped in the SUV and started toward the airport. Myron filled Win in on his conversation with Spark Konners. Win listened in silence. When Myron mentioned feeling bad about their franchise-coach deception, Win frowned, mimed sticking something under his chin, closed his eyes, gently sawed on his air violin.

"Funny," Myron said.

"Do you think Spark is lying to you?"

"I think he's being less than forthcoming."

"Me too."

"Not much we can do about it."

"Oh, that's where you're wrong," Win said.

The car drove down the Strip and through the gate that pro-tected the tarmac for the private jets. Myron saw Win's parked out to the right. The lights were on inside.

"Where is Spark?" Myron asked.

"Right there."

Another SUV pulled through the gate.

"How did we beat him here?"

"He hit traffic."

"It's the same route we took," Myron said.

"Come. Let's say goodbye to our guest, shall we? We can even apologize if you'd like."

Myron looked at Win. "You have another idea, don't you?"

"I'm taking a page from your playbook," Win said.

"Meaning?"

Win didn't reply. He got out of the car. Myron didn't like where this was going, but he also knew that sometimes when the "Win-Mobile" was swerving all over the road out of control, it was best to stay out of the way.

Win started toward the SUV carrying Spark. Spark got out. Again Myron was surprised by the sheer size of him. It wasn't just the height. His chest was broad enough to handle a paddleball match. Myron watched Win head toward the big man with his hand extended for a handshake.

"I'm sorry this didn't work out," Win said.

Spark looked as though he was on the verge of losing it. "I just want to get home."

"I understand."

Win, too, was a good athlete. He wasn't a pro-level one like Myron, but he made up for it with constant training and a detachment that made him border on the genius. He had learned self-defense, speed, strength, planning, coordination, takedowns, maneuvers, strikes, weaponry from literally the world's best teachers. He planned fast. He saw the angles. He coldly and mercilessly took advantage of every opening.

He also had remarkably fast hands.

Spark was carrying his phone. One second the phone was in his hand, the next moment, Win had snatched it away.

"Hey! What the—"

Win looked at the phone. "As I feared, the phone is locked. Facial recognition and all that."

"Are you kidding me?" Spark had had enough. "Give me that god-damn phone or I'll bust you wide open."

Win grinned at the much, much larger man. Myron spotted the look on Win's face. He didn't like it.

Myron said, "Win."

Spark stepped closer. It was always a mistake to crowd your oppo-nent. Even if you're the bigger man. You think it's going to intimi-date. It may. But it won't intimidate those who know how to fight.

Just the opposite in fact.

"I don't give a shit how rich you are," Spark said. "Give me back my phone, asshole. Now."

Win didn't move back a step. He craned his neck, looked up, and said, "I don't think so."

Myron again said, "Win."

Spark Konners was turning red with anger. His hands formed two sledgehammer fists. Win wanted that, Myron knew. Anger made you stupid. Spark was fed up. He had been insulted and humiliated by the little rich guy standing in front of him. The little rich guy had crossed a line. Heck, more than one line.

"Spark," Myron said. "Don't."

But Spark was too far gone. He loaded up for a big roundhouse swing that, if it connected, would have probably toppled a sky-scraper. It didn't connect, of course. Win saw it coming a mile away. He sidestepped, waited for the precise moment Spark was fully off balance, then Win swept Spark's leg.

Spark dropped hard to the tarmac.

Win moved fast. He grabbed Spark's hair, pulled his face to the phone, let go of the hair, stepped back.

The phone was unlocked now.

In a blind fury, Spark got to his hands and knees and bull-rushed

Win. Win waited until the very last moment, slid to the left, tripped Spark.

Again the big man fell hard.

Myron moved toward Konners, tried to put himself between the two men to prevent more physical confrontations. Win had so far been only defensive. If Spark tried again, that might change.

Win scrolled through Spark's phone. "Looks like you made a phone call after you left the hotel suite, my dear lad. Four-oh-six area code. Who were you calling?"

"None of your goddamn business."

"Hold on." He pressed a few more buttons. "Four-oh-six...that's in Montana."

Spark got to his hands and knees. He was planning another attack. Still staring at his phone, Win took out a large handgun and pointed it in Spark's direction.

"I'm a pretty good shot," Win said. "But you can test that if you so wish."

Myron tried once again. "Win."

Win sighed. "Your warnings are like your appendix—they're either superfluous or they hurt you."

Myron frowned. "Seriously?"

"Not my best analogy, I admit." Still reading off his phone, Win said, "Tracking the number now. Hmm. Got it. According to the location towers, the phone is currently emanating from a Budget Inn in someplace called Havre, Montana." Win glanced toward Myron. "Get on the plane. The flight to Havre is a little over two hours. I'll pin-drop you the phone's location."

CHAPTER TWELVE

Y ou park outside the home of Walter Stone.

It is two in the morning. The house is dark other than the dim glow from a computer monitor coming from the downstairs den. Walter is fifty-seven years old. His house is a three-bedroom Cape Cod of aluminum siding and faded brick on Grunauer Place in Fair Lawn. He has two sons, both in their twenties. One just had a baby, his first grandson. Walter is at his keyboard. He got laid off last April. The Foodtown supermarket he had worked at for thirty years shut their doors, and they won't find new work for an older white guy, no matter how good he is. That's what he tells people. It's the truth, in his mind. His wife is named Doris. She plays pickleball three times a week and does her best to find ways to keep out of the house most days. Right now, she is upstairs sleeping. After dinner, that's where Doris always goes. Upstairs. Walter stays downstairs. They're both good with that.

You sit outside in the Ford Fusion. You wear gloves and a ski mask. You have a gun on your lap.

Walter, you assume, is still giddily typing away.

He thinks he is safe behind internet anonymity.

Walter started off on social media like most people his age— poking fun at it, wary of the time suck, thinking it's something lazy kids do. He hates the new generations—Generation X or Y or Z or Alphas or whatever—thinking they're all soft and spoiled and that they'd rather suck off the tit of his taxes than do a day's honest work. Walter's youngest son Kevin is a bit like that. Into computers and video games and whatnot. A total waste of time, if you ask Walt. Still, at some point, Kevin signed his dad up with a Twitter account first. Not sure why anymore. Guess so Walt could see what the fuss was about. Maybe use it as a free news feed or something. Walter would be damned before he gave any money to the local paper or watched the lies on lamestream TV. Once he started checking out the site, well, maybe it was because Kevin created his account or maybe there was some weird algorithm, but Walter's Twitter feed filled up with tweet after tweet of the dumbest, most vile, naïve load of bullcrap you could ever imagine. How did people get so dumb? None of these idiots posting all day have a clue how the real world works. The only thing they were more full of than shit? Themselves. Man, they all thought they were the cat's ass, didn't they? Endlessly pontificating and condescending and yeah, Walter knew what those words meant. And don't even get him started on the thumb-up-the-ass, brain-dead women. Jesus H. Get a boyfriend or something. All whining anytime a guy said boo to them or bumped into their elbow. Man, that got Walter's goat. Everything a guy does nowadays pisses them off. Heck, just talking to them was an "act of violence." Oh, and not talking to them—ignoring them? That was disrespectful and sexist. When Walter was young, a girl liked to get a wink and a nod. It was flattering. Try that now and she'll blow a rape whistle in your face. I mean, get a grip, sweetheart. You're not all that.

That's kind of what happened at Foodtown too.

Once that foreign chick Katiana started working the deli counter—Katiana who on her very first day smiled at Walter and touched his arm, clearly flirting with him even though he sported a wedding band clear as day—ever since she complained to HR, it was over for him.

That's how it is. No one cares about the other side. A woman complains about you, you're cooked. And all Walt did was try to be nice. Katiana was a recent divorcée (smart guy her ex, escaping that bear trap of a bitch) and so Walt figured he'd make her feel better about herself, compliment her figure and whatnot. She wore tight clothes for a reason, no? Suddenly his transfer to the store in Pompton Lakes, poof, gone. Oh, they didn't fire him. They let him stay until the store closed. Three weeks' severance after thirty years. A week's pay per decade. Bastards. And now, months later, here on this goddamn computer, all these smug online bitches just like Katiana are spouting off these brain-dead rules about how men should act in defiance of all natural laws, as though the world just started yesterday. Jesus H. One bitch who calls herself "Fit Amy" if you can believe that, she keeps going on and on about how she's scared to get into an elevator alone with a man—that, get this, the man should wait and take the next elevator if he sees a woman is alone in one. Seriously? And so Walt wants to lay a little knowledge on her. Not a big deal, right? He sets up a second account because if you just tell the truth in this world, they come after you. That's how it is now. Fuck freedom of speech. You want to go online and tell this man-hating elevator rider, "You're so ugly you'd be grateful if a man raped you on an elevator," well, the truth hurts now, doesn't it, sweetheart?

So Walt, a smart guy, a quick learner, made up a fake account with the name Rotten Swale. Not because he was afraid to speak his mind. Not Walt. He wants everything out in the open, believes in the free flow of ideas, so that stupid feminazis get drowned in an avalanche of logic. But that's not how it works anymore. Not in today's sissified world. These chicks are zealots. If they find out who he is—"dox" is what they call it—they'll write to Stop-N-Shop or that new Green Grocery opening up in Ridgewood and threaten to boycott or sue or whatever if Walter gets a job there. That, my fellow Americans, is how nuts these people are. So yeah, he sets up the anonymous account on a whim. Like he won't really use it. That's what Walter thinks until the desire—no, the *need*—to set these bitches straight is too strong to resist. So that's what he does. Or should he say, Rotten Swale does. They get an earful of the truth from Rotten Swale. They may not listen. But they'll hear. And that one chick who calls herself Fit Amy, that my-shit-don't-stink profile with her fucking bio talking about BLM and rainbow flags, this chick with these giant knockers and the shirt buttoned low, always bending forward into the camera during her rants, inviting men to stare down her blouse, and so Rotten Swale tells her in subsequent comments that a) "No one would watch if you didn't have a big rack" and then b) "You're a dumb lying whore who sucks cocks at the truck stop" and then c) "Your seven-year-old daughter deserves to get ass raped," which, well, Walter doesn't really believe, but you need to say something that will get their attention, and boy, does this chick need a good solid fucking from someone like Walter, from a real man who will pin her down and show her what's what.

This goes on for a year.

Walt posts more and more. Worse and worse. Rotten Swale gets blocked after a while, but—no problem—Walter just takes on another identity. Late Towners. And then other. Seattle Worn. On and on. He remains anonymous.

That's what he thinks.

But you, sitting outside his house in the dark with the gun—you found Rotten Swale.

It took time to track down his real identity, but not as much as people might think. The Rotten Swale account could still be accessed. You check through all the posts. Not much there to give you a clue—Walter has learned to be careful—but one time he posts a photo taken through his front windshield driving past a sex shop he claimed was "ruining our neighborhood." Dumb. A quick google told you the shop was on Route 17 in Paramus, New Jersey. Okay, so now you know approximately where he lives.

Next step: Go to the bottom of his followers list. That's where the first profiles someone follows are to be found. You can learn a lot there because they are often people you know in real life. Walter had followed these people because when he set up the account, he fooled himself into believing he wasn't a crackpot, that this account would be legit in its own way.

This was a fairly common practice with budding stalkers.

When you look at Rotten Swale's first followers—when you cross-check these profiles against Rotten Swale's activity—well, this is when you hit bingo. Rotten Swale hit the "like" button on several Instagram posts by women he follows. Two posts are for women named Kathy Corbera and Jess Taylor, both of whom live in the Paramus, NJ, area— one in River Vale, one in Midland Park. You do a bit more digging and find a connection. The women follow one another plus a page called "Glen Rock High School 1980s alumni." Okay, cool. You go to that page. Now you search for the men who follow both that alumni page *and* Kathy Corbera and Jess Taylor.

You find three men who fit that criterion.

Closer.

So now you're down to three men. One, Peter Thomas, lives in New York City. One, Walter Stone, lives in Fair Lawn, close to Paramus. One, Brian Martin, still lives in Glen Rock, also close to Paramus.

Now you take a step back.

Why did this guy choose the name Rotten Swale?

It's never totally random. There is always a reason. And the reason here was easy once you had it down to three people. Rotten Swale, Late Towners, Seattle Worn.

They were all anagrams for Walter Stone.

How clever.

Game, set, match.

The problem for you then is a simple one. Walter Stone, the stalker you want to kill, lives in Fair Lawn, New Jersey. Amy Howell, the stal-kee you'd like to frame, lives in Salem, Oregon.

How can you pin Stone's murder on her?

Here you get lucky. Amy Howell has a brother named Edward Pas-coe who resides in Woodcliff Lake, New Jersey—a twenty-minute car ride from where you are now parked.

You like this. The one-step-removed killer. Something a little differ-ent. Something that requires new skills.

Edward Pascoe has a pretty sophisticated alarm system at his house. You debate waiting to find a way to break in to gather DNA and use his car—your semi–modus operandi—but you come up with some-thing that will work just as well. He drives a 2020 white Ford Fusion. It's a very common make, so you rent one under a fake ID. Pascoe parks in his driveway, which does not have the same security as the house. An hour ago, you sneaked up that driveway and switched his license plates with the ones on your rental. When this is over, you'll drive back to the house and switch them back. No one will be the wiser. Your white Ford Fusion with Pascoe's plates will have been spotted and recorded by several street cams during the drive.

Pretty clever, no?

You also have printouts of your legwork in figuring out that Rot-ten Swale, the troll threatening Pascoe's sister with violence, is Wal-ter Stone. They'll find that paperwork hidden behind Pascoe's garage. And finally, the closer: Before switching the license plates back, you'll drive the Ford Fusion to the Woodcliff Lake reservoir, making sure the license plate is picked up on CCTV, park the car, and toss the murder weapon into the water.

That should be more than enough for the police, but despite what you see on television, the police are not omniscient. So if all of this isn't enough for law enforcement to home in on Edward Pascoe as the culprit, if a few days pass and nothing happens, you'll make sure the police get an anonymous tip, a little nudge. In truth, you almost hope for that. You get to be involved again.

And you love that.

You leave the car door unlocked. You go to the window. You see Walter Stone in front of his computer. The lights are off, but the blue from the monitor illuminates his face into a ghoul mask. You push the barrel against the window opening. He is smiling, looking like some grotesque monster as he types away. You knock on the window. He looks up.

That's when he dies.

For Walter Stone, the horror is over.

For Edward Pascoe, it's just begun.

CHAPTER THIRTEEN

W hen Win's plane reached ten thousand feet, the Wi-Fi came on. Myron called a former client and retired basketball star named Chaz Landreaux. Chaz didn't pick up. Myron sent a text to give him a call when he had a moment, then he checked the notifications on his phone.

Terese had texted their standard emojis: a telephone and a heart. You didn't have to be a genius to figure out their complicated marital code. The telephone said, "Do you want to talk?" The heart said, "I love you." They often sent these emojis before calling because one (on the lighter side), the other may be busy or in a meeting or in some other way not alone and ready to talk, and two (the darker side), they both led lives where things went wrong and a phone call out of nowhere might cause a few seconds of unnecessary worry.

Myron opened his phone to Favorites and tapped the fourth one down. Myron's father held the top fave spot, Mom the second, his parents' home phone—yes, they still used one—was the third. Win had been fourth, Esperanza fifth, but both got knocked down a peg when Myron and Terese tied the knot.

Terese answered on the second ring and said, "How was your day?"

"Good." Then Myron added: "I almost lost my baby toe."

"Left or right foot's?"

"Left."

"Yikes. That's my favorite toe. What happened?"

"A bad man tried to cut it off with pruning shears."

"And what happened to the bad man?"

"Win happened to him."

"Is it okay if I'm okay with that?"

"It is."

"Myron?"

"Yes."

"I'm keeping it light to stave off my panic."

"I know," Myron said. "Me too. But it's okay."

"Do you want to tell me what's going on?"

"Maybe later. Right now, I just want to hear your voice."

"Is that code for phone sex?" she asked.

"I'm on Win's plane."

"That sounds like a yes."

Myron smiled and felt the warmth spread through him. "I love you, you know."

"I love you too. Are you free Tuesday?"

"I can be."

"I'll be in town to interview the Manhattan district attorney."

"Oh wow, great."

The phone clicked. Myron checked and saw it was Chaz calling him back. Through the line, Terese said, "Incoming call?"

"Yeah. Can I get back to you in a few?"

"I'm half asleep. Let's talk in the morning, okay?"

Terese was the least needy person he knew, far less needy than Myron, but he said okay and they both said love you again and then Myron clicked over to the other call. Mee brought him over a Yoo-hoo, already shaken and poured into a glass. Myron hoped she hadn't thrown in any absinthe.

"Myron!" Chaz said with the genuine enthusiasm that had made him such a popular player, sportscaster, and now coach. "As I live and breathe."

"Thanks for calling me back so fast."

"For you? Always."

There had been a time many years ago when Chaz Landreaux, so-called "street kid" (when that euphemism was too often used) from the South Ward, had gotten himself in trouble with mob-connected agents. Myron and Win helped him out of that mess, and Chaz had ended up as one of Myron's first clients. When Myron chose to close MB Reps and leave the business, Chaz had moved on to a new agency with young Black talent. When Myron returned, Chaz did not. Chaz was a loyal guy. He would never have left Myron of his own accord. But Myron had chosen to quit the business and so Chaz had found alternative representation, and his new agency had done good by him. It wouldn't be fair, Chaz explained, to move back. Myron understood.

"Congrats on the new job," Myron said.

Chaz had just landed the job as the University of Kentucky's new men's head basketball coach.

"Thanks," Chaz said. "But you already congratulated me about that."

"Yeah, I know."

"Even sent a gift basket of food."

"Was it any good?"

"Gift baskets of food are never any good."

"True," Myron said. Then: "I need a favor, Chaz."

"Okay."

"I'm hoping it'll end up being a favor for you too."

"Oh boy, what a pitch," Chaz said. "You're a great salesman."

Everyone's a wiseass.

"I hear you're looking for a head assistant coach."

"Ah. You want to pitch a client?"

"Not a client," Myron said. "But can you give Spark Konners an interview?"

"Funny."

"What?"

"I got his résumé on my desk here. Of course, I got about a thousand résumés. How do you know him? Oh wait. Greg Downing, right?"

"Yeah, I guess."

"You guess?"

"Greg liked him a lot. That much I can say. The truth is, I really don't know much about his qualifications other than that."

"Uh-huh," Chaz said.

Myron sipped the Yoo-hoo. He thought he'd outgrown the taste years ago. Now, maybe it was nostalgia, maybe it was fear of aging, maybe it was almost losing Terese's favorite toe, but he found comfort in the old nectar.

"So you don't know if he's any good," Chaz continued.

"I don't, no."

"So why are you making this call?"

"I owe him," Myron said.

"Like you owe him a favor?"

"Worse," Myron said. "I wronged him."

"How?"

"Long story and one I can't tell you. I just did him wrong."

"And you're trying to make amends?"

"This won't make amends. But maybe something is better than nothing."

Chaz didn't say anything for a few beats. Then: "I know you, Myron. You don't 'wrong' people without a reason."

"There was a reason. But it's not a reflection on Spark. He's an innocent."

"Fair enough," Chaz said. "His résumé looks pretty solid anyway. I'll interview him."

"Thank you."

"And I'll announce it publicly. Even if he doesn't get the job, that should get him some cred."

Myron told Chaz he appreciated it. They hung up. He sat back.

The plane began its descent. Myron looked out the window. Montana. A whole lot of beautiful nothingness. That wasn't a judgment. When you live on the East Coast, it's just different. Montana is twenty times bigger than Myron's home state of New Jersey. Twenty times bigger. Montana has about a million people while New Jersey has over nine million. Not to be all mathy, but that means that New Jersey has 1,260 people per square mile. Montana? About 7.5 people per square mile.

Different.

Myron checked the app. The phone he was tracking—he was still assuming it belonged to Spark's brother Bo/Brian—was still at the Budget Inn. A rental car waited for Myron at the airport. He put the Budget Inn into Google Maps. The app told him it would be a nine-minute ride.

You don't expect a lot from a place called the Budget Inn, and you don't get a lot either. The two-level motel didn't have the word "FLEABAG" spray-painted on the side of it, but maybe it should have. Myron parked and headed toward a sign saying MOTEL OFFICE. One thing struck Myron as odd right away. There were probably twenty vehicles in the lot, but he counted only eight rooms: four on top, four on the bottom. No lights on in any of them. Not one. The motel office was locked. A handwritten sign on the cracked glass door read: "PERMANENTLY CLOSED."

Myron checked his phone. As with most tracking apps, the location was approximate. Now as he looked at it again, the dot seemed to be somewhere in the corner of the parking lot. As Myron headed back toward the front, he spotted a red shack with a yellow sign aptly reading: THE SHANTY LOUNGE.

In another era, the Shanty had probably been the Budget Inn's watering hole, but whereas the lodging had ceased to exist, the lounge was still hopping. Two men stumbled out the front door, both clearly intoxicated. One jumped into a monster SUV, vroomed the engine, and took off over the curb. The other guy vomited on a Ford Taurus before walking it off. Myron checked the location app again. The answer was obvious now.

Whoever Spark had called was currently inside the Shanty Lounge.

Myron headed to the saloon door. He wasn't sure how to play it or what he expected to find here. Could Spark have called Greg Downing? Could Greg be in this bar? And then what? If it was Bo and not Greg, what was Myron's play here? Question him? Watch him and follow him back to wherever he lived?

He reached the door. The bar sounded happening from the outside. The old yacht-rock classic "Sailing" by Christopher Cross was playing, maybe on a jukebox, maybe karaoke. Several patrons were singing that sailing took them away to where they always heard it could be. Okay. Myron hesitated. If Greg was inside, suppose he recognized Myron. Would Greg—what?—run? Still none of it made any sense. Let's say Greg was here. Let's say Greg and his lover Bo had run away from Joey the Toe and decided to hide in Montana.

Why travel to New York and kill a former model he had barely known?

It made no sense.

Myron was missing something. That wasn't uncommon. Situations like this were always about missing stuff. His normal way was to keep shaking the box and hope more pieces fell out. But something here, something about the pieces he had already, made him feel as though he was shaking the wrong box.

So Myron just pushed open the door and entered. Spark had called someone. Maybe Greg, maybe Bo. Whoever—they might be on the lookout. Maybe Spark had warned them that people were looking for them. Maybe they were prepared.

Best to be on guard.

When Myron entered, he half expected the whole bar to go silent and turn toward him, like you used to see in old Westerns. Nothing like that happened. The aptly named Shanty was a classic small-town watering hole. That was a compliment. Oodles of neon beer signs shined bright against dark wood paneling. Coors Light dominated, but Budweiser had a pretty good showing too. There were deer antlers on the walls and a long mirror behind the bar. The specials were written on a whiteboard. The Shanty was small but happening. Four dudes with cowboy hats played darts. Two guys with trucker hats scrutinized a pile of giant Jenga blocks. A tall woman leaned on the corner jukebox and sang that fantasy, it gets the best of her, and three guys backed up when she noted that she felt this way when sailing. Shanty Lounge and the Pips. There might be a variety of tops—tees, flannels, polos—but everyone wore blue jeans. Myron counted three dogs—two golden retrievers lying on the floor like throw rugs, and a third dog, a French bulldog, slouching on a stool at the bar.

The corner jukebox transitioned from Christopher Cross to an old Doobie Brothers ditty. Soon Michael McDonald and the tall woman were urging the bar patrons to take it to the streets. No one in here seemed in the mood to take it anywhere. The clientele all seemed pretty content inside with their drinks and darts and billiards.

Myron took in the crowd. No Greg. No Bo/Brian.

Wait. Hold the phone.

One of the bartenders was working a Carter's Brewing tap into a Miller Lite glass.

Myron narrowed his eyes. The long, frosted locks were gone, replaced with a blending-in military-style crew cut. The carefully cultivated facial hair had been replaced with the old-school clean-shave look. He wore wire-framed glasses now, and where his outfits on his Instagram page were Technicolor and flamboyant, this bartender too wore the stock black-tee-blue-jeans uniform of the Shanty.

It was a disguise and a pretty good one. Subtle. If you weren't looking for him and looking for him hard, you'd never happen upon him and say, "Hey, aren't you Bo Storm?"

But it was Bo. No question about it.

Myron again debated how to play it—should he wait, watch, what?—but the direct route seemed best. He didn't want Win delaying Spark any longer than absolutely necessary. They'd done enough to the guy.

There was an empty stool next to the French bulldog. Myron took it. He was the only one not in jeans, sporting his crisper look of trousers and a blue dress shirt. No one seemed to care what he was wearing, though the French bulldog, who wore a nametag that read

FIREBALL ROBERTS, looked at him with disdain. Myron nodded at the dog and smiled. The dog turned away and faced the bar.

Can't please everyone.

Bo Bartender came over to Myron and gave him a smile. The smile was a bit of a tell. Not to stereotype, but his teeth were still the bright white of Vegas veneers, which didn't fit the norm of the Shanty Lounge.

"What can I get you?" Bo asked.

"What's good on tap?"

"I like the Carter's."

"Sounds good," Myron said. "But can you do me a favor first?"

"What's that?"

"Don't panic. Don't run. Don't even react. I got guys out front and out the back. You're safe right here. I promise. I'm not here to hurt you. You can make a big stink and try to get away, but that'll just draw attention and then Joey the Toe will hear about it. That will be bad for you. I mean you no harm. He does."

For a moment Bo just stared at him. Myron could see the wheels turning. He kept his eyes on Bo's. Steady. Calm. Confident. Bo could scream for help. He was a local. These people would jump in, Myron had no doubt.

"Yo, Stevie?"

It was someone at the other end of the bar. Bo said, "One second."

Bo looked lost.

"Pour my beer, Stevie," Myron said.

Bo nodded and turned to the tap. Myron looked to his right. Fireball Roberts was giving him the stink eye. Myron almost told him to mind his own business, but Fireball had been sitting here first and also Myron didn't want to get into a beef with a French bulldog.

The beer had the right amount of foam on top. Bo put it in front of Myron and said, "You work with those guys who harassed Spark?"

"I am the guy who harassed Spark."

"No way. You could never—"

"Private plane, Bo. This is big time. You might want to listen to me."

"I got a good life here."

"I don't doubt it."

"I kicked the drugs. I've been clean for four years now. I like my job. I got friends. People."

"And I don't want to ruin any of that."

"So what do you want?"

"I just need to talk to Greg."

Bo stayed quiet.

Patron One: "Yo, Stevie? You hard of hearing?"

Patron Two: "We're thirsty, Stevie. Man is not a camel, you know."

"Hold your horses, Darren," Bo/Stevie yelled out. Then to Myron: "I'll be right back."

There was one other person behind the bar, a mussed-hair barmaid in her fifties displaying both taut forearms and ample cleavage. She was down the other end of the bar, pretending she didn't see Myron to such a degree that Myron knew she was worried. Myron risked another glance at Fireball Roberts. Yep. Stink eye.

"I'm not here to hurt him," Myron told the bulldog.

The bulldog remained unmoved.

Myron kept his eye on the barmaid. She was staring so hard at a guy in a cowboy hat playing billiards that the guy must have felt it. Still holding the cue stick, Cowboy turned around and looked a question at her. The barmaid looked at Cowboy, then she looked at Myron, then Cowboy looked at Myron, then Cowboy looked at another guy with a beard so long he kept it under control with hair ties, and then both Cowboy and Beard Ties started toward him.

Oh damn.

Cowboy came up and stood behind Myron on his right. Beard Ties took the left. Fireball Roberts turned away as though he wanted no trouble. Bo came back over to Myron and said, "Okay, so what do you want?"

"You want me to talk in front of your friends here?"

The cowboy's voice was a deep, rich baritone. "I'm more than a friend."

Myron looked back at him now. "Oh."

"We don't have any secrets," Bo added.

Myron said "Oh" again.

"So what do you want?"

"I told you. I need to talk to Greg. If he wants to stay hidden after that, okay, fine. But I need to make sure he's all right. Tell Greg it's Myron. He knows me. I'm his agent. He can tell you I'm a man of my word."

"Your name is Myron," Bo said.

"Yes. Myron Bolitar."

"Myron, I don't know what the hell you're talking about."

Myron sighed, looked back at Cowboy and Beard Ties, and said, "I know about you and Greg Downing."

His eyes widened. "Greg Downing?"

"Yes."

"You're joking with me. Greg Downing? That's the Greg you're talking about?"

"Look, Bo, I saw the messages."

"Messages?"

"The romantic DMs on your old Instagram account."

And then Bo did something Myron didn't expect. He broke out laughing.

"Wait, you think Greg and I..." Bo laughed some more, shook his head. He smiled at Cowboy. "Whoa, man, this guy must have the worst gaydar in the history of the world."

Myron said, "Someone saw your DMs—"

"Greg wasn't talking to me."

Myron stopped. "Pardon?"

"That was my mom," Bo said. "Greg was DMing with my mom."

Myron sat there and blinked. In his mind's eye he saw the puzzle pieces. Then he saw himself sweep all the pieces off the table and onto the floor. His voice sounded far away in his own ears. "But it was your Instagram page."

"Yeah, duh. My mom ran all my social media stuff—Instagram, OnlyFans, whatever. When the Bucks came to town, Spark invited us to a game. My mom, well, it may sound weird for a son to say so, but she's hot. A total smoke show. Spark introduced Greg to Mom after the game—"

"That game," Myron interrupted, remembering the curvy blonde in the photo sitting next to Bo. "Was it in Phoenix?"

"Yeah, against the Suns. That's where we're from. Spark and I were raised in Scottsdale."

"So you and Greg aren't—"

"Are you serious?" Bo looked up at Cowboy. "We're good, Cal. I'll call you if I need anything." To Myron he added, "Take a sip of the beer. You'll feel better."

Myron did, trying to think it through.

"Can I ask you something?" Bo asked.

Myron nodded.

"Am I really safe staying here? Cal and I, we can move on if not."

"I won't tell anyone."

"And there's no way for Joey to track us down?"

"I don't see how," Myron said. "Did you kill Jordan Kravat?"

"Wow, not beating around the bush. Do you think I'd tell you if I did?"

"It might save us some time," Myron said.

"No, I didn't kill Jordan. I loved him."

"Jordan's mother thinks you had something to do with it."

"Donna? No, she doesn't. She may have said that to you, but that's because she doesn't want to face the truth."

"That being?"

"She let Joey into our lives. Invited him in really. Donna couldn't make enough money just running the nightclub. So she teamed up with Joey. He started pressuring us. Always wanting more money. It got out of control. Jordan tried to step in, and it got him killed."

"Donna said you and her son were on the outs."

He considered that for a moment. "We were, I guess. But I mean, we were young. It was all sort of volatile. Neither of us thought we were meant to be forever."

"Did you kill him?" Myron asked again.

"No."

"What about Greg?"

"What about him?"

"I'm thinking about the timing," Myron said. "Greg started DMing your mother. He travels to Vegas. Then Jordan gets murdered and Greg disappears."

"Greg didn't disappear," Bo said. "He and Mom fell hard for each other. They decided to travel the world. When he died, she was crushed."

"I don't think Greg is dead."

"Of course he is. You said you were Greg's manager or something?"

"His agent. We'd known each other since we were kids."

"Well, you must not have been very close," Bo said.

"Why do you say that?"

Bo started wiping the bar with a rag. "Why do you think Greg quit his job and ran off in the first place?"

"He said he wanted to get out of the rat race."

Bo shook his head. "No, man. Greg was sick."

Myron said nothing.

"He got a bad diagnosis. The Big C. That's why Greg quit coaching. That's why he and Mom ran away. Because he didn't have much time left."

CHAPTER FOURTEEN

———

The next step was obvious: Find Bo's mom.

They did. Fast.

By the next day, Myron was in Pine Bush, New York. Win had offered to come, but Myron decided to handle it himself. Pine Bush was classified as a hamlet rather than a town or a city and while the definition was confusing, it really just meant "pretty dang small."

Bo/Brian had put on a convincing performance, but something about it kept bumping Myron. The kid was lying. Not about everything. But once Myron realized that some level of deception was at hand, he stopped pushing him for information. He let Bo talk himself out. Myron nodded along as though he was buying every word, and then he apologized to Bo for the mistake. He never told Bo why he'd been looking for Greg. He didn't inquire—though man oh man he wanted to—where Bo's mom resided now that Greg was dead. He figured that Bo either would lie to him or tip her off or more likely, both.

He wanted to catch Bo's mom unawares.

They—Myron, Win, and Esperanza—found clues fast. Bo and Spark's mom had been named Grace Konners. Five years ago, right around the time she and Greg presumably ran overseas, she changed her last name to Conte. She kept the Grace. That was not uncommon. It is hard to change first names, to not react when you hear your name called and, of course, to react when you hear a name that was not yours. It can trip you up.

Once Grace changed her last name, boom, she vanished off the so-called grid. No credit cards. No mortgages. No employment records. No social media accounts. All Grace Konners activity stopped, and no Grace Conte activity took its place.

That fit.

But more recently, probably because several years had passed and she felt somewhat safe, Grace Conte risked using her Social Security number to open a cash management account with Bank of America. She was still careful. The account had been opened online, and the address used was a post office box in Charlotte, North Carolina, right near the bank's headquarters—clearly a move to hide her whereabouts on the rare chance someone would discover the account.

It took a bit more digging and triangulating locations and history. Your life is on your mobile phone. Most people realize this by now. It's not much of a shock. But perhaps we don't quite recognize the depth of that technology. Companies know everything. All movement. Bo used burner phones, so he was somewhat less conspicuous. It made sense. Bad guys like Joey the Toe were searching for him. His brother Spark was more of an open book. He traveled a lot, but it almost exclusively fit into the Amherst College basketball schedule. If the team was playing Bowdoin, his phone showed that he was in Brunswick, Maine. When the team played Middlebury, Spark was in Vermont.

But there was no reason for him to have visited Pine Bush, New York, three times.

The rest fell into place. Grace Conte never wrote checks. She never used the credit card that came with her account either. But she did make cash deposits at a variety of bank branches in New-burgh and Poughkeepsie—both larger towns near Pine Bush. Grace Conte also owned car insurance for a blue Acura RDX. She used the North Carolina address, but now that they had zeroed in on Pine Bush, it was just a matter of time.

Myron hadn't gotten an exact address yet, though judging by Spark's phone, she lived on a large rural plot of land off Route 302. He'd driven by it and spotted two possible driveways that could lead up to a house that might match the coordinates. One had a chain-link gate blocking the entrance. The second was open, so Myron risked driving up. Near the house, he spotted four cars—none of them a blue Acura RDX—and he figured that with that many peo-ple and that many non-Acura cars, this was probably not the right house. He took another look at the chain-link fence property from a distance. There was a camera attached to a tree.

Hmm.

He texted the address to Esperanza. She texted back.

Back to you within the hour.

No reason to wait here and look conspicuous. Myron drove back to the "hamlet's" center to grab something to eat. He chose Lar-ry's Chinese Restaurant and Bar because it had over four hundred Google ratings and 4.5 stars and because, to quote Elton John sing-ing "Levon," he "likes the name."

Myron took a seat at the bar. Larry's reminded him of the Shanty Lounge in Havre, Montana. It didn't look the same, other than the neon beer signs, but local American taverns all have the same feel. There is a comfort for the regulars and a try-to-be-comfort for the strangers, but he still felt like a tourist and that was okay. The menu was, as expected, Chinese, but there was also more classic Irish-pub fare like buffalo wings and burgers.

Chinese food at an Irish pub. Who said Myron wasn't willing to take risks?

A big burly man behind the bar introduced himself as "your host and barkeep, Rick Legrand." Full name. Odd. Myron asked Rick for a recommendation. Big Rick suggested a Chinese dish called Charlie's Angels. Myron asked what was in that. Rick Legrand made a face and said, "Do you want a recommendation or do you want me to read you the whole menu?" That, Myron thought, was a fair point. He ordered the Charlie's Angels and whatever beer was cold on tap. Rick wearily told him all the beers on tap were cold. "What, you think we keep warm beer here?" Then Rick shook his head and asked whether this was Myron's first time in a bar.

Everyone's a wiseass.

Myron spun the barstool around to check out the clientele. Hey, he could get lucky again. Maybe Grace Conte would just be here. His eyes scanned the place. Myron could hear the sizzle from a wok. The place reeked of MSG. Myron could almost feel his arteries harden. He checked all the faces.

Nope, no luck.

But when the bar door swung open again, allowing sunshine and a brief view of the outside, perhaps even greater luck hit him.

He spotted a blue Acura RDX.

"Rick Legrand?" Myron said.

Rick turned toward him. "Sup?"

"Cancel my order," Myron said.

"It's almost done."

Myron dropped two twenties on the table. "Give it to someone worthy."

Rick shrugged. "I'm almost on break."

"Then I deem you worthy, my man."

Myron hustled to the door and pushed it open, blinking into the sunlight. The blue Acura RDX was parked across the street in front of a place called, according to the sign, the Blush Boutique, the kind of shop Myron's mother would have described as "cutesy."

Now what?

Myron hustled back to his rental car. The ride up from Manhattan had been a little under two hours. Win had made sure that Myron had come prepared. That meant a locked Kevlar bag that contained a handgun (over the years, guns had come in handier than Myron wanted to admit), zip-tie handcuffs (not handy), and a magnetic GPS tracking device (somewhat handy). Myron figured that if he could stick a GPS tracker on Grace's blue Acura RDX he could follow at a safe distance.

He slid into the front seat and grabbed the Kevlar bag. He'd started working the spinning combo lock when a woman emerged from the Blush Boutique. Myron stopped. In every photo Myron had seen of her, Grace Konners had long, white-blonde hair. This woman had a short auburn cap. In every photo, Grace Konners had worn cropped and fitted flex-da-bod see-through summer whites. This woman wore high-waisted dad (or were they also mom?) jeans and a loose green sweatshirt with a cartoon camel on it.

Again, like with Bo, you wouldn't recognize her unless you were really staring, but Myron had little doubt. This was Grace Konners now Grace Conte or whatever.

Bo/Brian and Spark's mom.

Grace moved with purpose toward her Acura. Myron had little chance of cutting her off before she drove off. And did he even want that?

Better, he figured, to follow her.

She started the car and pulled out onto Main Street before turning left onto Route 302. Myron followed in his car. If the coordinates they'd gotten off Spark Konners's phone were correct, the ride would be a short one. Three minutes later, the blue Acura RDX, yep, pulled into the driveway with the chain-link fence. The fence slid open. Grace Conte drove in. The fence started to slide back into place. Myron tried to pull in behind her, but the fence was already too closed for his car to fit. Myron threw it into park, turned off the engine, hustled out, and slid through before the fence completely shut again.

Now what?

There was no reason to hide anymore. She would see him. He started trekking up the driveway. He decided not to take the handgun. Win would have scolded him over that. Win always carried a gun. Always. More than one usually. He'd told Myron repeatedly to do the same because of situations like these. But Myron didn't like carrying a gun. They were bulky. They were heavy. They chafed.

Not much to be done about it now.

He trudged up the dirt driveway. He had no idea how far up the house was. Also dumb. He could have probably checked that on Google Maps. As he continued, he cupped his hand around his mouth and started to call out.

"Hello? Grace? Ms. Conte? I just want to talk to you, okay?"

When he came to a turn about a hundred yards up the drive, he saw the house. He'd expected something rustic and charmingly decrepit, but the renovations on this particular A-frame were impressive. The house was pristine, white, with huge windows. There was something whimsical about it. The dirt road was gone now, replaced with a carefully laid brick drive. The yard was asymmetrically landscaped, as though the overgrown fauna and shrubbery were both completely natural and perfectly planned. It was a welcoming home. You could easily see yourself living here. Relax. Unwind. Enjoy a cup of coffee on the front veranda and watch the morning sun rise. That kind of thing.

"You're trespassing."

She was standing next to the Acura with the car door still open as though readying for a quick escape. She held up her phone. "I'm going to call the police."

"I'm not here to hurt you, Grace."

"Do I know you?"

"My name is Myron Bolitar. I was—I am—Greg's agent."

"I don't know what you're talking about."

Myron gave her a somewhat theatrical sigh. "Do we really have to play this game? Go ahead. Call the police. Let everyone, including Joey the Toe, know where you are."

She didn't move.

"I don't want to get you or your family in trouble. And by family, I mean your son Brian aka Bo aka Montana bartender Stevie."

Grace swallowed and finally lowered the phone. "How did you find me?"

"It doesn't matter. No one else is onto you. Yet."

"So what do you want?"

"I need to talk to Greg."

"Greg is dead."

"Yeah no," Myron said.

"What?"

"He's not dead." Myron started walking to the house. "Is he here?"

"No, of course not. He's dead. You're his friend. You know that."

Ah, so now she knows who Myron is.

"This house is awfully big for one person," Myron said.

"Greg bought it for me before he died."

"When?"

"That's not your—"

"I can get the tax records."

"I have a new boyfriend now."

"Uh-huh. So how did Greg die?"

"He had cancer."

"What kind?"

Slightest of hesitations. "Kidney."

"Painful," Myron said. "So was he hospitalized? In palliative care? Where did he die exactly?"

"I don't have to answer your questions."

"I spoke to his doctor. A mutual friend of ours named Ellen Nakhnikian. She said Greg was healthy."

"Doctors can't say anything. Patient-client—"

"Well, maybe. But Greg is dead, so Dr. Nakhnikian had no issue talking to me."

She stuck out her chin. "Greg went to another doctor."

"Did he now?"

"He didn't want anyone to know."

"Noble," Myron said. "But that's not what happened. Dr. Nakhnikian saw Greg two months before you two ran off. Gave him a clean bill of health." Myron switched gears, hoping a sudden change might throw her. "Do you know who Cecelia Callister is?"

"No." Then: "Wait, the name is familiar."

"She was a big model. She was recently murdered along with her son Clay."

"Oh right. I read about that. What does that have to do with—?"

"The police think Greg did it. That's why I'm here. They want to question him."

"That makes no sense. Greg is dead."

"Yeah, Grace, that's not going to fly. I'll keep digging. But worse—the cops will keep digging. Heck, Joey the Toe will keep digging. I beat them all here, but they'll find you too. It's just a question of time."

"I'm telling you—"

And then from behind Myron, another voice, a familiar male voice, said, "Let it go, hon. Damn, Bolitar, you always were a stubborn son of a bitch who didn't know when to quit."

Myron turned around. He had a full beard now covering up his famous baby face. His straight hair had been permed to a curl. But there was no doubt.

It was Greg Downing.

CHAPTER FIFTEEN

"Yeah, look, I didn't lie to you. I planned to run off, just like I told you."

Greg and Myron sat at an ash-wood kitchen table. The kitchen was white, except for the raw-wood ceiling beams. The refrigerator and freezer had glass doors. Grace was working some kind of gleaming espresso machine.

"I needed to quit coaching. Just like I told you. The game...I mean, you know better than anyone, Myron. It consumes you. It takes everything you have. I had spent my life doing it. The fire just wasn't burning anymore."

Grace placed the coffee cup in front of Myron. Myron smiled a thanks.

"Wow, I'm sorry," Greg said.

"Huh?"

"All that talk about being tired of the game," he continued. "That probably sounded insensitive. I get how lucky I was. I had a long career. And...and I took that away from you. I'm sorry, man. You know that."

Myron wasn't sure how to reply to that, so he went with, "No reason to rehash the past right now."

"Yeah. Yeah, I guess you're right. How did you find us anyway? Or is that a state secret?"

The room filled with the aroma of top-echelon coffee beans.

Myron ignored the question. "You don't have cancer, do you?" he said.

"No, I'm fine."

"So what happened, Greg?"

"A lot of things."

"Like?"

"Like quitting basketball. Like wanting to start over."

"I got those."

"Like meeting Grace." He gazed up at her and smiled. She put her hand on his shoulder and smiled back. With his eyes still on her, Greg said, "Is it too corny to call her my soulmate? Doesn't matter. She is."

"I feel the same," she said.

"She changed my whole life."

They held the lovey-dovey gaze to the point where Myron almost told them to get a room, but that line would be too expected.

"So that's the main reason I wanted to start over," Greg said. "I fell in love."

"Lots of people fall in love," Myron said.

"Yeah, I know, and I would say, 'Not like us,' but everyone says that too." He shifted in his chair. "Look, it's pretty simple. Grace and I met at a time when both of us needed change. We fell hard. I'd had it with basketball. I was burnt out. So we decided to run off and travel the world for a while. We planned to do it for a year, maybe two, and then see what's what."

"You went to Vegas first," Myron said.

"Right. That's where Grace's son lived."

"Brian."

"He likes to go by Bo," Greg said. "Anyway, Bo was having problems."

"What sort of problems?" Myron asked.

"You and I, Myron, we grew up in way different times."

Myron waited.

Grace said, "His boyfriend was abusing him."

"That would be Jordan Kravat."

"Yes."

"When you say abusing—"

"Physical, emotional, in every way," she said.

"The boyfriend owed money to some bad people," Greg explained. "So he was paying it back by pimping Bo out."

"It was awful," Grace said.

"Anyway, Grace and I wanted to help. So we flew down to Vegas. I figured that maybe I could pay off the kid's debt, and he'd leave Bo alone. That was our plan. Make sure Bo was safe. Then, poof, we would take off for parts unknown."

"Like we originally intended," Grace added.

She moved to the chair next to Greg. He took her hand.

"So then what happened?" Myron asked.

"This guy Jordan. I try to talk some sense into him. But he won't listen."

"The mob owns him," Grace said. "Him and his mother." Her face started to redden. "His mother's the real criminal."

"Yeah, that's where it really went sideways," Greg said. "Jordan's mom. I forget her name."

"Donna," Myron said.

They looked up at him. Then they glanced at each other.

"You know her?" Grace asked.

"We met. When I was looking for Bo."

"She owns this mobbed-up club, you know."

"Owned," Myron said, stressing the past tense. "Yeah, I know."

"She teamed up with this awful mobster."

"Joey the Toe," Myron said.

"Wow," Greg said. "You've been busy."

Their eyes met and for the briefest of moments, they were back on the court, Greg dribbling, Myron low in a defensive stance, trying to force him right. It was Greg's weakness. He was a great player and despite being a righty, he preferred penetrating the middle using his left. The memory was a moment, no more, but it was there, and Myron could tell that they both sort of experienced it.

Myron leaned forward, keeping all his attention on Greg. "Why didn't you come to me?"

Greg said nothing.

"You know me. You know Win. You know what we can do."

Greg nodded. "I thought about it." Then, glancing next to him, he said, "*We* thought about it. But in the end, Grace didn't think it was the right move."

"Violence is never the answer," Grace said.

Myron said nothing. Greg said nothing.

Grace shook her head. "Men."

"No, no, you're right," Myron said. "So what did you guys decide to do?"

"Grace convinced her son to turn state's evidence. Wear a wire. All that."

Makes sense, Myron thought. "And then?"

"Somehow Joey the Toe gets wind of it. He breaks into the house at night. He murders Jordan."

"Why?" Myron asked.

"What?"

"You said Jordan was part of his operation. Bo was the one who was the threat. So why kill Jordan?"

"We wondered about that too," Grace said.

"Want to know our theory?" Greg asked.

Myron nodded for him to go ahead.

"It was an accident."

"An accident?"

"Turant meant to kill Bo. Bo and Jordan lived together. It was dark."

"Bo was home at the time," Grace added. "He heard a commotion and ran."

"You know the rest. Joey the Toe gets arrested. Bo testifies against him. Suddenly we are all on the run from the mob. Grace and I make sure Bo has a new identity, and then"—Greg turned and looked at Grace—"we just followed our original plan."

Myron nodded slowly. "And you faked your death."

Silence.

"Why?"

"That's not really your business, Myron." Greg shifted in his chair, suddenly agitated. "Why are you here anyway? Why couldn't you just let us be?"

"Because the feds came to me looking for you. Do you know Cecelia Callister?"

"She was murdered, right?"

"Did you know her?"

"A little, a long time ago. She was friends with Emily. We went out a couple of times as couples."

"Anything more?"

"Like?"

"Like, anything more. Like, did you sleep with her? Like, when was the last time you saw her?"

"I didn't touch her, and I haven't seen her in years."

"Because your DNA was found at the crime scene."

Greg froze. "Are you serious?"

"No, I'm being funny. I tracked you down and did all this because I thought it might make a good comedy bit."

"I don't get it," Greg said. "How could my DNA be at her murder scene?"

"You tell me."

"It has to be a mistake."

"They found it under the victim's fingernails."

"My DNA? Bullshit. I mean, absolute and utter bullshit. They're lying to you."

"Who? The cops? Wait, why would the cops lie?"

Silence.

"And why did you fake your death? You just let everyone who cares about you think you were dead."

Greg chuckled then. "Who cares about me?"

"What?"

"Who cares about me? Come on. You may have mourned a day or two, then went back to your real life. Emily? Ha. My mom is dead, my dad has advanced Alzheimer's."

"What about Jeremy?"

"Ah, now we are getting to it." Greg smiled. "You mean, our son?"

Myron didn't take the bait. Not right away anyway. He stayed silent. Win was good with silence. He could hold it a long time. Myron on the other hand was not so good. So eventually he said, "Yeah, fine, our son. How could you not let him know?"

And then Greg smiled again. "Who said I didn't?"

It was then, as Myron was struggling to take in what Greg was saying, that they heard the crackle of the bullhorn. Myron looked out the kitchen window. Greg and Grace did the same. At least a dozen armed officers were positioned in the backyard.

"Oh shit," Greg said.

There, in the center of the backyard holding a bullhorn, was FBI agent Monica Hawes with FBI agent Beluga Whale by her side.

Greg muttered "Oh shit" again as the bullhorn sounded again.

"Greg Downing," Hawes said into the bullhorn. "This is Special Agent Monica Hawes with the Federal Bureau of Investigation. You're surrounded. Come out with your hands up."

CHAPTER SIXTEEN

S till seated at the kitchen table, Greg swiveled his head as though searching for an escape route. But that lasted only a few seconds. Grace put a calming hand on his forearm and shook her head. Greg deflated, nodded. Myron started shouting that they were surrendering peacefully. As the police swarmed in, Myron warned Greg not to say anything, not a word, that he'd follow Greg and get him the best legal counsel available. By the time Hawes and Beluga stepped into the kitchen, Greg was cuffed, his stomach on the kitchen floor.

"You're not to question him without his counsel present," Myron said.

Beluga patted his mouth for a fake yawn.

Three officers lifted a stunned Greg to a standing position. As they hustled him out the kitchen door, Myron shouted out reminders for Greg not to say anything. Shocked, Greg didn't so much as nod. Grace started to follow, but an officer blocked her path.

Grace glared over her shoulder at Myron. "You brought them to our door."

Myron opened his mouth to defend himself, but Grace pushed past the officer and rushed out the back.

Beluga slapped Myron on the back. "Tough break, pal."

"Were you following me?" Myron asked.

"We don't discuss our methods," Beluga said, the smug smirk firmly locked on his smooth, pale face, "so I can neither confirm nor deny that we tracked your movements to Nevada and Montana and eventually here."

Myron bit back a rejoinder and asked, "Who authorized the tail?"

"I think his name was…" Beluga looked up in the sky as though in deep thought, tapped his chin with his index finger for emphasis… "Special Agent Lick My Balls. Who cares anyway? You were about to call us, right? A law-'n'-order guy like you, Bolitar, would never harbor a wanted fugitive. That's a crime, you know."

The next few hours and indeed days passed in something of a blur.

Greg was denied bail. The prosecutor started in with the "if he were poor or marginalized, he would never get bail" optics argument, and while that may be true, the judge seemed far more persuaded by the fact that Greg Downing had been off the grid for five years and even faked his own death to stay that way. There was no way to make a convincing argument that Greg wasn't a huge flight risk. Perhaps someone as skilled as Hester Crimstein, the famed trial attorney and host of television's *Crimstein on Crime*, could have gotten him off, but Hester, who had gone to law school with Myron's mother, wouldn't take the case.

Hester had been Myron's first call:

"He needs a good lawyer," Myron had told her. "The best."

"Oh my, you called me the best. I'm now a malleable puppet who will bend to your will from all your charming flattery, *bubbe*."

"So you'll do it?"

"No, sorry, this case isn't for me."

"It's going to be a huge story. Worldwide press."

"And, what, you think I'm some attention-seeking media whore?"

Crickets. Crickets.

"Well, yeah, sure, okay, I am. But not this time."

"Why not?"

"I'm down in Miami on vacation. Did your mother tell you we're having lunch on Thursday?"

"You can fly up for the arraignment and right back down. Win can send his plane."

"Not going to happen. I'm too old for that." Then Hester hesitated, something she almost never did, and added, "And I don't want to."

"Why?"

"I don't like him, okay? There. I said it."

"You never even met him."

"But I know what he did to you."

"That was a million years ago," Myron said. "I did worse."

"No, you didn't."

"I forgave him."

"I didn't," Hester said. "You're my guy, not him. And may I give you a piece of advice?"

"I think I know what it is."

"I'll say it anyway. Your relationship with this guy is what the kids today call toxic. Now let's forget all that because I have a question for you."

"What's that?"

"Tell me the truth," Hester said. "How's Mom doing anyway?"

Myron swallowed. He opened his mouth, closed it, tried again. "I don't know."

Hester heard the thickness in his voice. "It's okay," she said softly.

"They don't tell me everything."

"They don't want you to worry."

"I'd prefer to."

"But they don't want that. Your mother and father. That's a parent's prerogative. You have to respect that. You know I love your mother like a sister."

"I know."

"And you like a nephew. But this Greg Downing business? It just isn't our fight. I'll call you after I see them."

In the end it didn't matter that Hester wouldn't take the case. When Myron tried to reach him, Greg wouldn't talk to him. He wouldn't see him. The media attention surrounding the case, as expected, was overwhelming. Not only had a former basketball star faked his own death—but now he was accused of murdering a supermodel who had once graced the covers of *Vogue* and *Cosmo*. It made for juicy headlines and snarky social media posts. The story trended everywhere. No one knew any of the details, but that never stopped anyone online from voicing fully formed opinions of guilt or innocence.

Myron was staying at Win's place on Central Park West. By the time he arrived it was close to midnight. Win was waiting for him in the parlor. Parlor, Myron had learned, was what rich people called a den or living room.

"Cognac?" Win asked.

"Why not?"

"Because for one thing you never drink cognac."

"It's a new me," Myron said. Then, thinking about his parents' last phone call: "Got an edible?"

"Is that a joke?"

"My parents swear by them."

"Your parents are rarely wrong," Win said. "I can get us some."

"Nah, a cognac will be fine."

"Good man."

Win's face was already red from the drink. Myron had noticed that Win now drank more than he used to, or perhaps it was just showing up on his face now. They both held their drinks and sat in burgundy leather chairs. A nineteenth-century pashmina wool carpet from northern India covered the floor between them. The carpet was a deep scarlet with gold stars and azure lotus blossoms.

"I spoke to PT," Win said.

Many years ago, when Win and Myron had done "favors" for the FBI, PT had been their contact. The public didn't know him, but every president and FBI director since Ronald Reagan considered him an intimate.

"What does PT say?"

"Greg did it. The DNA evidence is overwhelming."

"A little too overwhelming maybe."

Win shrugged. "Sometimes the simplest answer."

"And sometimes not. What else did PT say?"

"He didn't know the feds were tailing you."

"Would he have warned me if he did?"

"I don't see why. You were doing the legwork for them." Win put down his drink and steepled his fingers. "There is one other wrinkle."

"Oh?"

"PT insists it has to remain confidential."

"Okay." Myron took a swig of the cognac. He didn't want to know the price per swig. "So what's the wrinkle?"

"The murder of Jordan Kravat."

"What about it?"

"That's the reason for the FBI's involvement."

Myron nodded. He had already put that together. "Two murders, two different states."

"Ergo the FBI involvement," Win added. "Correct."

"Let me guess," Myron said. He took another swig and realized that he was already feeling it. Happened fast with Win's cognac. Maybe the rich even have ways of speeding up the alcohol-effects process. "Even though Joey the Toe was convicted of Jordan Kravat's murder, they aren't sure he did it."

"You should drink cognac more often," Win said. "Clears your thinking."

"They think, what, Greg killed them both?"

"Something like that."

"Do they have a motive?"

"Not a one."

"A connection between the victims?"

"Not a one," Win said again.

"Other than Greg."

"Other than Greg, yes."

"And they want to keep this, uh, was 'wrinkle' the word you used?"

"It was."

"They want to keep this wrinkle confidential because if it gets out that Joey's conviction isn't completely righteous..."

"It would be *très* embarrassing," Win finished for him.

They sat in silence for a moment.

"So where do we go from here?" Myron asked.

"Nowhere," Win replied. "Greg no longer wants our involvement."

"He never wanted our involvement."

"True. Still, we did what we could."

"'What we could,'" Myron repeated, "was getting our client arrested."

Win spread his hands. "I was being kind when I said 'we.'"

Meaning, correctly, it was on Myron. "Why would Greg murder Cecelia Callister, Win?"

"No idea. But it's not our concern. You've offered to help. He refused it. In sum, it is over. For us. We are done."

Win had a point. Myron tried for another sip, but the glass was empty. He reached for the crystal decanter and refilled it. He let his thoughts bubble up, but he could feel the haze of exhaustion and drink start to wear on him. Myron rarely imbibed because despite his size, he'd always been what one might call a lightweight. Two drinks and he was toast.

He looked over at Win. Win's eyes were closed, and there was a gentle snoring. That never used to happen. The two of them would sit up and talk all night or, if they were tired, just enjoy the comfortable silence. More and more often now, one of them fell asleep. Myron didn't like that.

He felt the buzz from his phone. It was well past midnight. He checked the screen and saw the text was from Emily Downing.

Emily's message was one word: Awake?

He let loose a breath and typed a reply: Yep.

The three moving dots that indicated Emily was typing appeared. Then:

I'm in the Hamptons. You might want to drive out.

Myron frowned and typed: Why?

Jeremy will be here soon. He wants to see you.

CHAPTER SEVENTEEN

The first thing Emily said when she opened the door was, "I knew Greg wasn't gay."

She was in a very-white nightgown at her very-white summer house in the tony (very-white?) Hamptons. She and Greg had bought the beach house for $18 million. Myron knew this because Win had helped with the financing.

"Where's Jeremy?" Myron asked.

"Where's your car?"

"I took a car service. Where's Jeremy?"

"His plane landed half an hour ago. He should be here soon."

"Where is he flying in from?"

"He would only tell me it was someplace overseas. You know his rules of engagement." She backed up so Myron could step inside. "So what happened?"

"I searched for Greg."

"Right, I figured that."

"The feds were tracking me. When I found him, so did they."

"And he was with a woman, right?"

"Yes."

"So my husband ran off with another woman."

Myron looked at her. "I thought you were married in name only."

"We were, but I was—am?—still his wife. Why not tell me he

met someone? I would have been fine with it. Why would he just run off like that?"

"I don't know. He said something about running away and escaping."

"Do you think he killed Cecelia?"

Myron ignored the question. "I need you to think, Emily."

"About?"

"What's Greg's real connection to Cecelia Callister?"

"You asked me that on the phone. I've been racking my brain."

"And?"

"I don't think he was sleeping with her."

"Okay."

"But he might have been."

"Helpful," Myron said.

"Hey, what do you want from me? I don't know."

"If it matters, Greg told me he hadn't."

"Yeah, what else is he going to say? But . . ." Emily hesitated. "This is probably a big nothing."

"But?"

"But you know how everyone keeps talking about how Cecelia the supermodel was murdered?"

"Right."

"I was thinking—what about her son? Clay. Clay was killed too."

"The theory is that he was trying to defend her."

"Right, I know. And that's why I don't think this is a big deal."

"But?"

"But I'm just trying to connect all the dots," Emily said. Then, thinking better of it, she said, "I don't mean connecting. There's no connection. Just dots."

"But?" Myron tried again.

"Cecelia was married to Ben Staples. Greg and I went out with them a few times. I told you that."

"Right. And you said Greg liked him."

"Yes. Look, you're asking for something, right? Anything?"

"Go ahead."

"Cecelia and I had lunch at the Palm Court. This was, what, twenty-five years ago? She told me she'd been raped. That wasn't the word she used. I mean, being a supermodel back in that era. The shit men did to you. The shit she took."

"Who raped her?"

"She wouldn't say."

"Did you ask?"

"Of course I asked," Emily snapped. "But it was a different world back then. Cecelia was trying to move into acting. A producer invited her up to his hotel room. Now we know all about it, but back then? Me Too wasn't even a glimmer in the eye. Cecelia actually tried to laugh it off. Like it was no big deal. I remember taking her hand, telling her we should go to someone. Get her help. She shook me off. She forced up a smile on that beautiful face and insisted she was fine. But she wasn't. She withdrew. I tried to call her a few times, but she stopped talking to me. Next thing I know she's pregnant and getting divorced from Ben."

"So you think...?"

"I don't think anything," Emily said. "But you asked me to rack my brain, and I started thinking back. I should have done more for her. Why did she confide in me, Myron? We weren't all that close. It had to be because she wanted help, right? I should have made her go to the police, but the truth is, nobody would have cared. She'd have been ruined. That's what I thought too at the time: If she goes forward...I mean, they would have said she went to a man's hotel room voluntarily, what did she expect?"

Emily hugged herself then, standing there in the very-white nightgown, looking up at Myron with something he couldn't quite read in her eyes. Myron wasn't sure how to play it, so he went with the obvious straight-up question.

"Did you tell Greg about it?"

"About Cecelia being raped?"

"Yes."

"No, not a word. She told me in confidence. But when Cecelia and Ben got divorced, like I said, Greg liked Ben. We got him in the divorce, as they say. Ben couldn't believe she'd do something like this to him—divorce him while having his child."

Myron said nothing.

"Anyway, Greg was pissed off about it."

"But not so pissed off he'd carry a grudge for, what, more than two decades and then kill her?"

"Uh no. Like I said, dots. Nothing connecting them."

Myron nodded. "Thanks. I appreciate you telling me."

"Sure."

"Any idea where Ben Staples lives now?"

"I think he's in the city."

They both saw the headlights as a car pulled into the driveway. They walked together toward the front door. Emily opened it and stepped out onto the front yard. Myron followed her. They stood side by side as the back car door opened and their son stepped out. Jeremy wore a blue suit. The driver popped the trunk. Jeremy circled to the back to retrieve his duffel bag. As he did, Emily, her eyes on her son, her only son, tapped Myron's hand with hers. Myron looked at her now. There were tears in her eyes. There were tears in his too.

He knew what she was thinking because he was thinking the same thing. They had messed up. They had done some terrible wrongs in their life. But if they hadn't, if they had done the right thing back then, this boy, this spectacular boy, would not be here.

Jeremy thanked the driver and started up the walk. When he spotted his biological parents standing side by side in the front yard, he pulled up. First, he looked at Myron. Then he looked at Emily.

"Ooookay," Jeremy said, stretching the word out. "This is weird."

Then Jeremy's face broke into a smile, a huge smile, a smile that echoed the best part of both of his parents.

"Don't worry, guys. It's a good weird."

———————

Myron and Emily sat on opposite ends of the couch and waited in silence while Jeremy quickly showered and changed into jeans and a T-shirt. When he was ready, he came tripping down the stairs fast. Myron watched him. His hair was military-cropped and that made his ears stick out a little. Myron's ears stuck out a little too. When Jeremy hit the bottom step, he looked straight at his mother.

"Mom, do you mind if Myron and I talk alone for a minute?"

"Oh," Emily said. "Uh, sure."

"It'll only be a second."

"Okay, no rush. You two talk."

Emily rose from the couch. She kissed her son on the cheek as she passed him. Jeremy gave her a hug in return.

"I love you," she said to him.

"I love you too, Mom."

"I'm happy you're home."

"Me too."

She headed up the stairs. Jeremy watched her until he heard

her bedroom door close. Then he turned back to Myron with the hazel eyes of Al Bolitar, his paternal grandfather. Myron tried to turn it off, his constant searching for genetic echoes. He hadn't seen his biological son in three years. The rules of the relationship had been set when Jeremy first learned the truth at the tender age of thirteen:

"You're not my dad. I mean you might be my father. But you're not my dad. You know what I mean?"

Myron had managed to nod.

"But . . . but maybe you can still be around."

"Around?"

"Yeah." That winning smile. "Around. You know."

Age thirteen. So damn wise already.

In the present day, Jeremy said, "Myron?"

"What?"

"You're doing it again."

"Huh?"

"Giving me those googly eyes."

"Right. Sorry."

"I get it. You can't help it. It's sweet, really. Except we need to make this fast." He took the seat across from Myron and leaned forward, elbows on his thighs, just like . . .

"You look good," Myron managed to say.

"So do you," he said. "How's Terese?"

"She's good. Busy."

Jeremy nodded. Then, as was his wont, he took over. "Tell me everything."

Myron did. Jeremy had been a sickly kid. He'd been diagnosed with Fanconi anemia and needed a bone marrow transplant. That was the reason Emily had eventually been forced to confess the truth about Jeremy's paternity—she'd been searching for a donor. For the first thirteen years of the boy's life, Emily had kept Jeremy's paternity a secret, neither telling Myron he had a son nor telling Greg the boy he was raising was biologically not. That wasn't so much a secret as a lie, but the big shock was that Greg knew the truth:

"You remember my father?" Greg had asked Myron. "Screaming on the sidelines like a lunatic?"

"Yes."

"I ended up looking just like him. Spitting image of my old man. He was my blood. And he was the cruelest son of a bitch I ever knew. Blood never meant much to me."

It was a shocking moment for Myron—and maybe the beginning of the strange bond between the two men. Greg's marriage unraveled; his role as Jeremy's father did not.

But while the illness was purportedly gone, Fanconi anemia never fully leaves. There was still some paleness to Jeremy's skin. He had to frequently screen for new cancers, and part of the kid's wisdom and insight, Myron didn't doubt, came with living his entire life under this mortality umbrella. So far, the bone marrow transplant had held. It might hold forever. But no one knew for sure.

When Myron finished filling him in, Jeremy had follow-up questions, drilling deeper into some of the crazier details. When he was done with that, Jeremy asked, "So what's our next step?"

"There is no next step. Greg doesn't want to see me."

"Forget that. He'll see us." Then he called up. "Mom?"

Emily appeared at the top of the stairs. "Everything okay?"

"Can Myron stay tonight in the guest room?"

"I guess so, sure."

"Great. You can borrow some of my clothes. We'll head in to see Dad in the morning."

———————

Emily had a guest wing more than a guest room. Right now it was too dark to see the ocean out the window, the moon barely a slit, but Myron could hear the waves crashing. He lay on his back and closed his eyes. A few minutes later, he heard the light knock on the door and before he could say, "Come in," Emily opened it. The hall light was still behind her, so she stood in the doorway in perfect silhouette.

"Hey," she whispered.

"Hey."

"How do you feel?" she asked.

"Tired."

Emily stepped into the room and sat on the bed. "It's lonely out here," she said. "This big house."

"I imagine you have a lot of guests."

"Oh, I have my friends. And sure, I go on a lot of dates. But it's been a long time since I felt a connection."

She still wore the very-white nightgown. She looked down at him.

Myron said, "Emily."

"I know." She smiled. "It wouldn't be cheating, you know."

"Yeah, it would."

"It would just be something between you and me."

"I'm not sure Terese would see it that way."

"She might. We have something. Apart from her. You know this."

"No, I don't."

"I hurt you."

"A long time ago."

"I loved you. I don't think I ever loved anyone as much as you."

"We were in college. It was a long time ago."

"Does it feel that long ago to you?"

Myron said nothing.

"That's the funny thing, isn't it? I read a line once: 'You are always seventeen waiting for your life to begin.' It's true, don't you think?"

"In some ways."

"You were just..." Emily looked up, blinked away the wetness in her eyes. "Back then, you were so sure of what you wanted. Like you had it all figured out. I was your first real girlfriend. We'd get married. We'd buy a house in the suburbs and have two-point-six kids and a barbecue in the yard and a basketball hoop in the driveway. Just like your family. You had it all planned out, but to me, it felt..."

"Claustrophobic," Myron said, knowing there was truth in her words. "Suffocating."

"In part, I suppose. But it was more like I'd won the audition to play this part in your life."

Myron shook his head.

"You don't agree," she said.

"I loved you, Em. I may have been young. I may have been romantically immature. But I loved you."

She swallowed, looked off. "Do you remember the last time we had sex?"

The night before her wedding. The night they conceived Jeremy. "It would be hard to forget."

"It changed everything, didn't it? Do you feel shame?"

"I feel a lot of things."

"I often wonder what my life would have been like if I had said yes when you proposed. I would have been too much drama for you, but you'd never have left me. That's not how you're built. Do you want to hear something?"

"Can I say no?"

She smiled and lay down on the bed next to Myron. Her back was to him so he couldn't see her face. She curled her knees up.

"If I could go back in time to the moment you asked me, I'd still say no."

Myron stayed on his back, staring at the ceiling. He could feel the heat coming from her body.

"Because if I had said yes, we wouldn't have slept together the night before my wedding. And we wouldn't have had Jeremy. Oh, I'm sure we would have great kids. Wonderful adults now. We'd be proud as all hell of them. But there'd be no Jeremy. Think about that."

Myron closed his eyes. Emily rolled over and put her hand on his chest. Myron didn't move. She leaned toward him and kissed his cheek. Then she rolled away so that her back was to him again.

"Is it okay if I just stay here and sleep? I won't—"

"Yeah," Myron said, his voice thick. "You can stay."

CHAPTER EIGHTEEN

Early the next morning Myron and Jeremy headed back to New York City in Emily's car. Myron drove.

"So," Jeremy said. "About last night..."

Myron's grip on the wheel tightened.

"Mom probably thought she was being quiet when she tiptoed back from the guest wing. She forgets I'm military."

"Nothing happened."

"Uh-huh."

"She just fell asleep."

"If you think I'm upset by it—"

"Doesn't matter what I think. She slept next to me. That's all."

"Okay."

"We will always be connected," Myron said.

"Let me guess. Because of me?"

"It's a good reason to be connected."

"The best. But she needs someone."

"That someone won't be me."

"Don't you have any friends who'd be good for her?"

Myron thought about it. "Not one. I know a lot of terrific single women your mother's age. I don't know one single guy my age worthy of them."

"Sad but true," Jeremy said. "So about my dad."

My dad, Myron repeated in his head. "What about him?"

"Visiting hours start at eleven a.m."

"We'll be in the city by nine."

"Where's your office again?"

"Park and 47th Street."

"I have an army pal who works in the MetLife Building next door. Okay if I visit him before we head over?"

"Sure."

Jeremy took out a set of AirPods and put them in his ears. "I'm still adjusting to the time change. Do you mind if I close my eyes?"

"No," Myron said, his heart sinking. "Of course not."

Myron parked in the garage below Win's building. When they got on Park Avenue, Jeremy headed left toward MetLife. Myron watched him walk away before heading into the Lock-Horne Building. He hopped on the elevator and took it to the top floor.

Big Cyndi greeted him in a spandex Batgirl suit, custom-made from the design used for the "original" Batgirl costume—the "real" Batgirl—from the old 1960s Batman TV series. Years ago, when Big Cyndi was professionally wrestling as Big Chief Mama, she befriended the iconic actress Yvonne Craig, who played that original Batgirl/Barbara Gordon role as well as Marta the green Orion girl in *Star Trek*. Yvonne had loaned Big Cyndi the Batgirl costume she still owned so that Big Cyndi could design her own. When Yvonne Craig died in 2015, Big Cyndi had made another one, entirely in black, and wore it every day for three months in mourning.

As the kids would say, Big Cyndi always goes hard.

She twirled when Myron entered. She always twirled to start her day. "You like?"

"I do," Myron said to her. "You look ready to save Gotham."

"Do you know what Batgirl's catchphrase is?"

"I do not."

Big Cyndi normally spoke in a high falsetto, but now she made her voice lower than a basso profundo at the Philharmonic. "I'm Batgirl."

She looked at Myron. Myron said nothing.

"I googled it," Big Cyndi said. "That was her catchphrase."

Not sure what to say about that, Myron went with: "It's easy to remember."

"Right?" Big Cyndi tilted her head and grinned. "Anyway, there's another quote from Batgirl I wanted to share with you, Mr. Bolitar."

She always called him *Mister* Bolitar, never Myron, and she insisted that he called her Big Cyndi, not Cyndi or, uh, Big.

"Something Batgirl once said to Batman."

"I'm listening," Myron said.

"'You don't have a monopoly on wanting to help.'"

Myron was six four. Big Cyndi had two inches on him, plus the Batgirl boots probably gave her another two inches. Big Cyndi never shied away from her size. She never toned down her personality. Many people will tell you that they don't care what people think, which is bullshit by definition—if you're *telling* me you don't care what people think, you *want* me to think you're the kind of person who doesn't care what people think and thus you care what I think—but Big Cyndi genuinely did not. She lived life out loud and was the most authentic person Myron had ever met.

"Is it okay if I give you a hug?" Myron asked.

"Not if I give you one first."

Big Cyndi stepped forward and swept him into her thick arms.

"I always need your help," Myron said.

"I know," Big Cyndi said. "It's true."

That made Myron laugh. His phone buzzed, telling him he had an incoming FaceTime. He stepped back and checked the screen.

"My parents," Myron said.

"Please tell them I said hi."

"Will do."

Myron hit the answer button. A shaky video appeared. Myron could make out startlingly bright sunlight and then the pool at his parents' condo. The screen jerked, and now Myron could see his mother's face. She wore huge sunglasses that looked like someone had glued two manhole covers together.

"Myron?" his mother said. "It's your mother."

"Yes, Mom, I have caller ID. Also I can see you."

"I'm outside by the pool."

"I can see that too, Mom. You know this is a video call, right?"

"Don't be a wiseass with your mother."

"Sorry." Myron headed into his office and closed the door behind him. "How are you?"

"I'm good. Let me see your face."

"Okay."

"Sheesh, I can barely see anything on this screen."

"Take your sunglasses off," Myron said.

"What?"

He repeated himself and told her to go into the shade. She did so.

"Oh, that's better," she said.

"Where's Dad?"

"What do you mean, where's Dad?" That was his father speaking now. "I'm right here."

The camera stayed on Mom, so Myron couldn't see him.

"Hey, Dad."

"So the reason we're calling," Mom said, "is that your father made a new friend."

"Ellen, stop."

"His name is Allen too. He spells it just like your father. Allen Castner. The two of them met at the poolside breakfast buffet and guess what? Allen Castner wants to teach Allen Bolitar how to play pickleball. Can you imagine such a thing?"

From off-screen, Dad said, "What's the problem?"

"You're going to hurt yourself, that's the problem. You're an old man. And what kind of name for a sport is pickleball anyway? Who came up with that? Myron, do you know who came up with that name?"

"I don't."

"Pickleball," Mom said again. "A grown man playing a sport with that name. And your father is no great athlete, let me tell you."

"Thanks for the support, Ellen."

"What, I'm not telling the truth? You, Myron. You got my genes. I come from a long line of great athletes. Shira, she got them too. Your brother? Not so much."

"Is there a point to this call, Mom?"

"Don't rush me, I'm getting there. So, like I said, your father made a friend."

"Allen Castner," Myron said.

"Right, Allen Castner. They're going to play pickleball together and then—get this, Myron—they both love trivia so tonight they're going to compete as a team at the local trivia contest at the JCC."

"Sounds fun," Myron said.

"It's not, but never mind that. Guess the name of their team."

"Allen and Allen?"

"Close," Mom said.

Dad took the phone. "Allen Squared," he said. "Kind of hip, right?"

"Kind of," Myron said.

Dad made a face and handed the phone back to Mom—or

maybe she just grabbed it back. The video's constant jerking was making Myron dizzy.

"So anyway," Mom said, "Dad's new friend Allen Castner is a huge basketball fan. Truth?" She lowered her voice to a conspiratorial whisper, which in Mom's case meant they'd hear her in Fort Lauderdale. "I think this other Allen made friends with your dad because of you. Anyway, your father was being all modest, but the reason I'm calling is Allen really wanted to meet you."

"Allen the friend," Dad said with a chuckle. "Not Allen the father."

"Good one, Al," Mom said in a voice dripping with sarcasm—something else Myron had inherited from her. "Anyway, here he is."

She turned the phone's camera now, so Myron could see his father crowding into the screen with a bald guy who looked to be in his late seventies–early eighties. Both Allens wore big smiles and, like Mom, all-encompassing sunglasses. Big sunglasses seemed to be haute couture amongst the Florida retirees.

Allen Castner said, "So nice to meet you, Myron. I'm a big fan."

"Nice to meet you too, Mr. Castner."

"Mr. Castner," he repeated. "What am I, your father?"

Everyone laughed at that. Myron didn't get it. Who calls their father Mister?

"Call me Allen. Look, Myron, I don't want to keep you. You wouldn't guess it looking at me now, but I was a big player back in the day. I even did some scouting for the Celtics. I was friends with Clip Arnstein."

Clip Arnstein was the famed basketball general manager who drafted Myron in the first round—one of the few major mistakes in Clip's long and stellar career.

"Anyway," Allen Castner continued, "I know it was a long time ago, but you were a great player. I saw every game when you were at

Duke. I know your career was cut short, but since when is time the deciding factor in how brightly someone shines? You were a joy to watch. So thank you for that."

Everyone went silent. Even Myron's parents. Dad's eyes started to well up. A song by the Moody Blues played over the pool speaker. Myron could make out the lyrics "Just what I'm going through, they can't understand." There were the happy squeals of kids at a pool, someone's grandchildren probably.

"That's very kind of you to say, Mr.—"

"Uh-uh."

"—Allen," Myron said, correcting himself. Then: "Listen, I have to take this other call."

"Go, go," Allen Castner said. "I've taken up too much of your time. But really, such an honor to meet you. Here, Ellen, say good-bye to your son."

He handed the phone back to Mom. She pointed the camera right into the sunlight. "You know I'm having lunch with Hester this week."

"She told me," Myron said. "Have a blast."

"Blast. What, you worried Hester and I are going to find some young guys and run off?"

From off-screen, Myron heard his dad shout, "I wish."

"Very funny."

"I'm kidding," Dad said. "If your mother ran off, I wouldn't know what I would do...first."

The two Allens yucked it up at that one.

"It's like Rodney Dangerfield is still alive. See what I live with, Myron?"

"I got to go, Mom."

They said their goodbyes. Myron hung up the phone and sat back and wondered what the hell was bothering him about that call.

CHAPTER NINETEEN

Two hours later, Myron and Jeremy sat in a visiting room waiting for Greg.

Myron said, "Can I ask you something else?"

"I'll skip the old 'you just did' joke," Jeremy said.

"Thank God." Then: "Did you know Greg was alive?"

"Not at first," Jeremy said. "He told me later."

"When? How?"

"He visited me. When I was stationed at Camp Arifjan in Kuwait."

"And, what, he just showed up?"

Jeremy nodded. "He had Grace call first."

"You knew about Grace?"

"I didn't before that call."

"So you saw him in Kuwait?"

"Yes."

"Why did he do it?"

"Fake his death?"

"Yeah," Myron said. "For starters."

"I think it was a combination of things."

"Like?"

"Like how he needed to escape the world."

Myron frowned. "Didn't running away do that already?"

"That's what I thought. But he didn't tell me about the murder in Vegas. That probably pushed him too."

Myron was about to ask a follow-up when the door opened. Greg entered. Myron expected him to be cuffed, but he wasn't. He wore a beige prisoner jumpsuit. Jeremy leapt from his chair and shouted, "Dad!" Myron tried not to let that sound pierce his chest. The two men embraced hard. Myron could see Greg's face over Jeremy's shoulder as he held tight. His eyes were squeezed shut. Jeremy clung to Greg as Greg gently assured him that everything was going to be okay. Myron wondered whether he had ever felt like such an awkward intruder in his life. He concluded that the answer was no.

Still holding one another, the two men—father and son, Myron thought, let's be honest about it—found their seats. Both had tears in their eyes. Myron just waited. He didn't want to be the first to speak. When they got a little more settled, Greg broke the silence.

Glaring at Myron, Greg said, "You're only here because Jeremy asked me to see you."

"Hey, don't do me any favors." Myron started to rise. "I can go right now."

"Guys," Jeremy said.

Greg continued to glare at Myron. "Did you set me up?"

"Are you serious?"

"Did you bring the feds with you," Greg asked, "or were you just a witless dupe?"

"I was trying to help you," Myron said.

"Guys," Jeremy tried again.

"Did a great job of that, didn't you?"

"I almost lost a toe," Myron said.

"A *baby* toe, don't be so dramatic."

"Guys," Jeremy said again, but this time there was some steel behind it. He wasn't the son of either of them in that moment. He was the military leader. Both men shut up.

Jeremy nodded as though satisfied. Then he said, "I'm going to leave you two alone."

Greg: "What?"

Myron: "Wait, why?"

"Because," Jeremy said, again adding that authority to his voice that didn't leave room for any protest, "Myron is an attorney. Anything you say to him falls under attorney-client privilege. You don't enjoy that same protection with me." Jeremy rose, turning his attention to Myron. "Signal me when it's okay for me to come back." He knocked on the door. A guard opened it. Jeremy slipped out.

Greg was still staring at the door. "That kid," he said.

"I know."

"Makes up for a host of sins," Greg said. Then, turning his gaze to Myron, "Makes it easier to forgive."

"For me or for you?" Then Myron raised his hand in a stop gesture. "We don't want to dig up old grievances, do we?"

"Or even new ones," Greg said. "So let's get to it, okay?"

He didn't add "for Jeremy's sake." He didn't have to.

"Emily said you knew Cecelia Callister," Myron began.

"I told you that," Greg said. "A long time ago."

"Emily says you were upset when Ben and Cecelia got divorced."

"'Upset' is a pretty strong word."

"What word would you use?"

"I thought it was scummy on her part. Leaving her husband after getting pregnant. Not telling him whose baby she was carrying."

The echo with their past clanged loudly and obviously. Myron pushed through it.

"Did you ever sleep with her?"

"Cecelia Callister?"

"Yes."

Greg smiled. "Wait. You don't think—"

"I'm just trying to find connections."

"No, I never slept with her."

"So there's no chance that her son Clay..."

"Was mine?" Greg shook his head. "Wow. All kinds of weird karma stuff going around here, isn't there? No, Myron. There's no chance Clay was mine."

Myron sat back. "They found your DNA at the scene."

"That's what they say."

"You don't believe it?"

"I wasn't there. I didn't kill her. I haven't seen Cecelia Callister in thirty years. So when my lawyer told me that they had my DNA under her fingernails or something—I assumed that it had to be a mistake. I know the science doesn't lie. But sometimes humans do. Or labs mess up. There had to be something wrong. That's what I thought."

"Thought," Myron repeated. "As in past tense."

"Yes."

"So now you think...?"

"My lawyer had his own expert redo the DNA test from scratch. Took my DNA, compared it to the lab sample. It's definitely my DNA under the fingernails. It's too crazy. Do you want to know where my mind went at first?"

Myron nodded for him to tell him.

"I wondered whether I had a twin brother or something. Then I wondered whether, I don't know, I gave blood somewhere. Like years ago. Like maybe I gave a donation to the Red Cross and someone stole it."

"Twins don't have the same DNA profile, and they can't use stored blood—"

"Yeah, I know all that now. I didn't really believe any of it either. I'm just trying to show you how crazy my mind started to go."

"So what then?"

"I kept thinking someone has to be setting me up."

"Who?"

"Cecelia Callister was murdered on September fourteenth."

"Okay," Myron said.

"So look, I've been keeping a low profile for a long time. The beard. The hair. It's all a disguise. I've been careful. But there are things I still miss. About my old life." Greg inched a little closer. "Tell me your favorite basketball memory. Not a big shot or a championship. Tell me when you enjoyed just playing the most."

Myron was going to mention the one time he got to suit up in a Boston Celtics uniform, his one and only preseason game, the game where Big Burt Wesson, paid off by Greg Downing to avenge his wife's infidelity, slammed into Myron and ended his career. But now was not the time. It wasn't water under the bridge, but it was water best not to navigate through right now.

When Myron didn't reply, Greg said, "What I remember most, what I loved about the game, were those pickup games in the off-season. Remember?"

"At the JCC," Myron said.

"Right. Nowadays the kids play competitive ball all year around. AAU. All these leagues, all these scheduled games. They're a nice moneymaker for someone, but it hurts the game. And the kids. My favorite part of basketball? The part I missed? Old-school pickup games. A gym that smelled like old socks. Guys choosing sides. Shirts and skins. Calling winners."

"Yeah, Greg, I know what pickup basketball is."

But it was hard not to agree. Myron loved pickup. He still played it occasionally, when his knee could handle the strain.

"Okay," Myron said. "So you started playing in pickup games."

"I was careful about keeping a low profile. A different court every time. I found a church league game one week. I found some guys who played at a local Y the next. I dialed my game down, so, you know, I wouldn't dominate."

He wasn't bragging. Myron did the same. Guys think they are good. But they aren't pros.

"I'd even play lefty," Greg said.

"Yeah, but you always drove to the hoop with your left."

Greg smiled. "You used to overplay it."

"The rare righty who wants to go left," Myron said. Then: "Nice to reminisce but Jeremy is waiting. What's your point?"

"I played in a game sometime early September."

"Okay."

"It was one of those games where the guys get out of hand. You know. Too much testosterone."

Myron knew exactly what he meant. "It got physical?"

"Very. A guy elbowed me in the nose. I started bleeding. Another scratched me. At one point, someone hit me in the back of the head. Hard. I went down. I may have lost consciousness, I don't know. I don't remember much."

"When was this exactly?"

"I don't remember. Like I said, I'm pretty sure it was early September."

"So what you're saying is—"

"Yeah, maybe it makes no sense, but if my DNA is at that murder scene, like skin under Cecelia's fingernails or blood...I mean, I was bleeding pretty good that night. My nose might have even been broken."

"Did you go to a doctor or ER?"

"No, of course not. Come on, you remember what it was like. You shake it off, right? That's how we were raised."

Again that was true. If you could walk home, you didn't complain. Dumb but there you go.

"But I'm thinking about it now. One of the guys handed me a towel to stop my nosebleed. I don't know where that towel is now. And the scratch marks. You can ask Grace. They were pretty deep. So if I am being framed, if someone planted my DNA at a murder scene..."

"This pickup game," Myron said. "Where was it?"

"There's an outdoor court in Wallkill. I don't remember the name of it."

Myron nodded. "Okay, I'll check it out. Anything else?"

"I didn't do this, Myron."

"It's weird though," Myron said. "Jordan Kravat, Cecelia Callister. You knew them both."

"Tangentially," Greg countered. Then he added, "How many murder victims have you known tangentially?"

Touché.

"I know you don't owe me anything—"

"You're still my client," Myron said. "So I'll do what I can."

CHAPTER TWENTY

Y ou point the rifle at his chest.

Ronald Prine stares at you. You see the question come to his face. He doesn't know who you are. He has never seen you before. He is wondering who you are and what you want and which one of his brilliant go-to lines will work for him.

Because life has always worked for him.

You smile. You love this part.

"Take my watch," he says to you. He is rattled, sure, but not as rattled as he should be. There is still the faux bravado of a soft man who has never known tough. This is just a small problem, he thinks, because all his problems up until now have been small, inconsequential. He'll get out of it, he's sure. He always has in the past. For guys like him, things just seem to go right. They live in a delusion of meritocracy. They believe that they have supernatural charisma, charm, and innate talents that separate them from the rest of us mere mortals.

"It's a Vacheron Constantin timepiece," he tells you. "My father bought it in 1974. Do you know how much they go for?"

You shouldn't be enjoying this so much. "Tell me," you say.

"Probably seventy-five grand."

You give a soft, impressed whistle. Then you say, "I'm not here for that."

"Why are you here then?"

"I'm here," you say, "for Jackie Newton."

You watch for a reaction. This, you are sure, will be your favorite part. He doesn't let you down. Bafflement crowds his face. It's not an act, which makes it all the better or worse, depending on where you stand. "Who?"

He really doesn't know her.

Should you tell him?

When Jackie Newton was eight years old, her mother ran off with Gus Deloy, a coworker at the old Circuit City on Bustleton Avenue in Philadelphia. Jackie remembered her mother sitting on a suitcase to close it, the lipstick smeared on her teeth, telling her daughter, "It's best this way, I'm a shit mom," before hurriedly dragging that suitcase along with her dad's old army duffel bag down the cracked front walk and piling it all in the back of Gus's Jeep. She didn't look back as they sped off, but Gus did. He gave Jackie a reluctant half salute, an almost apologetic look on his face. Maybe Jackie's mom would have changed her mind or regretted abandoning her daughter eventually. Maybe she would have come home or asked to see Jackie again. But for three years, there wasn't a word. Then Jackie's dad, Ed Newton, got a call that Mom had died in a car crash in Pasadena.

No word on the fate of half-salute Gus.

It wasn't all bad for Jackie. Ed Newton raised Jackie the best he could. He was a good man, surprisingly gentle and patient with her. She was his whole world. You could see it every time he trudged through the door at the end of his shift. His face lit up when he saw Jackie. The rest of the world? It could go to hell, as far as Ed was concerned. He didn't hate. He just didn't really care. His daughter was his everything, and like the best of fathers, he somehow managed to make her feel that without suffocating her.

Ed Newton worked long hours doing hardwood flooring for TST

Construction, mostly on new residential complexes on the outskirts of Philly. He didn't mind hard work. He loved tools and making things with his hands, but his bosses were cheap rat bastards, always trying to cut corners, always trying to squeeze the last bit of juice out of anyone who worked for them.

"It sucks working for someone," Ed Newton oft repeated to his daughter between bites as they sat at the Formica kitchen table. "Be your own boss, Jackie."

That was the dream.

When Jackie was ten, Ed Newton bought her a leathercraft suede tool belt. It was the most beautiful thing Jackie had ever owned. It smelled like pinewood and sawdust. She treated the leather with oils three times a week. She wore it all the time. Even now. Even more than a quarter century after he first gave it to her. When she was eleven, Dad managed to buy a small plot of land outside the Poconos. Every weekend father and daughter would go out there and build Dad's dream hunting-and-fishing cabin. Jackie always wore the tool belt. Ed was a patient teacher, and she was a quick study. They worked mostly in silence. The work was Zen for them both.

The two of them had plans too. One day, Ed said, they'd open their own contracting company. The two of them. They'd work for themselves. They'd be their own bosses.

When she was eighteen, Jackie got a full scholarship to Montgomery County Community College. She took finance courses, something her father encouraged so they could shore up the fiscal side of running a construction firm. Jackie worked various construction jobs after graduation to learn the business inside and out. The hope was that if they scrimped and saved, they'd be able to open their own shop in three to five years.

It took longer than they anticipated.

Ed put a second mortgage on the house in Philadelphia and despite Jackie's protests, he sold the dream cabin they'd built outside the Poconos. By the time they raised enough capital to get a business loan, Jackie was thirty-three, Ed was sixty-two—but a dream delayed is not a dream denied.

One day, Ed Newton burst through the front door with a stack of business cards that read:

Newton and Daughter Construction Services, LLP

Ed Newton

Jackie Newton

General Contracting, Home Remodeling, Flooring

The logo on the upper right-hand corner was a little house with windows as eyes and a wide door as the smile. Jackie had never seen her father so happy, and for the first six months, things went surprisingly well. The Nesbitt Brothers needed last-minute help with a housing development in Bryn Mawr. Newton and Daughter kicked ass on the project, bringing it in under budget. That job got them some good referrals. Other jobs followed. Ed and Jackie hired three full-time staff and leased office space in a warehouse on Castor Avenue.

Newton and Daughter were still small-time with a lowercase *s*, but they were moving in the right direction.

After a year, their fine work and excellent reputation got on the radar of Ronald Prine, a major Philadelphia real estate mogul. Prine's people invited Ed to put in a bid on hardwood floor work for the new, upscale Prine skyscraper on Arch Street. It was a huge job, too big for them really, but it would be a prestigious get and a chance to put Newton and Daughter on the map.

Ed and Jackie spent two weeks working out the numbers and

creating a full PowerPoint presentation for the Prine conglomerate, but their initial bid, according to Prine's people, came in too high. Ed Newton went back to his office. He sharpened his pencil and lowered their bid. Prine's people still balked.

They're smart businessmen, Ed explained to his daughter. That was why conglomerates like Prine's were so successful—they know how to squeeze every dollar. Jackie wasn't so sure. The job was too unwieldy, and now the margins were far too low. She didn't like or trust Prine's people. She had heard stories about smaller contractors like them being stiffed.

But Ed wouldn't hear of it. A prominent job like this would be incredible publicity for them. It would give Newton and Daughter legitimacy that money couldn't buy. If they could break even on something like this, Ed told her—heck, even if they lost a dollar or two—they'd come out ahead.

After lowering their numbers one more time, Newton and Daughter won the bid.

The job was all-consuming. It took everything out of them in every way, but hey, they were playing in the major leagues now. Dad loved that. He walked into O'Malley's Pub with his back a little straighter, his smile a little wider. He got congratulatory slaps on the back from his old coworkers. They wanted to buy him drinks.

Like so many things, it was all good until it wasn't.

First off, Prine was late on the down payment. The money was coming, they were repeatedly told. This was the multinational conglomerate's standard operating procedure, they were assured. Just get started on the job. And so they did. Ed took out another loan to buy the flooring from his favorite sawmill in Hazlehurst, Georgia. A little more expensive but worth it. Ed and Jackie turned down other jobs, good jobs, to focus solely on the Prine skyscraper. It was a hard job with lots of red tape, delays, overruns, cost issues.

In the end, they'd lose money, but the hardwood flooring was top-notch, impeccable. Ed and Jackie took tremendous pride in what they'd done. They'd had their backs to the wall and showed they could play with the big boys.

You can guess the rest, can't you?

Prine stiffed them. Not a little bit. Not a chisel. He simply didn't pay them. When they finished the job and presented the final invoice, Prine ignored it. He didn't even bother to lie, to say the money was coming, to claim it would just be another week. He didn't even offer up the hoary chestnut that the check was in the mail. Ed Newton sent another invoice. Then another. Weeks passed. Then months. Ed and Jackie made phone calls, but no one with any authority would get on the line. They showed up at the office, but security wouldn't allow them on the premises. Left with no other option, Ed and Jackie ended up hiring an attorney appropriately named Richard Fee. Prine ignored the attorney too. More months passed. They eventually had no choice but to sue the Prine Organization. It wasn't David versus Goliath—it was David versus a thousand Goliaths. Prine's lawyers, a massive team of them, swarmed and overwhelmed them. They drowned Ed and Jackie in paperwork. They submitted constant motions. They made outrageous demands on discovery. Ed and Jackie's legal fees started piling up. Richard Fee dropped out once the money ran out. When Ed and Jackie tried to dig in their heels, Prine's people bad-mouthed their work, just straight-up lied about shoddy craftsmanship and needing to redo. Newton and Daughter's reputation was left in tatters. After two more months, Prine finally offered to settle for twenty cents on the dollar. Ed refused.

You know the rest, don't you?

They lost their business. They lost the house. Eventually, to pay off a small percentage of their growing debt, the bankruptcy courts forced them to take a deal that gave them fourteen cents on the dollar. As part of the settlement, Ed and Jackie were forced to sign nondisclosure agreements, so that they couldn't tell anyone what Prine or his organization had done to them.

In April of this year, Ed Newton suffered a debilitating stroke. Maybe it was just his age or a lifetime of not eating right. Maybe it wasn't connected at all to the lawsuit or all the losses. But Jackie didn't believe that. It was Prine. What he had done to her father. What he had done to them.

She fantasized about revenge, but of course, that would never happen.

They moved into a low-income housing development. Jackie ended up working for Ed's old bosses at TST Construction at a reduced hourly rate.

They had nothing. Almost nothing. But one thing Jackie kept:

Her father's hunting rifle.

You—you who learned her story and saw an opportunity in it—have the rifle in your hands now.

You are pointing it at Prine's chest.

"Who are you?" Prine asks. "What do you want?"

You had wanted this mission to go in reverse—kill Jackie, pin it on Prine—but that would have been very difficult. Prine had never even known the woman whose life he had ruined. He didn't even know Jackie's name.

There'd be no motive.

"Look," Prine says to you, "whoever you are, we can make this right. I have a lot of money—"

You pull the trigger.

You anticipated a big recoil, and you got one. The slug blows a giant hole through the rich man's chest. Money does a lot for a man, but it doesn't stop a bullet. Prine is dead before he hits the ground. You drive back to the low-income project in Philadelphia. You have a key to the Newton place. When Jackie left her key at work one day, you took it, duplicated it, and put it back without her ever knowing. You can enter and go as you please now.

And as always, you planned.

That's how you got her father's rifle this morning. That's how you got access to Jackie's dated computer where you could send the Prine Organization emails threatening violence for what they had done to Jackie and her father.

You use the key again now. The TV is on. It always is during the day. You tiptoe past the bedroom where Ed Newton will probably spend his final days.

You found the unloaded rifle in the closet toward the back. You return it there now.

You didn't add a DNA tie-in this time. The rifle and threatening emails and messages should be enough. Jackie might have an alibi— you couldn't cover all the bases, what with the rush to get this done— but you know that's unlikely to sway anyone.

Ironically, if Jackie Newton were rich, if she had Prine's money, this wouldn't be enough. She'd probably get off. She'd hire a team of top lawyers who would buddy up to the right judges and cops and politicians and heck, it might not even go to trial.

Still, Jackie might get lucky. She might have an airtight alibi. She might get assigned a public defender who cared. She may not end up spending the rest of her life in prison.

In short, you are giving Jackie Newton a fighting chance.

And that's something you've never given to anyone else.

CHAPTER TWENTY-ONE

———

The cemetery overlooked the schoolyard.

Myron could not believe, after all these years, he was back. He took a few deep breaths before getting out of the car. Ben Staples, Cecelia Callister's ex, had asked to meet here because, his assistant explained on the phone, it was now Cecelia and her son Clay's final resting place. That reasoning didn't seem to track, but here Myron was.

He could see Ben Staples up ahead in a grassy clearing where the cemetery remained mostly unoccupied. Myron didn't plan it, didn't even want to, but he found himself veering over to the older graves, as though guided by some higher power. He had not been to this cemetery in years, but he still knew exactly where to go. His body started to tremble as he walked, and soon he was there. The name on the tombstone was Brenda Slaughter. Myron read her birthdate and then let his eyes travel right to the date of her death. So young. So terribly, awfully, tragically young. The familiar pain came back to him all at once, like a stab, and Myron felt his knees buckle.

Myron stood there for a moment and let all the bad memories wash over him. Had he loved Brenda? No. Too early for that. But after her death, he'd had something akin to a mental breakdown. He drank too much, ran away from everyone, and met a strange woman who was hurting too. Their mutual misery bonded them, and so they'd run off together to a private island for a quick, therapeutic fling. A rebound, if you will. A way to heal.

That woman's name was Terese Collins. She and Myron were married now.

Man plans, God laughs.

It wasn't worth it, of course. If he could go back in time, he'd rather have saved Brenda and never met his current wife, awful as that might sound. But that's what he'd do. And the best part, one of the many reasons he fell so deeply and passionately in love with Terese, is that she would get that too.

We are our mistakes. Sometimes they are the best part of us.

Ben Staples had neatly groomed salt-and-pepper hair. He wore a black turtleneck under his overcoat. For a man who had once been married to a woman who was on every "Most Beautiful" list, Staples was nondescript in the looks department. If a sketch artist tried to prompt you, there would be little to say. Normal nose. Normal chin, maybe a little weak. Oval face. Average height. He held a plant in front of him with both hands like an offering. He stared at the two mounds of dirt. No tombstone yet. Still too soon.

"Thanks for meeting me here," Ben Staples said.

Myron moved next to him so that they stood shoulder to shoulder, facing the dirt.

"Cecelia is on the left. Clay is on the right. There were name placards here on Monday. Now..." Ben Staples gave his head a world-weary shake as if the missing placards explained everything. "I told the guy in the chapel over there." Ben gestured with his chin. "But he says it was probably some kids who took them as souvenirs." Another shake of the head. "Souvenirs."

"I'm sorry for your loss," Myron said.

"Thank you." He looked down at the plant in his hands as though it had suddenly materialized there. It looked like a cactus of some kind. "She didn't like flowers. Cecelia. I mean, she liked them, but she thought they were a waste. That they died too soon. She liked things that lasted, so she preferred when I sent her succulents. Like these. So that's what I bring."

"Nice," Myron said, because he had no idea what else to say.

"I still loved her."

"I'm sure you did."

"Did you know that Joe DiMaggio sent roses to Marilyn Monroe's grave for twenty years?"

"I think I read about that somewhere."

"He felt guilty when Marilyn died. Supposedly his last words were 'I finally get to see Marilyn'—even though they'd been divorced over forty years by then."

"Do you feel guilty?" Myron asked.

"I don't know. I guess. But I couldn't save Cecelia from herself."

"What do you mean?"

He shook his head. "You represent Greg Downing."

"Yes."

"I haven't seen him in forever. Haven't really thought about him even. And now he's in jail for murdering the love of my life."

Myron was going to remind him that it was just an arrest and it was all alleged, but that seemed like the wrong move. "You knew Greg, right?"

"Yeah, way back when."

"Do you think he killed Cecelia?"

He gave Myron a half shrug. "The cops say they have solid evidence."

"I want to know what you think."

"I don't know. I find it hard to believe. I mean, what's his motive?"

"You have another suspect?"

Ben gave a firm nod. "Lou."

"Lou Himble, Cecelia's husband?"

"They were separated. Cecelia hated him. You know what he did, right?"

"Some kind of Ponzi scheme."

"Like Madoff. Not that big. Lou isn't that heavy a hitter. But yeah, he stole a lot of people's money. The feds wanted Cecelia to testify against him. She agreed right away. Didn't ask for immunity because she knew she was innocent. She just wanted to do the right thing. Then suddenly, poof, Cecelia ends up dead." He shrugged. "So you tell me."

"Sounds like you were in regular touch with Cecelia."

"We were still close. You married?"

Myron shifted his feet. "Yes."

"A long time?"

"No," Myron said. "It's new."

"I bet she's pretty."

"She is."

"But I hope she's not"—Ben Staples made quote marks with his fingers—"'a supermodel.' That's what they called my wife. Not a model. A *super*model. Like she was in the Avengers." He smiled. "Anyway, don't marry one. It's a mess in so many ways. She walks in a room, she knows everyone's looking at her. Judging her. Hoping her looks will be a disappointment so they can say, 'I don't get what the big fuss is about.' Supermodels worry about aging all the time. Everyone hits on them. Even your closest friends."

"Did Greg?" Myron asked.

"Probably. I don't know. Everybody wanted to screw my wife. I'd be lying if I didn't say that was a high too. I had what everybody else wanted. You know what I mean?"

Myron gave a small nod.

"But I was so naïve, so overconfident."

"In what way?"

"You have a wife like that, you can't even trust your friends. But I did. Cecelia was the ultimate notch on the belt. I loved her. I really did. But did I like the jealous stares from other guys? Who wouldn't? I thought it didn't matter. No way she'd give in to that. But now, after what happened to us, I was just so dumb. Now it all seems so…"

Ben Staples turned his attention to the pile of dirt on the right now. "Clay wasn't my son, you know. Cecelia confessed that to me right away. Didn't pretend otherwise. It was the worst day of my life. We're married, I'm a naïve happy dope, she comes in, she sits me down, she takes my hand, she tells me she's pregnant and it's not mine. Just like that."

Ben Staples swallowed, looked away. A bird started cawing. A car drove by with its windows open, blasting something with a heavy Latin beat.

"That must have been awful," Myron said, knowing the words were inadequate, but again what else can you say? Then as gently as he could: "Did Cecelia tell you who the father was?"

"No."

"Never?"

He shook his head. "And I never let the public know Clay wasn't mine. He was a good kid. We had a nice relationship. Not father-son obviously. But I wasn't just his mother's ex either."

"Did Clay know who his father was?"

"Not until years later. It's complicated."

Myron waited.

"I don't know why I'm telling you all this," Ben Staples said.

"They were murdered. I want to find out who killed them."

"You're not a cop."

"No."

"But I asked some friends," Staples said. "They told me you're good at this—that you're on the side of the righteous."

"I try," Myron said. "You were saying something about Clay finding out about his father?"

"Cecelia didn't want him to know. She said it wasn't relevant. But when Clay was old enough, he put his DNA into a few of those genealogy databases."

"And he matched with his father?"

"It wasn't that simple. I don't know the details. Clay found a first cousin. He talked to them. He sought out relatives in that cousin's circle. Process of elimination. Or maybe once Clay got close, Cecelia told him. She didn't want him knocking on the guy's door."

"Did Clay knock on the guy's door?"

"I don't know. It seemed to me once Clay found out, he let it go. But I don't know."

"Was your divorce with Cecelia amicable?"

He turned to Myron. "Do you think—?"

"No, not at all. This is about Greg. I heard that Greg seemed upset about the divorce. Did you notice that at all?"

He thought about it. "Now that you mention it, yeah. Greg trashed Cecelia a bit. But he wasn't alone. To the world, she got pregnant with another man and dumped me. That's what everyone saw. Hell, that's what happened, when you think about it."

"Ben?"

"Yes?"

"I don't know how to ask a lot of this delicately, so I'm just going to dive in, okay?"

He nodded. "Part of the reason I agreed to see you."

"I'm not following."

"I figure you are here because you know more than you're saying," Ben explained. "So here's the deal: You want to learn from me—and I want to learn from you. So go ahead. Don't pull punches."

Fair enough, Myron thought. Then: "Was your wife acting differently before she asked for the divorce?"

"Yes."

"How so?"

"She was moody, withdrawn. Depressed, really. I wanted her to see someone. She wouldn't. I think she was taking pills a friend got for her."

"When was this exactly?"

"A month, maybe two before she told me she was pregnant. Hard to remember. But if an affair is supposed to lift a woman's spirits, this was doing the opposite. It seemed to be crushing her."

Myron didn't know how to soften the blow, so he said it: "Did Cecelia ever tell you that she was raped?"

His head snapped as though someone had punched him in the jaw. For a few long moments, he didn't say anything. He just stared at Myron. Tears filled his eyes. When he finally spoke, his voice was soft.

"Was she?"

"That's what she told a friend."

"Oh my God." He closed his eyes and lifted his face toward the sky. "What friend?"

"Emily Downing."

"Greg's wife."

"Yes."

Ben Staples stood there, frozen, staring at the mound of dirt. "Does she know who . . . ?"

"No," Myron said.

It took some time for Ben Staples to process this. Myron gave him the space.

Then Ben asked, "Why wouldn't Cecelia tell me?"

Myron figured that he was asking himself that more than he was asking Myron, but he still said, "I don't know."

"And Emily told you this?"

"Yes."

"What else did she tell you?"

Myron filled him in as best he could. Ben's expression moved from anguish to anger. There was a reckoning of some sort going on here or, at the very least, something dawning on him. When Myron finished telling what he knew, he didn't give Ben Staples a chance to ruminate.

"You know who did it," Myron said.

"I think so, yes."

Myron waited.

"He kept talking to her about getting her a lead in a new Broadway play. I knew it was a come-on. I mean, so did she. Every male producer suddenly had the perfect role to launch her as a serious actress. But a lead in a Broadway play? Cecelia couldn't act. I told her that once too. I'm like, 'You get what's going on here, right?' I shouldn't have said that. Even if it was true. I should have been more supportive."

"Who raped her, Ben?"

"I'm not sure I should say."

"Why not?"

"Because obviously she didn't want the world to know. I don't know if her death changes that."

"This guy, this rapist, he may be connected to her murder."

"He's not."

"How can you—?"

"Because he's dead. It was Harold Mostring. She had a late-night"—again with the sarcastic finger quotes—"'audition' with him a few months before our divorce. I even thought, I mean, it crossed my mind—this was before all the awful stuff about him coming out—I actually did wonder if he was Clay's real father. Like maybe she just wanted the role so badly."

Howard Mostring had been a well-known Broadway producer/predator who, by the time he got into a courtroom, had more than fifty accusations of sexual assault over the past quarter century. Howard's lawyers got him out on bail under the condition he wear an ankle bracelet. Howard went home to his swanky penthouse apartment on Park Avenue, opened up the sliding glass door to his terrace, and jumped. It may have been the perfect ending except that destructive people too often end up being destructive to the very end. He landed on a young woman who had just gotten engaged, killing her too.

"One last victim for Howard Mostring."

That was what the media called that poor woman.

"I still don't get it," Ben Staples said.

"Get what?"

"How does Greg Downing end up taking the fall for all this?"

CHAPTER TWENTY-TWO

When Myron got back to the Dakota, Terese Collins, his wife, ran up to him and greeted him with a kiss that could knock a movie up a rating.

"Whoa," Myron said, when they finally came up for air. "That was...I mean...wow."

"You are so smooth," Terese said.

"Right?"

"I'm so happy to see you," she said.

"Me too."

"God, stop with the smooth lines."

"Can't help myself," Myron said. "I thought your plane didn't land until late."

"I caught an earlier one. Happy?"

He smiled. "Ecstatic."

She moved in closer and arched an eyebrow. "Win won't be home tonight."

"He told you that?"

"He told me that."

"Win's a good man."

"Not really," she said, "but he's good in this case."

"Do you want me to take you out to dinner?" he asked.

Terese put her lips by his ear. Myron felt the jolt. Then Terese whispered, "I'm not really hungry, are you?"

"Uh, not for food anyway."

"Again with the smooth," she said.

"I'm on a roll."

"Or you soon will be."

They stumbled their way into the bedroom. Much later, they ordered burgers and fries from Shake Shack and devoured it all in bed. Hours passed. The rest of the world stayed away. At some point, very late into the night, when they were both lying in the dark staring at the ceiling, Terese said, "I have to leave tomorrow. Ends up I'm covering the Prine murder."

"Oh," Myron said. Not a surprise. He had seen something about it on the news this morning. Real estate mogul Ronald Prine had been gunned down in Philadelphia. They lay there for a few more minutes, both on their backs, their breathing starting to sync up. Then Myron said, "I have something to tell you."

Terese didn't move.

"Before I say anything, nothing happened."

"Myron?"

"Yeah?"

"That's not the reassuring opening you think it is."

"I was at Emily's last night," he said.

"Her place on the Upper East Side?"

"No, her house in the Hamptons."

"Uh-huh."

"She slept in the same bed as me for a few hours. Nothing happened. Jeremy flew in so I went out to see him and then we were going to see Greg together in the morning so I ended up staying overnight in the guest room. Emily came in when I was in bed. We talked. She sort of laid down next to me and asked if she could just stay."

"You said yes."

"It was just...the emotions of the day, all the upheaval. I think she was just lonely."

Terese kept her eyes on the ceiling. "You two have a bond."

"Yes. But not that kind."

"You share a son."

"Yes."

"And a past. You proposed to her."

"I was twenty-two."

"So you didn't mean it?"

"It would have been the greatest mistake of my life. I don't have feelings for her."

"It's funny," Terese said. "Do you know what I was thinking before you said that?"

"Tell me."

"How great we are together."

"We are."

"Two damaged souls who heal each other when they connect." She sat up. "You and Emily are the opposite: Two damaged souls who destroy each other when they connect."

"A long time ago, Terese."

"The wounds are all healed then? No lasting scars?"

"She doesn't mean anything to me."

"Still, you wanted to comfort her. When she was there. In that bedroom."

"Not like that."

"So why tell me about it then?"

He wondered that himself. "It felt like something you should know."

"I didn't need to know."

"Oh."

"Knowing everything is overrated," she said.

"Are there things that you don't tell me?" Myron asked.

She sighed. "It will sound like tit for tat."

"I'd still like to hear it."

She rolled over so that her head rested in her hand. "When I was in Rome last month, I had a drink with Charles."

Myron didn't like what he was feeling. "Ugh," he said.

Terese said nothing.

"Did he hit on you?"

"Of course he hit on me."

"But you weren't going to tell me."

"No," she said.

"Why?"

"Because it doesn't matter."

"I don't get it." Myron sat up. "You know what Charles is like."

"I do."

"So why the hell would you go out to drinks with him in the first place?"

"You're kidding with that tone, right?"

Now it was Myron's turn to stay quiet.

"Last night, you slept in the same bed with an ex you share a son with—an ex you once asked to marry you. Why didn't you just drive back?"

"I was meeting Jeremy in the morning."

"Which you could have done from the city," Terese said. "You chose instead to stay at Emily's house on the beach."

"She needed someone."

"And suppose I told you Charles needed someone?"

"Oh please. It's not the same thing. You know that."

Terese smiled. Myron could see it in the moonlight coming in from the window. She looked so beautiful right now. He wondered whether he'd ever seen anyone look quite this beautiful before.

"Why are you smiling?" Myron asked.

"I know it's toxic, but it's kind of cute when you're jealous."

He couldn't help but smile back. Then: "I also met with Cecelia Callister's ex-husband today."

"Big day for various exes."

"He was telling me how having a supermodel for a wife was tough. Everyone always hitting on her. I get what he means."

"You comparing me to a supermodel?"

"No," Myron said. "You're way hotter."

"Very smooth," she said. "For real this time."

"I kept thinking about that 'When You're in Love with a Beautiful Woman' song."

"Who sung that?"

"Dr. Hook, I think."

"Right," she said. "Dr. Hook and the Medicine Show. They also sang 'Sylvia's Mother.'"

"See why I fell so hard for you?"

"What about Cecelia's ex and that song?"

"This ex, he kept telling me how naïve he'd been—thinking that men hitting on her was cool and was kind of a high."

"And it's not a high for you."

"No. And then one day, this ex—his name is Ben Staples—out of nowhere in his mind, his wife tells him she's pregnant with another man's kid and she's leaving."

"Well, we both know you have no fear of that happening with me."

Myron closed his eyes, silently cursed himself. "Terese."

"Don't."

"I'm sorry. I didn't mean—"

"I know. It's okay. Really."

"I love you."

"I know," she said. Then Terese turned to face him. "But are you good with this?"

"Yes."

"I'm not what you wanted."

"You're better."

"You always wanted the wife, the kids, the picket fence, the family barbecues, the kiddy sports league—"

"Terese."

"You can't have that with me."

"I know."

"You did not plan for this."

"Do I have to say it?" Myron asked.

"Ugh," Terese said, doing her best Myron impression. "Please no."

"*Der Mensch Tracht, un Gott Lacht.*"

She handled the translation. "Man plans, God laughs."

"It's not what I planned. It's better. I love you, Terese. I want this. I want you. Okay?"

"Okay." He wasn't sure she believed him. "Myron?"

"Yes?"

"Don't make love to Emily."

"No interest."

"Yeah, you do. That's why you said something, and I didn't. You still have feelings for her. It's how you're built. You give someone your heart, they always have a little piece of it."

"And you don't feel that way about Charles?"

"Not even a little bit."

Myron considered that. "Can I still punch him in the face?"

"No," she said. "But I'm glad you want to."

CHAPTER TWENTY-THREE

Myron slipped out of bed at five a.m.

He often lived out of the main guest bedroom in Win's apartment, the one that overlooked Central Park near 72nd Street. There was an eight-foot-tall Chagall—yes, a real one—on the wall between two windows that faced the park. From the George III–era antique four-poster bed of Jamaican mahogany, Myron's view (from left to right or right to left) was window overlooking Central Park, gorgeous Chagall, window overlooking Central Park.

There were worse places to stay.

Win was already awake, fully dressed, and reading a newspaper— a real-life actual newspaper made from paper—in the parlor. He drank his Earl Grey from a fine bone china teacup with the family crest on it. Myron took the burgundy leather chair next to him.

"How was your night?" Win asked.

"Pretty awesome. I didn't hear you come in."

"Probably because your night was—how did you so skillfully describe it?—'pretty awesome.'"

Win was a night owl. He took walks in the wee hours. He drank a bit too much and womanized, if that was still the term people used, to all hours, but somehow, he always woke up early looking fresh and ready. Or he used to. Not that it would be noticeable to anyone else, but Myron could feel the years starting to surface just a bit on his old friend. The eyes were slightly more lidded. The hand lifting that cup of tea wasn't quite as steady. Maybe that was Myron's imagination. Or maybe Myron was projecting—he wasn't getting younger either—but he didn't think so.

"Did you, uh, use your app last night?" Myron asked.

"I did," Win said.

Win had a super-rich, super-exclusive, super-anonymous, super-luxurious sexual hookup app—Tinder for the uber-wealthy kinda thing. Myron didn't know all the details—didn't *want* to know all the details—but in sum, two mega-rich people match, meet in a clandestine gorgeous penthouse somewhere in midtown, and, well, do the sheet mambos.

"Don't ask for details," Win said.

"I won't."

"Everyone on the app is sworn to secrecy."

"Terrific."

"I mean, I could tell you about it without giving names. Make it a hypothetical."

"Hard pass."

"Why did you ask in the first place?"

"I was just wondering that myself."

Win smiled, turned the page of the newspaper, and refolded it. He did this with great precision, like a mathematician working geometric shapes or Myron's aunt Selma dividing a lunch check.

"Esperanza needs to see you this morning," Win said. "Her office. They're waiting for you now."

Myron glanced at the fancy Louis the Something clock on the marble fireplace mantel. "Kinda early."

"Yes."

"You said they're waiting," Myron said.

"So observant."

"They. As in plural."

"Not in today's world."

"Fair enough, except I know Esperanza's pronouns are she/her. Ergo she's not the 'they' to which you refer."

Win smiled, nodded approvingly. "The 'they,' my clever boy, refers to both Esperanza and Sadie Fisher."

Sadie Fisher was the founding partner of the FFD law firm—the first F, as it were, where Esperanza was the D.

"So Sadie wants to talk to me," Myron said.

Win didn't reply.

"Why didn't Esperanza just text me?"

"Because she didn't want to interrupt you and Terese in flagrante delicto."

Myron shook his head. "How old are you?"

"She preferred that I give you the message in person."

"Any idea what's up?"

"Some," Win said. "But it would only be conjecture."

An hour later, Win's limo pulled into the special entrance below the Lock-Horne Building. They entered the private elevator. Myron got out alone on his old floor. Back in the days when MB Reps ruled this land, this foyer had been painted in the we-are-serious-professionals neutrals of gray and beige. When Fisher, Friedman and Diaz moved in, they painted the walls a harsh rouge seemingly inspired by the lipstick color Esperanza and Sadie both now sported.

The law firm's receptionist was a young man named Taft Buckington III, who looked exactly like his name. Taft's father, Taft Buckington II—and this won't shock anyone, what with a name like that—was a member of Win's ultra-exclusive golf club on the Main

Line known as Merion. The FFD law firm was all-female. When Win, an investor in said law firm, suggested that Sadie hire a token male attorney, her response had been blunt: "Shit, no." Instead, she hired young Taft to be both a receptionist and paralegal. It seemed to be working.

"Hey, Taft," Myron said.

"Good morning, Mr. Bolitar. I'll let Sadie and Esperanza know you've arrived."

"No need."

It was Sadie speaking. She and Esperanza strutted toward Myron side by side, heads high, shoulders back, as though on a runway, Myron thought, which was undoubtedly sexist thinking, but there you go.

Esperanza greeted Myron with a kiss on the cheek. He didn't know Sadie very well, but she did the same. They moved into what had once been Myron's office. It belonged to Sadie now. She had kept his old desk, but that was about it. The minifridge that held Myron's Yoo-hoos had been replaced by a printer stand. Gone were all his Broadway musical posters and sports artwork and keepsakes from his own playing career. Instead there was nothing on the walls. Nothing on the desk.

"Feels weird, right?" Sadie said.

"A little."

"I don't like having anything personal in here," she explained. "I'm not trying to make an impression. I don't want them to think I have a personal life or any life outside of this office. When a client comes in here, I want nothing to distract them. I want them to think I only exist to help and represent them."

Sadie took Myron's old seat behind the desk. Myron sat across from her. It was weird, this view. Esperanza stood and paced, metaphorically and nearly literally sitting on the fence. Sadie adjusted her librarian glasses and said, "Our firm is now handling Greg Downing's defense."

That surprised Myron. "Oh." Then: "Who specifically did Greg hire?"

"Me," Sadie said. "But we are all on the team, including as of right now, you. You're a bar-appointed New York City attorney, correct?"

"Correct."

"So everything we say to one another is covered under attorney-client privilege. We clear?"

"Crystal."

"That's the reason why Win wasn't invited to participate. Just to clarify. I would never leave him out otherwise."

Myron looked at Esperanza then back to Sadie. "I know you guys have done great work protecting your clients from rapists and stalkers, but have you done much criminal defense work?"

"Much? No. Some? Yes." Sadie took off her glasses and put one earpiece in her mouth. "And to answer your next question, no one at the firm has done a murder trial. I explained this to Greg."

"So if you don't mind me asking—"

"Why us?" Sadie finished for him.

Myron nodded. "I don't mean any disrespect."

"None taken. That would be my first question too, if I were you. And I asked Greg that. To cut right to it, Greg knows me, he likes me, he trusts me. He knows I'm good and I'll fight like hell for him, and even though I've never done an actual murder trial before, he knows I'll find the right people to help."

"Greg knows me, he likes me, he trusts me," Myron repeated.

"You want to know how," Sadie said. "Understandable. You are familiar with Greg's ex, Emily."

Myron glanced again at Esperanza. Esperanza shrugged.

"I am."

"Of course you are. I was being facetious. Greg told me the whole sordid tale that is your history. Do you remember Emily's younger sister?"

"Judy."

"Judy Becker now. Judy was my college roommate. We're very close. Like you and Win at Duke, I guess. That's how I met Greg. I've done light legal work for him and Emily for years. In fact, Greg introduced me to Win a few years back. It's why I thought of him when I needed office space."

Myron took this in for a moment. He looked once again at Esperanza.

"Why do you keep looking at Esperanza?" Sadie asked.

"We're close friends."

"I know. What do you think I'm not telling you?"

"Nothing."

"Then knock it off. It's distracting."

"Sorry. Old habit. I assume you talked to your client."

"Yes."

"And?"

"And—shock of shocks—Greg says he didn't do it."

"Do you believe him?"

"Is this the part where I say it doesn't matter or I don't care or whatever? I'm not getting into that right now, okay?" Sadie checked her watch. "I'm taking too long to spit this out, so let me just get to it. There's something weird about this case. Right now, the FBI is keeping it very hush-hush but there's a bizarre rumor going around."

"The rumor being?"

"They think this isn't the first time Greg murdered someone."

Myron almost turned to look at Esperanza, but then, remembering Sadie's reaction, he thought better of it. "Who else do they think he murdered?"

"Don't know."

"Do you know about the murder of Jordan Kravat in Vegas?"

Sadie nodded. "Esperanza filled me in."

"That's probably the murder the rumors are about, no?"

"I think," Sadie said slowly, chewing on the earpiece of her glasses, "it may be more than that."

"What do you mean?"

"Those FBI agents came to your office."

"So?"

"So the FBI doesn't usually handle murders."

"That's a little bit of a TV cliché," Myron said, "that whole 'crossing state lines' thing. They help out a lot. Also, Greg was high-profile and supposedly dead. I figured that put it in their jurisdiction."

"Did you look up Special Agent Monica Hawes?"

"No."

"Her area of expertise is profiling," Sadie said. "As in serial killer profiling."

Myron blinked. "They think Greg is a serial killer?"

"Don't know. But I'm getting a vibe. Not a good one either." Sadie put her hands on the table and leaned forward. "That's why you're here. I'm hoping you could help us."

"How?"

"I know you and Win have a past with the FBI, and yes, I know that from Esperanza so you can now turn your head and look at her for confirmation. You have a contact in the FBI. An upper-echelon one, right?"

Myron immediately thought about his old boss PT. "I may."

"You're cute when you're coy. Actually, you're not. Anyway, please give your contact a call. We need to know what we're up against. Then please report back to us what he tells you."

————————

Myron filled Win in on his conversation with Sadie and Esperanza. He understood why Sadie had to be careful about attorney-client privilege, but in the end, there was nothing said in that room that needed to be kept quiet anyway. Not that Win would talk. Not that they could ever get a guy with his resources on the stand. But even if they did, at the end of the day all Sadie wanted to know was what the FBI had on her client. There was nothing incriminating about that.

"I know you already spoke to PT," Myron said.

"And he made it clear he knows more," Win said. "No harm in reaching out."

Win put his office phone on speaker and dialed PT's number. He threw his feet up on the desk as the first ring trilled. Myron sat across from him and waited. On the third ring, the familiar gruff voice came through.

"Is Myron with you?" PT asked without preamble.

Myron said, "I am."

"Lunch at Le Bernardin. Just the three of us."

He clicked off.

"It's like he was expecting our call," Myron said.

"Indeed."

"What do you make of it?"

Win thought about it a moment. "The FBI must have a hell of an expense account if he's taking us to Le Bernardin."

CHAPTER TWENTY-FOUR

P T was one of those old men who seemed to get stronger with age. He was big, bald, and intimidating. His hands looked like baseball gloves, his fingers thick as sausages. Win's hand vanished into the baseball glove when they shook. Then Myron's did the same.

"It's been too long," PT said to Myron.

It was an odd comment. Myron hadn't seen PT in nearly two decades. Even back in the day, PT had mostly been a voice on the phone. There are men who live in the shadows of our government. PT *was* the shadow. Myron didn't even know his real name.

"It has," Myron agreed.

"You look good, Myron."

"So do you."

"I hear you got married."

"We invited you to the wedding."

"Yeah, I know."

PT didn't say why he couldn't attend. Then again, Myron hadn't expected him to. Some might think that odd, but a relationship with PT was never a normal one.

They were in a private room above Le Bernardin's main restaurant. One wall was taken up by a Ran Ortner painting of the ocean. Ortner's work seemed to be more marine photograph than painting—simplistic and minimalistic in most ways, and yet Myron found it hypnotic, beguiling. Myron took a moment and stared at it. There was something about Ortner's oceans that slowed Myron's heartbeat so that it matched the imagined rhythm of the waves.

PT put a hand on Myron's shoulder. "Good, right?"

Myron nodded.

"Always take that second to appreciate art," PT said. "Our lives have too much chaos in them as it is. It's a reminder of why we do what we do."

Myron smiled. "Aren't we philosophical today?"

"Comes with age. You happy, Myron?"

Weird question, Myron thought, but: "Sure."

"Win?"

Win spread his hands. "It's good to be me," he said.

PT smiled. "Truer words."

"Why do you ask?" Win asked.

"Because I changed the trajectory of your lives," PT said.

Myron never really thought about that, but it was true. PT had recruited them young for a brief and clandestine stint with a subgroup of the Federal Bureau of Investigation under the code name Adiona. There were reasons PT had selected them, trained them, put them out in the field, but that was long ago. Still, PT was right. That was where it started for Myron and Win. It had forged them, made them think they could do this. They had saved many. They had lost some too. Myron flashed back to that tombstone, the name Brenda Slaughter, but then he blinked and moved on. Great competitors had that ability—to move on. To be the best in any sport, you must have the reflexes, the physical ability, the mental attitude, the scary-ass competitive drive—but you also had to hone the simple ability to forget. Did you blow the save? You forget it. Miss the putt? Forget it. Make a big turnover down the stretch? Shrug and onward.

The great ones know how to forget.

"Sit," PT said.

There was a round table in the center of the room that could probably hold ten, but right now there were only three place settings.

"I took the liberty of asking Eric to order for us," PT said.

Eric, Myron assumed, referred to Eric Ripert, the co-owner and head chef. Myron didn't know him. Win did. So, Myron guessed, did PT. A waiter appeared and poured white wine. Myron didn't like drinking wine during the day. It made him fall asleep. But if PT had ordered it at Le Bernardin, it was probably worth trying.

"What brings you to Manhattan?" Myron asked.

The one thing they did know about PT was that he lived in the Washington, DC, area—close enough to reach the president with a moment's notice.

"Work."

"I thought you retired," Myron said.

"I often retire," PT said. Then he added, "But my help is needed here."

"Does that happen often?"

"Almost never," PT said, taking a sip of the wine. "Only when an important matter requires great sensitivity."

"And the Greg Downing case fits that category?" Myron asked.

"It does indeed," PT said.

"It's a murder case," Myron said. "A double murder. That shouldn't be enough to bring you out of retirement."

"A double murder would not be enough, no."

"Then it's not a double murder?"

"Before we get into that," PT said, "I assume you reached out to me here because Greg Downing is a client of yours."

"That's right," Myron said.

"So we all know what's what: You wish to help his defense. You're on Greg Downing's side."

"I guess," Myron said. "What side are you on?"

PT grinned. "I have no dog in this fight. I just want to get to the truth. If that means Greg Downing fries, he fries. If it means he is innocent, I'm all about clearing him too." The waiter came in and served the first course. "So I have a bit of a dilemma."

"That being?"

"There are things you should know. Check that. There are things I want to tell you, even though our new director would not like me confiding in you."

"Do you like the new director?" Win asked.

"I do not," PT said. "But I still respect his office. So to be clear: If you are here as advocates for Greg Downing—"

"We are," Myron said.

"Then we should just enjoy the lunch."

PT picked up his fork.

"I'm not an advocate for anyone," Win said.

"Win."

Win turned toward Myron. "I'm not here to protect Greg," Win said to him. "He ended your career. He faked his own death. His DNA was found at a murder scene. If he murdered Cecelia Callister and her son Clay, then I don't want any part in getting him off. You don't want that either, do you?"

"No, of course not. But—"

"You also are *not* his attorney on this. Greg hired Sadie, not you."

"She made me part of his legal team."

"Then you should leave," Win said. "I'm not here to help Greg Downing get away with murder."

PT took a bite, closed his eyes, murmured something about gods and ambrosia.

"Neither am I," Myron said. He turned to PT. "You know our situation."

"I do," PT said.

"You knew when you agreed to meet with us."

"True."

"So let's stop with the semantics," Myron said. "You know me. I won't obfuscate justice to free a murderer."

PT looked over at Win and arched an eyebrow. "Obfuscate."

"I bought him a daily vocabulary calendar for his birthday," Win said.

PT put down his fork and dabbed the sides of his mouth with his napkin. Nothing in the room seemed to change, but everything seemed quieter now, still. This was one of the things about PT. He had almost supernatural magnetism, charisma, the kind that made you sit up and listen no matter how mundane his words might be. When he was ready to speak—as he was now—everything else around him seemed to stop.

"When we first started studying serial killers seriously at Quantico—I'm talking about the seventies, eighties—I would estimate there were hundreds, perhaps even a thousand, serial killers across the United States. But now? We estimate there are only five, ten at the most who are active. That isn't because we have fewer psychopaths or that people have somehow grown kinder as a species. It's because it's harder to get away with being a serial killer in today's world. There is so much technology, inescapable CCTV, tracking tools, surveillance methodology—you are seen hundreds of times a day by the government or private enterprise. Big Brother is indeed always watching. Plus our citizens—the serial killer's desired victims—are more cautious nowadays. They are educated on that matter via TV or movies. They don't let themselves be easy targets. No one hitchhikes anymore, for example. If someone is involved in sex work, it isn't as clandestine as it used to be. They tell their friends or coworkers where they are. They carry smartphones that track their movements. Our computers can analyze all the clues, the DNA, the fingerprints, the surveillance, all the mountains of information in seconds nowadays. In short, modernity has made the serial killer nearly extinct."

Myron and Win waited.

"But I feel one may be at work here."

The door opened. The server appeared, but PT waved him away. He slipped back out, closing the door behind him.

Myron said, "You think Greg Downing is a serial killer?"

"Before I get ahead of myself, let me say this: Most of my colleagues in the FBI believe that this is indeed a normal murder case. We don't have a strong motive yet, but Greg Downing knew Cecelia Callister, albeit tangentially. That's enough for most. We stick with what we know. We follow the evidence and when we do, when we adhere to protocol and procedure, what we have on Greg Downing is overwhelming. He will go down for it."

"And your other colleagues?" Myron prompted.

"Others believe that Greg Downing is a serial killer and that the Callisters are just two more of his victims—"

"—I don't see how—"

"—while still others—a somewhat small yet wise group—believe that Greg Downing may be a victim."

"A victim?" Myron said. "Of a serial killer?"

PT took another sip of wine.

"How can Greg be a victim?"

"Here is where I need your expertise." PT pushed his plate to the side. "I know that you two took a good look at the murder of Jordan Kravat in Las Vegas."

Myron nodded. "You told Win that you think Greg may be connected?"

"Oh, he's definitely connected. That doesn't mean he did it. But that's the thing. Let us suppose that there is a serial killer at work here. We are still tracking it all down, but right now we have seven murders we believe he's responsible for."

"You said 'he,'" Myron noted. "The serial killer is a man?"

PT sighed. "I said 'he' because I'm an old man, and I don't want to make this more convoluted by saying 'he or she' all the time or making you think it's the plural by using 'they.' Plus, ninety-one percent of serial killers are male. So for the sake of simplicity, I'm going to say 'he' for right now, okay?"

PT bent down and picked up an old-school briefcase. He placed it on the table, opened the latches with his thumbs, took out a folder. He took his reading glasses out of his suit jacket pocket and put them on.

"You know about the murder of Jordan Kravat, and you know about the Callisters. So keep those in your head as we go through this. There's also the murder of a woman named Tracy Keating in Marshfield, Massachusetts. She was hiding in a rental unit from an abusive boyfriend named Robert Lestrano. He found her and killed her. Easy conviction. We also have a wealthy tech entrepreneur from Austin, Texas, who was killed by his own son over a money dispute. There was a man abusing a woman online from New Jersey who was killed by the woman's brother. A farmer who was murdered on his soybean farm near Lincoln, Nebraska, by two migrant workers."

"How are they connected?" Myron asked.

"You tell me," PT said. "What stands out in what I just told you?"

Myron nodded. He was starting to see it. "The cases are solved."

"Good," PT said, like a pleased mentor. "Go on."

"You caught the perpetrators. They were tried and convicted."

"Some are still going in the trial stage," PT added to clarify. "But yes."

Myron shook his head. "My god."

PT couldn't help but smile.

"Explain," Win said.

"Don't you see?" Myron replied. "That's how a serial killer would get away with it in today's era."

"Elaborate," Win said.

"These aren't open cases. Just the opposite. They are closed right away. So there's no way to discover a pattern." Myron leaned forward. "When a serial killer murders someone or makes them disappear, the case remains unsolved. Eventually, you start seeing patterns. Or an MO. Or a bunch of unsolved murders. You start searching for links between victims. But in this case, if I'm following the logic here, this serial killer isn't just murdering someone—he's setting up someone to take the fall. He's done it in Las Vegas, Texas, New York, wherever. The cases are then"—Myron made air quotes with his finger—"'solved.' In the case of Jordan Kravat, for example, it's pinned on Joey Turant via DNA. Joey takes the fall. Case closed. With the Callisters, the DNA points to Greg Downing. He takes the fall."

"Case closed," Win said, nodding, seeing it now.

Myron turned to PT. "I assume the same thing happened in the other cases you mentioned—the soybean farmer, the father-son from Austin?"

"Yes."

Myron sat back. "So someone set Greg Downing up."

"Not so fast," PT said.

"Isn't that the obvious take?"

"No, Myron, it is the one that best suits your narrative." PT shifted his large frame in his chair. "Another take is that the FBI has been painstakingly searching for strands that connect the various cases. Combing through the evidence for overlaps. The murders happened in different states. The victims are from various backgrounds and genders. Nothing connects any of them—nothing at all—except we've now found one overlap between the cases of Jordan Kravat and the Callisters. And that overlap is . . . ?"

PT stopped and waited.

"Greg Downing," Myron replied.

"Bingo, Myron. Do you believe it's just bad luck that Greg Downing is the only connection we can find between any of the victims?"

"It could be," Myron said.

"But do you believe it?"

"No," Myron said. "I don't believe it."

"So that means we know what one thing for certain?" PT asked. "Whatever is going on here, whoever or whatever is responsible for all these murders—it's directly connected to your old nemesis, Greg Downing."

CHAPTER TWENTY-FIVE

———✦———

Y ou stand under the red awning for the Michelangelo Hotel on 51st Street near Seventh Avenue. A rain so light it is barely a mist falls. The wind blows it under the awning. For a moment you close your eyes and enjoy the feel of it on your face. It brings you back to your childhood. You're not sure why. You always liked the ocean. You remember sitting on the edge of the jetty rocks, the waves crashing near you, closing your eyes like this and feeling the spray. You'd open your mouth and stick out your tongue so you could taste the salt.

You open your eyes and wait. You are patient. It is one of your learned strengths. It didn't come naturally to you, but you could now be called detail oriented, overcautious, plodding even. But you know. One mistake could end it for you. That has never been clearer.

And a mistake has been made.

Half an hour goes by. You have walked up and down 51st Street from this awning on Seventh Avenue down to the Major League Baseball flagship store on Sixth. There is a line to get inside the baseball store. You scowl at that. Grown men buy baseball jerseys for two hundred dollars. Not children. Grown men. They wear baseball jerseys of their "heroes" in public.

You shake your head over that.

You can't help but think it would be nice to pop one of these guys in the head just for the fun of it.

And you do have a gun on you.

You didn't used to think that way. Or wait, maybe you did. Maybe we all do. Just for a fleeting second. Look at that douchebag in the sports jersey, we all tell ourselves. Be nice to... But then we stop, of course. We smile to ourselves. It's all just fun and games. We don't really want to hurt anyone. We don't ever let ourselves go there because if we do, if we go there even once, we may not ever come back.

That's what happened to you, isn't it?

You hear this about the addictive quality of, say, heroin. You may be tempted to try it, but if you do, if you get even one hit, they say you may never come back. That may be true, that may not be true. You don't know.

But for you, it was true about murder.

It is then, when you look back down toward Seventh Avenue, that you see Myron and Win leave Le Bernardin.

You turn toward the baseball store and pretend to window-shop. There are mannequins in full gear, including cleats and those bizarre stirrup socks. You wonder whether some losers actually buy the entire uniform of a favorite player. You remember a long time ago going to the US Open tennis tournament in Queens and seeing some spectators dressed in full tennis gear—collared shirt, shorts, sweatbands— as though one of the playing pros might call them out in mid-set to join them on the court of play.

Pathetic.

Stop, you tell yourself. You're getting distracted.

You step closer to the window. Your collar is turned up. You have on a mild disguise because you are always smart enough to wear a mild disguise. Nothing flashy. But no one who knows you would recognize you. It would be hard for witnesses to accurately describe you.

Myron and Win cross Sixth Avenue. They don't talk. They don't seem to need to. They just walk side by side.

You have the gun.

You mostly watch Myron Bolitar. You wish you had more time. You are rushing and that is never a good thing. But there is no choice now. It is all moving fast. You wonder.

Shoot him now, a voice inside tells you.

The streets are crowded. The gunshot would cause panic. You could even kill another person or two, get something of a stampede going. That would be a distraction. You'd get away.

Sometimes it pays to play. Sometimes it pays to just act.

Perhaps now was a time for action.

You have a long coat. You reach into your pocket and take hold of the gun. No one can tell, of course. If anyone bothered to look, you are but another pedestrian strolling with your hands in your pockets.

Your hand finds the gun—and when it does, when your palm slides onto the grip, when your finger threads its way onto the trigger, you feel the surge. It runs through you like a lightning bolt. You feel the power course through you—the power of life and death. Everyone who owns a gun, everyone who has ever even held a gun, has experienced this. Maybe it's a small hit. Maybe it's something bigger. There is a thrill to holding a gun. Don't let the naysayers tell you differently.

Myron and Win continue to head east on 51st Street.

You know their destination. The Lock-Horne Building on 47th Street and Park Avenue. Will they cut through Rockefeller Center? Perhaps. You rush and get to a spot closer to their final destination, wait, take aim. Fire. The Lock-Horne Building is close to Grand Central Station. You could shoot, cause panic, run toward it.

You start to move, keeping your eye on the two men.

Then Win stops and turns around.

You are safe. You are disguised. You are at a great distance.

But you still turn toward another shop window so that there is no chance you can be spotted. Your heart thumps in your chest.

Not now, a voice inside of you says. There is too much risk involved. Too many pedestrians. Too much CCTV. And there is also Win. Even now. Even as Win starts walking again with that nonchalance, his sunglasses blocking his eyes, he seems to be looking everywhere at once, like one of those Renaissance portraits whose gaze follows you around the room.

You know Win's reputation. You know what he did in Las Vegas.

Too risky.

Stick to the plan.

For Myron, the horror will soon be over.

For him, the nightmare will have just begun.

CHAPTER TWENTY-SIX

I t was a fifteen-minute walk from Le Bernardin back to the Lock-Horne Building. Win threw on a pair of badass mirrored sun-glasses that reminded Myron of his parents' except for being in fashion terms the direct opposite. For the first few minutes, Myron and Win didn't speak. They headed east on 51st Street.

Finally, Win said, "Interesting."

"What's interesting?"

"You don't trust PT."

Myron knew where Win was going with this. "You're wondering why I didn't say anything about Greg getting roughed up in that bas-ketball game."

"It could explain how his DNA ended up at the crime scene."

"I think revealing that would be a violation of attorney-client privilege," Myron said.

"And you want to save that information," Win said.

"Yes. There'll always be time later to say something."

"Like as a courtroom surprise."

"Probably nothing so dramatic," Myron said, "but I don't know the FBI's agenda here, do you?"

"I don't, no."

"I don't see why we'd give them a head start on this."

"Even if it exonerates Greg."

"If it does," Myron said, "then we can be the ones who find it and control it."

Win nodded. "Makes sense."

They continued down 51st Street.

"There are too many hidden interests at play here," Myron said.

"Like?"

"Like, if the FBI believes a serial killer is out there, why are they keeping it a secret?"

"To avoid panic."

"The public should know," Myron said. "Sadie Fisher, as Greg's attorney, should know."

"We both know why," Win said. "We discussed this before—with Joey the Toe's conviction."

"Exactly," Myron said. "That's what I mean about hidden interests. The FBI is afraid that if this gets out, then all those convictions— especially Joey the Toe's—would get overturned."

"So," Win said, "it is prudent for them to wait."

"But is it? Why? So they don't embarrass some overzealous DAs? There may be innocent people serving hard time in prisons for crimes—murders no less—that they didn't commit. Can you imagine a greater nightmare for them?"

"If the FBI reveals it now, they create a big issue. If they keep it to themselves, well, the same." Win thought about it. "Neither option is desirable when you think about it."

"So side with being open."

"And create panic by telling people there's a chance a serial killer is on the loose?"

"You underestimate the common man."

"You overestimate him," Win said.

"Ben Franklin said that it's better that a hundred guilty men go free than one innocent man suffers in prison."

Win nodded. "Blackstone's ratio."

"Yes."

"And you agree with that?"

"Blackstone actually said ten guilty men, not a hundred," Myron said. "But yeah, if the feds harbor the slightest doubt about these people's guilt, they should speak up now."

When they reached St. Patrick's Cathedral at Fifth Avenue, the foot traffic picked up and conversations in myriad languages wafted in the air.

"I trust PT," Win said.

"So do I."

"So for now, we honor that. We can't say anything."

"Why do you think he told us?" Myron asked.

"You know why."

"He's already thought of all the things we are saying now," Myron asserted. "About revealing the truth to the public."

"Yes."

"And the only way out of this dilemma for him is to solve this fast."

Win stopped, spun slowly, looked around.

"You forget something?"

Win frowned. "I never forget something."

"I've seen you forget umbrellas in downpours."

"I don't forget them. I leave them behind for others."

"You're such a man of the people."

Win took out his phone and checked it. He frowned and started typing a reply.

"Problem?" Myron asked.

"No, just a family business matter. I'm going to helicopter down to Philadelphia. I should be back in a few hours."

Within seconds, Win's limo was on the scene. The driver opened the back door for him. Win started toward it, stopped, turned back to Myron. "Is it wrong that I want it to be a serial killer and that the serial killer is Greg Downing?"

Myron smiled. "You don't forgive easily."

Win said nothing.

"Yet you still worked with him," Myron said. "You helped him with his finances."

"It wasn't my place to forgive or hold a grudge."

"It was mine."

"Yes."

"I don't know about right or wrong," Myron said. "I guess it would be easiest."

"We never get easy."

"Never," Myron agreed.

Win disappeared into the car.

When Myron got back to his office, Big Cyndi met him at the elevator. She kept her voice low.

"You have a visitor, Mr. Bolitar."

"Who is it?"

"Ellen."

"Ellen what?"

Big Cyndi was whispering now. "She wouldn't give me her last name."

Myron moved into the waiting area by Big Cyndi's desk. An elderly woman—Myron guessed her to be about his mother's age—stood holding her purse in both hands. She was tiny—what some might call wizened—with short hair and a buttoned-up cardigan of matching grays. She wore pearls and cameo stud earrings. A white shawl was wrapped around her neck, held in by a brass brooch of a butterfly.

"Can I help you?" Myron asked.

"Yes please," the woman said. "Can we speak alone in your office?"

"Do I know you?"

She gave him a smile so big that he almost took a step back. "Call me Ellen."

"That's my mother's name."

"My stars, what a coincidence," she said with a little too much enthusiasm. Then she lowered her voice and said, "I just need a moment. It's important. It's about my grandson. He was recently drafted by the Dodgers, but..." She looked past Myron and up at Big Cyndi. "Please," she implored. "It won't take long."

Myron nodded and led her into his office. The old woman moved slowly toward the big picture window overlooking the city. "This view is magnificent," she said.

"Yes, I'm lucky."

"Views don't make you lucky," she said. "You get used to them. That's the problem with views. They are nice when you first have them, but we get used to them and take them for granted. That's true of most things, of course. When I was young, my parents had the most exquisite home. It was a Queen Anne built in the early 1900s. We lived in Florala, Alabama. You ever heard of it?"

"No, I'm sorry."

"Anyway, I remember when we first drove up to it. I was eight years old, and you'd never seen any home as grand as this one. Sixteen rooms. Curly-pine wainscoting. The most gorgeous wraparound porch. Second-story balconies, one off my own bedroom. I loved it for, oh I don't know, a month. Perhaps two. But then I got used to it. So did my family. It just becomes the place you live. It was why Father liked having company. He loved to see the expressions on a newcomer's face, not because he wanted to impress them. Well, maybe that was it a little. All humans like to show their feathers, don't they? But mostly, when we saw someone else's reaction to the house, it brought us back to our own. We all need that now and again, don't you think?"

"I guess so, Ms. . . ."

"I told you. Call me Ellen."

Myron took the seat behind his desk. Ellen sat in front of it. She put her purse on her lap, both hands still on it.

"You said your grandson had been drafted by the Dodgers."

"I did say that, yes, but it isn't true. I just said that for the sake of your receptionist."

Myron wasn't sure what to make of this. "So what can I do for you, Ellen?"

She gave him a smile, a big smile, the kind of smile that—Myron was trying not to be ageist—gave him the creeps. Then she said, "Where is Bo Storm?"

Myron said nothing.

"My name isn't really Ellen. I work for some people who have close ties with a man named Joseph Turant. Do you know who that is?"

Joey the Toe. Myron still said nothing.

"I understand you had an encounter with Mr. Turant's colleagues recently in Las Vegas. In exchange for your safe passage out of that sinful place, you were supposed to provide the current location of Bo Storm, a young man who did Mr. Turant great harm. I'm here to collect that information for him."

Myron just stared at her.

"Before you reply," the old woman continued, "may I make a suggestion?"

"What's that?"

"You're eventually going to tell me what I need to know." Her eyes bored into his. "It will be much easier on all of us if you just do it now."

"I don't know where he is," Myron said.

She gave him an exaggerated faux pout. "You don't?"

"I'm still looking for Bo."

"Mr. Bolitar?"

Myron almost said, *"Mr. Bolitar? What am I, your father?"* but it didn't seem the time.

"Yes."

"You're lying to me."

"No, I'm not. If there's nothing else—"

"Private aircraft routes can be easily tracked, as I'm sure you and Mr. Lockwood are aware. We know you flew from Las Vegas to Montana on his aircraft. Why the stop at Havre Airport?"

Myron opened his mouth to answer, but Ellen raised a silencing finger.

"I asked you to make this easier," she said in the voice of an elementary school teacher who has been disappointed by a favorite student. "That's all. Just one small thing." She sighed theatrically. "I suspected you wouldn't listen. But I did ask you, didn't I?"

Myron figured the question was rhetorical, so he said nothing. She kept her eyes on his. Finally, Myron broke the stalemate.

"Look, whatever your name is, I don't know what you want from me."

"Haven't I made myself clear?"

"I don't know where Bo Storm is."

"Pity then." She shook her head and opened her purse. Myron half expected her to pull out a gun—it was that kind of day—but instead she took out a smartphone and said, "Allen, did you hear all that?"

A newly familiar voice came from the phone speaker: "Every word, Ellen."

Myron felt his blood freeze.

The old woman turned the screen toward him, so Myron could see. There, on FaceTime or whatever video app she was using, was Dad's new pickleball/trivia pal, Allen Castner.

"Hey, Myron!"

Myron just sat there. He felt a rushing in his ears.

Allen Castner moved his face very close to the screen. He had AirPods in his ears. "Your father invited me over after our pickleball outing for a little pinochle. He's just in the bathroom, taking a piss. Something's up with his prostate. It's like the fourth time he's been in there."

Myron swallowed. "What the hell is going on?"

"Oh, I think you know, Myron."

The screen jerked as though Allen Castner had dropped the phone. When it came back into view again, he was holding a Beretta M9A3 with a silencer screwed on the end of the barrel.

"Talk to us, Myron."

It was Ellen who said that. He understood, of course, that it wasn't her real name. And that this guy's name wasn't really Allen. They'd used his parents' names to mess with his head. Like he needed that.

"By the way," the old woman said, "Allen is wearing headphones."

"Ear pods," Allen said, correcting her.

"I stand corrected, ear pods, thank you. The point is, Allen can hear you. Your father won't be able to."

And then Myron heard his father's voice. "Who are you talking to?"

Allen Castner said, "Sit down here, Al."

"What the hell? Is that a gun?"

"Dad!"

"Don't shout," Ellen said. "Your receptionist will hear and that will be a problem. Where is Bo Storm?"

Myron's eyes were glued to the screen, to his father. "I told you. I don't—"

And then, on the screen, Myron saw Allen Castner whip his father in the face with the gun. His father grunted in pain and fell back.

"Dad!"

"I told you," the old woman said in a calm, almost soothing voice. "He can't hear you."

Myron's father crumpled to the floor, his hands covering his face. Blood seeped through his fingers. Myron looked across at the old woman. She just smiled.

"I asked you, didn't I? I asked you *nicely*."

Myron almost jumped across the desk—almost throttled her right then and there. Forget that she was an old woman. Damn the consequences.

But she just gave him a simple shake of her head.

"That would be Daddy's death warrant."

On the screen, Myron heard his father moan.

"Tell us where Bo Storm is," the old woman said.

"He's in Montana."

Myron could hear the panic in his own voice.

"That much we know already. Where in Montana? Be very specific."

Through the phone, Myron's father stubbornly shouted, "You bastard! You broke my nose!"

Ellen met Myron's eyes. Myron tried to regain some kind of leverage here or at least slow things down a beat, give everyone a chance to breathe. "Let's just talk about this a second."

Ellen sighed and leaned forward closer to the phone's speaker. "Allen?"

"Yes, Ellen."

"Shoot him in the head and wait for the mother to come home."

"No!" Myron shouted.

"Just do it, Allen."

Then Allen Castner said, "Ellen, turn off the video."

The old woman hesitated a moment before pulling her hand back across the desk, taking the phone off speaker mode, removing one earring, and putting the phone up to that ear so Myron couldn't hear. She listened a moment, nodded, and said, "Understood."

Then she disconnected the call.

"What happened?" Myron asked.

He could still hear the panic in his own voice.

"We sit and wait."

"For?"

"It won't take long."

The hell with that. Myron took out his own phone.

"Put it down," she said. "If you contact anyone . . ." The old woman shook her head. "Do I really have to make the threat? I thought you'd be smarter than that."

Myron's leg started shaking. "I don't know who you are," he said, "but if anything happens to my father—"

"Wait, let me guess." She stroked her chin. "You'll go to the ends of the earth to find me and make me pay. Please. Look at me, Myron. Do you think this is the first time I've done this? Do you really think I don't have all the bases covered?"

Myron had never felt so helpless in his entire life. "So what do we do now?"

"We wait."

"For?"

"For as long as it takes."

"Don't hurt him. Please. I'll tell you—"

She put her index finger to her lip. "Shh."

They sat there. Myron had never imagined time could move so slowly.

"This would have been easier if you'd just cooperated."

"What does that mean? What's going on right now?"

Her phone finally buzzed. She picked it up. "Hello?" She listened for a moment and then said, "Okay." She hung up and put the phone back in her purse. Using both hands for leverage, the old woman pushed herself into a standing position.

"I'm leaving now."

"What's going on? Is my father okay?"

"If I don't get down to my car in the next ten minutes, it will get worse for you. Much worse. Sit there. Don't move. Don't call anyone. Ten minutes."

And then she was gone.

CHAPTER TWENTY-SEVEN

M yron hit full panic mode.

He called his father's phone. No answer. He called his mother's. No answer.

He debated calling the lobby of the Lock-Horne Building and telling security to follow the old woman, get a license plate, something, but how would that help his father? It wouldn't. It might bring justice later, but for now that whole idea was something his brain didn't even want to entertain.

So what should he do?

Call the Florida police? Call someone who worked at his parents' retirement village?

It all felt so futile. Myron felt helpless and scared and vulnerable, and man oh man, he didn't like that.

He sprinted into the waiting area. Big Cyndi wasn't there. He could feel the panic in him rise to yet another level.

From behind him, Big Cyndi said, "Mr. Bolitar?"

"Where were you?"

"In the little girl's room," she said. "It was only a number one."

He was about to tell her what happened when his phone buzzed. The caller ID read MOM.

He hit the answer button with the speed of a gunslinger in an old Western. "Hello?"

"Guess what klutz broke his nose playing pickleball?"

Then he heard his father's voice: "Oh stop it, Ellen, I'm fine."

Relief flooded Myron's veins.

"You were the one who insisted I call him right away, Al."

"I didn't want him to worry."

"How would he worry? He didn't even know you were hurt."

"Mom," Myron said, fighting to keep his tone even, "just tell me what happened."

"Cousin Norman, that's Moira's boy. You remember Cousin Norman, right? We went to see him in *Where's Charley?* when he was in seventh grade?"

"Mom."

"Anyway, Cousin Norman is driving us to urgi-care, but your father is fine. Seriously, Myron, who breaks their nose playing pickleball? You know that new carpet in our living room? The one we bought at . . . Al, what was the name of that place?"

"I don't know. Who cares?"

"I care. It was that home store off Central Avenue. Myron, you know the one. It's next to that diner you took us to lunch at last time in February."

"Ellen."

"It begins with a D. Demarco Home and Carpeting? Deangelo? Anyway, that carpet. It's covered in blood now. Like our living room is that shower scene in *Psycho*. Who comes back home when they're still bleeding and, what, takes a nap on the floor?"

"I didn't know I was still bleeding," his father said.

"How could you not know? Anyway, he's playing pickleball. Then someone—your father won't tell me who—"

"Because it doesn't matter!"

"—smashed the ball at your father. Your father, being a regular Jim Thorpe, used his nose instead of a paddle."

Myron said, "Mom?"

"Yes?"

"I'm going to catch the next flight down."

"No, you're not."

That was his father.

"I'm fine," Dad said. "You have work. You're busy."

"Oh, right," Mom said. "We read about Greg Downing getting arrested. Did he really kill that pretty woman and her son?"

"Don't ask him that, Ellen. You're a lawyer. You should know better."

"What, I can't ask him mother-to-son?"

"Myron," Dad said, "don't come down."

The voice left no room for argument. Myron got it. Dad didn't want Mom to worry. If Myron flew down, Mom would know something was seriously wrong.

"Who were you playing with, Dad?"

Mom took that one. "He was playing with his new friend Allen. You remember him, Myron? He's that big fan of yours."

"I remember."

"He's gone," Dad said.

"Oh, Myron?" Mom again. "We just pulled into the urgi-care. I'll call you later."

When Mom hung up, Myron realized that his entire body was shaking. He called Win and filled him in on what happened.

"They just suddenly backed off," Myron said at the end. "I don't get it."

"I do."

"What do you mean?"

"Let me get people on your parents. I'll be back at the office in fifteen minutes."

"I thought you were flying down to Philadelphia."

"I canceled."

"Why?"

"Fifteen minutes, Myron."

Win hung up. Myron took his phone and stared at it for a moment as though he were expecting it to ring again.

What now?

He called Terese. She answered on the third ring. "Hey, handsome."

"Hey."

"What's going on?"

"I just wanted to hear your voice," he said.

"Shit, what happened?"

He didn't reply for a second.

"That bad?"

"Tell me about the story you're working on."

"I would say, 'You first,' but it seems you need a second."

Myron couldn't help but smile. "I love you, you know."

"I do, yes. Ronald Prine was murdered by a contractor he ripped off. Her name is Jacqueline Newton. Tons of evidence. She swears she's totally innocent. The only hiccup for the police is that her sick father is confessing."

"Trying to take the fall for her?"

"Yes," Terese said.

"Any chance he really did it?"

"I don't think so, no." Then Terese added, "We done stalling?"

"They went after my parents."

He spilled it all—about the meeting with PT, his theory that a serial killer may have set up Greg, the walk back, the attack on his father, all of it.

When he finished, Terese asked, "Do you want me to come back up?"

Yes. "No," he said.

"I can get someone else to cover this murder case."

"Don't come up. I'm okay."

"Hmm," she said.

"What?"

Myron's phone buzzed, telling him another call was coming.

"Terese, it's my father."

"Go."

He switched over. "Dad?"

"I'm fine. I'm waiting for the doctor to see me, but it's a broken nose, that's all. I'll be fine. Look, I'm not keeping things from you, but I'm not telling you everything either."

"About?"

"About your mother."

"What about her?"

"She's okay most days. And she's at her best when she's on the phone with her children. She has anxiety. She's scared a lot, Myron. I don't want her scared, okay?"

Myron swallowed. "Okay, Dad."

"We keep this between us for now, understood?"

"Understood."

"And don't come down, Myron. Your mother reads you like a book. Always has. It's why you never got away with anything when you were a kid. I assume this all involves something you and Win are working on?"

"Yes."

"So protect your mother and get on with it. Don't get distracted."

"Already taken care of," Myron said. "What happened after they hung up?"

"Allen that rat bastard—by the way, I've been in fights. I grew up in a tough neighborhood. I had the factory in Newark. Anyway, I saw the gun coming. I turned my head and rolled with it. So really it's not so bad, okay? Trust me on that. It's just the nose. I didn't get dizzy or anything."

"Okay, thanks for telling me that."

"So anyway, after Allen hung up, he just held the gun on me. He was waiting for something to happen."

The same thing as the old woman who called herself Ellen.

"Any idea what they were waiting on?"

"Someone called him on the phone. Allen mumbled something about letting him know if they find him and then he said something about a shanty."

Myron felt the hairs on the back of his neck stand up. "A shanty?"

"Yeah, I didn't get it either."

But Myron did get it. Shanty. The bar where Bo/Brian/Stevie worked in Montana. Myron nodded to himself, seeing it now. Turant's people knew that Myron had flown to Montana. They'd sent men there, started canvassing where Myron had gone, maybe asked around, maybe there had been a tracker on Myron's rental car, whatever. They'd somehow found out where Bo was at the same time as they were threatening Myron's dad. So they held up, kept the gun on Dad, waited until . . .

Joey's people must have found Bo.

"Doc, I'm talking to my son. Okay, I'll hang up now. Myron, I'll call you later. Don't worry, I'm fine."

Click.

Myron quickly googled the Shanty Lounge in Havre, Montana. He hit the link and heard the phone ring. Three rings later, someone picked up and said, "Who is this?"

"I'm looking for your bartender Stevie."

"And I asked, who is this?"

Myron didn't reply right away.

"We see your phone number on the caller ID. Why is someone with a New Jersey number calling?"

The voice was a deep, rich baritone.

Like Cal the Cowboy's.

"You're Cal, right? My name is Myron Bolitar. I was there the other night."

"You promised we'd be safe."

Myron's grip on the phone tightened.

"He even asked you," Cal continued.

"Am I really safe staying here? Cal and I, we can move on if not."

"I won't tell anyone."

Myron swallowed. "What happened?"

"You sold us out, that's what happened."

"Cal, where is Bo?"

"They took him, you son of a bitch. They came in here with guns and took him away."

————

When Win arrived, they moved into Myron's office. Myron closed the door.

"Turant's people got Bo," Myron said.

"I have people watching your parents as a precaution," Win said. "But now that they have Bo, your parents should be safe."

"What do we do about Bo?"

"Nothing. He isn't our issue."

"We revealed where he was."

"That doesn't make him our responsibility. For that matter, Greg isn't our responsibility either. If we have a task in all this—and I'm not sure we do—it is to help PT apprehend a serial killer."

"So we just, what, wash our hands of it?"

"In terms of Bo? Yes."

"We don't even contact the authorities?"

"He has family. He has loved ones and friends. They will call the authorities if they believe he's in danger. We need to think this all the way through for a moment. An hour ago, PT informed us that there may be a serial killer out there."

"Okay."

"He also informed us that this particular serial killer has covered his tracks by implicating someone else—a scapegoat, if you will—as the killer. The only connective tissue they've found so far..." He waited.

"Is Greg Downing," Myron finished for him.

"Precisely. He connects the Callisters and Jordan Kravat," Win continued. "Ergo, if Kravat was a victim of the same killer as the Callisters, who is the innocent man serving time for that murder?"

"Joey the Toe."

"And who was the witness who helped put Joey away?"

"Are you saying Bo Storm lied on the stand?"

"Bo lied to you. He lied about Greg having cancer. He lied about Greg dying."

"And the other evidence found at Jordan Kravat's murder scene," Myron said. "The DNA or whatever. That fits into this serial killer's MO."

"In light of this, the official explanation of the murder makes little sense. Joseph Turant, the gaffer—if you will allow me my Britishism—of a major crime family, has avoided arrest for decades by being careful. Does it seem logical that he would suddenly become stupid enough to murder this stripper-slash-sex-worker or his pimp—let's call them what they are; if they were women victims, that's how people would label them—and leave behind a witness like Bo Storm and so many clues?"

"It does not," Myron agreed.

"One more thing: Joey the Toe went after us hard. Really hard. He has been searching high and low for Bo Storm for five years. If someone testified truthfully about him, even if it put Joey behind bars, do we really think he would go to these lengths just for revenge?"

"He might, but it does seem a lot. Hiring those killers to threaten my parents. Sending his soldiers to Montana. Scouring the area. I don't even know how the Turants found Bo."

"They didn't find him," Win said.

"What do you mean?"

"Joey's people didn't find Bo Storm. I told them where he was."

Myron just stood there.

"It was the only way," Win said.

"You gave him up?"

"We aren't bulletproof."

"I know that."

"We killed Turant's men."

"To rescue me."

"And you think he understands that distinction?" Win asked. "I made a deal with Turant when we were in Vegas. Safe passage in exchange for information. Once I saw they had your father—"

"You were on that call too?"

Win nodded. "They would have killed him. They would have killed your mother. They would have gone after us too. In simple terms, Bo Storm isn't worth that. So yes, I gave him up."

"That's why they stopped hurting my father," Myron said.

"Yes."

"And, what, they stayed with him and checked out the Shanty to make sure you were telling the truth."

"Yes." Win rubbed his face with his hand, a gesture Myron had never seen him make before. "I messed up," he said. Also words Myron didn't think he'd ever heard Win utter. "I should have realized that they might track my plane. I miscalculated Turant's desperation until I saw the gun on your father."

"And giving up Bo was your only option?"

Win put his hands on Myron's shoulders. "We are good, Myron—but no one is that good. I had no choice. It's over now."

"And what about Bo Storm?"

"A casualty of war."

"I don't know if I'm good with that."

"Doesn't matter if you are or not. You understand the stakes. If it makes you feel any better, killing Bo won't help Turant. He needs Bo to tell the truth without appearing coerced."

"It doesn't make me feel better."

"I didn't think it would."

"You're okay with all this?"

"This isn't about my personal comfort. I made the choice. I don't think it was a difficult one."

"Suppose Bo was telling the truth. Suppose Bo did see Joey the Toe murder Jordan Kravat that night."

Win smiled. "You do love your moral dilemmas."

"I want to know if it bothers you at all. I want to know if you still sleep well at night."

"It doesn't bother me at all," Win said. Then he added: "And I never sleep well at night."

Myron shook his head. "You're something."

"I don't care about Bo Storm. I care about your parents. We all feel that way. Strangers don't matter to us except in a theoretical way. We just pay the notion lip service."

"You made the decision, so I didn't have to."

"This was an easy call for me. I would sacrifice a hundred Bo Storms to save your parents. And while you don't want to admit it, so would you."

It was an uncomfortable truth. "Dangerous way to think," Myron said.

"Then you probably don't want to know how many lives I would sacrifice to save you," Win said. "Or maybe you would."

CHAPTER TWENTY-EIGHT

A few minutes later, Jeremy called. "Where are you?"

"I'm at my office," Myron said. "How about you?"

"At Mom's apartment," his son said. "Can you come over?"

"Sure, what's up?"

"Grace is here."

Myron tried to conjure up the mental picture: Greg's current soulmate at the apartment of Greg's ex-wife Emily. "Grace is at your mom's place?"

"She just arrived. She's pretty upset. She says it's urgent she talk to you."

No doubt this was about her son Bo. "I'm on my way."

He called his father's phone on the way. No answer. He was tempted to call his mom, but Dad had made it clear that was not what he wanted. He didn't like the idea of keeping the truth from her. When he was growing up, Mom had always seemed the stronger of the two, a force of nature, the one who argued and stood up for you and gave anyone in her way an earful. But Myron also got what his father was saying. There was a fragility there now, one both obvious from her Parkinson's and one that seemed vaguer to him, something to do with aging and fear and perhaps seeing her own mortality. Either way, Myron was not about to go against his father's wishes.

When he arrived at the apartment, Emily opened the door. Myron waited for her customary quip, but she looked at him with concern etched on her face. "Are you okay?"

"I'm fine, why?"

She put her hand on his arm. "Tell me what happened."

Seemed it wasn't just his mother who could read him like a book. "No time now. It's all okay." He spotted Jeremy standing behind her, so he politely pushed past her. His son offered him a handshake. Myron took it and resisted the urge to pull him in close, settling for an awkward slap on the shoulder.

Grace Konners had her smartphone pressed against her ear. She turned away from them and kept her voice low. Myron looked a question at Jeremy.

"She's staying at a hotel down the street under a pseudonym," Jeremy said.

"And you've already met her?"

"Yes. I told you. They visited me when I was in Kuwait."

Myron looked over at Emily. He remembered how concerned Emily had been, how she didn't want to get Jeremy's hopes up before they knew for certain Greg was alive. But he'd known. Jeremy had known for years. Emily met Myron's eyes and gave a half shrug.

Grace hung up the phone, stood, and moved toward Myron. "Let's you and me take a walk."

"Don't bother," Emily said, her hand already on the doorknob. "I'll take the walk. You guys stay."

She didn't wait for a reply. She headed out and closed the door behind her.

"You lying son of a bitch," Grace said. "You sold out my son."

"That's not what happened, but we'll have time for assigning blame later. Right now, we need to contact Joe Turant's people."

"That was Bo on the phone," she said.

That took Myron by surprise. "Is he okay?"

"They haven't hurt him, if that's what you mean."

"Where is he?"

"They're taking him back to Vegas."

"But they let him contact you?"

Grace nodded. "They didn't want me calling the police."

That made sense, Myron thought.

"And they wanted to assure me that they had no intention of harming Bo."

"How did he sound?"

"How do you think he sounded?"

"What can I do to help?" Myron asked.

Grace half chuckled at that. She looked over at Jeremy. "Now I know where you get it from."

"Get what?" Jeremy asked.

"Your hero complex. It's genetic. Your father—and by that, I mean—this is confusing as hell but I mean Greg—he only cares about us. That's how most people are. But a few, like you two, insist on helping even if it hurts others. On the surface, you seem the better, don't you? Sacrificing yourself for others and all that. But you're not. You need to be the hero." She turned to Myron. "You found out Greg was alive?"

"That's what the FBI told me."

"So you guessed that Greg faked his own death, right?"

"What's your point?"

"My point is, you realized that Greg had made the conscious decision to let you and the rest of the world think he was dead. And did you then honor his choice? Did you think, 'Oh, Greg must have his reasons, I shouldn't interfere'? No. Instead you turned his world upside down trying to rescue him. And now he's in prison, and a bunch of sadistic mobsters have my son—all because you had to 'help,' consequences be damned."

Myron had had enough.

"Hey, Grace?" he said.

"What?"

"Someone is murdering people out there. You and Greg and Bo are all tangled up in this. So if you're trying to lay some guilt trip on me—"

"That's not what I'm trying to do."

"Then why don't we instead focus on getting Bo back safe?"

"Did you tell Turant's men where Bo was?"

"No," Myron said. "You have my word on that."

It wasn't a lie. It wasn't necessarily a full truth. But it wasn't a lie.

Jeremy pitched in. "Maybe we can help, Grace."

Grace moved toward the window and looked out over Central Park. "You said someone is out there murdering people. What do you mean by that?"

"You know about Jordan Kravat. You know about Cecelia Callister and her son Clay. There are others."

Grace turned away from the window. Jeremy looked at Myron.

"What do you mean, others?" Jeremy asked.

Myron moved toward Grace, wanting her to turn and make eye contact. "Joey Turant didn't grab your son just to get revenge because he testified against him. If he had, your son would be dead by now. He wants Bo to change his testimony."

"And once he does?"

"What really happened to Jordan Kravat?" Myron asked. "We need the truth now. It's just us in the room here. I'm an attorney. You can hire me if you want that kind of protection. Jeremy can leave—"

"No," she said. "I want Jeremy here."

"Do you need some water?" Jeremy asked her.

"I'm fine, Jeremy."

"You can trust Myron," Jeremy said. "Maybe he should have minded his own business or whatever. I get that. But you need to tell us what really happened."

"Your father," she said. "He didn't want you involved in any of this."

"I know," Jeremy said. "But it's too late for that now. You need to talk to us."

Grace sat down. Jeremy took the seat across from her. Myron stayed standing, trying to move out of her eyesight. Grace clearly trusted Jeremy. She might open up more if Myron faded into the background.

"What Greg and I told you before was all true," she began. "Donna Kravat's club got all mobbed up. Jordan was a big part of it. Bo got caught up in it and couldn't find a way out. It got bad between them. One night, Jord said he had a plan for how to get them both out from under. He said that he still loved Bo and if they could just make this one last move, they'd be free from the mob and could be happy again. I didn't know any of this at the time. If Bo had come to me, I would have told him not to go that night. And I think even Bo didn't believe it. By now, he had already decided he was going to work with the cops. We told you this. Bo was going to turn informant. That was his way out."

Grace looked now at Myron. Myron nodded, keeping his face even. He wanted her to keep talking.

"Some of this is speculation on Bo's part. So bear with me. As soon as Bo got back to the house that night, he felt like something was wrong. Jord poured them both bourbons. That was the Kravat drink—Jord and Donna are from Louisville and love bourbon. They were big Maker's Mark drinkers. But Bo...he knew that Jord used to roofie guys at work to make them, uh, compliant. Some customers got off on that. Jord used to joke about it, call it a Gay Cosby. Sick, right?"

"Very sick," Jeremy said. He leaned forward. It felt odd to see his son in this position, but of course his son was a highly trained military officer. Myron watched in awe and pride but there was also a pain here, pain for what he had missed, pain for what he realized he'd never get back or know.

"So when Jordan wasn't looking," Grace continued, "Bo switched their glasses. So if the drink was spiked..."

"I get it."

"And sure enough, Jordan started getting sleepy. He kept muttering to himself. Bo said at one point Jordan was smiling and his head was lolling back and he kept saying 'Bye, bye, toe' and 'Joey's coming' and laughing."

She sat back now. Her hand fluttered up toward her face. She blinked away tears.

Jeremy's voice was soft, confident, soothing. "What happened next, Grace?"

"He left."

"Bo left the house?"

She nodded. "After Jordan passed out from the sedative, Bo left."

"What time?" Jeremy asked.

"I don't know. Around midnight maybe? Does that matter?"

"No. Go on."

"He'd been renting an extended stay on East Harmon Avenue."

"Okay, so that's where he went?"

"Yes."

"And then?"

"He watched TV. He tried to sleep. He called me at one point and said he was scared. I told him to come over and stay with us, but he said he'd be okay."

"Where were you?"

This was all Jeremy asking the questions. Myron just kept silent and tried to make himself invisible.

"Greg and I were staying at a suite at the Bellagio. We told you before. We'd come to town hoping to help Bo get free before we headed overseas."

"Right," Jeremy said. "Of course. Go on."

"At five in the morning, the police knocked on Bo's door. They told him Jordan Kravat had been murdered."

"In court," Jeremy said, "Bo claimed to have seen Joe Turant leaving the house."

"That..." She stopped, took a deep breath. "That wasn't true. They made him say that."

"Who is they?"

"The police, the district attorney...I don't know. One of them, all of them. Once the DNA tests came back tying the murder to Joey Turant, the cops went nuts. They'd been trying to nail Joey for so long and now they had the goods. But the DNA wasn't enough. All science and no emotion or something like that. They wanted to make sure it was a slam dunk. So they went back to Bo. They wanted him to testify that he'd witnessed Turant leaving the house that night. When Bo said he didn't want to, they added threats. They'd tell Turant that he cooperated. They'd prosecute Bo on the lesser charges they had on him before all this. So really, what choice did my son have? You tell me." She looked up at both men. "What else could he have done?"

"Nothing," Jeremy said. "Your son had no choice."

"He didn't want to testify."

"I understand."

"And remember," she said. "Turant *did* kill Jordan Kravat. The cops made that clear. It wasn't like he was putting an innocent man away. They had the evidence. There was no doubt in anyone's mind."

Jeremy nodded. "Okay, so let's skip ahead to a few minutes ago. You talked to Bo on the phone?"

"Yes."

"And?"

"And he's with Joey's people. They want him to tell the truth to the press. Show the corruption of the police. And if he goes public, they promise not to hurt him. And yes, I believe them. If they hurt him now, then the police can claim Joey the Toe forced him to change his story."

Myron couldn't tell whether this argument was coming from a place of hope or reason. She seemed to be trying to convince herself, which made total sense. But so did the argument. Win had said something similar. Bo changing his testimony would only work for Joey Turant if Bo stayed alive, healthy, and did not appear to be under duress.

A phone buzzed. Jeremy grabbed it, looked at the screen, frowned.

"Everything okay?" Myron asked.

"Fine. But I need to take this. I'll be back in a second."

He headed into the other room, leaving Myron and Grace alone.

For a moment they both looked away. Myron felt awkward standing there. He wasn't sure what to do here, so he stayed quiet.

"He's a good man," Grace said. "Jeremy, I mean."

Myron nodded.

"As soon as I called him about his father, he caught the next flight out. He was here in three hours."

They sat in uncomfortable, heavy silence.

Then she said, "I know biologically he's your son."

Myron didn't reply.

"I know what you and Emily did," Grace said with something approaching disgust in her voice. "Greg just told me a few days ago."

Myron said nothing.

"That crushed him, you know. It took Greg a long time to get over the trust issues."

Myron kept quiet.

"I'm talking about how you and Emily slept together the night before the wedding."

"Yeah," Myron said, "I kinda guessed that."

"I'm not saying what Greg did in response wasn't wrong—"

"Hey, Grace?" he said for the second time today.

She stopped.

"I'm not rehashing the past with you, okay?"

Myron stepped away and tried his father's phone again. This time it was answered on the second ring by his mother.

"Your father is fine," Mom said. "It's a broken nose."

"Where is he?"

"He's still with the doctor. But he's fine. And the nose? It'll have a new bump. Don't tell him, but I think it's kind of sexy."

"I bet it is," Myron said.

There was a pause.

"Mom?"

"What's going on, Myron?"

"What do you mean?"

"I tell you it looks sexy, you usually say something like 'I don't need to hear this' or 'Ew, Mom, stop.'"

Man, Dad was right about how well she could read him.

"He broke his nose," Myron said. "I'm worried about him. Did he fall? Did he hit his head? Make sure the doctor checks for a concussion. Is someone there to help you guys? Not just Cousin Norman. Call Aunt Tessie too. Also I want you guys to hire a nurse."

"A what?"

"A nurse. Just to stay the night."

"Do you know how expensive a nurse is?"

"I'll pay."

"Thank you, Daddy Warbucks, but I don't want a stranger staying in my house."

"They wouldn't be a stranger—"

"And I'm supposed to entertain now too?"

"A nurse, Mom. I said a nurse, not a houseguest."

"Speaking of which, the house is a mess. Your father is a slob. I don't want a strange nurse just coming over—"

"Okay, fine, no nurse. I'll call Aunt Tessie and—"

"Already done. We have plenty of help. Too much, in fact. Speaking of which, Tessie just arrived. I'll call you later."

CHAPTER TWENTY-NINE

fter Grace left, Jeremy said that he was hungry, so Myron asked him in as casual a voice as he could muster whether he'd like to go out for a bite. Jeremy answered in the affirmative and they were now ensconced at a corner table at Friedmans on 72nd Street, not far from the Dakota.

"What did you make of what Grace said?" Jeremy asked.

"Not sure," Myron said. "You?"

"Hard to read her. I was trained in interrogating enemy combatants. When they've been captured, there are obviously high levels of stress. They're nervous, afraid, often young. We factor that in. We don't get too much practice interrogating a middle-aged woman in a Fifth Avenue luxury apartment."

"But?"

"I don't think she's lying, do you?"

Myron tilted his head back and forth in a yes-no gesture. "Something was off with her story."

"Like what?"

"That detail about what brand of bourbon they drank."

"Does that make it more or less true to you?" Jeremy asked.

"It feels like an odd detail. But the part about Bo switching the glasses..."

"So that Jordan Kravat got the spiked drink?"

Myron nodded. "Like out of a movie. Then the stuff about him muttering 'bye, bye, toe.'"

"So you think she's lying?"

"Or was lied to," Myron said.

Jeremy looked off in thought, and when he did, something in his expression echoed Myron's own. You don't see yourself too often, but this man in front of him had never felt more like his own flesh and blood.

"What?" Myron asked.

"If we believe what Bo told Grace, then Jordan Kravat was abusing him and forcing him into committing crimes."

"Right."

"To the point where Bo was willing to become an informant to get out from under. You still with me?"

Myron tried to keep the tears from his eyes. He got that way when he was emotional. His eyes welled up. Here he was, talking over a case with his son, talking to him in a way he never had, and every part of him felt overwhelmed.

"I'm with you," he managed.

"So maybe the answer is far simpler," Jeremy said. "Maybe Bo killed Jordan Kravat. Maybe he planned it or maybe it was spur of the moment or even self-defense."

Myron nodded. "And then Bo makes up the whole story about switching bourbons and leaving the scene. It would also explain why he'd testify against Joey Turant."

"One hole," Jeremy said.

Myron arched an eyebrow. "Only one?"

Jeremy smiled at that. "If Bo was the killer, how did Joe Turant's DNA end up at the crime scene?"

The waiter came by to take their order. Both opted for the hand-cut pastrami sandwich with cups of tomato soup.

"I just realized something else," Jeremy said when he left.

"What's that?"

"This is the most time we've spent together in a while."

In ever, Myron wanted to add, but he kept that thought to himself. "I guess that's true."

"Myron?"

"What?"

"Don't get emotional on me."

Myron waved his hand. "Who me?"

They both said nothing for a moment. Jeremy broke the silence.

"I want to know," Jeremy began, "what you found out about... is it okay if I just say 'my father'?"

Myron nodded. "Of course."

"I don't mean to make a big thing of it or anything."

"No, I get it."

"But I don't call him Greg or anything like that."

"He's your father," Myron said, his mouth suddenly dry. "Call him whatever you want."

"Thanks. I appreciate that."

"Sure, no problem," Myron said, hearing how hollow his voice sounded in his own ears. "I met with an old contact at the FBI before I saw you."

Jeremy leaned in and gave Myron his full attention.

"In short," Myron continued, "the FBI thinks there's a connection between the Jordan Kravat murder and the Callister murder case."

Jeremy frowned. "I don't see how. Kravat was killed, what, five years ago in Vegas. The Callisters were a month or so ago in New York. Could the connection be the son?"

"The son?"

"Cecelia Callister's son was murdered," Jeremy said. "Clay, right? How old was he?"

"I think around thirty."

"I guess Jordan Kravat would be about the same age."

"That's not the link," Myron said. "Or, I don't know, though maybe someone should look into that."

"So what is the link?"

"It's not just those murders."

"What do you mean?"

"They think there were more."

Myron filled him in as best he could. He tried to keep away from the details, which wasn't very difficult because he didn't know that many himself. He knew that Esperanza would dig into this whole idea of a serial killer in a deeper way. They needed to learn about the other victims, the other cases, but Myron also understood the limitations. The FBI were not fools. He didn't fancy himself a better investigator than professional law enforcement. They had the resources and the contacts.

Jeremy's eyes were wide when Myron finished. "Wow."

"Yes."

"But I still don't see why they think Dad is behind this."

"I'm not sure they do," Myron said. "But right now, he's their only link."

"Yet they can only connect him to two of them?"

"So far, yeah."

"We need to dig into this."

"I agree."

The sandwiches and soups arrived. Myron dunked the edge of his pastrami sandwich into the tomato soup before taking the first bite. What had PT muttered at Le Bernardin? Gods and ambrosia.

"You're staying with Win at the Dakota?" Jeremy asked.

"Yes."

"Where's your wife?"

"She was here last night. She left on assignment."

"She's good on TV."

"Yeah, thanks."

Jeremy hadn't met Terese yet. He hadn't been at the wedding. Myron wanted to say that he hoped they'd meet, get to know each other better, but it didn't feel right.

Myron watched Jeremy dig into his sandwich for a moment and then said, "Can I ask you something?"

"Shoot," Jeremy said.

"Where did you fly in from last night?"

"Classified," he said.

"Overseas?"

Jeremy stopped midbite and looked at Myron. "Why do you ask?"

"Your mother told me you were coming in from overseas."

"So?"

"So Grace said you got here in three hours."

A half smile came to Jeremy's face. "Which means I couldn't have been overseas," he said with a shake of his head. "Always the detective, eh, Myron?"

"I just...I just want to know more about you, I guess. I don't mean to pry."

"Don't worry about it. I didn't tell Mom 'overseas.' But she probably assumed it."

"Okay."

"I'm actually stationed domestically right now."

"Oh. And you can't tell me where."

"And I can't tell you where," Jeremy echoed. "And I just got called back. I leave in the morning for two days. But I'll be back, okay?"

"Okay."

Jeremy put down his sandwich. "It's funny."

"What?"

"When I was a kid, I wasn't much into the whole sports world."

"Because of your illness," Myron said.

"Mostly, yeah. The Fanconi anemia should have killed me. We both know that. You saved my life, Myron."

Myron stared down at his plate.

"Did I ever really thank you for that?"

"Yeah," Myron managed, keeping his head down. "I think you did."

"Anyway, my point is, once I was healthy and able to exert myself, I realized, I don't know, that I must have inherited some of your athletic genes. And of course, Dad. I mean, he's not my biological father, but I was raised by a professional basketball player. So in terms of athleticism, on the nature front, I have you. On the nurture front, I have him. You get it, right?"

"I get it," Myron said, wondering where he was going with this.

"So that's why I was a later bloomer. When I was seventeen, I realized that I had the potential to be an elite athlete, but since I never played any sports as a kid, I was too far behind to catch up skill-wise. So I had these—shall we call them physical gifts?—and no outlet for them. I think that's why I ended up channeling those skills into what I do now."

"In the military?"

"Yes."

Myron nodded. "Sounds like you put your 'physical gifts' to work in a much more meaningful way than me or . . . or your father."

Jeremy smiled. "Your father," he repeated. "You really dug deep for that one, Myron."

Myron shrugged, also smiled. "Trying."

"I appreciate that."

"So while I'm digging deep," Myron began.

Jeremy looked up.

"We never talked about what it was like for you," Myron said. "Finding out about me."

"Yeah, we did."

"You're not my dad. I mean you might be my father. But you're not my dad."

"Okay, that one time. When you first found out. But you were thirteen."

"It's a little late now."

"Is it?"

"I said all I wanted to say. Look, Myron, you did nothing wrong. Well, okay, hold up, you clearly *did* something wrong, you and Mom, but as she's pointed out to me ad nauseam, that mistake made me. It was a long time ago. Can we just move on now?"

"Yeah, sure." And then Myron realized that he couldn't turn back. Not now. "But I have a favor to ask."

Something in Myron's tone made Jeremy pause. He put down the sandwich. "Okay."

"It's not a favor exactly. I'm not sure what it is."

"You're kinda scaring me, Myron."

"It's not scary. It's the opposite of scary."

"Myron."

"You wanted to keep your paternity private out of respect for Greg. I got that. And I always respected that."

"And now?"

"Now your grandparents—your biological grandparents—are getting old. Your grandmother is not well. And today your grandfather..." Myron stopped.

"My grandfather what?"

Damn eyes welling up. He blinked.

"Myron?"

"I want to tell them, Jeremy. About you. And I want you to meet them."

Jeremy took a second. Then he said, "It's a hell of a time to ask."

"I know."

"With my father in jail."

"I know. I didn't plan on asking."

Jeremy looked off again. Myron gave him the space. After some time had passed, Jeremy said, "Can we talk about it when I get back?"

"Of course. Yeah. No pressure."

CHAPTER THIRTY

Esperanza read from the tablet on her lap.

"So the only names PT actually said were Tracy Keating and Robert Lestrano?"

They sat in Win's parlor, all three ensconced in the burgundy leather armchairs.

Esperanza looked up at Myron and sighed. "What?"

"When was the last time the three of us were here like this?"

"Last month," Esperanza said. "Ema's birthday party. Your nephew was here."

"I don't mean for a party. I mean, just the three of us." Myron motioned with his arms. "Like this."

Esperanza shook her head. "You're such a wuss." She turned to Win and held up the snifter of cognac. "This is pretty good stuff."

"Remy Louis XIII Black Pearl Grande Champagne Cognac," Win said.

"You say so."

Win frowned. "Myron?"

"Uh-hmm."

"It's gauche to check prices on your phone."

Myron stopped typing. "Is the bottle more expensive than a car?"

Win considered that. "Not *my* car."

Touché.

"Can we get back to this?" Esperanza asked. "Hector comes home tonight."

"Where is he?"

"Down in Florida with his father."

Esperanza split custody fifty-fifty with her son's father.

"How old is Hector now?" Win asked. "Nine, ten?"

"He's fifteen, Win."

Win considered that. "Nothing ages you faster than someone else's child."

"Deep," Esperanza said with the slightest hint of sarcasm. All three of them favored a pinch of sarcasm in their voice, but none could deliver the full potpourri of sarcasm's spices and herbs like Esperanza. She was a sarcasm savant. "Speaking of sons, how's it going with Jeremy?"

"It is what it is," Myron said. Then: "I told him I want him to meet my folks."

"Good," Esperanza said. "He should have them in his life."

"He's also not stationed overseas anymore."

Win arched an eyebrow. "Since when?"

"I don't know."

"Where then?"

"It's classified."

Win didn't like that. "But somewhere in the United States?"

"That's what he said."

"Can we get back to this?" Esperanza asked. "Like I said, I have to get home."

"Of course." Win put the snifter down and stood. "Do you need the large screen?"

"It would be helpful."

Win approached what appeared to be a bronze bust of

Shakespeare on the marble fireplace mantel but was, in fact, a prop used in the 1960s Batman television series. Bruce Wayne (Batman) or Dick Grayson (Robin) would tilt the head of Shakespeare's bust back, revealing a hidden switch. Once the switch was hit, the bookcase behind the Caped Crusaders would slide open and reveal two poles (one pole said "DICK," one pole said "BRUCE," as though they might forget which pole was whose) and then Bruce Wayne, played by the brilliant Adam West, would exclaim, "To the Batpoles!"

Like the famed Caped Crusader before him, Win now tilted back the Shakespeare head, flicked the switch, and voilà, the bookcase slid to one side. Instead of Batpoles, there was a large flat-screen television mounted to the wall. Blackout curtains automatically lowered over the windows, converting Win's parlor into a man cave–styled theater room—albeit one serving Remy Louis XIII Black Pearl Grande Champagne Cognac.

Myron looked over at Win. Win smiled and arched an eyebrow. The man loved his gadgets.

Esperanza quickly mirrored her tablet to the television so they could all view the files on the big screen.

"Okay, so here's what I put together from what PT told you," she began. "We already know about Jordan Kravat in Las Vegas. And we have the Callisters in New York. Adding to that"—she clicked the pad and a new slide appeared—"PT told you about Tracy Keating. I got this off her LinkedIn page."

A photograph appeared of a woman with curly blonde hair and dark glasses and the kind of smile that hit every part of her face and made you want to smile back.

"Tracy Keating was allegedly killed in Marshfield, Massachusetts, by a stalking ex, a guy named Robert Lestrano. She was in the process of getting a restraining order. PT already filled you in on some of this, but I was able to make up pretty extensive files on these three cases—Kravat, Callister, Keating. Win, you may be happy to know your pal Taft Buckingham's kid was helpful in putting this together for me."

"I'm ecstatic," Win said. "Enthralled even."

"Super. So next we dug a little deeper to unearth the other cases. PT mentioned an online abuser getting murdered by a brother. I think we found the case." Esperanza tapped the iPad and a man's face appeared. "The murder victim was Walter Stone. Age fifty-seven, two grown kids, a wife. Spent most of his days abusively trolling online and really went hard after a woman named Amy Howell. She lives in Oregon."

Myron read the file. "Sheesh, this guy was pretty sick."

"You have no idea what we see at the law firm," Esperanza said. "People spiral. They'd never act this way in person. But online? Not to get too deep into it, but social media wants eyeballs. Period, the end. The best way to get that? Divide people. Make them angry. Turn them into extremists."

"Not unlike cable news," Myron said.

"Exactly. Fear and divisiveness offer engagement. Agreement and moderation do not. Anyway, here is the evidence against Howell's brother Edward Pascoe."

Myron read down the list. "Car spotted, CCTV of the car by a water reservoir, murder weapon found there.... It's a lot."

"Yes. The cops consider it open and shut. Two things in Pascoe's favor though. One, his wife was home that night. She said that her husband never left the house, but she also admitted that she was up in the bedroom and that he was downstairs watching television. The DA claimed that—one—she's the wife, she could be lying to protect her husband, and—two—he could have sneaked out without her knowing. The wife testified that the second was impossible, that they have alarms on the house and every time the door opens it pings, but of course, the DA will argue that those can be easily switched off. I have all the details on the case, but let's move on for the moment."

She touched the iPad.

"PT also told you about a father-son murder in Austin, Texas. What's interesting is, it really wasn't hard for me to figure out the cases from what he told you. We think murders are common, but these kinds are pretty rare. I literally just put in my search engine 'father son tech executive murdered in Austin' and the right case came up."

The screen filled with crime scene photos and articles.

"From what we can tell, the murdered father was a rich guy, his son a ne'er-do-well. A few months before the murder, the father—Philip Barry—disowned the son, Dan. In return for what the son saw as a huge betrayal, the police theory goes, Dan Barry killed his father with a knife. The police got an anonymous call purportedly from a neighbor about a man screaming for his life. They went to the house. The front door was open. They found the dead dad in the kitchen, throat slit. They found the son upstairs still asleep. A bloody knife was under his bed. There were also blood traces on the clothes and sheets, on the stairway, on the path from the kitchen to the son's room. DNA would show they all belonged to the victim. Only one set of fingerprints on the knife—you guessed it, the son's."

"Dumbest killer in history," Win said.

"There were plenty of drugs in his system. The police theory was old-school—he was hopped up on coke, remembered how he'd been disinherited, killed the dad, and probably didn't even realize it."

"Still," Myron said. "An easy conviction."

"To be fair, the son's attorney offered an alternative theory—someone broke into the house while the son was sleeping, killed the dad, planted the knife upstairs, and then called the police anonymously. He pointed out that when the police called, no neighbors admitted making the call and none heard a scream. The call came from an untraceable line."

"So maybe the killer made the call," Myron said.

"Yes."

"That didn't fly in court?" Win asked.

"It didn't fly enough. Dan Barry was hardly a sympathetic witness. He had a record, including vehicular manslaughter. He killed someone in a DUI."

"Did the police look into that?" Myron asked.

"What do you mean?"

"Like, maybe the DUI victim's family was seeking revenge?"

"I don't know. But you hit on a good point."

"That being?"

"Motive. In all these cases, the person convicted of the crime had a motive, so when they claimed that they were framed in some outlandish schemes..."

"It was easy to dismiss," Myron said.

"Right. Imagine, like in this case, the time and planning it would take to get in Barry's house, drug the son, whatever—well, who would buy that someone would go to all that trouble? What would be the killer's motive?"

"Unless," Win said, "there was no motive."

"Like in the case of a serial killer," Myron added. "It all makes horrible sense. Anything else?"

"Not much. PT mentioned a soybean farmer killed by two immigrants who worked for him. The media was quieter on this. I don't think they wanted to arouse trouble for other immigrants in the area. I'm still going through it, but again, blood from the victim was found in the immigrants' bunkhouse."

Myron and Win spent a few moments studying the information on the screen.

"The evidence," Win said. "It's overkill."

"Agree," Esperanza said.

"Murderers are oft careless, of course," Win continued. "And if we view these cases separately, yes, the convictions are solid. But when we group them together, one must marvel at the overall stupidity. Who in our modern world doesn't know your phone location can be tracked? Who doesn't know about CCTV or E-ZPass or DNA?"

"And the gun found in Robert Lestrano's toolshed," Myron added, rising and pointing to the photograph on the screen. "According to the police report, he readily admits to the police that he owned a gun. He tells the police he kept it in a locked case next to his bed. They even watch him open the drawer to retrieve it, and by the cops' own admission, he looks genuinely shocked to see it's missing. How dumb do you have to be to use your own gun and say it's next to your bed and then just hide it in a shed in your yard?"

"Overkill," Win said again.

"Except prosecutors never question overkill," Esperanza added.

"Because," Myron said, "it plays into their preconceived narrative."

Win nodded. "And again to be fair, viewing any one case in a vacuum, there would be no reason to doubt anyone's guilt here."

Myron walked toward the screen on the wall. "Something else is bothering me."

Win and Esperanza waited.

Myron's eyes moved from case to case. Then he asked, "How did the FBI put it together?"

No one replied.

"I mean, think about it. Nothing links these cases. No strands of hair. No locations. No victim type. The killer has been careful about that. Ingenious even. So what made them put it together now?"

"Greg Downing?" Esperanza asked. "Isn't that the point? He's the link."

"Yes, but only in two of the cases set, what, five years apart? How do you go from that to a serial killer? Chronologically, the first murder was Kravat. Greg is linked to that murder because his girlfriend's son was involved with the victim."

"Pretty loose link," Win said.

"And again, going in chronological order, the, what, third or fourth murder, is Cecelia Callister's. Okay, that's a big link obviously. DNA and all that. But how did the FBI link those two murders to Keating or Barry or Stone or . . . ? Wait, hold the phone."

Myron stopped, looked up, didn't move.

Win leaned toward Esperanza and said sotto voce: "I think our boy has a thought. I wish he'd cry 'Eureka' so we could be sure."

"Funny." Myron suddenly took his phone out of his pocket and hit the fourth number on his speed dial. Terese answered right away.

"Hey," she said.

"I have you on speakerphone," Myron said. "I'm with Win and Esperanza."

Everyone did the quick-greeting thing.

"So what's up?" Terese asked.

"The Ronald Prine murder case."

"What about it?"

"He was killed, what, two days ago?"

"That's right."

"And you said they've already arrested someone?"

"A woman named Jacqueline Newton," Terese replied. Then she

said, "Oh, I see where you're going with this. I was starting to won-der the same thing."

"Tell us."

"Newton insists she had nothing to do with it, but the murder weapon is her father's hunting rifle."

"Where did they find the rifle?"

"In her closet. Right where she said it was. Newton claimed that it hadn't been fired in years, but a quick lab test showed it'd just been used."

"Any DNA tying her to it?"

"Not yet, but it's really early. Prine was murdered only forty-eight hours ago."

"Where is Newton now?" Myron asked.

"Being held overnight. Bail hearing is in the morning."

"Do you know her lawyer?"

"Very well. A guy named Kelly Gallagher. He's a solid public defender. He'll do his best."

"Any chance you can get me in to see her?"

"You mean see Jacqueline Newton?"

"I do."

Terese thought about it. "I'll call Kelly."

"I love you, you know," Myron said.

"I do too," Win added.

"I just think you're hot," Esperanza called out.

"I'll take it," Terese said through the speakerphone. "Group hug next time we are all in the same room. Myron?"

"Yes."

"I'm staying at the Rittenhouse Hotel, room 817. I just checked my traffic app. You can be down here in one hour and forty-eight minutes."

"Start the timer," Myron said.

———————

Myron made the drive in about ninety minutes.

Terese had left a key for him at the front desk. He took the elevator up to the eighth floor. When she opened the door, Terese was drying her dirty-blonde hair with a towel. When she smiled at him, Myron felt it in his toes and forgot all about dead bodies and serial killers. For the moment anyway. She wore the hotel's terry-cloth robe. Myron flashed back to the first time he'd seen Terese in a terry-cloth robe, when they'd met up at the Hôtel d'Aubusson on the rue Dauphine in Paris.

"Well, hello," Myron said.

"I love how you always open with the smoothest lines."

"It's the 'well' before the 'hello.'"

Forget your merry widows, your frilly lace, your G-strings, your baby dolls, your camisoles, your bodysuits, your whatevers. There is nothing sexier than the woman you love drying her hair in a hotel-room terry-cloth robe.

"Want to see something that will really turn you on?" she asked.

Myron managed a nod.

She moved to the side. There was an overstuffed binder on the bed.

"Are those photos of you in a terry-cloth robe?"

"Close," Terese said. "It's a copy of the murder file on Ronald Prine."

"Take me now."

"God, you're easy. Shall we?"

They sat on the bed. Terese paged through the file and told the story. Myron listened intently and resisted the impulse to untie her terry-cloth belt. When they got to the emails Jackie Newton sent to Ronald Prine, Myron began to see a pattern. In the beginning, while the Prine Organization was stalling, Jackie Newton's emails were professional but firm. They increased in frustration and anger in a completely organic way. For the most part, Jackie Newton was contacting a Prine vice president named Fran Shovlin and copying in Ronald Prine.

The Newtons had done the work. She offered up evidence in photographs and videos, in invoices and pay stubs. The Prines didn't care.

"How do companies get away with stuff like this?" Myron asked.

"You're cute when you're naïve."

"Am I?"

"Not really, no," Terese said. "I wish the Newtons had come to me. I mean, as a journalist."

"Now who's being naïve?"

Terese considered that before nodding. "Fair."

Still, the story arc of emails, evolving from desperation to anger to finally despair, felt natural. Then a week ago, after months of no contact, Ronald Prine received an email that police claim came from Jackie Newton's home ISP. It simply read:

We haven't forgotten what you did to us.

And then, two days before the murder, one final email:

You think you can just destroy our lives and not pay any price. Get ready.

"Overkill," Myron said.

"Come again?"

He explained what Win had said. "Did Jackie Newton make any statement?"

"Just that she insists she's innocent."

"And her father?"

"He tried to take the fall, but he doesn't have the physical capacity to have done it."

"That can't be good for her," Myron said. "The dad thinking he has to take the fall. Makes her look guilty."

"Right. Gallagher got him to retract."

"That's her attorney, right? Speaking of which, can I talk to Jackie Newton tomorrow?"

"Gallagher said if you'll sign up as part of her legal team, yes, you can speak to Jackie. First thing in the morning." Terese checked the time. "It's getting late. Why don't you take a shower and we can get into bed?"

"You're good with the ideas."

"There's another terry-cloth robe in the bathroom. You can put it on if you want."

"And if I don't want?"

"You be you. Go."

Myron didn't have to be told twice.

An hour later, when they lay spent in the dark, Myron pulled Terese in close for that perfect drift-off-to-sleep spoon.

Terese whispered, "What are you thinking?"

"That you smell good."

She smiled. "What else?"

He thought about it. "For tonight, can that be enough?"

"Hold me closer."

His arm was loose around her waist. He pulled her in tight, closing his eyes, feeling the warmth of her skin.

"Closer," she whispered.

"Any closer and I'll be in front of you."

"Now you're catching on."

CHAPTER THIRTY-ONE

"You need to sign these."

Kelly Gallagher, the public defender assigned to Jackie Newton, clicked the pen and handed it to Myron. Gallagher was younger than Myron expected, probably no more than thirty, with a wet-pavement-gray suit that seemed to be fraying in live time. He wore a tie loose enough to double as a belt. His white shirt may have been some newfangled cream color, but it looked more like it had suffered a laundry accident.

"What am I signing?" Myron asked.

"It's like I told Terese," Gallagher said. "If you want to get in and talk to Jackie, you need to be part of her defense team. I know you passed the bar in New York, but Pennsylvania has bar reciprocity. So I need you to sign here. And here."

Myron skimmed it over as he took hold of the pen.

"So you're married to Terese Collins," Gallagher said.

"Yep."

"If the situation for my client wasn't so dire, I'd hate you for that right now."

Myron bit back the smile. "Yeah, I don't blame you." He signed the papers and handed them back to Gallagher.

"So what are you hoping to accomplish here, Myron?" Gallagher asked.

"What's your take?"

"Take on . . . ?"

"Terese says you're a great public defender."

He shook his head. "Like she wasn't already the perfect woman."

"She also told me you're cynical."

"Does she find that attractive? If so, yes."

"What percentage of your clients do you think commit the crimes of which they are accused?"

"Seventy-three percent."

"Pretty specific."

"If I say three out of four, you'd think I was making it up. Seventy-three percent gives the illusion of specificity and thus believability."

"So between us—and understanding that either way I will defend Jackie Newton to the nth degree—do you think she killed Ronald Prine?"

"No."

"That was quick."

"You don't think I thought about it before you asked? Look, when I got assigned this case, I figured she'd be guilty as sin. Didn't even consider the possibility she didn't do it. And I almost didn't care. See, like most rational, thinking, breathing people, I hated Ronald Prine. The guy was a heartless prick who got off on ruining people's lives. So before I even met Jackie, I was already planning a Robin Hood–like defense of justified homicide or temporary insanity or diminished capacity, that kind of thing. The prick ruined her life, she has a sick father, she snapped. You get that idea, right?"

"I do."

"So that's what I thought."

"And what changed your mind?"

"Jackie. Look, I can be fooled by a charming client, no question about it. But this time? It's not even a close call in my eyes. She didn't do it."

"How do you explain the evidence?"

"By 'evidence,' you mean the rifle and the threatening emails sent from her ISP?"

"Yes."

Kelly Gallagher smiled. "That's why you're here."

The guard gave them a wave.

"Showtime," Gallagher said.

He got up first. Myron followed. When they entered the small interrogation room, Jackie Newton was already seated. Her eyes looked up at them, hollow from fear and lack of sleep. Perhaps Myron was projecting, what with knowing her story, but there seemed to be both disbelief and defeat in her face. She couldn't believe where she was—and yet she also understood that life rarely worked out for someone like her. The world was capricious and random and cruel.

"Jackie, this is Myron Bolitar. He's come on to help me with the case."

She turned her eyes toward Myron. "Why?"

"Why what?"

"Why do you want to help?"

"I think you're innocent," Myron said.

Tears suddenly filled her eyes, like she'd been surprised by that. She held them back, wouldn't let them fall. "And again I ask," she said in a voice fighting to remain steady. "Why?"

"I owe you an explanation, but we don't have time," Myron said. "So let me just dive into this, okay?"

She glanced at Kelly Gallagher. He gave her a small nod.

"Go ahead," Jackie said.

"Do you have an alibi for the time of the murder?"

"I was working."

"Can your employer verify that?"

"You know I'm broke, right? I mean, I can't pay you if—"

"I am not here for the money," Myron assured her.

She looked wary. Understandable. People don't do things out of the kindness of their hearts. That had been her life experience.

"I don't have an employer per se," she said. "My father is sick. I'm taking care of him, so I can't work a regular gig. I hire myself out as a handyman mostly. Odd jobs via apps like TaskRabbit, that kind of thing."

"And that's what happened on the day of the murder?"

She nodded. "I got a job, yeah. It was to put together a kid's cedarwood playset in a backyard for forty dollars per hour, maximum of three hours to do the job. That's the deal I negotiated with the owner."

"So the person who hired you can back this up?"

Jackie looked over at Kelly. Kelly said, "Some of it. Yes, a woman named Leah Nowicki confirmed that she hired Jackie over the Task-Rabbit app. But once Jackie arrived and they met, Nowicki went to work and left Jackie alone in her yard to finish the job."

"So theoretically," Myron said, speaking to Jackie now, "you could have left and come back."

"But I didn't."

"We're still working on it," Kelly Gallagher added. "Maybe there was nearby CCTV or something that can lock in the alibi."

"So what next?" Myron kept his attention fixed on Jackie Newton. "You finish the job and go home?"

"Yes."

"What time was that?"

"I got home around seven o'clock."

"Anyone else there?"

"Carol DeChant had stopped in for five minutes but she was gone by then."

"Who's that?"

"A neighbor. She's a widow. She comes over sometimes and keeps him company. She watches him for me when I'm gone too many hours. It pisses Dad off though, having someone watch him." Jackie Newton actually smiled. "So what Mrs. DeChant does is, she pretends she's interested in him. Sexually. She does that just so he won't get angry when she stops by to check on him."

"Some neighbor," Myron said.

"There are a few good people in this world, Mr. Bolitar."

"There are," Myron said. "Okay, and Mrs. DeChant was gone when you arrived?"

"Yes."

"For how long?"

"I called her fifteen minutes before I got back. She said she was just leaving, that Dad was down for a nap."

"So you get home. What happened next?"

"I started making dinner for when Dad woke up. I was home maybe half an hour when the doorbell rang. It was two police officers. They said that a Remington rifle had been stolen from someone in the building. They asked if we owned one. I told them yes. They asked if maybe it was mine. I said let me take a look. I think that surprised them."

"They probably figured you'd jump on the stolen-gun story," Myron said. "They figured you'd disposed of the rifle after the murder—that's what most killers would do—and would come up with some weird excuse that would help them get you. So what happened? Did they ask to come in?"

"Yes. I told them I kept the rifle in my closet."

"And they followed you there?"

Jackie Newton nodded. "I opened the closet and pushed back the big overcoat in the back and yep, there it was, the rifle, leaning against the wall. Then I said, 'Nope, the stolen one isn't mine,' but they were already freaking out. One took out his gun."

"What did you think was happening?"

"I didn't have a clue. I said, 'Whoa, whoa, calm down, the rifle isn't even loaded.' Then I saw that they had gloves on. The cop with the gun called for backup. The other told me not to move. I asked him what was going on. He asked me if I knew Ronald Prine. At that stage, I figured this was just more Prine harassment—that he'd sent them to torment me. I got mad and said, 'Yeah, I know the prick. What, do you guys work for him or something?' And then the cop asked again, slower this time, 'Do you know Ronald Prine?' and now I really didn't like the tone in his voice. So I stopped talking. I said I wanted a lawyer."

"They tested the rifle," Myron said.

"Yeah, I know."

"Had you fired it lately?"

"No. No one has fired that gun since Dad took it to a shooting range maybe five, six years ago."

"You said the rifle was in the closet."

"Yes."

"Like readily visible?"

"No, it's way in the back behind my dad's old overcoat."

"So how often do you see it?"

"What do you mean, the rifle?"

"Yes," Myron said. "We know you were set up. We know that rifle was the murder weapon. This means at some point the killer gained access to your house and took the rifle. So I'm asking when was the last time you saw the rifle."

"I'm not sure. Months ago probably."

"Okay, so the killer could have taken it anytime in the past few months. We won't really be able to narrow that down, but we do know that they had to have returned it sometime between the murder and the time you got home. That's a pretty narrow time frame. Our best guess is, the killer shot Prine, drove straight to your place, and put the rifle back into the closet. I assume your father's home alone a lot. Would he hear someone sneaking in?"

"He sleeps a lot," Jackie said. "He's in his room most of the time with the door closed. Someone could have sneaked in if they had, I don't know, a key or something."

Myron turned to Gallagher. "The building have CCTV?"

"Only on the street."

"We have to comb through all that footage."

"It's a busy street," Kelly Gallagher said.

"But how many people would be carrying a rifle?" Myron asked. "I don't mean out in the open. But they'd have to have it in a guitar case or something. It's too warm for a long coat to cover it, but we could look for those people too."

"Wait, if we can find video of Jackie taking public transportation to her TaskRabbit job and she's not carrying a rifle—"

"Won't help," Myron said. "They'll say she carefully planned this. She took the rifle from her closet days or weeks ago. She planted it near the spot where she would commit her crime."

"Sorry," Jackie said, "but this whole scenario is insane. Why me? I don't mean this in a whiny way—but I'm a nobody. I mean, I'm less than a nobody. Why pin it on me?"

Gallagher looked at Myron. "That's a good question. And I suspect you have a theory."

"I do, but let me get to it my way, okay?" Myron turned back to Jackie. "Do you have any enemies?"

"Ronald Prine," she said. "But my guess is, he didn't do it."

"Any others? How about an ex?"

"The last guy I dated was a pharmacist from Bryn Mawr. He dumped me because I spent too much time with my dad. Mr. Bolitar?"

"Call me Myron."

"What aren't you telling me?"

"I'm trying to help you, Jackie."

"Why are you so sure I didn't do it?"

It was then that Myron felt his phone buzz. He had turned off all other settings. The buzz could only be used by his wife, parents, Win, or Esperanza and only for something urgent. He pulled out his phone and checked. It was a text from Terese.

Come out now. I'm across the street.

CHAPTER THIRTY-TWO

W in stood in front of four Vermeer paintings.

"What do you think?" Stan Ulanoff, the curator, asked him.

He was at the Frick museum, the original one located in the Henry Clay Frick mansion, on Fifth Avenue between 70th and 71st Street. The Gilded Age mansion was currently closed to the public for an expansive renovation project that was finally reaching completion.

There are debates on how many Vermeers exist worldwide. Some claim thirty-four. Others say thirty-five or maybe thirty-six. The Metropolitan Museum of Art, a stone's throw away from the Frick (if you had an arm that could throw ten blocks), has the most Vermeers on planet Earth—five of them. The far smaller Frick owns an impressive three, all of which are now on the wall in front of Win.

"We used to keep the Vermeers in the West Gallery," Stan explained, "but for this very special exhibition, we've moved them to this new spot. Our reopening gala will be the event of the season, and we hope you will accept being our guest of honor."

"No, thank you," Win said.

"I'm sorry?"

"No, thank you."

"You don't want to be our guest of honor?"

"That's correct."

"But we would like to recognize your generosity—"

"No, thank you," Win said again. "Please continue your presentation."

The smile faltered a little, but he got it back. He raised his arm, curator/guide style, and continued. "From the left to right—and also in chronological order from oldest to newest—we have *Officer and Laughing Girl*, then *Girl Interrupted at Her Music*, and *The Mistress and the Maid*, and of course, on this wall, by itself so as to highlight it, we can't thank you, Mr. Lockwood, enough for loaning us..."

His voice tailed off as he looked at the Vermeer placed on its own wall next to these three. The Met owned five, the Frick owned three—and Windsor Horne Lockwood III, aka Win, owned one.

"...*The Girl at the Piano*."

A voice next to Win whispered, "Great painter, not so clever with names."

Win turned. It was his personal assistant Kabir.

The curator frowned. "Vermeer didn't name his paintings. Others later attributed names to them based on—"

"Yeah, I know," Kabir said to him. "I was joking."

Kabir had just turned thirty years old. He had a long beard and as a Sikh American he wore a dark blue turban. Because we still jump to conclusions based on appearances, people often expected Kabir to speak with an accent or bow or something, but Kabir had been born in Fair Lawn, New Jersey, graduated from Rutgers, loved rap, partied like, well, a thirty-year-old living in Manhattan, but still, to quote Kabir, "You always have to explain the turban."

Stan frowned at Kabir for another second before turning to Win and lighting up the smile. "Do you like it?"

Win would be honest enough to admit *The Girl at the Piano*, the centerpiece of the opening, was the smallest and least impressive of the paintings, but then again, Win's Vermeer was the most notorious. Stolen decades ago, *The Girl at the Piano* and the tragic mystery behind the heist had only recently been unearthed. When Win finally got the Vermeer back, he decided to send it on a tour so that the world could enjoy it. The painting's first stop had been Win's cousin's historic mansion-museum in Newport, Rhode Island. Alas, that too had ended in tremendous controversy, thus adding to the painting's mysterious and dark allure.

"I do like it," Win said.

This pleased the curator.

"If you'll excuse us one moment," Win said.

He and Kabir slipped into the next room. They stood before another one of the Frick's gems, *La Promenade*, the masterpiece of a mother with her two wide-eyed young daughters, by Renoir. The wide-eyed girls looked well-fed and well-to-do in their fur-trimmed overcoats. The mother had her hands on the girls' backs. Was the mother protectively escorting her children or pushing them ahead? Win didn't know, but something felt amiss in that promenade.

"Articulate," Win said to Kabir.

"First up, those pickup games where someone might have gotten Greg Downing's blood or whatever," Kabir said. He read off his phone. That was how he took notes. Many young people did this, of course, but it still always looked strange to Win. "We had one of our best investigators go up to Wallkill. There is only one outdoor court that hosts pickup games. It's near Wallkill High."

"And?"

"Nothing. It's a game that features mostly regulars, though like most of these things, anyone can show up. There's a lot of trash-talking and arguing over calls, but no one remembers any incident

involving blood spilled in the past year. Also no one remembers Greg
Downing showing up."

"Downing claimed that he went in disguise."

"Yeah, like what? Fake mustache? Wig?"

Win said nothing.

"I personally talked to a guy named Mike Grenley. He's like the
commissioner of the Wallkill pickup games—knows everybody in
town, selects the teams, brings a ball, keeps the score, that kind of
thing. Total basketball nutjob. He's a huge fan of Myron's, by the way."

"I'll let Myron know."

"Anyway, he says he would have recognized Greg Downing, even
if Downing played with both his hands tied behind his back."

"Mr. Grenley might have missed that night."

"He says he hasn't missed one since 2008 when he tore his
meniscus."

"Try pickup games in neighboring towns."

"Already on it, boss."

"What else?"

"You wanted me to do a deep dive into Greg Downing's son Jeremy."

Kabir, like everyone outside the very inner circle, had no idea
that Jeremy Downing was Myron's son. Only biologically, of course.
It was important for Win, even in his own mind, to make that distinction. It made what Win was doing now feel slightly less like a
betrayal to think of it that way.

"What did you find?"

"Here's a summary," Kabir said, handing him a sheet of paper. "I
sent the entire file to your email."

Win began to scan the text when he spotted the discrepancy. He
was about to read more when Kabir touched him on the shoulder
and said, "Whoa."

Kabir stared wide-eyed at his phone.

"Whoa what?"

"We need to watch this pronto."

———————

Terese met Myron in the coffee shop across the street from where Jackie Newton was being held. She had a laptop open, and after Myron came through the door, she handed him one AirPod and put the other in her own ear.

"Sadie's about to go live," she said.

"But you don't know what she's going to say?"

Terese shook her head. "But my network would never go live unless she guaranteed something big." Terese pushed the cup at him. "Black. Darkest roast."

"I love you, you know."

"You're not so bad yourself."

"Kelly Gallagher has a crush on you."

"Really?"

Myron made a face. "Like you didn't know."

"I'm way older than Kelly Gallagher. It can't work."

"Plus you're married to a dreamboat of a guy."

"Oh right," Terese said. "That too."

The white-bearded news anchor with the wire-framed spectacles announced that they had breaking news. Myron sat up and leaned forward. The woman at the podium was none other than the founder of Fisher, Friedman and Diaz, Sadie Fisher. On Sadie's right, no more than a foot behind her, was the recently abducted Bo Storm. Myron couldn't help but feel relief. The kid looked healthy enough.

Sadie, ever in her element, looked out into the audience as though she might devour it. Bo looked the direct opposite of all that.

On the bottom of the screen, the banner conveyer-belted the words BREAKING NEWS: LIVE FROM LAS VEGAS across the lower part of the screen.

"Thank you all for coming," Sadie Fisher began.

She wore the fashionable eyewear and bright lipstick. Her hair was pulled back into a tight bun, giving her even more of the fetish librarian vibe. Her white blouse was extra white against the form-fitting black suit. Her chin was high.

"Our judicial system is founded on certain bedrock principles, none greater than the presumption of innocence. In our country, you are innocent until proven guilty. This idea is sacrosanct in our society. No man or woman should ever, *ever*, be denied their free-dom, unless and until the government proves their case beyond a reasonable doubt. No exceptions."

Terese leaned close to Myron. "I feel like 'The Star-Spangled Banner' should be playing in the background."

"And of course," Sadie-on-the-screen continued, "few things shock the senses of all decent people more than an innocent man or woman serving hard time for a crime that they didn't commit. If an overzealous or, worse, an overly ambitious prosecutor convicts someone wrongly by accident—takes away their freedom—that, to me, is still a crime. It may not be murder, but it is still very much manslaughter. But if we find out that prosecutors not only wrongly convicted a human being but let them languish in prison after—*after*—they learned the conviction was a mistake, it is unconscio-nable. Correct the mistake—don't cover it up. Own up to it. Do not let your victims spend even one more day behind bars."

Sadie put her hands on both sides of the podium and gripped the wood.

"We are here to talk about an outrage and a danger to the entire public."

Terese whispered, "She has a gift for hyperbole."

"She's a lawyer," Myron replied.

On the screen, Sadie nodded toward Bo. He slid forward a bit, his eyes darting everywhere but straight ahead.

"This young man was forced by an overzealous prosecutor to testify falsely in a murder trial. The Clark County District Attorney's Office threatened him with criminal prosecution, even though they knew that they were demanding he lie. But the corruption goes deeper than one rogue prosecutor. The Clark County DA, in conjunction with other law enforcement agencies, have colluded to keep innocent people incarcerated. They know, for example, that not only did they force my client to testify falsely but that Joseph Turant, who has been imprisoned for four years for the murder of Jordan Kravat, is innocent. If they didn't know it at the time of his trial, they know it for certain now."

She paused, fixed her glasses, turned her eyes back toward the camera.

"There are at least six other murder cases nationwide where innocent people are currently languishing in prison—and the FBI knows it. The latest involves the murder of Cecelia Callister and her son Clay Staples—a case where the innocent man currently being railroaded is my client Greg Downing. And I stress this—the FBI *knows* he didn't do it."

There was a sudden burst from the reporters at the press conference. This was how it always happened. Most people are followers, staying in check until one of them breaks the fence. Then they all flow in...

"Where's your evidence?"

"Why would the FBI do this?"

"Are you saying the FBI is intentionally imprisoning innocent people? Why?"

Sadie Fisher held up her hand and waited until everyone was quiet. When order was somewhat restored, she continued. "It is my belief that most of these prosecutors originally tried these cases in good faith. They believed that they had the right perpetrators, and that the convictions would be righteous. Not here in Clark County, however. Here, they were so blinded by the idea of convicting a man who they believed had significant ties to organized crime, that they ran afoul of all rules and ethics. They used Bo Storm to gild the lily, to make sure a strong case was a slam dunk."

Sadie Fisher raised her hand again, preempting the next explosion of questions.

"But now, as I stand here today, the FBI knows that those incarcerated for these murders are innocent. They are doing nothing about it. They are dragging their heels—"

"Why?" a reporter shouted. "Tell us why."

There were murmurs of agreement from the press corps. Sadie looked out at the sea of reporters. She had strung them along long enough.

"They are dragging their heels," she repeated, "for two reasons. One"—she raised her index finger—"overturning and admitting error in those murder convictions will cause tremendous embarrassment and damage careers. Yes, I find this disgusting and so do you, but we all know it's often the reason for prosecutorial cover-up, but—"

"Any evidence?"

"But two," she continued, making a peace sign with her fingers now, "the bigger reason for their silence is . . ."

Sadie paused now, making sure that the world was listening.

"Damn," Terese said to Myron, "she's good."

Myron nodded.

When Sadie was ready, she dropped the bomb: ". . . is because there is a serial killer on the loose."

Myron expected yet another outburst from the press; instead, there was dead silence.

"The FBI now knows that a serial killer is responsible for the murders of Jordan Kravat, Walter Stone, Tracy Keating, Cecelia Callister, and Clay Staples—and several more that are still unknown—and that the people in prison or being held for these murders—Joseph Turant, Dan Barry, Robert Lestrano, and Greg Downing—were framed."

"Wow," Terese said under her breath. "She's taking no prisoners."

Myron's phone buzzed. It was a message from Win: Watching?

Myron: Yes
Win: PT is not going to be pleased.

Myron gave the message a thumbs-up.

A bubble with dancing dots played for a few seconds.

Win: When you get back, we need to talk.

Myron read the message again. He didn't like it. Once again, it wasn't like Win to be coy or cagey—or if you say that enough, do you just have to accept that maybe he is? Before Myron could think of a response, Terese nudged him back to Sadie and the press conference.

"In fact," Sadie Fisher continued, "we believe that real estate mogul Ronald Prine, who was murdered only two days ago, was also a victim of the Setup Serial Killer—"

"Setup Serial Killer?" Terese repeated.

"Too wordy a nickname," Myron agreed.

"—and," Sadie continued, "that the young woman arrested just last night, Jacqueline Newton, is the killer's latest frame job."

"I guess she just did our work for us," Myron said.

Terese nodded, her eyes glued to the screen.

"In closing," Sadie said, "I would like to address the FBI and its current director, Harry Borque, directly."

Sadie Fisher turned and faced the camera straight on, adjusted her glasses, and drove hard to the ending salvo.

"If you want to deny what I am saying, please go ahead. Your excuses won't hold water. Not anymore. The public has the right to know that there is an odious serial killer working across this country who not only kills people but then frames others for his crimes. My guess is, you will claim that you were holding back on the serial killer revelation to prevent public panic or to somehow help facilitate their capture. That's nonsense."

Her anger grew now, feeling on the edge.

"I might have been somewhat sympathetic to such a phony PR move if it wasn't for the fact that you are knowingly—*knowingly*—keeping innocent people behind bars to mitigate the embarrassment of prosecutorial mistakes. Sorry, that's criminal conduct and for that, I will not stay silent. I will not let innocent people spend even one more moment behind bars. Free them. Free them now. And shame. Shame on all of you who allowed this. You are the serial killer's co-conspirators, and I will not rest until the truth comes out and all who are truly guilty are brought to justice."

On that note, Sadie stormed off stage.

"Wow." Terese leaned back. "I think I need a cigarette."

The reporters on hand started shouting questions in her wake. Bo didn't move at first, looking like the classic "deer in the headlights" before bolting away, to keep within the metaphor, like a deer who finally realizes the headlights signal that a car is indeed heading toward them.

"Will there be much blowback?" Terese asked.

"On me?"

"Yes."

Myron shrugged. "I'm not sure. It doesn't matter."

"She's telling the truth, right?"

"As far as we know it."

"What was Sadie's goal here?" Terese asked.

"To get her client released."

"Greg Downing?"

"Yes."

"Still," Terese said, "she's not in the wrong."

"No," Myron agreed, "she's not."

"Greg will be kicked free," Terese said.

"Probably."

"And Jackie Newton too."

"I hope so, yes."

"Then it's over, isn't it?"

Myron said nothing.

"You got involved in this to help Greg."

"Yes."

"Mission accomplished."

"True."

"So I repeat: It's over, isn't it?"

Myron thought about that. "Would it sound arch if I say, 'There's still a serial killer out there'?"

"It would," Terese said. "The entire FBI is on this now. The public will be on the lookout. It isn't on you to capture this guy."

"True."

"You don't have the resources they do."

"True."

"And it would be dangerous."

"True again."

Terese looked at him. "It's not over for you, is it?"

"I don't think so, no."

CHAPTER THIRTY-THREE

M yron kissed Terese. "I have to head back," he said.

"And here I got a late checkout at the hotel."

"Or I can stay a little longer."

"No, you can't."

"No, I can't."

"You have to go back to New York and, I don't know, catch a serial killer or something."

"Even though you don't like it."

Terese put her arms around his neck. "You tilt at windmills, my love. I've been the beneficiary of that. It's one of the reasons I love you."

"The other being my prowess in the sack?"

"Or your susceptibility to self-delusion."

"Ouch."

She kissed him again. "You are the best thing that ever happened to me."

"Same."

"Please be careful."

"I will."

Myron got in his car and crossed the Ben Franklin Bridge into New Jersey. To people outside the area, New Jersey is a mystery; to people inside the area, New Jersey is an enigma. In truth, New

Jersey is a dense, jigsaw-puzzle, defined-by-being-undefined mass squeezed between two large cities. The top half—northeast New Jersey—is the suburbs of New York. The bottom half—southwestern New Jersey—is the suburbs of Philadelphia. Sure, there are edgy beach towns and proof that despite the industrial, postmodern hideousness or the maze of crumbling factories and dilapidated warehouses, New Jersey still earns the moniker "The Garden State." It's all there. But most travelers are passing through and really, what are you going to put on your major interstates—ugly oil refineries or pretty farmland?

Myron hit a number he almost never hit. PT answered on the third ring.

"Are you calling to apologize for that press conference?" PT asked.

"No, not really. Something occurred to me."

"Like an epiphany?"

"Just like an epiphany."

"And you've deigned to share your epiphany with me?"

"And only you. For now."

"So tell me what it is."

"You set this up," Myron said.

"That's your epiphany?"

"It is."

"Care to elaborate?"

"Sure," Myron said. "The FBI realized that a serial killer was at work, but someone—probably the new director you don't like—wanted to keep it quiet. He knew that it would be a huge brouhaha, what with all the innocent people falsely convicted and serving time in jail."

PT asked, "Did you just use the word 'brouhaha'?"

"You hang around Win long enough . . ." Myron replied. "Anyway, you told Win and me. You didn't swear us to secrecy. You gave us enough information to figure out a few of the other cases. You knew we would act on it, and it would get out into the world, just like this."

Silence. Then: "No comment."

"I'm not a reporter," Myron said. "There's no need to comment."

"I believe that my role should always be clandestine, but the Bureau itself should be transparent," PT said. "Does that make me a hypocrite, Myron?"

"It makes you a man of principle who doesn't like innocent people languishing in prison for the sake of optics."

Myron drove the car past the Port of Elizabeth, which had one of those oil refineries that probably inspired the set for the *Terminator* movie, then past Newark Airport. A few miles later, the Manhattan skyline rose into view.

"By the way," PT said, "I didn't know the Ronald Prine murder was connected."

"There hadn't been an arrest yet."

"Still," PT said. "Good work on that."

"Thanks."

"Are you and Win going to stay on this?"

"I can't speak for Win."

"Yes, you can."

"I have a question for you."

"I'm listening."

"We took a hard look at these cases last night," Myron said.

"When you say 'we'—"

"Win, Esperanza, yours truly."

"Go on."

"We see the patterns, of course, but what we don't see are the connections."

PT said, "Ah."

"Ah what?"

"The—what did Sadie Fisher call him?—the Setup Killer?"

"The Setup *Serial* Killer."

"Terrible name."

"That's what I said."

"I hope the media comes up with a better one," PT said. "Look, I despise calling serial killers 'evil geniuses,' but let's face it—this guy is close. He was careful. He was smart. He took his time, not only in staking out the murder victim but more so in framing the—shall we call them second victims?"

"Ruining two lives for the price of one," Myron said.

"Yes. It's one thing to enjoy killing people. That's a sickness we are somewhat familiar with at the FBI Behavioral Analysis Unit. But to also get a thrill out of sending an innocent person to prison? That's a true double hit of psychotic behavior."

"Unless it wasn't for thrills," Myron said.

"Meaning?"

"Unless they did the framing just to cover their tracks," Myron said.

"Do you think that's likely?"

"I don't, no," Myron said. "I think the killer enjoys that part too. It's about power often. A kill is quick and strong, a full-on rush. Incarcerating an innocent is slow. A double whammy. But that's not my point here."

"What is your point?" PT asked.

The car sped past the Lautenberg Rail Station in Secaucus. Myron remembered driving this route not long after 9/11. He could still see the Twin Towers in his mind's eye. For years he would do that—drive by this stretch of the New Jersey Turnpike, look to his right, see exactly where the towers had stood. Then one day, he couldn't see the towers in his mind's eye anymore. A month later, when he drove by here again, he couldn't remember where the towers had even stood. That angered him.

"My point is," Myron said, "we couldn't find any connections between the cases."

"Right."

"So how did the FBI put together that it was the work of a serial killer?"

"They didn't," PT said, "until Greg Downing was caught."

"Yes, but that would only give you a connection between the Kravat case and the Callister case."

"Agreed."

"So?"

"So an anonymous source dropped enough hints."

Myron thought about that. "Someone leaked it to the FBI?"

"The new director won't admit that. He claims it's their clever investigating. But yes."

"Who would do that?"

"Could be the killer himself bragging. Could be the killer wanting attention. Could be the killer wanting to get caught. Could be a lot of things."

Myron headed through the E-ZPass lane at the Lincoln Tunnel. The traffic slowed him down. He stared at the tunnel's opening, a mouth widening to swallow the car whole.

"Sounds like you're staying on this," PT said.

"My wife thinks I should stop now. I was in this for Greg, she said. The FBI has the resources. I don't."

"She makes a good case," PT said. "But?"

"But something feels incomplete."

"To me too," PT said. "Myron?"

"What?"

"Greg Downing is connected to two of these cases."

"I know."

"Then you know that's not a coincidence."

———————

When Myron got back to the Lock-Horne Building, he took the elevator to the fourth floor—his old one, which now houses the law firm of Fisher, Friedman and Diaz. Taft Buckingham the Whatever greeted him with a blue blazer, khaki pants, pink tie, boat loafers. Myron half expected him to don a white captain's cap and deejay a yacht rock set.

"Esperanza is waiting for you," Taft, son of a grown man Win called Taffy, said.

Taft led Myron into the conference room. Esperanza stood by the window and stared out. "Should I have warned you about Sadie's press conference?"

Myron shrugged. "Not a big deal."

"Sadie wanted to handle it this way."

"I get it."

"She's in the right, you know."

"I do."

"She's on her way back now. She wants to be there when they let Greg out."

"She knows how to get her face on television."

"For all the right reasons," Esperanza said.

"I know. And I agree."

"We are doing good work here."

"I know that too."

"But I'm not sure it's for me."

Myron nodded slowly. Esperanza finally turned to him to gauge his reaction. Myron tried to keep his face neutral.

"How's business upstairs?" Esperanza asked.

"Shitty," Myron said.

"But you still want me back?"

"I do. We can starve together."

Esperanza smiled. She crossed the room and kissed Myron gently on the cheek. "I miss being around you every day."

"Same."

"And we can't forget Big Cyndi."

"No matter how hard we try," Myron said. "When do you want to start?"

"Let's table that for now," she said. "So what's up?"

"Something about this serial killer isn't adding up," Myron said.

"I thought Sadie did a pretty good job of explaining it all."

"She did. But no one can explain why Greg is the only connection to two of the cases."

"You have a theory?"

"Just a simple one: The killer is connected to him."

"Or out to get him."

"Or someone close to him," Myron said.

"So what's your next step?"

"When Greg was hiding, you found Grace's hidden bank account in Charlotte," Myron said. "I think we need to do more digging."

He explained what he wanted her to do. She listened in silence. When he finished, Esperanza said, "I'm on it."

"Have you spoken to Win?" Myron asked.

"No, why?"

"He sent a cryptic text."

"Does he send any other kind?"

"I checked with Kabir," Myron said. "He told me Win's down in the basement training."

She checked her watch. "Yep. Like clockwork. Talk to him. I'll start on this."

CHAPTER THIRTY-FOUR

The only way to get to Win's secret space was via the private elevator. There was no button to call the elevator. You could only access it with a key. Once inside the elevator, there was no button that would take you down below street level—you had to put the right code into the keypad. Myron always typed in the code very slowly for fear that if he got a number wrong, the elevator might self-destruct or the walls would slowly start closing in like the garbage disposal scene in *Star Wars*.

Win liked his gadgets.

Myron hit the lower floor. The elevator doors opened. Myron never knew what to call the room. Win's gym? Workout room? Training space? Exercise area? All felt inadequate. There were the expected items you'd find in a classic workout gym—weights, barbells, pull-down-type machines, leg presses, a heavy bag, a Wing Chun fighting dummy, that kind of thing. The lights were kept low, giving the place a cave-like atmosphere. Right now, Win was barefoot and shirtless, sweating, running through a series of traditional katas. Win trains every day. His origin story is nothing as dramatic as Batman's (murder of his parents) or Spider-Man's (insect bite mixed with murder of his uncle), but when he was young, Win had felt unsafe and scared—the details are best saved for another time—and so he decided that he never wanted to feel that way again. That meant constant learning and training. He has studied with master fighters and top-level weapons experts from around the world. He is almost supernaturally knowledgeable about pretty much every hand-to-hand fighting discipline, knows his way around various blades better than anyone Myron knew, was a marksman with handguns and more than adequate with riflery. Win is always armed, though perhaps not right now where he was only wearing some kind of bathing-suit-like shorts. The room temperature was set at ninety degrees.

"A moment," Win said, continuing through the kata, a flowing dance of kicks, blocks, blows, somehow both violent and meditative, "unless you want to join in."

Over the years, Myron had trained with Win, most notably in tae kwon do and street fighting. It wasn't a competition between them, but it would be hard to say who would come out victorious in a real fight. Win was smarter, more knowledgeable, better trained, more ruthless. Myron was bigger, stronger, and had the reflexes of an elite athlete.

"Pass," Myron said.

"A sparring session. A quick workout. A hot shower. You'll feel better."

No doubt. "You said you needed to see me."

Win finished the kata with a flourish, moving both hands and feet at blurring speeds. When he finished, he bowed to a mirror (not surprisingly, Win's workout space had lots of mirrors), grabbed a towel and a bottle of room-temperature water. Win didn't believe in drinking cold water when he worked out.

"Kabir is still tracking down Greg's basketball game in Wallkill," Win said, "but so far, no one remembers playing with him."

Win filled Myron in on what Kabir had told him at the Frick. Myron listened. He didn't like it. Myron had played in basketball pickup games his whole life. Pickup games were celestial, magic, nirvana, a place where everyone starts anew, where your wealth or status are meaningless, where your game matters and only your game, where you can suddenly form a bond and even a friendship with people you've never met before. You didn't know what your fellow players did for a living. You didn't know if they were married or had kids or anything about them, except that maybe they couldn't dribble with their weak hand or they played too lax on defense or man, could they jump high for a rebound. They were Ronnie or Ace or TJ or if there were two guys with the same name, they'd be Big Jim and Little Jim, and most of the time, even if you played with the guys for years, you might not know their last name. Because it didn't matter. Nothing mattered but the game. It was childish and warm and competitive and a bubble. There was the stale smell of a small gym, the dribbling of the ball, the squeaks of sneakers on the wood floor. You called out screens and high-fived and argued whether the contact constituted calling a foul and most of the time, nah, forget it and get payback on the next play.

But even when Myron dialed his game back, even when he saw the competition was not good enough for him to go more than 20 or 30 percent, the other players still knew—this guy had game. This guy was great. Myron could never hide that.

And neither could someone like Greg.

It was bothersome, no doubt, but when Win finished, Myron said, "You didn't text me about Greg's basketball game."

"No, I did not."

"So?"

"Jeremy Downing is not in the military."

It took a few seconds for Myron to register what Win said. "Wait, what?"

"After you told me that Jeremy had not flown in from overseas, I began an extensive background check on him."

"On him," Myron repeated.

"Yes."

"On my son. You ran an extensive background check on my son."

Win put a black long-sleeved shirt over his head. "Is this how we are going to do this?"

Myron said nothing.

"You say he's your son, I remind you that it's only biological, that you barely know him, you say that doesn't matter, that I should have asked you before I did anything like this, I say there is no harm in doing a background check, that if I found nothing you would be none the wiser, you say yes but you should have, I interrupt you and remind you that there is no one on this planet I care about more than you, that I would never do anything to harm you, that whatever I do, I do to protect you because I love you. Is that how we are going to have to play this?"

Myron shook his head. "You're something."

"I am. Can we skip past all that now?"

Myron nodded. "We can. But one thing first."

"Go on."

"You gave up Bo without telling me. Then you did a background check on Jeremy without telling me. This keeping things from me— it needs to stop."

Win considered that. "You are correct. I will stop."

Nothing more bizarre than a reasonable Win. "So tell me what you found," Myron said.

"Jeremy did indeed serve in the military in various elite and clandestine divisions. Just as he told us. But he was discharged three years ago."

"Voluntarily?"

"I don't know yet. This is the top echelon of our military apparatus. There is intentional misdirection and confusion in any kind of records."

"So maybe he's still there," Myron said. "Maybe saying he was discharged is a cover."

"It could be," Win said.

"But you don't think so."

"His discharge wasn't announced. I had to dig deep to find it."

Win picked up a barbell and started to do Zottman curls. The up move is a standard bicep curl, but then you flip your wrist so that the downward move, slow and under control, works the forearms.

"Jeremy also lives in New Orleans under the pseudonym Paul Simpson. 'Paul' works in IT at a Dillard's department store in nearby Gretna."

"Again: Could be a cover," Myron said.

"Again: Could be indeed. I draw no conclusions. We report, you decide."

Myron frowned. "You did not just say that."

"I wish I hadn't now that I think about it. Either way, Kabir will continue to dig unless you tell me to call him off."

Myron thought about it. "There's probably nothing to this."

"Then there's no reason not to continue," Win said. His watch vibrated. He checked it. "Sadie just landed."

"You loaned her your plane?"

"Not loaned. Chartered. I will bill her for it, and she in turn will bill Greg Downing."

"Makes sense. How did she hook up with Bo Storm?"

"This will interest you," Win said. "She got a call from our hefty friend Spark Konners."

"Bo's brother."

"You felt bad about that, didn't you?"

"Conning Spark into coming under the pretense of a job offer and then holding him against his will?" Myron asked. "Yeah, a little."

"So you recommended his services to Chaz."

"I asked Chaz to interview him. That a problem?"

"Not for me, no. Apparently, when Bo was released by Joey the Toe's men, Spark flew into Vegas to help."

"Help how?"

"I don't know. Be a supportive brother. You might be able to ask him yourself. He and Bo just landed with Sadie. Oh, one other thing. The Vegas DA's office says it will look very closely at Joey's conviction, but they denied pressuring Bo into lying."

"Not surprising," Myron said. "It's not like they would just admit it."

"True, but they claim to have audiotapes, proving that Bo Storm is lying. In fact—and this is where it gets interesting—they claim the only reason they homed in on Joseph Turant in the first place was because Bo claimed he saw Joey that night."

Myron thought about that. "A lot of moving parts."

"Yes."

Myron's phone rang. He checked the caller ID and looked up at Win. Win spread his hands. "Well?"

"It's Jeremy."

———

Myron clicked the answer button. "Jeremy?"

"I assume you saw Sadie's press conference."

There was a lilt in Jeremy's voice.

"I did, yeah."

"I just talked to her on the phone. They're going to release Dad in a few hours."

Dad.

"Yeah, that's great."

"I'm coming back."

"To New York?"

"Yes."

Myron switched hands. Win had moved to a corner to give Myron space. He was doing push-ups on closed fists, his body a perfect plank.

"Didn't you just get home?"

"Yeah, but I didn't expect this to happen this fast. I want to be there for him."

"I understand," Myron said.

"I want to thank you. For helping him and all."

"You're welcome," Myron said.

There was a brief silence.

"Something wrong, Myron?"

Win was still doing push-ups. His torso moved up and down with piston-machine-like precision. He did three sets of one hundred, twice a week. "If you do more than that," Win had explained, "you will injure your rotator cuff."

"Where are you coming in from?" Myron asked.

"I told you before—"

"Classified, I remember." Then: "Are you still in the military?"

Silence. Long silence.

"Or were you discharged three years ago?"

More silence.

"Are you still in the military," Myron continued, "or do you work IT at Dillard's department store?"

Still more silence. Myron's grip on the phone tightened.

Finally, Jeremy said, "You've been busy."

"Do you want to explain?"

"Over a phone? No, I don't think so."

"When you arrive?"

"Sure," Jeremy said. Then: "Myron?"

"Yes?"

"You're probably expecting me to get all indignant and snap, 'How dare you dig into my past' or 'I can't believe you don't trust your own son' or something like that."

Myron nodded. Of course, Jeremy couldn't see it, so it was more to himself. But that was exactly what he'd been thinking.

"I'm not upset. I get why you did it. We'll talk about it when I see you, okay?"

"Okay."

"So don't worry," Jeremy said. "It's all good."

CHAPTER THIRTY-FIVE

The Metropolitan Correctional Center is a twelve-story high-rise in the Civic Center of Manhattan, near Chinatown, Tribeca, and the Financial District. John Gotti was held here. Sammy the Bull was held here. Bernie Madoff was held here. El Chapo was held here. Jeffrey Epstein was held—and purportedly killed himself—here.

And now, with a ton of media fanfare around the edifice, Greg Downing was being released from here.

Myron and Win watched from a spot across the street.

"Greg could just exit from inside," Myron said.

"He could."

"It's a correctional center. There are ways in and out besides the front door."

"True," Win said. "But we both know Sadie won't let that happen."

"You like her, don't you?"

Win nodded. "She's very effective in advocating for the bullied and battered."

"Look at you," Myron said. "Finding a cause."

"And she's profitable. Insecure, violent narcissists are a growth industry."

"Sad but true."

"Sadie's also a total smoke show."

Win.

There was a podium set up on the sidewalk. On the right, just far enough away to not be a part of the proceedings, stood the Konnerses—Grace, Spark, Brian/Bo. Grace seemed to be hiding behind her hulking older son, Spark. Spark turned and spotted Myron. Their eyes met. Spark's eyes narrowed. He said something to his mom and moved toward them.

"Uh-oh," Win said.

Spark beelined straight to Myron. "Chaz Landreaux," he said.

Myron didn't reply.

"You called him for me, didn't you?"

"I may have told him to give your résumé a look," Myron said.

"You think that makes up for what you did?"

Win took that one. "He didn't do anything to you," he said. "I did."

"Win," Myron said.

Win put his hand up to let him handle it. He slid in between Myron and Spark, his chin facing Spark's paddleball-wall chest, once again daring Spark to make the first move. "You lied to us, Sparkles. You knew Greg was alive. You knew your brother committed perjury on the stand."

"You better take a step back," Spark said, puffing out the chest.

"Oh my." Win smiled and Myron didn't like the gleam he saw in Win's eyes. "Do you want to play this game again?"

"Win," Myron said.

"Don't sweat it," Spark said, looking at Myron over Win's head. "I just came by to make sure you're the one who put me on Chaz's radar."

"I am, yes."

"Then I'm not going to the interview."

"I'm sorry to hear that," Myron said. "Chaz would have given you a fair shake."

Win pouted and mimed rubbing his eyes and said, "Wah." Pause. "Wah."

Spark shook his head, turned carefully to avoid touching Win, and headed back to his mother and brother.

When he was far enough away, Win said, "I told you to let it be."

"We kidnapped him, Win."

"Kidnapped," Win scoffed. "Don't be so melodramatic. And could we stop with the 'we' please? 'We' didn't do anything. I came up with the ruse of a fake coaching job offer. I flew him to Vegas in my plane. I am the one who put him on his ass on that tarmac."

"And I'm just an innocent?"

"In this case? Yes. How is that hard to understand?"

Myron stared off across the street. "There was a time . . ." Myron stopped, starting again. "There was a time when I thought you went too far."

Win waited.

"And I called you on it. I told you that you couldn't do that again. Do you remember what you told me?"

Win still did not reply.

"You said: 'You know what I do—and yet you always call me.'"

"Look at you, quoting me verbatim."

"You were right though. I don't get off the hook by blaming you."

Win shook his head. "Such an idealist."

"No, not anymore. I wish I were. But I get you better now."

"And that's a bad thing," Win said.

Myron wasn't sure whether Win meant that as a statement or a question.

"You try to shield me from the squishier morality moments,"

Myron said. "But I'm right there with you. So yeah, maybe it wasn't my idea, but that doesn't mean I can wash my hands of what you did."

"So," Win said, "you figured that by calling Chaz, you might mitigate our, uh, squishiness, a bit."

"Yes."

Win thought about it. Then he shook his head. "Weirdo."

There was a commotion by the front door now. Greg Downing stepped out with Sadie Fisher. Sadie, no surprise, wore a killer outfit—bright red blazer over black blouse, black pencil skirt. Greg wore the same jeans and flannel shirt he'd been wearing when he was arrested back at that A-frame house in Pine Bush. He blinked into the sun as though he'd just emerged from solitary and into bright sunlight. The move felt a tad performative, but Myron let it go. Greg gave a half smile and a half wave—he, too, knew how to work a press conference.

"Thank you all for coming," Sadie Fisher said.

Win nudged Myron and gestured with his chin. Myron looked and saw Spark and Bo vanish into one of those large black vans Myron normally associated with party travel. Grace was by the door too. She turned and glared at Myron. Myron didn't look away. Then Grace too slipped inside.

Sadie Fisher continued: "I said everything I needed to say at my press conference this morning from Las Vegas. I'm not here to grandstand, so I won't repeat myself. Mr. Downing is grateful to be set free, but he worries about the other victims still incarcerated. He and I both hope for their speedy exoneration. We also hope that the Federal Bureau of Investigation will conduct an open and transparent investigation, so that the American people understand the threat and we can all help to bring the perpetrator to justice." Sadie gave the crowd a tight smile. "My client asks that everyone please respect his privacy after this harrowing ordeal. Thank you for your time."

The expected cacophony of questions erupted from the media. Sadie and Greg ignored it and hurried toward the same black van.

"Hmm," Win said.

"What?"

"Jeremy didn't make it."

———————

Emily Downing was watching her ex-husband's release on television when she heard a strange buzzing.

You hear the hoary chestnut that there are moments when it seems your entire life passes in front of your eyes. The imagery here was not violent enough for what Emily was about to experience. The past few days have felt like her entire past clenched into a massive fist that won't stop pummeling her. She had made mistakes. She had regrets. Who didn't? She didn't dwell on them. Her life was good. She thought about Myron. She thought about Greg. But mostly, despite modernity, despite everything, despite her own rebellion, she was first and foremost a mother. She didn't say that to her friends when they gathered. She barely admitted it to herself. It felt too old-fashioned, too out-of-vogue, but the best of her, the most important role in her life, involved being a mother. Her own mother had told her that, way back when, before Jeremy was born. Your life is one thing before you have a child. It is forever something else after. Nothing is the same. Emily had pooh-poohed that canard. Of course, there would be changes, but she was steadfast in the fact that her path would not deviate from its intended course. How silly of her. The giant world she had known before the birth of her child had been reduced to a six-pound, fourteen-ounce mass on the day Jeremy was born. It was celestial and loving and feral.

The buzzing sounded again.

It wasn't so much a buzzing, she realized, as a vibrating noise, and while that thought would normally make her smile—that thought might even lead to a dumb double entendre she would laugh over with friends—she didn't move because, even though she had no reason to believe this from a simple vibrating buzz, the sound made her blood run cold. The sound was a precursor, she thought. The sound, like her first baby being born, was going to change her life forever.

Stop with the hyperbole, Emily told herself.

After college, Emily had gone to Iowa to get a master's in creative writing. Yep, she'd wanted to be a novelist. It was not lost on her that the next love of Myron's life, the one he'd fallen for after they'd broken up and she'd married Greg, was the novelist Jessica Culver. Culver had been one of Emily's favorite writers, living the life that Emily had sometimes imagined could have been her own. In the end, Jessica Culver had left Myron too, and Emily realized that was something else the two women had in common. Not merely writing, not merely breaking it off with Myron, but a streak of self-destruction in the guise of independence.

The buzzing was coming from Jeremy's room.

When she was twenty-four, Emily gave up writing completely. She didn't even journal. The idea of putting pen to paper repulsed her. She didn't know why. It was only lately, in the last year or so, the craving came back. She had started a novel. She wasn't sure what fueled that—the need to reach people, the need to tell a story, the desire for fame, glory, immortality?

Did you need to know your motive?

The buzzing was coming from under Jeremy's bed.

Emily got down on her hands and knees to see better. Her Upper East Side apartment had three bedrooms. One for her, one for Jeremy, one for Emily's younger daughter Sara. The vast majority of the time, it was just Emily here. Jeremy was, well, wherever he was. Sara had taken a job in Los Angeles working as a production assistant for a major streamer.

The buzzing stopped.

Didn't matter.

It took another minute or two, but Emily found the phone. And when she did, her heart sunk. She stood and walked zombie-like back into the kitchen. The live coverage of Greg's release was over. A commercial played exalting the virtues of selling your own gold by mail. A little while later, Emily sat heavily at the kitchen table and stared straight ahead. Then she picked up her mobile phone and hit the number.

Myron answered on the third ring. "Emily?"

"I'm at my apartment," she said, her voice sounding very far away in her own ears. "Please come over right away."

CHAPTER THIRTY-SIX

s you watch Myron Bolitar, two competing, disparate thoughts ricochet through your brain.

One: You have lost control of the narrative.

Two: It is going exactly according to plan.

You no longer know which is true. You wonder whether there is a world where this paradox could be made whole, where the contradictions become harmonious. In a sense, it doesn't matter. You are coming to the end of the journey.

That means killing Myron.

You wonder whether you are being analytical here or if you are looking for a rationalization. The truth—the *hard* truth—is you are still sane enough to know that you are not sane. You enjoy killing. You enjoy it a lot. You also believe that there are many people who feel—or would feel—exactly the same as you. You are not so different from them, but they have never let themselves "go there," to use a popular modern idiom, so they don't know what monster may lie dormant within them.

You have.

It changed you.

You hadn't expected that. If you'd ever been asked to ponder what killing another human would have been like, you'd have honestly said that idea holds no appeal to you, that the thought of murder repulses you. Like anyone would. Like a so-called "normal" person. You were one of them. You'd never cross that line. And you never meant to. But once you did, well, things changed, didn't they? For a moment you were a god. You felt an exhilarating rush like nothing else before. It knocked you down in surprise. And that's when you knew.

You would seek the feeling again and again.

Even now, you don't consider yourself a psychopath. You feel like someone who had an epiphany, a rare insight with almost religious undertones, and so now you see the world with a clarity that mere mortals can never quite understand.

And yet.

And yet, with that same clarity, you also know that you are unwell. You just don't care. Circular reasoning but there you go. Human beings are selfish creatures. We want what we want, and the rest of the world is window dressing, background, extras in a movie in which we are the only star that matters. And so you recognized that you are trying to justify what you've become, all the while knowing that at the end of the day, you don't really care.

You watch Myron take the phone call.

You have the gun. You have the plan.

Before the sun rises again, it will be over for Myron Bolitar.

And for others...

This time, you really aren't sure.

CHAPTER THIRTY-SEVEN

yron sat on one side of the kitchen table. Emily sat on the other side. The only item on the table between them was a phone. It was small and black and a flip model. Myron knew the type. Some people called them "no-contract" or "prepaid" or "pay-as-you-go." Others, like Myron, knew them as disposable or burner phones.

He had not touched it yet.

"Do you have a pair of latex gloves?" Myron asked Emily.

"You mean like surgeons wear?"

"Yes."

"Does this look like a hospital?"

"How about to clean?"

"You mean like rubber gloves?"

"Yes."

"I can look. Why do you need them?"

"Why do you think, Emily?" His voice had a little too much edge in it. He dialed it back and said, "I don't want to leave or smudge fingerprints."

"But I already touched it," she said.

"Tell me about that."

"Tell you what?"

"Where exactly did you find it?"

"Jeremy's room. I told you that. It was taped to the bottom of the bed."

"And you heard it vibrate?"

"Yes. But for all I know, it could have been there for months."

Myron frowned. "And stayed charged?"

"It wasn't like someone was using it. Can't phone batteries last a long time if it's never used?"

Myron saw no reason to get into it with Emily.

"Myron?"

He looked up at her. There were tears in Emily's eyes.

"I'm really scared."

He reached across the table and took her hand. "Step at a time, okay?"

She nodded.

"How did you get the phone out from under the bed?"

"I tried to pull it off with my hand, but the tape wouldn't give. So I went back to the kitchen and got scissors."

"Did you flip it open or anything?"

"No. I called you right away."

Myron nodded. "Could you get the gloves?"

She found them under the sink, but they were far too small for his hands. Myron gave up on them pretty fast—if he messed up some DNA or whatever, so be it. The phone had been taped. Emily had grabbed it. The contamination was already there.

"Wait," Emily said. "Should we call Jeremy first?"

"Okay," Myron said. "But let's not ask him about the phone right now."

"It's probably nothing."

"You're probably right."

"He's in the military. He does a lot of clandestine work. The phone could be a part of that."

"Yes," Myron said. "I agree."

They both stared at one another for a long moment.

"He's our son," Emily said, her voice a plea. "You get that, right?"

Myron said nothing.

"Maybe we shouldn't touch it," she said. "We should wait until he gets here and let him explain."

"Call him," Myron said.

She dialed Jeremy's number, but the call went straight to voice-mail. The voice on the message was machine-produced, not Jeremy's. Emily didn't bother leaving a message. She hung up. They sat at the table together. The room was silent. Myron stared at the phone. He glanced up at Emily and then reached across the table and picked up the phone. He flipped it open and checked incoming calls. There were four calls in total, all over the past three days, the most recent being an hour ago.

The caller ID on all of them read Anonymous.

Not helpful.

Myron looked for an option to call the number back. There was nothing there. He clicked the arrow on top of the screen and moved to outgoing calls. Bingo. There were two calls listed. Same number. When Myron saw it, he stiffened.

"What?" Emily said.

He didn't reply. *Don't jump the gun*, he told himself. *Step at a time.*

"Myron?"

The number had a 215 area code. That was what had startled him. He put down the phone and picked up his own.

"What are you doing?" Emily asked.

He put the 215 phone number into his own phone. He was about to dial the number, but then thought better of it. Why leave a record of his call? He moved over to the Google app and entered the number in there. If this didn't work—if the number was unlisted or not online in some way—he would send it to Esperanza. She'd be able to find the phone's owner right away.

But no need. The google worked.

The 215 phone number, according to Myron's web search, belonged to the Prine Organization.

Myron closed his eyes.

"What?" Emily asked.

The intercom buzzed, startling them both. Emily pushed back her chair and stood. "I'll be right back."

Myron slid the phone off the marble-top table. It dropped into his palm. He leaned back and jammed the phone into his front pocket. Myron heard Emily tell the doorman to let him up. Myron rose and headed toward the door.

"When I found the phone," Emily explained, "I called you first. Isn't that odd?"

"I don't know. Is it?"

"It was just a gut reaction. But when I hung up, I felt weird."

"So you called someone else," Myron said.

"Yes," she said. "And he's here now too."

———

The three of them—Myron, Emily, and now Greg Downing—sat at the same kitchen table with the flip phone in the middle, equidistant from all three of them.

Greg spoke first. "It's a setup."

"Yes," Emily said, leaping at Greg's explanation.

"That's what this serial killer has been doing, right?" Greg turned to Myron, ready to make his pitch now. "They kill someone and then they frame someone else for it. This time, they framed Jeremy."

"Exactly," Emily said.

"That would be two separate frame-ups then," Myron said.

"What?"

"The killer framed a woman named Jackie Newton. She was arrested already. Jeremy would be the second person."

Greg locked eyes with Myron. It brought back the memory of the first time they met. Sixth grade. When Myron's Kasselton All-Stars got to play Greg's Glen Rock Greats at a high school gym in Tenafly, both kids had already developed reps as two of the best in the state. Myron had dominated every game so far that season. The Kasselton All-Stars were undefeated. But that day, a few of the guys had come up to him and said Glen Rock got a kid as good as him. Myron and Greg never spoke before the game. They shook hands and played hard. Myron got the better of that battle, though he remembered envying Greg's cool under pressure. Myron showed emotion on the court. Greg never did.

And here too sat the first woman Myron ever loved. She had been an awakening, an explosion, an eruption of pathos. Perhaps it hadn't been built to last, but at the time, when he lost her, Myron had felt as though he would never feel this way again or with anyone else. How wrong he'd been, but hey, youth is wasted on the young. Still, even now, even after all these years, it made no sense. He understood Emily's (frankly) mature decision not to marry him. It had been too soon. So why didn't she just say that? Why break it off altogether? And even if that made sense—and he got that it did, that it is hard to go back after a rejected proposal—why move on so fast to Greg Downing? There were a million guys out there. Why Myron's rival?

When Myron was in middle school, his mom continuously played Jim Croce's album *You Don't Mess Around with Jim* on repeat in the car. Her favorite song from the album, which she always sang along with, was "Operator," a heartbreaker about a man futilely tracking down the lost love of his life with the help of a phone operator. It was a tough listen sometimes, this man who wanted to show his ex-love that he had moved on, that he was doing well, though clearly he hadn't and wasn't, but what made the song extra heart-wrenching for Myron even back then, even when the only thing he knew about relationships were schoolyard crushes, was that the love of this man's life had run off with his "best old ex-friend, Ray." Not bad enough she'd broken his heart. She had made it so damned personal.

"We tell no one about this," Greg said. "Jeremy is innocent. We all know that. If the police accuse him or arrest him, his life will be severely damaged. We can't have that."

"Should we destroy the phone?" Emily asked.

"Whoa," Myron said, "let's slow down here."

"We don't destroy it," Greg said, ignoring Myron. "I'll keep it for now. If push comes to shove, I'll say it's mine."

"And if Jeremy is involved somehow?" Myron asked.

Greg looked at him. "You're not his father."

"Yeah, I know."

"No, I don't think you do," Greg said. "If it comes down to it, I'll take the hit for him. This"—he raised the phone—"officially belongs to me. I bought it. They already have my DNA at one of the crime scenes. So I'm the bad guy. I'm the one who did it."

"Either way, we get Jeremy the help he needs," Emily added. "I don't believe he's involved. Not for a second. But if he is, well, maybe something happened to him overseas. He's experienced horrors we can't understand. We get him the best care possible."

"Myron," Greg said with a nod, "we need to know you're with us on this."

Myron looked at Greg, then back at Emily.

"You're not thinking straight," Myron said. "Neither of you."

Greg now turned his focus on Emily. He shook his head and said, "Why did you call him?"

Emily didn't reply.

"We could have handled this on our own. As his parents."

Emily put her hand on Myron's arm. "I thought you'd understand."

"I do," Myron said to her. Then he turned to Greg. "Take a second. Your strength as a coach was your ability to draw up the perfect game plan. You watched game film tirelessly. You read scouting reports. No one prepared for a game like you did."

Greg leaned forward. "It's why I know this will work," he said.

"Will it?" Myron said. He pointed to the phone. "Calls on that phone were made to the Prine Organization."

"Right."

"Ronald Prine was murdered while you were in custody. Are you going to say you shot him from your prison cell?"

Greg turned his gaze toward Emily. Emily gave a helpless shrug.

"I need you to listen to me," Myron said to Greg. "The FBI doesn't know how many people were murdered—and framed—by this serial killer. At least half a dozen, probably a lot more. There was one in Texas, one in New York, one in Las Vegas, one in Nebraska... all over. There were zero connections between all the cases. Zero. Nothing the FBI could put their finger on. Not a clue. The killer could have continued to operate like this for years. They may have never been caught, except one thing blew open the case."

They both waited. Greg reached across the table and took Emily's hand. For the briefest of moments, she looked unhappy about it, even repulsed by his touch, but then it was as though she realized that they were in it together, as Jeremy's parents, the two of them against the suddenly strange interloper named Myron.

"You, Greg. Don't you see? Your DNA ends up at the Callister murder scene. And you are connected to Jordan Kravat."

"How?" Greg asked. "Jordan Kravat was, what, my girlfriend's son's ex-boyfriend. I mean, that's not much of a connection."

"But it isn't a coincidence, Greg. I need you to stop and think about this. Who else is connected to both? Who could have framed you for Cecelia Callister and framed Joey Turant for the murder of Jordan Kravat?"

"What are you trying to say?" Greg asked. "That Jeremy is the connection?"

"No. I'm asking—"

"Because I hadn't seen Jeremy in months before I went to Vegas." He turned to Emily. "You remember. He was on some mission and incommunicado for four months."

"I remember," Emily said.

Greg folded his hands and put them on the table. "Myron, listen to me. We need to buy a little time, so we can sort this out between us—before we tell anyone else, okay? Maybe you're right. Maybe I need to take a step back and do what I do best. Scout. Plan. Get methodical. The three of us."

It was then that Myron's phone rang.

He checked the caller ID.

It was Jeremy.

Everyone at the table froze.

"Why is he calling you?" Emily asked.

Myron didn't wait for Greg or Emily to offer advice on how to handle the call. He hit the answer button.

"Hey," Myron said.

"Hey," Jeremy replied.

There was an awkward silence. Myron switched the phone from his right hand to his left. Emily and Greg stared at him.

"I thought I'd see you at Greg's release."

"I got held up," Jeremy said.

His voice, Myron realized, was probably loud enough for Greg and Emily to make out what he was saying. Myron debated whether that mattered or not and decided to let it go.

"Are you at Win's?" Jeremy asked.

"Not right now, no."

"Oh, sorry. Am I interrupting anything?"

"No, not at all."

"I'm about an hour out," Jeremy said. "Can we meet?"

"Sure."

"I want to explain . . . well, you know. About the discharge and IT job."

"Yeah, okay, sure." Myron felt numb. "Win's place work?"

"That'll be perfect. I'll see you in an hour."

When Myron hung up, Greg said, "What was that all about?"

"He's an hour away. We are going to meet at the Dakota."

Emily pushed her hair back behind her ears. "What was he talking about with the discharge and IT stuff?"

Myron rose, their necks craning up to follow him. "It's not my place to say."

"What the hell does that mean?" Greg asked.

"It means you can ask him yourself."

"Discharge?" Emily said again. "So he's not in the military anymore?"

"He came back to New York when he heard you were being

freed," Myron said to Greg. "That's what he told me a few hours ago. I'm sure he'll reach out to you both."

"Wait," Emily said.

"What?"

"You can't just..." Emily began. She stopped and started again, her voice firmer now. "He's our son, not yours."

"Yeah, you keep telling me that," Myron said, "except when it's convenient."

"What is that supposed to mean?" Emily snapped.

"When he was thirteen and needed to find that bone marrow donor, suddenly I'm his father. Just now, when you found that phone hidden in his room, suddenly I'm his father. Look, I didn't raise him. I get that. I'm just a sperm donor or an accident of biology or whatever. I've been respectful. I've kept my distance. It may not be up to me what my relationship is with Jeremy, but it certainly isn't up to you two either. He called me. He wants to talk to me. I'm going."

Myron started to the door. Emily and Greg followed him.

"Are you going to tell him about the phone?" Greg asked.

"I don't know."

"Don't, okay?" Greg said. "Just trust me on this."

"I don't trust you on anything," Myron said, and then he left.

CHAPTER THIRTY-EIGHT

Y ou stand on the Central Park side of the street and watch
the door.

The Downing apartment is on Fifth Avenue and 80th Street. It offers breathtaking views of Central Park, the Metropolitan Museum of Art, and even the former Payne Whitney residence on 79th Street, which now serves as the Cultural Services Center for the French Embassy.

You wear a black baseball cap. You are "disguised," though again it isn't an elaborate one. It's just enough.

You have your eye on the front door, so you don't miss Myron's exit.

This part isn't exactly rocket science.

The Downing apartment is on the eastern side of Central Park. The Dakota, where Myron often resided with his friend Win, is on the west side of Central Park. This means, of course, that Myron will most likely cut through the park for his walk home.

There is a chance he might take a taxi or Uber, but that seems unlikely.

You were counting on this.

It is getting dark. You see him come out. He says something to the doorman, and then you see him move to the corner and wait for the traffic light. You move through the park's entrance before the light changes. There is no need to follow him.

You know what route he will take.

You've weighed the options. Should you kill him someplace more remote on this route, or is it better to shoot him in a crowded area? Logic would tell you that it would be better to find a more secluded place, though this is Central Park, one of the most popular parks in the world, and secluded spots are something of a rarity. You and he are soon "mid-park," if you will, far from park exits and accessible escape routes. There is also the other issue of catching Myron off guard. When you walk through Central Park's quieter spots—when you feel most alone here—that is when you are most wary. That's just natural survivalist thinking. It isn't that the park isn't safe. It is just that when you hit the darker and less inhabited spots, you naturally look around more.

Your answer?

Whatever route Myron takes through the park—via Belvedere Castle or past the Bethesda Fountain or perhaps south down past Conservatory Water and the Alice in Wonderland sculpture—he will undoubtedly exit out on the west side at 72nd Street near Strawberry Fields. You know this. That is where Win lives. The Strawberry Fields area, a memorial to John Lennon, is popular and happening and always has a busker singing Lennon tunes and a lively crowd.

So it will be ideal.

You decide to hurry to the thicket tunnel opening off the path. Your plan is simple. Myron will walk right past where you are lurking. You will fire several bullets. That will cause panic. There will be screams and pandemonium. The crowd of tourists and dog walkers will scatter. You will scatter with them. You will exit out on Central Park West, just a few yards away. Across the street is the subway entrance for the B and C trains.

You'll be gone before anyone can do anything about it.

You have the gun. You have the plan.

You pick up your pace, find your spot, and wait.

CHAPTER THIRTY-NINE

―――――――

Myron crossed Fifth Avenue and entered Central Park just south of the Met. The walk, he knew from experience, would take fifteen minutes. He headed around the back, past Cleopatra's Needle, an obelisk commissioned by Pharaoh Thutmose II nearly 3,500 years ago. Years later, Cleopatra supposedly used the obelisk in building a Roman temple dedicated to her main squeeze Julius Caesar, ergo the nickname Cleopatra's Needle. It has been in Central Park since 1881.

Myron knew all this—and distracted himself with thoughts about it—because Win was a history buff and loved this park. He hurried on. The fairy-tale Belvedere Castle rose over the Ramble, a seemingly magnificent hybrid of Romanesque and Gothic, though in reality the building was merely a "folly," oft defined as a costly ornamental building with no practical purpose. This one had an observatory, a visitor center, and a weather tower, but the idea of a folly—something created to look like something more impressive—kept weighing on Myron.

He thought about the phone Emily had found. He thought that maybe, in its own way, it was a folly too.

He took out his own phone and called his mother. She answered on the first ring.

"I'm glad you called now," Mom said to him.

"Everything okay?"

"Oh yes, fine. But your father and I just took our edibles, and you know what that means."

Myron closed his eyes. "Yeah, no."

"We haven't taken one in a week."

"Uh-huh."

"They'll hit soon, and then your father will start chasing me around the apartment."

"Hello? This is your son on the phone. Your son doesn't need to hear this."

"Truth be told? I'm not hard for him to catch."

"Mom?"

"Oh stop being such a prude. Be happy for us."

"I am. Really. I can just do without the visuals."

"What's wrong with the visuals?"

No point. "So I guess Dad is feeling better?"

"Yes. Everyone called. Your brother. Your sister—oh, and she's coming in from Seattle tomorrow."

"That'll be nice."

"It will be. And Terese called."

Myron started south along the path.

"She's growing on me, Myron. I like her a lot."

"I'm glad."

"She's substantial."

"She is."

"You know I had worries."

He did. Terese can't have kids. His parents already had three grandchildren—his brother Brad's son Mickey being the oldest—but Mom and Dad knew that Myron had always wanted children too.

His phone beeped that another call was incoming. He checked the caller ID and saw that it was PT.

"Mom, I have to take this, okay?"

Mom picked up on the tone of his voice. "Go," she said quickly. She hung up before he did.

"PT?"

The gruff voice did not sound happy. "Anything you need to tell me?"

"Like?"

"Like we found a receipt for a burner phone bought at a Walmart in Doylestown. Do you know where Doylestown is?"

Doylestown was, Myron knew, an hour north of Philadelphia.

"Yes."

"Oh good. This particular burner phone called the Prine Organization and made threats. With me so far?"

Myron did not like where this was going. "I am."

"Guess what we just did, Myron?"

"You pinged the burner phone?"

"We did more than that. We woke up the phone and then geographically pinpointed the location through triangulation using the nine-one-one and one-one-two emergency beacon provisions on the network."

"Didn't know you were so up on your techno."

"I'm not," PT said. "I'm reading verbatim from a report sitting on my desk. Do I need to explain the rest?"

"Give me an hour," Myron said.

"You're joking, right?"

"The phone is at Emily Downing's apartment. I know."

"So you're going to lie to me?"

"I'm not lying—"

"The phone isn't at the apartment anymore," PT said. "And neither are you."

"What?"

"The phone is in the middle of Central Park. And guess what? We've also geographically pinpointed your phone, so we know that you're crossing the park with it."

Myron's eyes widened. He did not break stride. He did not look behind him.

"You have my exact location?"

"It's on my screen. You're traveling southwest through Central Park."

Myron swallowed. "And the burner phone?"

"You don't know?"

"I don't know."

"Are you telling me you don't have it on you?"

"I don't."

"Shit."

"How precise are the locations?"

"A hundred meters maybe."

So someone was following him. Only two possibilities here. Greg or Emily.

"Look, we got agents on the way," PT said. "It shouldn't take long. Tell me about the phone."

Myron debated a subtle turn-and-look to see if he was being followed. But then what? Suppose it was Greg. What was the plan here? Myron reached the walkway up to Strawberry Fields. Through the trees up ahead, he could make out the fortresslike exterior of the Dakota. Almost there. This was good. He would hurry up the path. He would get to the end of it and duck behind a tree. Then he could wait and see who was following him.

"Myron?" PT said. "What's with the phone?"

"It's a long story."

Myron walk-ran up the path, glancing behind him as he did.
There was a family of four. Two parents and two girls who looked to
be twins. There was a tour group of maybe thirty behind them being
led by a woman holding up a French flag so she was easy to follow.

No Greg. No Emily.

On the bench up ahead, Myron spotted a bearded busker with
a guitar and microphone and amp, and QR codes so you could tip
him by Venmo or Zelle. Street musicians had gone high tech too.
He sang about a banker who never wore a mac in the pouring rain,
which he found very strange. Great lyrics until you really thought
about them. Myron rushed past him. There was a large group of
people lined up to take photos with the "Imagine" mosaic. Dave, the
button vendor Win sometimes chatted up who also scheduled the
Strawberry Fields buskers/musicians, was gone from his usual spot.
That's where Myron veered off the path. He found a thick tree and
hid behind it.

He looked out. No Greg. No Emily.

"Where's the phone now?" Myron asked PT.

Before PT could answer, Myron's phone buzzed again. It was a
text from Esperanza in full caps. Esperanza never uses caps.

CALL ME NOW!!!!

Myron didn't bother saying goodbye to PT. He just hung up and
hit Esperanza's line.

"What's up?"

"Oh shit, you were right."

"What?"

"That hidden bank account," Esperanza said. "The one Greg and
Grace used for the house in Pine Bush. You told me to look into it."

"And?"

"They got a credit card issued in the name of Parker Stalworth. Someone using that card rented a car in Horsham, Pennsylvania, two days ago."

Horsham, Myron thought. Not far from Doylestown or Philadelphia.

It was suddenly all coming together.

"How do we trace this down?" Myron asked.

"Already done," Esperanza said. "A screenshot from the rental-car surveillance video is coming to both of us now. Check your texts."

Myron heard the buzz from the incoming photo. He glanced again down the path. No Greg. No Emily. No one he knew. Then he put the phone on speaker and looked down at the screen. The screenshot was too small to see. He tapped the photo to enlarge the image. It took a few moments to load.

The image, like all CCTV surveillance images, was shot from above. Myron saw the back of the rental-car employee's head. The person renting the car wore a black baseball cap and kept their face down.

But Myron knew who it was. Suddenly all the pieces fell into place.

Esperanza said, "Myron, is that—?"

At that same moment, Myron sensed more than heard or even felt it:

Someone had sneaked up behind him.

He didn't hesitate. He spun to his right, his arm coming up, deflecting the gun mere inches from the back of his head. In that split second—less than a second, less than a tenth of a second maybe—Myron spotted the same black baseball cap.

The gun fired.

The bullet hit Myron.

And Myron went down.

CHAPTER FORTY

From your spot by the tunnel opening, you watch Myron hurry up the path.

Why so fast? you wonder.

Strawberry Fields is bustling. Tour groups huddle up while guides speak in a variety of tongues. The pedicabs—think a mix of bicycle and rickshaw—are lined up on the seemingly always-closed-to-cars 72nd Street ramp. The drivers hustle for the tourist trade, cajoling pedestrians with smiles and maps and photographs of the park wonders they would encounter should the driver be hired. Several horse and carriages await new riders. The horses, you realize, will freak out when they hear gunfire.

That's good. It will cause more chaos.

Myron Bolitar walks past the Imagine mosaic.

So close.

You pull down the bill of your cap, more out of habit than for anything approaching security. You are hiding at the mouth of a tunnel made from twigs and branches. Plenty of foot traffic passes you. Dog walkers stroll by for their pets' nightly relief.

Myron Bolitar has his phone pressed against his ear.

Does that matter—that he might be talking to someone on the phone when you shoot him?

You can't see how.

Your plan is not complicated. He walks by. You put the barrel of the gun against his head. You pull the trigger.

Myron is thirty yards away from you.

You now don a surgical mask. Better safe than sorry. They are rarer today—surgical masks—but far from uncommon, a hangover from the Covid era.

You are already wearing gloves, of course.

Twenty yards away.

You take out the Ruger LCR. You keep your arm at your side, your dark pants camouflaging your black gun.

Fifteen yards.

You snake your finger onto the trigger.

Seconds away now.

You feel the rush start coursing through you. The anticipation. No, this part isn't as satisfying as the actual kill. That's the sweetest—the moment the eyes close and the life leaves the body. But this, the fore-play of murder, is still a heady concoction.

And then, without warning, Myron deviates from the path.

What the . . . ?

He slides quickly behind a tree and presses his back up against it.

Why, you wonder, would he do that?

Is he . . . hiding?

So it seems.

Does he know you're here, waiting?

You can't see how. You watch now as Myron turns his head left and right. Then he cautiously leans out just a little, just enough to look out.

You duck.

But he isn't looking in your direction.

He is looking back down the path.

As if he knows you are coming for him. Except, of course, he's looking in the wrong direction.

Did that make sense?

He's still on his phone.

Who is he talking to?

That doesn't matter.

You don't know what's going on or why Myron is hiding behind the tree. You debate your next move. Should you wait for him to start walking this way again?

No.

You can't risk that. You must act and act now. Suppose Myron is being followed. Or suppose he doubles back in the opposite direction, back toward Emily's apartment. You'll be out of position. You may lose him entirely. Your plan will be jeopardized.

Go! you tell yourself.

So you do.

You abandon the safety of the tunnel entrance and hurry toward him. His back is still turned. He keeps glancing in the direction of the Imagine mosaic while talking on the phone. That's good. He's distracted. He isn't looking toward you.

You're only a few yards away when Myron suddenly takes the phone away from his ear.

He looks at something on the phone's screen.

A lot of things happen at once now.

You raise the gun to shoot him in the head.

You also see what he's looking at on his phone. When you do, you freeze.

It's you.

How the . . . ?

You stay frozen. But not for long. Barely a second. You push away the panic and snap out of it. You put the muzzle of the gun up to the back of his skull.

You start to pull the trigger—and as you do, Myron spins around and knocks your arm.

But it's too late for him. The bullet fires.

And his blood splashes on your face.

CHAPTER FORTY-ONE

M yron dropped to his knees first. Then he fell forward onto his hands.

Blood poured off him. Myron stared down and watched it pool on the pavement below him. There were screams and shouts and everything seemed to be in motion.

Myron blinked and felt the cold.

He realized that he had been hit—that he was heading into a state of shock.

Move, he told himself. *Move or die.*

There was no plan, no conscious contemplation beyond the simple idea of not staying still. He knew that he'd been hit and hit badly. The pain came at him in a roar and spread. It felt as though a giant animal had taken a huge bite out of his neck. From his hands and knees, he tried to get up. No go. He pushed instead off one leg, a wounded sprinter in the blocks.

"We aren't bulletproof..."

Hadn't Win said that just the other day?

Apropos.

Still, he managed to lurch forward a foot at a time.

CHAPTER FORTY-TWO

Y ou are stunned but also feel delirious joy.

He surprised you, Myron Bolitar that is, when he swung his arm and threw off your aim.

Good for him.

Still, the bullet landed in the cusp between his neck and his collarbone. Blood gushes, splashing you. You wonder whether you hit an artery.

Will he simply bleed out?

You wanted chaos and you got it. You hear screams. You see people rush for the park's exit on the west side. You swim with the tide of people, another salmon heading upstream.

But then you remember: He had your photo on his phone.

Somehow Myron has put this together.

You can't just wound him. You have to make sure he's dead.

There is no time for you to think it all through. If you did, if you had a few more seconds, you'd probably realize that someone must have sent him that picture, that Myron never works in a vacuum, that if Myron has put it together, others, like Win, will know too.

But right now, you don't have time for nuance.

You need to kill him. No matter what. If this is the end for you, if this is your goodbye, it will be his too.

Myron is badly wounded. He crawls away from you like a crab with no equilibrium. The stream of people heads in the other direction, getting in your way. You debate just firing, but your weapon is a six-shooter. No reason to waste the bullets. When you lose sight of Myron for a moment, panic sets in. You fight harder now, pushing past the crowd.

And there he is, still crawling by the benches. He starts to rise up a little.

You aim and fire. You miss. You aim and fire again.

You hit him in the back.

Myron's body jerks. He falls hard now.

CHAPTER FORTY-THREE

A fter the first bullet hit him, Myron tried to straighten up, but the pain made his head reel in protest. He stayed low, more slithering than running. He stumbled to the left. His head screamed in protest. He had no balance, no stability.

People ran by him, bumped into him, pinballed him to and fro. Everyone was screaming. Myron tried to keep moving away from the general direction of the shooter. He heard another gunshot. Myron blinked hard, felt the blood pouring off him. He kept stumbling ahead. Another shot rang out.

A hot searing pain entered the small of his back.

The impact knocked Myron forward, his arms splayed. His spine bent backward as the air rushed out of his lungs. He couldn't breathe. His cheek landed hard on the corner of a bench.

Blood filled his mouth. Not from the fall. Not from banging his cheek on the bench.

The blood was coming up from his chest into his throat.

Drowning him.

Myron started to feel the darkness on the edges moving in. He was losing consciousness.

Hang on, he told himself.

But his body wouldn't listen. Even his primitive survival instinct had faded away, grown distant. He rolled away, rolled under the bench. The darkness was starting to swim in front of his eyes now. Something inside of him was shutting down.

He wondered whether he was dying.

He lay now on his side, his cheek on the pavement. He couldn't move. He could barely care. He could still see feet running by, but he couldn't hear the screams anymore. The only sound now was a high-pitched whirring in his head. Why was that? Why couldn't he hear anymore?

It felt as if some powerful force was dragging him down into the cold, into the black.

Two feet appeared in front of him. They stopped and bent down.

The face from the screenshot, complete with the black baseball cap, came into view and stared right at him.

It was Grace Konners.

His phone was still in his hand. She reached for it and pried it out of his weak grip with ease. Once she had taken possession of it, Grace pointed her gun at the center of his face. Myron couldn't move. He could only look on helplessly. He saw the gleam in her eye, the way her lips curled into a smile.

He had found the killer. Too late. But he had found her.

Myron tried to do something in the second of life he had left. A final gesture. A way of ending it all with resistance or bravery or something. But his body wouldn't obey. His gaze locked on the gun, only the gun.

Time slowed down.

Then the rest happened all at once:

A male voice shouted, "No!"

Grace pulled the trigger.

A man's hand landed on the barrel of the gun, the palm covering the muzzle.

The voice and the hand belonged to Jeremy.

Myron wanted to wave him away, to tell his son that it was too late, to let go of the gun and move to safety.

The gun fired.

Myron heard Jeremy scream in pain.

No...

Myron wanted to cry out, wanted to help, wanted to do anything.

He couldn't move. He felt cold, frozen. The high-pitched whirring became a death hum in his head.

Grace aimed her gun again. But not at Myron.

At Jeremy.

No...

Two shots rang out. The bullets didn't hit Myron. They didn't hit Jeremy either.

They hit Grace.

She pirouetted to her left, held herself up for a moment, and then went down like a marionette with her strings cut. And when she did go down, Myron could see someone standing on the other side of the "Imagine" mosaic.

Greg Downing.

He stood with a stunned look on his face, still pointing the gun at the spot where Grace had been standing.

Myron couldn't hang on any longer. He felt his hands slide down whatever internal rope he'd been gripping. His eyes rolled back into his head.

"Myron?"

It was Win.

"I'm here," Win said, and Myron could hear the unfamiliar panic in his friend's voice. "Hold on, Myron. Stay with me."

But Myron couldn't.

"Myron? Myron, stay with me."

He wanted to listen. He really did. But he was plunging into that humming void now, and there was only blackness.

CHAPTER FORTY-FOUR

WIN

M yron?" I say again, hearing the alien pleading in my tone. "Myron, stay with me."

But he isn't. I can see that now. His skin is gray, his lips already blue. Blood bubbles up and pours freely from his neck. I clamp my hand over the spot, apply pressure. I turn to a man who is standing next to me, filming this.

"Call 911," I say in my most commanding voice. This is what you do. You don't just yell out randomly for someone to make the call. Too many people will stand around and assume someone else will do it. You assign someone the task and make sure they act on it. "Call now."

The man nods and starts to dial. I don't know whether it matters because I imagine someone has already notified the authorities. Chaos reigns. I keep my hand over the gushing wound. Myron's blood is trickling through my fingers.

He is losing too much blood.

"Hang on," I tell Myron, the tone sounding faraway and unfamiliar in my own ears. He isn't conscious anyway. He can't hear me.

I can see several things going on at the same time in my periphery. Grace Konners is on the ground. She is dead. Her eyes are open and unblinking. Her blood slowly leaks toward the Imagine mosaic. Greg Downing, the one who shot her, sprints toward Jeremy. Jeremy's complexion, like his biological father's, is ashen. Jeremy is wisely holding up his bloody stump of a hand above his head, like it's a torch, staring at it as though surprised it's there. Greg rips off his coat and wraps it around the wound.

I don't know how long we all stay there.

At one point a woman kneels next to me. She is maybe fifty years old with reddish hair tied back in a ponytail. "I'm a doctor," she tells me. "Keep applying pressure." I will later learn that her name is Dodi Meyer, and that she works in the Emergency Room at New York-Presbyterian. She rolls Myron onto his back. I don't dare move my hand from his neck until the paramedics arrive and relieve me.

I pull my hand away then and climb into the ambulance with him. I stare down at my hands as the ambulance speeds away. My hands are drenched in Myron's blood. Later, I will wonder when I cleaned off the blood, because as many times as I have replayed that night in my head, I have no recollection of doing so.

And yes, that's an odd thing to be wondering about.

Myron dies twice. Once in the ambulance on the way to the hospital. Once again while on the surgeon's table. We oft hear how tough humans are, how we are built for survival, but it never fails to startle me how fragile and subject to the whims of fate we end up being. Here is Myron Bolitar, one of humanity's best specimens on so many levels, an empathetic soul from hardy stock who has also been imbued with remarkable physical strength and intelligence. And yet. And yet despite doing everything right here, doing the moral thing, the courageous thing, the wise and careful thing, all it takes is a madwoman with a readily available weapon to snuff out such a force. We like to think the universe is just or orderly, but we all know that it is not. It is cruel and random. We think that we have evolved as a species, that it is the survival of the fittest, but in fact, the best of us, the strongest of us, the most intelligent and brave, were sent to battle centuries ago and died no matter how, like Myron, brave and skilled they were, while the feeble and cowardly stayed home and reproduced. That's who we are. The byproduct of the feeble and weak. The fecal wreckage, if you will, of history. We want to believe that there is an ethical center to our being, that our world is peaceful and kind, and yet anyone who has seen even five minutes of a wildlife documentary is reminded that we must kill to survive. All of us. That's the world whatever higher being you believe in created—a world of kill or die. No one gets a pass on that, including you smug vegans, who plow fields and in doing so sacrifice living creatures so that you too may survive.

This isn't a pleasant realization, but do you want pleasantries or truth?

And now, as I watch the life force drain from the man I care about most in this world, I beg to a higher being that I don't believe in and I know isn't listening, as many of you sit there and tell me this is part of some master plan.

Imagine being that naïve.

You want to sleep at night, so you tell yourselves fairy tales. Like a child.

But I digress.

Myron is in the hospital. He still has trouble communicating.

That is why, with your permission, I am finishing this story for him.

His road back will be a long, arduous one. There are few guarantees. A full recovery, whatever that might look like, seems unlikely. A full month after the shooting, when he's no longer comatose and in the ICU, Myron is moved into a private corner room in the Milstein Building at New York-Presbyterian. I arrange this via a sizable donation. A cot is placed in the corner near the window. Terese sleeps there. She has taken a leave. She rarely leaves his side.

I won't go into the details of his injuries because I don't see the point. Myron spends most of his time in a fog of pain and medications and procedures. It is hard to know what he comprehends and what he doesn't. I try to explain to him what I can. It is hard for him to focus for long stretches. I repeat myself because I fear that he either forgets or the material doesn't quite stick.

So let me answer the questions that I can. I have told this to Myron too, though I am condensing dozens of conversations with him into this summary for you:

First off, Myron's biggest concern: Jeremy.

As soon as the first bullet hit Myron, Esperanza realized that something was very wrong. She hit my speed dial, patching me into the line as a three-way. Oddly enough, I was already up and moving. I had heard the shot and the ensuing pandemonium from my apartment across the street. I didn't know Myron was the victim, but perhaps something instinctive inside of me realized that it was a strong possibility. I knew that Myron should be crossing the park around that time to see Jeremy, who was seated next to me when Esperanza called.

I reacted fast. Jeremy, having perhaps inherited some of his father's gifts, reacted faster.

It was Jeremy, not me, who arrived on the scene first. Youth, I suppose. I can run, but Jeremy shot past me with ease. Seemingly with zero concern for his own safety, Jeremy acted the hero that he obviously is. He dove straight for Grace's gun—and he paid for it when Grace pulled the trigger.

Jeremy lost the ring finger and pinkie on his right hand.

They are working on some kind of prosthetic device for him down at Walter Reed. No, Jeremy was not discharged three years ago, and no, he did not work in IT at Dillard's. As Myron had theorized—perhaps more out of hope than cold analysis—the discharge, the name change, and the IT job were all part of Jeremy's elaborate cover. He did indeed work clandestinely to keep this country safe. I can't say more because I don't know more.

It is, in the words of Jeremy, classified.

Second: The Setup Serial Killer.

According to the official FBI statements, the investigation remains ongoing. According to PT, the "unofficial official" conclusion is that Grace Konners was that rare (though not completely unknown) bird known as the female serial killer. The FBI has so far tied her to six murders and subsequent frame-ups, but there are at least three other cases the FBI is confident will circle back to her.

PT believes—and I concur—that there are probably more, and that law enforcement, despite its best efforts, may never know how many victims. Awful, I know. I think about that—that there are innocent people in prison for murder who will most likely remain there.

What makes this investigation even more unwieldy for the FBI is that dozens, perhaps hundreds, of convicted killers now claim that they, too, were framed by Grace Konners. She is their get-out-of-jail-free card. They are demanding that their own verdicts be overturned. You can imagine the headache, can't you? Almost all are lying, of course, but the FBI cannot afford to make a mistake. The task of looking into the claims is a time-consuming resource suck, overwhelming even the most seasoned of investigators.

Three: Why was Greg Downing's DNA at the Callister scene?

There are two schools of thought here. The main one, the one the FBI believes is most likely, is that like most serial killers (or addicts of any kind), Grace Konners needed a stronger dopamine hit as time went on. In short, she wanted to both "up her game," if you will, and rid herself of the one person in the world who could stop her.

Greg Downing.

Greg also controlled their wealth, which would be hers and hers alone if he were to end up in prison. She would be off the hook for what she'd done, able to start completely anew. And talk about a psychotic's rush— imagine being able to not only kill a former supermodel but frame your own partner for the crime.

Myron makes a face when I tell him this part. I don't know if I buy it completely either, but it seems close.

Four: How did it all start?

I think some of this is hindsight being twenty-twenty, but I will tell you what the FBI believes. When they investigated Grace Konners's past, they found a lot of troubling signs. As a child, she had been abused by a violent uncle. Pets and animals in her neighborhood went missing. Both Spark and Bo, her sons, spoke of physical trauma at her hands and their belief that their father, who died after purportedly falling in the shower, may have met a more devious end at the hands of their mother.

After their father's death, Grace would go into her sons' beds at night. The less said about that, I think, the better.

In terms of the chronology, the first Setup Serial killing victim was Jordan Kravat. Grace had originally chosen to kill Kravat, not because she was a budding serial killer but for the most basic of reasons—Kravat was tormenting and destroying the life of her son. But somewhere along the way—perhaps before she killed, perhaps seeing an opportunity after— she realized that she could kill two birds with one stone by murdering one nemesis (Jordan Kravat) and framing the other (Joey Turant).

Grace's children back this theory, by the way. Bo Storm has admitted that the Vegas district attorney did not pressure or threaten him. His mother told him that she had killed Jordan Kravat to protect him, and that now she needed him to point the finger at Joey the Toe.

Finger, toe. I made a funny.

Anyway, the FBI behavioral heavies believe that Jordan Kravat was the Patient Zero that led to the outbreak known as The Setup Serial Killer.

Next question (I lost count—what number is this?): How did it end?

You probably know this, but I'll spell it out: Greg shot and killed Grace. When Myron left Emily's to confront Jeremy, his two parents—that is, Greg and Emily—worried that Myron might have too strong a bout of ethics and report the found phone to the FBI. For that reason, Greg decided to go and try to join them. He had the burner phone in his pocket, which was why PT geolocated it as being near Myron in the park. Greg heard the gunshots, he ran toward the sound . . .

. . . and when he saw Grace turn the gun on his son . . .

Kaboom.

I wonder though: If Greg had run up and seen Grace about to shoot Myron again, would he have shot her?

Hmm.

I also wonder: Did Greg, in fact, arrive a few seconds earlier? Did he just choose not to shoot until his own son was in jeopardy?

Answers: I don't have any, ergo my use of the term "wonder."

Last question: What about Greg Downing? Surely, he must have known the truth.

Once again, there is more than one school of thought.

The first is that Greg didn't know at all. The couple had a strange relationship, according to Greg. He told the authorities that he and Grace often traveled separately and lived apart for months at a time. There were only—and I realize "only" in this sentence is extraordinarily relative—six definitive kill scenes over the course of five years. That is a little more than one per year. How hard would it be to keep that secret from your partner? There are many instances where a male serial killer has kept his thirst for death from a partner. Most recently, the wife of Rex Heuermann the

Long Island killer has claimed no knowledge of her husband's barbaric crimes. Most of us accept that she is being truthful. Might it be sexism to think that Grace Konners wouldn't be able to keep all of this from her boyfriend?

Good question.

The second school of thought is that Greg did suspect what was happening, or perhaps Grace worried that he was getting too close to the truth. That, of course, would contribute to her decision to plant his DNA at the Callister murder scene.

It adds up, I suppose.

There may be holes, I say to Myron (and by extension, you), but if so, they seem small to me. I have never seen a murder case that didn't have at least a few discrepancies. If a case is too solid, well, haven't we all just learned a valuable lesson about murders that seem too open and shut?

Either way, I tell Myron, it is over. We may learn a few more things, like how the victims were found or chosen or if there were additional motives. But I don't see how that will change things in a material way. The FBI seems more interested in putting out the fires this murder spree created rather than adding fuel to them. Greg is traveling again, having purchased a ticket to Cairns, up by the Great Barrier Reef in Australia. There are rumors he may get lured back to coach the New York Knicks, but for now, he is staying off the grid.

So that's the end.

I have compressed months of personal debriefings with Myron into those above few pages. You probably guessed most of it. I hope that I was able to scratch whatever last itch remained.

I give Myron this summary too when he is well enough. He stays silent throughout, which is something I'm still not used to. Myron is normally a talker. He likes to interject, probe, distract, interrogate, cajole, agitate.

But talking exhausts him now. Today he just sits up in bed and listens without uttering a word.

When I finish, when I say to him, as I have above to you fine people, "So that's the end," Myron speaks up for the first time:

"No it isn't."

CHAPTER FORTY-FIVE

I t is six weeks later.

Myron sits alone in the dark in room 982 at the Royal Mansour hotel in Marrakech. Yes, in Morocco. I am next door, in a connecting room with Terese. If Myron needs me, I can be with him in seconds. Cameras and audio are in place. Myron's health is somewhat better, but nowhere near a hundred percent. Or even fifty percent. We could have put this off a bit longer—Myron's doctor pretty much insisted upon it—but I know that doing so was robbing Myron of sleep. I detest the word "closure," but there is little doubt that for Myron to heal, he will need it.

My man watching the elevator sends me and Myron a one-word text:

HERE

Terese reads the text over my shoulder. "I don't like this."

"He's safe," I tell her.

She doesn't seem satisfied with that. I understand.

Room 982 has been booked for the last six nights under the name Arthur Caldwell. That's not his real name. He waves his key card in front of the lock and opens the door. The lights are out. He enters and closes the door behind him. He hits the light switch and walks into the hotel room.

He pulls up short when he sees Myron.

"Hey, Greg."

Greg Downing startles for a second but to give him credit, only for a second. "Is there any point in asking how you found me?"

It wasn't all that difficult, I think. When the FBI was done with him, Greg started his journey, as I mentioned before, in Cairns, Australia. I figured that Greg would want to change his identity as soon as possible. My people found three suppliers of fake identities working in Cairns. I offered a quarter million dollars to the first one who could tell me Greg's new identity. One came forward immediately, took my cash, and gave me copies of all the paperwork on Arthur Caldwell.

There is no honor amongst thieves.

"You look thin," Greg says.

That is an understatement. Myron has lost thirty pounds. His cheeks are sunken. There are times it is hard for even me to look straight at him and not wince.

When Myron does not reply, Greg asks, "So what do you want?"

"Did you know Grace planned to kill me?"

"Would you believe me if I said no?"

"I might," Myron says. "I think she might have gone rogue there."

"She was a killer, Myron."

"So are you."

Greg smiles. "Not like her though."

"Are you going to tell me about it?"

Greg takes a seat on the corner of the bed. "I don't have any choice really, do I? I assume Win is nearby. You wouldn't have come without him."

Myron does not reply.

"I don't want to spend my life looking over my shoulder," Greg says, crossing his legs, "so let's get on with this, shall we? For starters, where did I go wrong?"

"Small things," Myron says.

"Such as?"

"Grace killing Ronald Prine, for one. If Grace was the one who planted your DNA at the Callister murder scene to frame you, why would she be dumb enough to kill Prine while you were behind bars and couldn't have done? That would only guarantee your release."

"Because she's crazy?" Greg tries.

Myron frowns. "Are we going to play that game?"

"Old habit, I guess. What else?"

"Your explanation for how the killer planted your DNA at the Callister scene."

"You mean the pickup basketball game? I thought that was pretty inspired."

"It was," Myron admits, "but only on the surface. Some guy hits you in the nose during a game. You bleed. They collect your blood and leave it at the scene."

"I got that idea from a novel, actually. Or maybe a short story."

"Either way, we checked it out. No one at the Wallkill remembers you or a broken nose. The broken nose? That didn't bother me. But no one remembered *you*, Greg. That's what struck me. Win didn't pick up on it. No one else would. But you and I . . ."

Greg nods. "You're right. Someone would notice."

"Greg Downing in a pickup game? I don't care how you disguised yourself or dialed it back."

"A real hoopster would have spotted me," Greg says. "Dumb on my part."

"Another thing," Myron says.

He grins. "You sound like Columbo. What?"

"I saw you and Grace together at your house in Pine Bush. Briefly, I admit. And it could have been an act, but I don't think so. I think you genuinely loved her."

"I did." His eyes close for a moment, his voice softer now. "I still do."

"You even said it to me: Is it too corny to call her your soulmate?"

"I meant that."

"I believe you. It's why all these stories about you not knowing because you lived apart or weren't that close—"

"That was a lie, yes."

Greg looks up at Myron. This time there is no falling back to their youthful days on the court. It is just two men, grown men, men physically past their prime, who fate has forced into too many collisions.

"Have you ever been in love like that, Myron?"

"I like to think I am now."

"No, no. You're in love and you're married and that's all great. But you two aren't together all the time. You have separate lives. That's probably smart. Healthy. It's how I always felt before Grace. But—and yeah, I know how corny this will sound—I remember lying in bed with her one night. I was holding her from behind. My arm was wrapped around her waist. I could feel her heart beating and suddenly my heart started beating the same as her. Involuntarily. They matched up, and I swear that never stopped. It was like our two hearts had become one."

"Wow," Myron says.

"I mean every word."

"And yet you killed her."

"I had no choice."

"Because she was going to kill Jeremy."

"Yes." He shakes his head. "I sacrificed the woman I loved for our son."

"Oh, *our* son," Myron repeats. "You're not going to play that card with me now, are you?"

"I'm going to play every card I have," Greg says. "But oddly, I think my best play is to let you see the truth."

"It all went wrong with the Callisters, didn't it?"

Greg shakes his head. "It all went wrong way before that, when Grace came to that Bucks–Suns game in Phoenix," he says. "That's how the world works, isn't it? Everything is a chemical reaction. What are the odds you and I would meet, compete, fall for the same girl, end up ripping each other's lives to shreds? We were like two ordinary compounds that became toxic when combined. It's the same thing here with Grace, except much more explosive. There are a lot of what-ifs in life. What if I hadn't hired Spark as an assistant coach, for example? I almost didn't. I would have never met Grace, and if you think you and I were combustible when we collided . . ."

"What happened, Greg?"

He shrugs. "I fell in love. That's all it was at first. The same as I said to you—I was burned out. I wanted to leave the game, run away with Grace, see the world with her. But first, her son needed help."

"Bo."

"You know the whole sordid story. Jordan Kravat got him strung out on drugs, pimped him out. I mean, that guy was killing Bo a day at a time. Grace and I talked it out. We couldn't find a way to extract Bo from the situation. And then suddenly Grace suggested the obvious and yet forbidden."

"Killing Jordan Kravat."

Greg nods. "And once the idea was spoken out loud, once we used the word 'murder' . . . it's like we crossed a line and there was no going back. I started planning like, well, for a big playoff game. Scouting. Sizing up the opposition. Trying to guess what they might or might not do. That's when I came up with the idea of framing Jordan's mob boss."

"Joey the Toe."

"Right. We would eliminate our biggest threat and it would divert

attention. Kravat, Turant. These were bad people, Myron. This felt like
our only way."

"So that was your first team kill?"

"Yes."

"And what, you liked it?"

He chuckles. "More than that. Much more. How do I explain this?"

"Let me help you. You're both psychopaths. One psychopath walking down the road of life alone, well, that's bad. But when the two of you—
what's the term you used?—collided . . ."

"That's not far off," Greg says. "It was, well, it was a high, sure. A rush
like no other. But it was more than that. It was like we both went through
a complete transformation. We were heightened in every way. Food tasted
better. Sex was more intense. We experienced something mere mortals
could never comprehend."

"So cutting to the chase," Myron says, "you went on killing."

"Yes."

"And framing people."

"Yes."

"As a team. The two of you working together."

He nods. "Grace was the more violent of us. She loved to watch the
life force leave the person's face. Ending another human being's life—she
described it as the closest thing to being a god. I got that, but I was more
the plotter. I loved working on the frame-up, the slow burn of sending
someone to prison for a crime they didn't commit. But we both did both. I
killed some, she killed some. I did most of the planning, but she contrib-
uted a lot. We were a team in every sense of the word. My point is, many of
us have the potential to be killers, but once Grace and I tried it—"

"Yeah, Greg, I think I get it. You just went on killing."

"Yes."

"How many, Greg?"

"More than they know. That's all I'll say for now."

Myron can see that it won't pay to pursue that line of questioning right now. "You planned carefully."

"Yes."

"You always made sure someone else took the fall. You took your time. There was pretty much zero chance you'd get caught, until you messed up with the Callisters. I don't get it. Why go after someone you knew, even tangentially?"

"To up the game, I suppose. I also liked the idea of taking down Cecelia's scuzzy husband, Lou Himble. He stole a lot of people's life savings, you know. I don't want to make it sound like we were Robin Hoods. For the most part, we chose our victims coldly—how easy they would be to kill and did they have someone in their life who would want them dead."

"To make the frame work?"

"Yes. We moved around a lot. We often worked more than one victim at a time, and more often than not, we aborted when we realized that we wouldn't be able to pull off both the kill and the frame."

"So you had no connection to the victims?"

"None. Until Cecelia. But she was so ripe for it, what with her testifying against her husband. Oh, and I knew Cecelia's first husband."

"Ben Staples."

"Yeah, I liked Ben." Greg puts his hands on his knees and takes a moment. He lowers his voice because he wants Myron's full attention. "You see, Myron, Cecelia screwed Ben over good. She got pregnant by another man. Can you imagine a wife doing anything worse to her husband?"

Greg stops now and grins at Myron.

"Subtle," Myron says.

"I'm not trying to be subtle."

"And Cecelia didn't cheat. She was raped."

Greg shrugs. "I didn't know that."

"So you planned on killing her and pinning it on her husband."

"Yes. Except Cecelia's son Clay showed up. He was supposed to be on a one-week cruise in the Caribbean, but he ended up getting food poisoning, so he came home two days early." Greg swallows, looks off. "He walked in on Grace and me killing his mother. A fight ensued. I killed them both."

"And left your DNA behind."

"No choice," he says, "but I wasn't too worried. I was dead, remember? That's part of why I faked my death. To stay under the radar. So if people maybe 'thought' they saw someone who looked like Greg Downing, well, he was dead. It would go nowhere. And then I figured, well, even if they somehow track the DNA of a dead man, I'm hidden under another identity. There is no way they're going to find me on my little farm in Pine Bush." He leaned forward. "How did you find me?"

"The bank account in North Carolina."

"Ah."

"Still," Myron says, "you're a planner."

"I am."

"So you came up with a scheme in the event you got caught."

Greg smiles again. "You're good at this."

"No, not really. But I can get in your head a bit."

"It is what made you a tough competitor on the court."

"Right after I found you in Pine Bush," Myron continues, "you were arrested. Your DNA was at the murder scene. You'd be convicted. You knew all this. So your only play was to do what you'd always done—pin it on someone else. Grace called the FBI pretending to be an anonymous source. She pointed to the other killings. She said it was all the work of a serial killer who framed innocent people—and that you were the killer's latest mark. Grace even went so far as to kill Ronald Prine because then the FBI would know for sure that you, sitting in a jail cell, couldn't be the serial killer."

"It worked."

"Except Grace wasn't as good at planning as you."

"No, that was my forte."

"She decided to set up Jeremy for all of it. She'd make him out to be the serial killer."

"Stupid."

"She planted the phone in his room."

"Grace probably thought I'd approve."

Myron makes a face. "She thought you'd approve of framing your own son?"

"Grace found out that Jeremy wasn't really mine, Myron."

Greg gives Myron that smile again and waits for Myron to take the bait. When Myron doesn't, Greg continues. "Grace probably saw what she was doing as poetic justice. In her eyes, Jeremy was the evil spawn of my cheating enemy. Why not kill that enemy and pin it on his evil spawn?"

The two men sit there for a long time. Neither speaks. The silence is strangely comfortable. Both know that they've reached the endgame, but neither feels the need to rush it.

Finally, Greg slaps his thighs with both hands and says, "So now you know."

"Now I know."

"You also know me," Greg says. "You know me like no one else does."

"Meaning?"

"You know that I'm no longer a danger."

This seems to reach Myron, but he still asks, "How do I know that?"

"Because we both get love and loss."

Myron stays silent.

"Do you know what the problem is when two hearts become one?" Greg asks.

Myron shakes his head. Greg stands up and crosses the room.

"It means when one of you dies, the other does too. Whatever was in me that made me kill—it's gone. We both know that."

He moves to the window and looks out.

"So you think I can just let this go?" Myron asks.

"You?" Greg just stares out the window. Then he says, "I don't think so."

Myron waits. Greg still has his back to him.

"We've done a lot of damage to one another," Greg says. "Grace thought that whatever was broken inside of me was broken by you that night you were with Emily."

"Greg?"

"What?"

"You don't get to put that on me," Myron says.

"Maybe you're right."

Then Greg takes two steps back from the window.

"Greg?"

"It's okay."

"What's okay?"

"It ends now."

"Greg?"

But he doesn't listen. Greg Downing gives Myron one last smile before turning back to the window. Then he runs those two steps and hurls himself against the glass. Myron tries to rise to stop him, but his brittle bones scream out in protest. There is nothing he can do anyway. For a moment it seems as though the window won't give way. But it does. And Greg disappears forever.

CHAPTER FORTY-SIX

S hould I end this on a positive note?

It is three days later. We have answered all the questions the Moroccan authorities have asked of us. The American ambassador to Morocco is an old friend. He helps us navigate the legal entanglements.

The three of us are now walking on the tarmac toward my plane. I stand on Myron's left. Terese stands on his right. We have both threaded our arms through his to keep Myron upright. His gait is slow, though steady. Our days in Morocco have taken their toll. He is weak and exhausted and yet, as predicted, the closure has lifted a weight off him.

Myron winces, stumbles.

Terese tightens her grip on him. "Are you okay?"

Myron manages a nod.

"Anything I can do for you?" she asks.

Myron gestures at the plane with his chin. "Help me get into the Mile High Club?"

I laugh out loud.

I love this man.

Terese rolls her eyes. "You never change."

"Is that a yes?"

"It is most definitely a no."

"You were more fun before I got shot."

We fly from Marrakech to Fort Lauderdale. Myron sleeps the entire flight. I have a car waiting for us. We drive to his parents' condo development in Boca Raton. They have not seen their son since the shooting. They'd wanted to come up to New York, of course, but Terese and I, with the help of Myron's siblings, convinced them to wait.

We take the elevator up to their floor. Terese has sent Ellen and Al photographs, so that they are prepared for Myron's gaunt appearance. When the elevator door opens, Myron's father is standing there. He already has tears in his eyes. So does Myron. That's how it is with this family. Lots of tears. Hearts worn on the sleeves. It should annoy a cynical blue blood like me, but I'm oddly okay with it. Myron's dad doesn't wait for us to get out. He jumps into the elevator and grabs hold of his son. Al Bolitar starts to cry, this man who has spent nearly eighty years navigating this mortal coil, and then this father cups the back of his son's head in his palm. That's the move that almost makes me lose it. I have seen photographs of Myron's bar mitzvah. There is one taken of a thirteen-year-old Myron with his father on the bimah. It is the part, Myron explained to me, where the father blesses the son. Myron says he can't remember exactly what his father whispered in his ear that day—something about loving him and praying for his health and happiness—but he remembers the smell of his father's Old Spice and the way his father cupped the back of Myron's head with his palm, just like this, just like I am seeing now, a distant echo traveling over the years, a sign that one man is still the father and that one is still his son.

Myron closes his eyes and leans on his father.

"It's okay," Myron's father whispers in his ear. "Shh, I'm right here."

I hold the elevator button so that the doors don't close on them.

We all have our roles.

Eventually, Myron's father releases his hold on his son. He turns and hugs Terese. Then he turns and hugs me. I accept the hug while keeping my finger on the elevator button, so the doors don't close on us. Multitasking.

When Myron makes his way out of the elevator, I hear Ellen Bolitar, Myron's mother, let out a cry. She is down the corridor on the right. Myron's sister is behind her. His brother is there too. Terese and I give them space. There are hugs and tears and complaints about how Myron needs to eat more. Terese and I are then sucked into the family mass as though by a gravitational pull from a far more potent source.

Everyone sheds a tear. Everyone raises their fingers and swipes their eyes.

Everyone but me. I remain, as is my wont, dry-eyed.

Ellen Bolitar whispers to Myron, "We have a surprise for you."

I steel myself because I know what is coming next.

Myron's mother turns slowly and looks down the hallway. All heads turn with her, save mine. I keep my eyes on Myron. I want to see his reaction. Myron looks bewildered for a moment. Then he follows his mother's gaze to the door of their condo. I keep watching him, a small smile toying with my lips.

Jeremy steps into view. "Hey, Myron."

I see Myron's eyes widen as his face crumbles. Jeremy runs toward him.

And me? I raise my fingers and swipe my eyes.

ACKNOWLEDGMENTS

It's been a while since I did a complete acknowledgments section so bear with me.

The author (love using the third person here) wishes to thank the following:

Everyone involved in the publishing process, including the USA team: Ben Sevier, Michael Pietsch, Lyssa Keusch, Lauren Bello, Beth deGuzman, Karen Kosztolnyik, Jonathan Valuckas, Matthew Ballast, Staci Burt, Andrew Duncan, Taylor Parker-Means, Alexis Gilbert, Janine Perez, Tiffany Porcelli, Joseph Benincase, Albert Tang, Liz Connor, Rena Kornbluh, Rebecca Holland, Mari Okuda, Jennifer Tordy, Ana Maria Allessi, Nita Basu, Michele McGonigle, and Rick Ball. As always, I thank Diane Discepolo and Lisa Erbach Vance.

The UK team: Selina Walker, Venetia Butterfield, Rachel Imrie, Charlotte Bush, Claire Bush, Glenn O'Neill, Alice Gomer, and Anna Curvis. The French team: Diane Du Périer, Valérie Maréchal, Caroline Ast, and of course, Eliane Benisti.

Letícia Rodrigues and Flávia Silva are instrumental in their support and research capabilities. Thank you for all you do.

All mistakes are on these people. They're the experts, not me.

I'd also like to give a quick shout-out to Judy Becker, Allen Castner, Grace Conte, Carol DeChant, Kelly Gallagher, Mike Grenley,

Rick Legrand, Ellen Nakhnikian, Ed Newton, Edward Pascoe, Ben Staples, and Stan Ulanoff. These people (or their loved ones) made generous contributions to charities of my choosing in return for having their name appear in this novel. If you would like to participate in the future, email giving@harlancoben.com.

ABOUT THE AUTHOR

Harlan Coben is a #1 *New York Times* bestselling author and one of the world's leading storytellers. His suspense novels are published in forty-six languages and have been number one bestsellers in more than a dozen countries, with eighty million books in print worldwide. His Myron Bolitar series has earned the Edgar, Shamus, and Anthony Awards, and several of his books have been developed into Netflix original series, including the #1 global hit *Fool Me Once*, *The Stranger*, *The Innocent*, *Gone for Good*, *The Woods*, *Stay Close*, and *Hold Tight*, as well as the Amazon Prime Video series adaptation of *Shelter*. He lives in New Jersey.